AF094445

SINS OF SURVIVAL

LEGACY OF SHADOWS
BOOK 2

JEN KARNER

Robot Dinosaur Press
robotdinosaurpress.com

PRAISE FOR CINDERS OF YESTERDAY

"Smooth as a knife's edge and just as sharp, an exciting and sapphic new entry into the paranormal genre with plenty of scary monsters to go around."

— *LADZ, AUTHOR OF THE FEALTY OF MONSTERS*

"Hot-blooded and heartfelt, CINDERS OF YESTERDAY lives at the fiery crossroads where magic and trauma collide, the sweetest sapphic romance simmers, and a haunting villain awaits. An ass-kicking debut for fans of Supernatural and Buffy!"

— *ANN FRAISTAT, BESTSELLING AUTHOR OF A PLACE FOR VANISHING AND WHAT WE HARVEST*

"CINDERS OF YESTERDAY promises sapphic yearning, badass female characters, and epic battles all wrapped in a spooky packaging perfect for fans of Supernatural, Buffy, and Charmed and it delivers!"

— *LOU WILHAM, AUTHOR OF THE HEX NEXT DOOR*

CINDERS OF YESTERDAY is a riveting urban fantasy with paranormal elements, featuring a sapphic romance and two deeply sympathetic heroines living with magic (and its perils) on a daily basis. Karner doesn't shy away from using curses and dark magic as an apt metaphor for generational trauma—the layers of meaning are deep in this novel. The plot, world-building, and magic system are fully dimensional and immaculately rendered. I savored every word.

— *PAULETTE KENNEDY, BESTSELLING AUTHOR OF THE WITCH OF TIN MOUNTAIN, AND THE DEVIL AND MRS.DAVENPORT*

This book is for everyone who loves complicated, Dean Winchester-esque disaster lesbians and the investigative, monster-of-the-week parts of SUPERNATURAL—Destiel for sapphics. At times horrifying and heartwarming, CINDERS OF YESTERDAY is a crisp and sharply written paranormal fantasy with clever characters and visceral, precise action and imagery.

— MORGAN DANTE, AUTHOR OF PROVIDENCE GIRLS

Copyright © 2026 by Jen Karner
All rights reserved.
No part of this publication may be reproduced, distributed, or transmitted in any form or by any means, including photocopying, recording, or other electronic or mechanical methods, without the prior written permission of the publisher, except as permitted by U.S. copyright law. For permission requests, contact JenKarner.com.
The story, all names, characters, and incidents portrayed in this production are fictitious. No identification with actual persons (living or deceased), places, buildings, and products is intended or should be inferred.

NO AI TRAINING: Without in any way limiting the author's [and publisher's] exclusive rights under copyright, any use of this publication to "train" generative artificial intelligence (AI) technologies to generate text is expressly prohibited. The author reserves all rights to license uses of this work for generative AI training and development of machine learning language models.

Book Cover by Therese Andersen
Editing by Megan Dailey

ALSO BY JEN KARNER

Legacy of Shadows

Cinders of Yesterday

For everyone who was forced to shrink themselves. Never forget, you are magic.

1

EMILIE

Emilie swallowed and turned to her companion with a wry turn to her lips. "I was hoping that some of the wards would still be intact."

"No dice?" Dani leaned back against the truck and gave Emilie a lingering look. "I mean, I did say this was probably a fool's errand. But did you wanna listen? No." She tsked quietly under her breath, then winked and turned back to grab something from inside the truck.

A year on the road—and in her bed—their lives getting more and more tangled together with every breath, and she still managed to steal Emilie's heart in such small, frenetic ways.

Dani was tall and athletic, with dark wavy hair she only tamed when it was time to fight, whiskey-brown eyes that set Emilie on fire, and a trim frame usually hidden under a leather jacket and jeans. Today was no exception, but she'd added a grey knitted cap to the ensemble, muttering about cold ears. Emilie turned from the moldering building in front of her to watch her girlfriend as she rummaged through the truck.

Emilie looked like a pale shadow next to her. Her own white-blond hair was getting longer, brushing the tops of her shoulders and framing her face. Her plump frame hadn't slimmed down so much as adjusted to hours on her feet as she worked with Dani, one job after the next.

After her dip in the Styx, the cold didn't bother her much these days. It'd been one of many things she'd discovered last winter, her first as a mature talented, the depth and breadth of her magic waking all the way up. She'd wanted nothing more than to ask her Grandpa if it had been the same for him.

November was warmer than it used to be, but the wind was cutting through everything tonight. They'd lost the light, another reminder that winter was still on its way.

"Don't get snotty," Emilie warned, turning back to the decommissioned building, trying to work out the best way to get inside without being spotted.

The Johnstown Municipal Library had been closed, and the stony brick building staring down at her now didn't look particularly friendly. Broken wards tried to flicker and chain together but remained dull and useless where they'd been placed. Time and erosion were doing what magical means couldn't and erasing their protective bearing one tumultuous rainstorm at a time.

At some point, this had been a collective, one of the places where talented gathered to share magic and knowledge, their little games of power and society happening in back rooms filled with texts that required special gloves to open. For safety, of course.

What she needed to know was whether they'd left by themselves and how long ago it had happened. Too many collectives had gone dark lately. There had to be a reason, and she was determined to find it.

"Snotty? What are we, ten?" Dani closed the truck, stepping over to join Emilie, one hand draping around her shoulders.

She leaned into the contact, happy to tuck her head under her girlfriend's while they kept bantering. She might not get cold, but Dani was a solid force, and she appreciated her for what that was.

"No?" Emilie rolled her eyes in response, even though Dani

couldn't actually see it, before taking a step back and tucking an errant strand of hair behind one ear.

"So, have you worked out how we get inside?" Dani's lips curled up into a dark smile.

Heat rushed through her, and Emilie shot her a look before shaking her head, trying to ignore the flirtation. Instead, she turned toward the building, taking a few faltering steps closer. They had work to do, and she would not be distracted. She'd probably fail of course, but right now, it was the thought that counted.

"Not entirely?" Her voice was scratchy and higher than it should have been, but she tried to talk through it. That Dani could still do this to her with a look after a year was absolutely unfair.

Emilie wouldn't have had it any other way.

"Mmm." Dani mock frowned and stalked forward a few steps, closing the distance between the two of them. "See, I'd bet there's at least one window around back that's been busted in." Her voice dropped an octave. "You know how it goes with places like this." Slowly, she circled around so that her presence was at Emilie's back.

Her hands draped across Emilie's shoulders, voice barely a whisper as it slipped past her ear. She was so distracted by the sensation of Dani there, she missed her words entirely.

"What?"

From behind her, Dani snickered, but it soon morphed into a full-on belly laugh. She had to pull away from Emilie and brace her hands on her knees as she tried to catch her breath.

"You're terrible!" Emilie laughed and took a shove at Dani while she low-key lost it in the middle of the street.

Without any more thought, she marched away from her erstwhile girlfriend and her truck, bag swinging with her hips. Dani had been dragging her feet about coming out here at all, but Emilie had made it clear she was going. And her overprotective hunter girlfriend—who also just happened to be the holder of a legendary weapon—wasn't willing to just let her wander off and hope nothing happened.

Behind her, she heard the moment that Dani's laughter died off, her boots echoing Emilie's own footsteps. In general, they cased out jobs in advance. Made sure that each was something they were a good fit for. She couldn't speak to the way anyone else worked, but she followed Dani's lead, and after a year, they were both still up and swinging.

No thanks to you, a nasty voice in the back of her head piped up, and she smothered it mercilessly. There was no time for that kind of talk while they were in the field. As if they ever weren't. One job blended into the next, only long stretches of pavement and anonymous rentals to differentiate one from another.

It didn't take long for Dani's long strides to overtake hers, and if Emilie wanted to, she could time them by her heartbeat. She never made it far before her hunter was gliding in front of her in a peculiar sort of predatory way, ensuring there was nothing waiting for them bearing too many teeth.

Around the corner was a window boarded up badly, but nothing else waited for them, and for the briefest moment, Emilie wasn't sure whether she was disappointed or not. Dani kicked in the boards with barely a glance along the alley, as casual as if she was opening it with a key. It was a smooth action, and Emilie was reminded that this was nothing new for the other woman.

This little expedition was supposed to be checking on a hunch. There *had* been a collective here, and now they were gone, and nobody seemed to care too much. She hadn't asked Dani to come, but here she was anyway. Breaking and entering and all.

Ahead of her, she watched as her hunter easily ducked through the window and disappeared into the dim building for a moment before popping her head back out with a charming smile.

"Looks good. I'm guessing it's been empty long enough nobody is using it much anymore."

"If they ever were," Emilie murmured with a look around before following her girlfriend into the dark.

The library sat far enough away from the city center that it was easy to see why it had fallen by the wayside. She might have a certain kind of reverence for libraries, with their rows of books and organization that ensured things were generally in place to be found, but even she could feel the chill of isolation from the rest of town.

She'd grown up surrounded by libraries that went back two hundred years, with tomes and scrolls and folios. So much information that if she hadn't been introduced early, she might have drowned among the stacks. In a way, the tall rows of books were more familiar to her than the bars and shops that hunters tended to patronize when passing information back and forth.

This was different, though. For no reason she could put her finger on, when Emilie passed through the window into the library, it felt like entering a tomb.

***

Inside the building, the smell of mildew and wet paper permeated everything, a thick floral bouquet of decomposition that was difficult to ignore. As much as she might hear the voices of the dead, avoiding their bodies had stayed near the top of her to-do list.

Dani waited for her at the doorway, both of them flipping on flashlights as they ventured deeper into the building. Emilie stopped short when the hallway spit them out into a wide room that must have been wonderful once. Tall windows allowed the new moon to deliver weak light, showing off the collapsed stacks that had belched stacks of abandoned books onto the floor.

What had she been expecting? The dim academic libraries she'd encountered between childhood and university? This had been a public library, not a magical archive, but something about the broken stacks and the books left to molder picked at her incessantly.

The weak moonlight didn't illuminate much, but every bit helped this time of year when the dark encroached so early. It'd make the expedition a little bit less fraught, even if Dani still thought she was being ludicrous.

"So, what are we looking for in here?" Dani wandered to where a long wooden checkout counter dominated one wall.

"You saw the wards out front," Emilie answered primly, following her before weaving behind the counter. She started opening drawers, looking for something without knowing *exactly* what it was she was looking for.

"The broken wards?" Dani raised an eyebrow. "Yeah, killer, I saw 'em. But they're broken. Anything they were supposed to be hiding has been out in the open for a while now."

"Maybe." Emilie ducked under the drawer she was tugging at where something was stuck. From underneath, she could see the faint flicker of a ward that wasn't entirely broken. *Hide Me.* She traced a finger against the curved shape and felt a key fall into the palm of her hand. "Solitary talented are paranoid all by themselves. That sentiment is only amplified when you get more of them in one place. Groups make them easier to spot." She popped back up and shot Dani a sly smile as she dangled the key from a leather loop.

"You think a collective was working out of this place?"

"At least a small one. But they were being careful, not operating out in the open." She ran her fingers along the underside of the desk and felt the remains of more wards caved into it. "The wards outside were just the easy ones, but they've got spellwork hidden all over the place."

Emilie made her way to the hallway behind the desk, following it farther into the heart of the library. Instead of a locked door, she found the ruins of a doorframe with the remains of wards gouged out of the wood.

"See this?" Dani passed her, gesturing at the wood. "This is what I mean. Just because you found keys up front, just because there was somebody here at one point, doesn't mean anything is left. Doesn't mean anything is *here*."

"Humor me here. Hunters and talented come at things from different directions, true or false?"

"True." Dani's eyes followed her as Emilie ventured inside.

"And I happen to be talented and was raised around their stupid circuitous bullshit." Emilie's eyes scanned the room, looking for the wards she knew were hiding somewhere.

"True." Dani was frowning at her now, but Emilie refused to look up.

The problem with relying on nothing but gossip and stories, in Emilie's opinion, always came down to how much information she could cram into her skull all at once. People liked to lie or use subterfuge. Books and wards, however...they were much more straightforward, and she'd always appreciated that about them. Books never asked her to explain herself or how her brain made the jumps from one thing to the next. They simply handed over the information she needed to move on with her day.

The point here wasn't about proving that there was a sanctum past this single room. Or at least, it hadn't been initially. There had been a collective here, and if the buzz of magic against her skin was any indicator, something had happened. They hadn't just moved on of their own accord. She could feel it.

To pinpoint the magical residue and know for sure, all she needed to do was let down her shields and take a peek around the room. And there was no way she was about to do that; the murmur of spirits nearby warned her that if she lit up, she would not be alone.

"Then trust me when I say there is something else here. Or was."

She could feel Dani's eyes on her from the doorway, pinned at the base of her neck. This was why she'd initially tried to arrange for this on a day when she could get out on her own for a few hours. It was impossible to ignore the weight of expectation of finding—well, nothing.

Everyone liked to think that talented were people who could operate without fear. Money could only insulate them so well when things went very wrong. And they went wrong more often than any of the more esteemed families ever wanted to admit.

She'd traced Mama's family thoroughly in the first weeks after leaving Dawson. After claiming her life for what it could be instead of what it was. The Deveraux name went back further than plenty, had been known for the clarity of their talent, and they'd still been hunted like rats by Spectre while none of the other families did a thing.

Her control wavered for a moment, shields dropping long enough for spirit radio to surge around her in a deluge of voices. Emilie's magic, her talents, allowed her to hear the dead. To listen and interact with the spirits and things that dwelled on the far side of the veil. As a child, she'd thought of it like tuning a radio. Now, it was more like an entire radio network.

There were at least a dozen voices braided together, so many that she couldn't isolate a single voice, couldn't quite parse out anything they were saying. Her shields snapped back into place, quieting the noise, and Emilie turned back to Dani, who was now facing the way they'd come down the hallway.

"Did you hear that?" Dani turned to Emilie, head cocked a little to the side.

"No, there was a surge." Emilie waved a hand around. "I wasn't hearing what you were hearing."

Dani went quiet for a long moment before prowling the space between the two of them. "Be careful, and don't go wandering." She pressed a long, lingering kiss against Emilie's lips before pulling back and disappearing back into the library silently.

With no one left to watch her, Emilie let her eyes wander over every spare inch of the room again. She could spot the ruined glimmers of wards along the ceiling and the door jamb. The room was crawling with them, and not a single one was still active.

She kicked the rug underfoot out of the way, revealing a spell circle burnt into the middle of the room. Emilie paused, listening for a moment to make sure Dani wasn't causing a ruckus without her, before dragging the rug out of the way entirely so she could see what she was working with.

Old burns and chalk ground into the grooves of the wood waited for her. Emilie pulled a notebook out of her bag and sketched out the circle for later before tucking it away again, unfamiliar with everything she was looking at.

As she did, the pressure from spirit radio began to rise. If she kept her shields closed tight, she'd end up with a migraine by the time they got to the truck, but Emilie generally didn't let them down while they were on a job unless she had to. She'd learned her lesson the hard way last spring, when a spirit had tried to hijack her body for a thrill ride.

She took a deep breath, incrementally lowering her shields. Not enough to give anything access to her, barely more than was necessary for spirit radio's static to start up again. The voices started back up, but the panic that had infected them a few minutes ago was gone.

"We needed to recharge the wards." The voices began to speak, one voice picking up where another left off. Men and women alike, at least seven or eight people in all. *"Nothing crazy or intensive, but Miriam saw the Scions working in the area. It was a safety precaution since some of the wards went down during the storm last summer. They knew. They knew we were here, and they came for us in the night. The Scions came for us."*

Emilie peeled back another layer of shields, blinking as she took in the room, seeing it for the first time properly. Broken wards flickered from nearly every square inch, but the floor was covered in the spectral remains of blood. It pooled on the floors, it spattered the walls, and somewhere out front, she could hear a woman wailing before her voice was cut short. It was an echo that kept repeating every twenty to thirty seconds, a broken record, a memory of her last moments before they'd been cut off.

She turned back to the doorway and saw the echo of a tall blond man grinning before leaving the room. There was a cold cruelty behind his eyes, and he was liberally spattered in blood. When he left the room, he moved to the left in the hallway, not the right. Deeper into the library.

Emilie let out a heaving, shuddering breath and tried to get her wits about her. This wasn't happening because she'd been wrong the whole time. Her skills at pattern recognition had obviously been leading her astray for months because saying out loud that the Scions of Seraph were hunting talented would be too much.

But as she watched the echo of that man leave the room over and over and over again, Emilie knew that was exactly what had happened.

2

DANI

With Emilie safely behind her in what had been an office, Dani clicked off her flashlight and prowled through the darkness toward the room they'd come from. The sound of a truck swerving up outside had caught her attention. When she reached the doorway into the main room, she crouched, the sound of voices from outside the front doors making her go stock-still.

The front of the library was now lit by a bank of headlights—three vehicles, if she was counting right, all of them pointed at the doors and windows, sending too-bright LED light careening through the room. If they were lucky, it'd just be some local kids who'd been using this as a place to drink and get high.

"I thought Jackal cleared this place weeks ago!" a man yelled, and Dani froze like a deer in headlights.

In most cases, her body's reaction to almost anything was to fight back, to burst into movement and action. Throughout the course of her life, staying still and quiet had been far more dangerous than simply making a break for it. *Jackal* though.

It'd been years since she'd heard that nickname, and there was no way a second person had picked it up. If they had, Evan Campbell would have killed them where they stood. Soon as he knew about it, anyway. The shock faded as the doors rattled on their hinges, and Dani swore under her breath.

If there were Scions outside, they were in deep shit.

Carefully, silently, she moved to the end of the counter that was currently hiding her from being spotted by the goons outside. Which was exactly the way she wanted it. They'd parked nearby, but her truck was old and nondescript; it fit in perfectly around here. But she was still in a library that used to be a collective with her very magical girlfriend while radical hunters who believed talented were afflicted and needed to be cleansed caused trouble outside.

She peered around the edge of the counter, trying to get a better count of who was out there, praying to a god she didn't believe in that there was nobody she knew. It'd only complicate things, and right now, she didn't need complicated.

She could see bobbing lights through one of the windows around the side of the building and shadowy forms standing in front of the headlights in a few places. Unless things had changed drastically, there were at least six of them outside. Maybe more; it depended on why they were here.

Why are they here? Dani edged back behind the counter and took a breath. She didn't know the layout of this place, didn't know the easiest way out, and they'd need to get out and make it to the truck without any trouble. Easier said than done, but she was nothing if not resourceful.

The door rattled again, and she could hear a few people by the vehicles as they argued. A minute later, the door rattled again before she heard the telltale *thunk* as an axe bit into the wood of the front doors. She was out of time. If she couldn't get herself and Emilie out before they got in, she'd just have to make sure those lunatics never realized they weren't alone.

Staying crouched, she moved back to the hallway, closing and locking the door behind her. It wouldn't hold up for long, but they needed every second they could get. She booked it down the hall and found Emilie still standing in the empty office, looking pale and drawn. When her little medium caught sight of Dani, her eyes flickered bright with magic for a moment before fading to their normal pale blue.

"We have problems." Dani crossed the room in two steps and took Emilie by the arm, pulling her down below the sightline of the large windows that banked the wall.

"Scions." Emilie's voice was hoarse, and her gaze looked distant in her face. She shook her head and then met Dani's eyes. "What do we do?"

"Sometimes we fight, sometimes we run." Dani grabbed Emilie's hand and interlaced their fingers as she met her eyes. "They're coming in, and we need to not let them know we were ever here, yeah?"

"Yeah." Emilie shook her head and looked around the room. It was as destroyed as they had found it, and whatever her medium had been searching for, it didn't seem to be in this room. "We have to go deeper."

"Deeper?"

Emilie didn't answer as the sound of wood breaking out front cracked through the halls. Instead, she moved toward the door, tugging Dani along behind her. She clicked off the flashlight, moving to the left, down the corridor, where it made an L turn, hiding them from view. They weren't moving fast, Emilie opting for quiet instead, but she seemed to know where they were going.

"We need circulation," Emilie whispered, moving them past doors that were barely on their frames anymore. "The blond guy who butchered them was looking for something. Something they'd hidden. But they didn't hide it in a place a hunter would look."

"And you know this because…"

"There was a breach while you were checking. I saw some things, like him trashing the room while the people he killed bled out. There was something here, something he wanted." Emilie stopped and turned to Dani. "Something we can't let him find."

Dani swore but reached with her free hand into her jacket, feeling the outline of the veilblade where it was hidden. The urge to draw it and turn back to those lunatics was strong enough that she considered it. But if Evan had been here, it hadn't been by chance.

His daddy ran the Scions like a paramilitary operation, and if he'd sent his son here to handle a collective, there was a damned good reason for it. The Scions hadn't been active now in years, at least not back East, and this was messy.

"You know where we're going."

Emilie smiled and tapped the side of her head with her free hand. "I've got someone who wants to make sure that they don't find us or what they're looking for."

With that, she led Dani around another corner until they hit a T junction. Behind them, the crack of wood splintering echoed through the empty hallways, and Emilie looked over her shoulder as if they would appear out of nowhere.

"Stay with me, killer," Dani murmured, her own fears smothered ruthlessly in the moment.

Emilie let out a slow, shuddering breath, and her eyes glowed bright and white in the darkness for a moment. The temperature around them dropped a few degrees before Emilie got a handle on herself. "Right, okay, we go right."

From behind them, the sound of people arguing was audible. They'd breached the hallway, and unless Dani and Emilie found what they were looking for fast, it was only a matter of time until they were cornered where they stood.

#

The hallway wound around another corner, and Dani followed Emilie into a corridor with two doors, one on either side. There were plate windows set into the hallway showing two separate rooms. Most of the glass had been broken, and there were dark smears of blood across the floor and the glass on the left.

Emilie paused in front of the two doors, but instead of looking to the left, she turned to the right and moved into the room like she'd been here before. Dani followed carefully, clicking her flashlight back on so she could see where they were going.

A sign just inside the room told Dani they had entered document storage. There were rows of shelves and cabinets. Several desks had boxes with documents in them. It looked a helluva lot like the talented archives she'd visited over the course of her life.

Ahead of her, Emilie moved in a flash, ignoring most of the room and heading for the rack of storage cabinets on the far side. Utilitarian grey metal, several were dented up badly, but all of them had retained their structural integrity. And their locks.

Dani stayed close to the doorway, ears pricked for any sound from the Scions as they made their way deeper. She could still hear their yelling and the raucous sound of them tossing one room after another.

What were they looking for? Her gaze shifted back to where Emilie was turning a key in one of the units. Whoever had reached out to her knew exactly what they were coming for.

The Scions of Seraph were monsters in human skin, and they didn't work with talented. Not ever. The fact that they were rummaging through everything here and hadn't simply burnt it to the ground said something. She just didn't know what.

Across the room, Emilie tugged at the drawer she'd unlocked, then it slid open with a metallic screech that made both of them freeze in place. From the hallway, the sounds of the Scions stopped, silence blanketing them for a single moment before the yelling began again.

"We can hear you, little mice," a cruel voice echoed through the halls.

Dani flipped her flashlight back off and sprinted across the room.

Emilie crammed everything inside the drawer into her bag and cinched it down until it was closed. From the hallway, the sound of several people thundered toward them, and Dani pulled Emilie away from the drawer and into one of the deeper corners of the room, praying the shadows would hide them.

This room didn't have any exterior windows, and there were at least four Scions closing on their position. Emilie breathed out, and vapor hung in the air, her eyes glowing a brilliant white-blue in the darkness.

"Run little mouse, run, run, run..." The voice drew closer.

Dani peered toward the window.

They were still intact on this side of the hall, the light from a flashlight making it easy to see when the goons entered the hallway. She ducked back behind the shelf, gestured for Emilie to stay down, and held her breath. There was no reason for them to look this way. No reason for anyone to enter this room. If they stayed low, stayed quiet...

She didn't move. Dani barely fucking drew a breath, eyes glued to the shadows thrown by the light shining through the plate windows. With barely a whisper of skin across fabric, Dani reached a hand into her jacket, wrapping her fingers around the handle of the veilblade. It pulsed in her hand, and she felt the fear about protecting Emilie start to slide backward in her mind.

Dani balanced on the balls of her feet in a crouch and licked her canines, feeling the rush of adrenaline as it crashed through her system. Across the hallway, there was another crash and the tinkle of newly broken glass.

Her muscles seized, body getting ready for what she would be asking it to do, but before she could burst into action, Emilie grabbed onto her arm. She shook her head and held up a finger. From the other side of the building, there was a muffled thump, followed by a cacophony of metallic screaming.

The Scions in the hallway thundered away from them and toward it all at once. Emilie grabbed Dani's hand, and together, they scrabbled to their feet. Emilie led them across the hallway into circulation, to a small door that led to a receiving bay. Dani closed the door behind them but didn't let them slow down. The bay dropped them outside, around the back of the building.

The night had gotten cold fast, the bite of it nipping at her sharply. Dani shrugged off the cold and took the lead, moving them around the side of the building toward the block where she'd parked the truck.

Out here, it was quiet, but she wasn't taking any chances. Instead of heading directly for the truck, she took them over a block first, coming at it from the wrong angle. The Scion trucks were in front of the building, but getting cocky on the getaway was a good way to get killed.

And they were not going to die tonight.

By the time Dani got them to the truck, her nose had started to run, but they hadn't run into anybody outside. Moments later, she was gunning the truck back east, getting the hell away from Johnstown and whatever horseshit they'd just waded into. Next to her, Emilie clutched the bag to her chest, eyes too bright in a pale, drawn face.

"What the fuck happened?"

Emilie licked her lips and dropped the bag to her feet with a sigh. "The Scions are operating again."

"I noticed that, yeah." Dani's eyes flicked between the road and her rearview mirror, afraid they had a tail she hadn't noticed yet.

This would all have been easier if they were closer to home, but Illinois didn't have many places she liked stopping. The Humans First sentiment out this way had been getting worse in the last few years, and this was proof enough of that.

"They raided the place, looking for the collective that was working out of it." She shook her head. "But there was no reason for them to even ping a radar. I saw…some of it." Emilie tucked a lock of hair behind one ear before continuing. "This wasn't dark magic. They were just trying to re-up the wards. Nothing fancy."

"It doesn't have to be fancy with them."

"I know, but. It wasn't by chance. There was this…guy there. Tall, blond, eyes as dead as they get? He butchered them like animals, but they weren't telling him what he wanted to hear."

Dani twitched at the description Emilie had given, even though it tracked with what she'd heard earlier. She let out a long, slow breath and tried to keep her nerves at bay as she accelerated onto the highway.

"That's how the Jackal operates." Her eyes flicked to the rearview again, glad that it was still empty. "Let's get back to the cabin. It's safer there."

Emilie nodded and took Dani's hand when she reached out, the miles between them and safety bleeding away.

3

EMILIE

The current safe house was a rental that overlooked a picturesque grove of trees, which bled into the hills that hid the closest towns. Just far enough out of the way that there were no nosy neighbors poking their heads around and asking questions neither she nor Dani wanted to answer. Best of all, the property was owned by a talented family and came equipped with wards around the property, along with a second ring built into the house.

The fear that had been riding them from Illinois didn't dissipate until they crossed the property line. The cool wash of magic over Emilie's skin, and the knowledge of the exact wards that protected them, gave her a measure of comfort, but not enough. Spirit radio was a constant buzzing hum at the edge of her perception. She'd kept the volume low, but the chorus of voices was becoming more prevalent, not less.

Sometime over the last year, Emilie had gotten used to looking over one shoulder and not being sure what she'd find. As her talents settled into the shape of her, they'd grown. It had taken months to work out how to shield herself from the constant chatter of spirits trying to pull at her attention, the flicker of the past imprinted into locations.

This was different.

Something about what had happened in Illinois—it felt like the beginning of a rockslide. The slow rumble as pebbles dislodged, the only sign before boulders came rocketing down, annihilating anything in their path. She'd expected signs that a collective had been there, but what she'd gotten?

It was one thing to say that there were collectives going quiet and talented going missing for no reason. It was another entirely to stumble onto the memory of a grisly murder and watch it happen on repeat. Fear of what she'd just seen burrowed deep and made a home in Emilie where she couldn't root it out. Even behind a double salt line, with the curtains pulled and wards winking in her vision.

She wanted to pretend that she didn't want to scope out what had been waiting inside that locked drawer of the library. Her bag was on the floor in front of her, still firmly shut. It'd be so easy to open it up and start rifling through what she'd stuffed in there, her fingers were practically itching with it.

Except that Dani was checking and rechecking the salt lines, peering through the front windows as though someone was apt to pull up at any moment.

"Babe?" Emilie's voice cut through the silence in the room.

"Mm?" Dani shot her a look over her shoulder but didn't say anything else.

"The lines are good. We checked them before we left, yeah?"

"Yeah, I just..." Dani's voice drawled off as her shoulders slumped, and she made a face Emilie recognized intimately.

Her life had been charmed, right up until it wasn't. Whatever future she'd originally sketched out for herself had burned away the night of the fire. There was no returning to the before, only learning to live with the repercussions of the after.

Surviving something terrible had taken something from Emilie, leaving a strange darkness in its wake and the ability to recognize that same darkness in other people. Right now, it bled off of Dani, but Emilie didn't want to ask. Didn't want to interrogate it.

Hunting was a harsh life for adults, and Dani had still been young when it caught her in its teeth. Her lover had survived more tragedy than most people would ever see in a lifetime, and she kept showing up.

"It's fine," Dani finally declared, letting the curtains fall closed behind her. She moved across the house, snagging a beer from the fridge before turning back to Emilie on the couch. "So, what kind of loot was in the drawer?"

Tension ratcheted up Emilie's spine, sending electricity arcing through her bones with each breath, as though something had cracked between the two of them while they were casing the collective. Except, aside from their uninvited guests, it'd been a run like so many others they'd done over the last year. *What is going on?* Emilie could feel the way things were accelerating, beginning to spin inexorably out of her control—if they had ever been within her purview to begin with.

"Not sure yet," she admitted, toeing at the bag idly.

She was hoping for research notes, some idea of what their focus had been. What could have put a target on their back. When the Watchtowers were still around, there had been collectives across the country—the world. She'd been raised on those stories and histories, of the great works of magic that groups of talented were capable of.

That had been before the schisms between talented and hunters grew too large to easily bridge. These days, the collectives that were working in the states—outside the enclaves of old talented circles in the Northeast, the deep south, and the Northwest—kept to themselves. Secrecy allowed them to guard their research and spellwork like treasure.

She hadn't understood when she was younger. Collectives, solo practitioners, even hunters and trusted casters had moved through the auction house all the time. Emilie hadn't understood how rare that was until this past year.

Dani joined her on the couch and tugged the bag up into Emilie's lap.

Emilie leaned into the curve of her lover, letting herself relax a bit into the press of their bodies together. It wasn't the sharp tang of attraction from when they'd first met. Instead, there was a quiet comfort she took from Dani that no one else in her life had ever inspired in her.

From inside the bag, Emilie pulled out a small black shoe box adorned with runes that ran along each side. The ink was invisible, but she could see the glimmer of magic—*ignore me, I'm not here*, and *look elsewhere*—all telling her eyes to slip over the shape of it. She brushed away the cobwebs of persuasion and spellwork and opened the box to find a single dark red journal.

"Book in a box," Dani commented.

Emilie huffed a small sigh at her and flipped open the journal, running a finger across the creamy pages. She didn't know exactly what it was she was searching for, she only hoped she'd recognize it when she saw it.

"A research journal, by the look of it." She raised an eyebrow at Dani.

"What were you looking for?"

"Proof someone had even been there?" She smoothed a hand across the notebook. "With this, we should have everything they wanted. Including whatever the Scions were after."

Around her, spirit radio kicked on as though she wasn't shielding at all, a chaotic swell of voices all speaking over one another.

"They came in the night...golden hair and dark eyes...they were disciples to something dark. I could feel it on them."

In the supernatural community, there were plenty of cells and militias, collectives and circles of power, covens scattered from one coast to the next. People were tribal deep down; adding magic to the equation didn't change that. If anything, it might have exacerbated it.

"You still with me, killer?" Dani's voice cut through the static and noise.

"Yeah, I'm...Spirit radio is just...raucous right now."

"Did it get bad after you opened the box?" Dani eyed the shoe box accusingly.

"No. It piped up once I was in the collective's space. I saw what that militia did to them." She swallowed. "Tell me I was blind or dreaming or…something." Emilie's voice had gone quiet. "Tell me it wasn't Scions?"

Dani met her eyes but didn't say anything, and that silence was a blow all its own.

The Scions of Seraph. She'd been taught, even as a child, how to hide herself in plain sight. How to make sure that non-magical folks didn't really notice her, that her gifts remained hidden. Dad had been a Dawson kid, and he'd lived behind the protection it granted his entire life. Mama was another story all together.

She'd lived out in the world, and while Spectre had been an omnipresent threat, he was far from the only danger. There were plenty of Humans First hunters who thought magic was a physical manifestation of a kind of sin. They saw the magical talents that she had in her blood as proof she'd been touched by something dark. They even had a word for it: *afflicted*. As though they were infected with a kind of spiritual disease. The Scions of Seraph took "humans first" to the extreme, unwilling to compromise, driven to fanaticism.

"I wish I could," Dani finally answered.

Dani's cell began to rang, and she answered it, pacing as she talked with whoever was on the other end. Instead of paying attention, the buzzing of voices over spirit radio crescendoed, another screaming maw of voices all braided together. It was maddening in its incomprehensibility, but the screaming lasted for less than thirty seconds before it was gone once again.

As it disappeared, Dani turned to Emilie, her face gone serious and blank. "Pack your bags. We're headed for the mountains."

"Mountains?" Emilie frowned in confusion.

"That was Lu. Crossroads needs help."

4

EMILIE

M adness runs in her bloodline.
That's what people said about Mama when they didn't think she was close enough to hear the way they lowered their voices, murmured words barbed and aimed to draw blood. By the time she'd understood it was fear and mistrust coloring their words, the damage had already been done.

Magic could be magic, but people were still afraid of death. Afraid of what came after it too. They wanted Mama to tell them that their people had moved on happily or to try to reach out to important people that they'd lost. But what remained after a person died wasn't often the parts that they remembered. It was anger or fear that kept some part of them from moving on to whatever came next. Sometimes love or obsession, but all Mama could speak to were the pieces left over. She couldn't reach out and coax the whole spirit of someone back once they'd crossed.

Most spirits just didn't have the juice to reach out unless someone was already open to a transmission, the way Emilie was. The only times she'd ever heard of a spirit speaking through someone, it required either innate talent to act as a conduit or complicated rituals that aimed for similar results. Lu had said there were spirits hijacking the bodies of unconscious hunters, and that was new, even for Emilie.

Crossings Clinic was settled in a small business park in the foothills of the Appalachian Mountains that had been slowly dying for years. It might have been urgent care at some point, or one of those "furnish to suit" medical suites, but whatever it had started its life as, it belonged to hunters now.

At the far end of the ocean of parking lot was a Roses flanked by a liquor store and sub shop that hadn't gone out of business yet. The other half of the business park was dominated by the clinic and the rows of trucks and RVs parked outside of it.

A young man in all black met them at the door, stony faced, with eyes that bounced constantly, primed for a fight.

"Lu told us to keep an eye out for you," he explained brusquely as he waved them through the door, watching over their shoulder until the glass shut behind them. They moved through anonymous hallways without saying anything, and Emilie could feel the murmur of spirit radio brushing against her shields as apparitions reached out to her. They took a back stairwell up to the third floor, where the young man keyed in a code on a pad. It flashed green, unlocking the door and letting them into another hallway, this one with a handful of medical professionals bustling around.

Lu Callaway appeared from around a corner, and their guide disappeared without another word. Lu had opted for a green Army jacket rolled up past her elbows instead of a white doctor's coat, an array of pale scars visible against her olive skin. This week, her dark hair had streaks of orchid and electric blue, barely noticeable where she'd pinned it up, revealing shaved sides and ears filled with rings and chains.

She ran the clinic and had been expanding her operation here beyond the mobile units she'd started with a handful of years ago. She'd been working to stem the death rate of hunters in the field to stupid, fixable injuries. She was sharp as a knife, brilliant enough to make grown men weep, and she'd been an Army surgeon for five years before Uncle Sam sent her home with a *"thanks, but no thanks"* after she'd gotten injured.

"Security going up?" Dani raised an eyebrow and gestured in the direction of the kid who'd led the two of them up here.

"Things are degrading rapidly." Lu answered, her voice cold as a winter storm. "It's a clusterfuck is what it is." She shook her head, eyes pinned on Dani before they darted over to Emilie. "Hey, Emilie. Welcome to the shitshow." She nodded and turned back to Dani. "There's some folks downstairs who wanna talk to you. Head down to the welcome wagon and see what they want?"

Dani shot Emilie a look, and when Emilie nodded, she turned on her heel and headed back downstairs again.

Once the door shut and locked, Lu's attention settled on Emilie, eyes narrowed as she stood there in silence for a moment longer than the medium was strictly cool with.

"So, I'm gonna go out on a limb and say something is happening?" Emilie asked, voice pitched carefully.

Some of Lu's icy demeanor evaporated, and her ramrod posture loosened. "Dani is a bad influence on you."

"It isn't that you're wrong, exactly, just that I don't care." Emilie smiled a little and fought the urge to duck her head. The banter helped quell the panic she'd bricked up at the back of her mind, just a loop of screaming about the Scions over and over again.

Lu shook her head but started to walk and gestured for Emilie to follow. "Our capacity is almost always at max because we're only so big, and every magical injury under the sun winds up in our lap. Along with hunters who've gotten messed up and can't walk into a normal hospital for whatever reason." She shrugged and let the two of them through a door that required a keycard.

They were standing in a narrow room with a pair of small tables; a large glass window dominated the space. Through it was a longer room filled with ten beds, each one holding a patient and several machines to monitor them. It was quieter in here, blinds pulled down to mask the early morning sunlight outside.

There was a hushed murmur she couldn't quite hear, followed by a pause, before the murmur started up again. A susurrus of words from lips that barely moved, sometimes in sync with one another and sometimes not.

Emilie looked to Lu, who gestured for her to walk forward. "This is our…long-term ward." Her voice sounded too loud in the quiet, and the hair at the back of Emilie's neck stood straight up as if the pressure was rising around them. "Four months ago, there were only four, and now we have ten. They're all in comas but breathing on their own. Alive, with enough brain activity that the family isn't pulling the cord, but not awake or responsive."

Fear wrapped itself around her spine, keeping her planted on two feet as some part of her disconnected and tried to understand what she was hearing. They were obviously saying something, but she couldn't hear them, wasn't sure she wanted to know what they were saying.

"But they're talking."

"Listen." Lu pressed a button on the left of the window, and a speaker crackled to life, magnifying the sounds.

"—the call. Emilie Lockgrove can help us. Answer the call. Emilie Lockgrove can help us. Answer the call. Emilie—"

She waved her hand, ice crackling to life along her ribs and bracing her shoulders in armor. Fear spiked through her too fast to process, shards of cold lightning that seared her in place as her mind tried to untangle the puzzle that was staring at her. Their voices were wrong, a terrible scramble as each voice escaped from vocal cords unsuited to it.

Nobody needed to tell her that there were spirits squatting in those bodies reaching out and calling her name, and now that she'd heard them, there was no turning a blind eye. *Answer the call.* How many times had she heard those words and not entirely understood what they meant? Too many.

"I can't—" She breathed out a long, slow, shuddering breath. "Standing here, are there wards between us and that room?" Panic still swirling around her, she tried to focus on what was in front of her. This was something she could deal with—that *only* she could deal with.

"Nothing that would block anything, why?"

"We both know that something is speaking through them, yeah?"

"I can agree there." Lu narrowed her eyes. "Why do I not think I'm gonna like what you're about to say?"

Emilie cocked her head and stared through the glass, letting her shields down just a touch, then turned back to Lu. "I should be able to see them or at least sense them in there." She shook her head. "Except that I don't." She licked her lips. "I need to take a peek through the veil is all."

Lu's left eye twitched. Not much, but enough that Emilie noticed. The doctor took in a deep breath through her nose, eyes slipping shut before reopening as she exhaled in a long, controlled burst.

"You want to me to...what? Hang out while you just slip your skin when there is something clearly not great going on?" Her nose scrunched up as she got more animated. "Does that seem like a super great idea to you? Because, gotta tell you, not so much for me."

Emilie rubbed a hand over her face before answering. "You didn't call me in to help because I was gonna do the same thing as everyone else."

"It could be a trap."

"It could, but there are much easier ways to set a trap for someone like me." She smiled, and it was laced with bitterness she couldn't quite hide. "They're asking for help. *For my help*. I have to check." She let out a huff that was somewhere between a laugh and a sob.

"I'm going on the record that I hate this and I'm telling Dani on you when she gets back up here," Lu said as she took a seat on a stool that gave her a view of both Emilie and her patients.

Emilie took a seat on the ground, back against the wall and legs crossed in front of her. "That's fair. If it makes you feel better, she can't stop me when I'm like this either."

She let out a long breath and, with a practiced motion, let her spirit slip from her skin and take in her surroundings. Things on this side of the veil never looked quite the same as they did in the physical world. The room was softer at the edges, deeper shadows in the corners, and a few cosmetic differences that spoke to a different time than the one she inhabited.

Looking through the window was another story. Dozens and dozens of shades filled the room, clustered around the bodies. Most of them were so worn, they barely retained the shape of personhood about them. Facial features blurred and faded from definition, but something inside of them still burned, begging for help.

Emilie moved into the next room, and the shades stopped in unison. One by one, they extricated themselves from the bodies they'd pushed themselves into. The spirits regained some measure of self, but they were so thin, and not one of them still looked entirely like a person. How had they even managed to reach out?

"I'm Emilie." She shrugged. "You called?"

"Do you answer the call, lighthouse?"

"Lighthouse?" Emilie frowned and made her way deeper into the room, looking for any spirit that had retained enough self that she could find out who they were. "Do you mean me?"

"Do you answer the call, lodestone?"

She frowned again, turning as the shades moved around her, parting as if she was a rock in a stream. "I don't know what you're asking." Emilie shook her head.

Two spirits intertwined their hands, and both of them became a bit sharper around the edges. Dark eyes and red hair framed identical faces.

"We need help, and no one else can hear us. But you can. You heard Miriam at the collective. We need your help. Yours. You are the lighthouse and the lodestone."

Emilie heaved a shuddering breath and reached a hand out, palm raised. "Show me."

In unison, the spirits surrounding her tipped their heads back and screamed, voices turning to fire and ice before returning to smoke that coiled back around their spectral forms. As one, their attention snapped back to Emilie.

"There are such things to show you."

The closest spirit reached out a hand, and delicate fingers hovered above her palm. The air tasted like ozone, electricity sparking in the corners as the pressure spiked. She hesitated for a moment, but Emilie knew danger in the veil, and this was not that. This was the most precious thing a spirit could give her.

This was information.

"We apologize. This will be unpleasant."

Electricity sparked through her as their fingers connected, and Emilie felt something deep inside of her come to life. A cold fire lit her from the inside. The elemental force ripped a scream from between clenched teeth as wild images began to flash behind her eyes.

Give us justice. The voices of spirits wrapped together screamed through her, showing her what they'd endured. Scions killing people in their beds, running down parents as they shielded children, hunting them through day and night alike.

Give us a voice. More of their stories, but this time interspersed with lives that were no different than the ones so many others had lived. They'd been killed for the magic in their blood or charms on their wrists with no mercy.

Give us revenge. Over and over, there was one face at the forefront of the images being fed to her. Tall and handsome in a classic all-American way, with artfully disheveled blond hair, bright blue eyes, and a charmer's smile. He kept smiling even as he killed his way through entire families.

He'd smiled from the doorway of the collective too.

The spirits pulled back, electricity no longer lighting her up from the inside like an obscene art exhibit. Even without being in her body, Emilie gasped for breath because her brain remembered breathing. Right now, she needed the touchstone, needed to remember who she was separate from what she'd just seen and experienced over and over again.

When she looked back up, most of the spirits had diminished even further. Her fragile equilibrium was smashed to bits, and without saying anything, Emilie retreated to the fortress of her body.

Bracketed by blood and bone again, her breath was still too sharp in her chest, but now she had a name for the man she'd seen wreaking chaos.

She opened her eyes to find Lu watching her very carefully. Emilie didn't have time to consider whether maybe she should have kept her mouth shut for the moment.

"It's Evan Campbell. Something happened, and something got ahold of him. The Scions are his now, and they're on the hunt." She swallowed against a throat that tasted like copper and lightning, rough as sandpaper. "His victims are screaming out because whatever is riding him is worse than anything he could do by himself."

Lu's eyes widened in horror as Emilie slumped back, fully letting the wall hold her up.

"How do you know that name, Emilie?" Her eyes were still too wide and hands trembling just barely, but Lu was a doctor and already regaining her composure. Emilie envied her the ability.

She waved at the next room, where the mumbling had stopped now that she had done as they'd asked. "He's been killing us for a long time now." Tears pricked at her eyes, and Emilie blinked against them as if it was going to do her any good at all. "He kept hunting us for no reason other than that there was magic in our blood." She blinked against the tears. "Same way his daddy taught him, but he's not a hunter. He's a monster in human skin." She paused and took a fortifying breath. "They told me his name." Her focus settled on Lu, meeting her eyes as the tears started to spill down her cheeks. "When they showed me how he killed them. When I lived it with them."

5

DANI

Her feet moved on autopilot, taking her down the stairs and through the labyrinth of internal rooms and hallways until they spit her out the back door, where a few dozen vehicles were parked. A few loose groups of hunters were gathered, lazy clouds of smoke wafting from them as they chatted while the sun went down on the horizon.

No longer trapped by the smell of antiseptic and too many people crammed into too little space, something deep in her chest loosened, and Dani took a deep breath. It was sharp and cold, but it cleared some of the fog drifting through her. She kept replaying the night before, the way ice had rushed through her veins when she'd realized they were outside, the fear consuming her at the thought of the Scions being in the same zip code as Emilie, much less in the same building.

She'd hoped that they'd never pop their heads back up out of whatever hole they'd been living in for the last few years. Nearly running into them alone was a nightmare all on its own. Having Emilie with her made it worse. Much, much worse.

They were supposed to be gone. Supposed to be *done*. Hot anger surged through her, sudden and ferocious. The shock of what had happened, what *could* have happened, had worn away, and fury was left in its wake, too much to contain inside her chest. Dani snarled and stalked over to where a dumpster hulked at the edge of the parking lot.

It was darker over here, with nobody lingering close by. Hidden in the shadow of the metal, she paced frenetically, trying to smother the hot anger threatening to consume her. The Scions hadn't been seen east of the Mississippi in three years, and she'd been avoiding them since long before that. She'd kept away from their old stomping grounds, worked the job, and she'd stupidly thought that somehow, they'd fade into the darkness.

Instead, they were on her fucking turf, and from what Emilie had said at the library, they were right back to their old MO. Hunting down talented like animals to absolve them of their affliction. With a snarl, she threw a punch into the dumpster, feeling the metal flex as it screamed. Reverberations ran up the line of her arm and settled into her shoulder. Dani let out a long breath and stepped back, readjusting her jacket. Her knuckles burned with the impact, but she could already feel the skin itching as it knitted back together, courtesy of the magic gifted to her by her affinity with the veilblade. She ran a hand over her face and walked back into the light.

A few moments, later two hunters she hadn't seen since before Graham died appeared out of the shadows. Mateo and Nova approached her, their faces drawn and serious. Dani's eyes raked across Mateo's broad form, searching his rich brown eyes for some hint of what was going on. Instead of finding anything helpful, she watched him clench his jaw before speaking up.

"Reaper. It's been a while."

Dani's head twitched at the old nickname, but she swallowed her reaction. She'd met Mateo during the year she'd been running with Julia Campbell and the Scions.

"Mateo. Nova." She nodded to his companion.

Nova was a sharp slash of a Korean woman with soft features, a bob of dark hair lit up with deep green highlights, and an explosive temper. The two of them had been working together for years now, and they moved in tandem. Dani didn't run into them often, but it was rarely good news when she did.

"We ran into some trouble recently."

Nova elbowed him, and Mateo sighed, dramatically waving his hand. She narrowed her eyes at him, then looked at Dani. "Scions are hunting again. Like they did back in the day." She gestured to where their Bronco was parked at the edge of the pool of light and began walking as she continued. "We ran into two hunting parties. One in Missouri three weeks ago, another in Texas before that."

"Seriously?" Dani looked to Mateo for confirmation. "How many years since any of us saw them at all, and now three sightings in a month?"

"More than three," Mateo said quietly.

Nova unfurled a map onto the hood of the Bronco and started pointing out places marked with red ink. "Three towns in Texas. Plus Missouri, Louisiana, Georgia, Kentucky, Tennessee, and Indiana." She stabbed at the map as she talked. "Something is up."

Dani let out a shuddering breath and checked to make sure nobody else was hovering close enough to overhear their conversation. "That's for fucking sure." Her eyes flickered to the clinic then back to Nova. "Emilie and I nearly ran face-first into one of their goon squads yesterday in Illinois."

Mateo produced a red pen from one of his pockets without looking and handed it to Dani. "Mark it on the map. You're not our last stop."

"You think there's *more*?" She took the pen but blinked at Mateo, hoping that he was kidding. "This isn't bad enough on its own?"

"If they're operating this brazenly, then we need to know how many of them there are," Mateo said.

"Fine. But for the record, I hate everything about this." She looked at the map and made a mark on it.

"They didn't clock you?" Nova asked.

"Last night? No." Dani shifted her gaze to the clinic again for a moment. "No, Emilie got reception"—she tapped the side of her head—"and found us an out. But they were there for cleanup duty. They'd already iced a collective there."

Mateo and Nova shared a dark look, and Dani saw them speaking without saying a word. "You wanna share with the rest of the class?" She gestured at herself.

"The Scions were always fringe, but there's been a lot more Humans First sentiment floating around in the last few years," Nova said.

"What if the old man let his dog back off the leash?" Mateo asked. "You of all people have to recognize what this looks like."

"Jackal is fucking *rabid*," Dani hissed in return. "The old man was unhinged, but let him off the leash, and all hell breaks loose. And if he's out—" *His sister isn't far behind.* Dani bit her tongue, but the hunters heard the words she didn't say out loud.

Nova folded the map back up and tucked it into a pocket with a look on her face Dani didn't know how to decipher. Mateo made a noise low in his throat. "If it is, though, we can't overlook that. And this"—he tapped the map insistently—"paints a picture."

Dani began to pace again and rubbed a tired hand across her forehead. "Did you just come to ask me if I thought it was him, or to ask about Scion sightings?" She paused, then turned her head to Mateo again. "That's not why you came." She narrowed her eyes. "What is it? What are you actually here to ask?"

Nova took a half-step forward, her dark eyes flaring with light as magic flooded her system. Mateo threw out a hand to stop her from moving closer, eyes pinned on Dani as her lip curled back in a snarl. The veilblade hummed in her pocket, vibrating gently against her jacket, asking if it was needed.

"Someone was tracking us," Mateo said.

Nova shot him a dirty look then turned back to the Bronco, hopping up to sit on the hood with a sigh. "We lost them, but we're not the only ones." She jerked her chin at Crossings. "Lu upped security because they spotted someone watching the place, and someone tried to torch a hub that worked openly with a local collective out west."

"You think Jackal is off the leash and he's gunning for *us*?" Dani swore under her breath and resisted the urge to go punch the dumpster for a second time.

"I think that he's only gotten worse with time and that he has an axe to grind," Mateo said.

"Targets on our backs," Nova added under her breath.

"If there's one on mine, there's no way they haven't been looking for you too." Mateo sighed again.

Dani tipped her head back and stared up into the darkening sky, trying to find a way around what they were telling her. She'd been fifteen when she got caught up with the Scions, and it had taken two and a half years for her to wise up and get out.

She hadn't gotten out alone, but it hadn't been easy, either.

"Did they ID you? I mean…"

"I know what you mean, and I don't know."

"They were on our tail for a few hours after a job, but we might have just pinged their radar," Nova said. "We didn't go face-to-face, but we had a quiet tail for a few hours."

"And we were in Nevada," Mateo added. "Way out from their old stomping grounds."

Dani groaned and rubbed both hands over her face as she looked back to her friends. "This is very, *very* fucking bad."

"You did ask why we needed to talk." Mateo shrugged.

Dani suppressed the urge to punch him in the shoulder to make a point. With her luck, Nova would try to bite her over it, and the last thing she needed to do was tussle with a hunter who didn't want her dead.

"It's been years. Why now? Why not, I dunno, anytime in the last decade?"

"Fuck if I know!" Mateo winced and lowered his voice. "But it's our problem now, and you know it only means we're at the top of the list. I don't know what's going on either, but we need to figure it out. Fast."

"I know." Dani breathed out and let her eyes close for a moment before reopening them. "I need to go fill in Emilie and ask Lu why she didn't tell me shit was this bad. I'll text you when I have more to tell."

Mateo nodded, and Nova hopped down off of the truck.

"Sounds like a plan. We're headed south. Gonna swing through Joe's before we meet up with somebody in Florida."

Dani nodded. "Just keep your head on a swivel, yeah?"

"Yeah."

She watched them drive off before turning back to Crossings with a sigh. Twenty-four hours ago, there had not been a murderous cult, coded journals hidden by murdered talented, or a psychotic hunter with a grudge and a taste for torturing anyone with magic setting his crosshairs on her.

The Campbells, the Scions, and why she'd left were all tangled up in her past. One she tried to ignore whenever she had the chance because dwelling on it had never done her any good. Except that now it was back to bite her in the ass, and she wasn't running on her own anymore.

A lump at the back of her throat made it harder to keep her cool as she worked out what needed to come next. Isaac Campbell might have been unhinged, but he was absolutely docile compared to his son, and he'd always kept a tight leash on his dog. If Jackal was out hunting talented without a sitter, something had gone very wrong.

When she'd gotten away from the Scions, most of her contacts from that world had disappeared overnight. But not all of them. There were a few old haunts that weren't happy she was so friendly with talented, but they wouldn't pull a gun on her for it. Not while the lights were on, anyway.

It meant walking into a hub that would gut Emilie as soon as serve her a beer just for the magic that hid under her skin. Meant slipping into the shape of the woman they all still called *Reaper*. She didn't blame them after what she'd done, but her girlfriend wouldn't like it. Wouldn't like any of this.

Dani tipped her head back to the sky again and rolled her shoulders. Pulling out her phone, she shot a quick message to someone she knew who still frequented the spot she'd need before heading inside.

She didn't know how she was going to explain this to Emilie. Didn't have the first clue how to explain any of it. But she'd have to before she left to meet up with her contact. If she knew anyone who still worked with the Scions, it was him, and he owed her big.

6

EMILIE

The world rushed past her in smears of watercolor as Lu led her through the hallways until they reached her personal office. Emilie only knew it was her personal office when the doctor pulled out a bottle kept inside the desk. She demurred, mind still trying to process what she had just seen, just experienced.

The lives of the people who had shoved their memories into her sloshed inside her mind, one scene bleeding into another, Evan's cold eyes following her through a dozen deaths that hadn't been necessary. She understood when there were talented who needed to be put down. It wasn't something she got involved with when hunters talked about it. But Emilie knew better than most what could happen when a talented was consumed by their own power. The damage it could do to people and communities on a small scale, much less a large one.

"You with me, Em?" Lu's voice interrupted the stream of memories, and Emilie focused on where she was leaning against the desk, watching her.

The medium tried to focus, but it was like the world wasn't tuning all the way back in after she'd returned from her trip to the veil. No matter how many times she blinked, she was still seeing echoes of the world past what most people saw. There were shades hanging in the shadows, drawn by her presence, and in the hallway, there was an echo of a young man treading back and forth anxiously.

Emilie noted this distantly and without emotion. *Did I overload my circuit?* It had happened after Dawson. The raw amount of magic and power she'd funneled through herself in order to help Dani destroy Spectre had knocked all of her talents out of whack for weeks. Spirit radio had gone quiet for almost a month; briefly, she'd wondered whether it would show back up at all. Now, it was like the veil was bleeding through. Her usual shielding techniques weren't quite cutting it, and in the back of her skull, there was a low, deep throb.

"I'm here. Ish." She frowned and shook her head, vision swirling in front of her eyes.

In the distance, a low droning started. Three words repeated over and over, too far away for her to hear them. It was barely audible, and Emilie's eyes kept drifting out of focus as she concentrated on it, trying to hear what the words were. What they were saying. Emilie was unmoored, drifting through her mind and the memories foisted on her.

Something is wrong. The thought rang through her like a clarion bell, fear flooding her system, ice racing at its heels. Emilie pulled in a ragged breath that tasted like frost, and it was clarifying. Her vision finally sharpened in front of her, the drone dying away as she focused on where Lu was kneeling in front of her, one wrist in hand as she took Emilie's pulse. Her dark green eyes flicked up, and she scowled before shaking her head and dropping Emilie's wrist.

"Your pulse was going crazy, and I felt your temperature drop through the floor. Wanna explain?" Lu stood up in a single fluid motion, then leaned back against her desk, folding her arms across her chest.

Emilie blinked a few times, noticing the shade in the corner hadn't disappeared when she'd gotten ahold of herself, before answering. "That hit me harder than—" *anything else I've done before* "—I expected it would. I panicked a little, and some of my talents responded." She picked at a nail, not meeting Lu's eyes for a moment.

"Are you okay?"

"I think so?" Emilie ran a hand through her short curls. "Things are just louder than usual. They'll quiet back down."

Lu harumphed at her but moved back around to the other side of her desk. When Emilie looked up, she found herself under the intense gaze of the woman most of the hunters she knew had nicknamed Charon. She resisted the urge to squirm under her fierce gaze. After a long minute, Lu broke their impromptu staring contest and leaned back in her chair, still watching Emilie carefully.

"As a rule, I'm a fan of when people don't try to die on me."

"I wasn't trying to die, I swear." Emilie held up her hands in front of her. "I..." She trailed off and stopped trying to find the words to explain what had happened. In the distance, the droning conversation started back up. She tightened her shields again, and it faded from her periphery. "They were asking for help." She frowned. "I just didn't think I was gonna get whomped...and I did."

"You didn't think you were gonna get *whomped*," Lu repeated, face deadpan.

Emilie sputtered and tried to smile. She did not succeed. Lu melted in her chair until only her eyes were visible above the line of the desk. She groaned from her position before popping back up to sitting normally.

"New rule, then," Lu declared. "No more of whatever that was unless you know what you're getting into. I'm not explaining to Dani if you *bork* yourself by poking ghosts." She shook her head.

Emilie narrowed her eyes. "I thought I was just going to talk." She scrunched her face up. "And technically, at first, that's what I did."

"At first."

"Mm hmm." Emilie blinked innocently before looking down, fingers picking at an errant seam on her shirt.

"And then?"

Emilie grimaced. "And then they asked for help and offered up information. It's usually just a few glimpses."

"I take it things were a bit more than that."

"A bit. Yeah." Emilie bit her lip and looked up at the ceiling for a long moment. "The spirits showed me why they were calling for help. I saw..." She breathed out, and broken glimpses of memory flashed across the back of her eyelids, Evan Campbell sneering down at her.

"Emilie?"

"I'm here, I'm good. I promise." The droning became audible somewhere in the background again, and Emilie felt her eyebrow twitch. "It was. I didn't just see what they had seen. For a few seconds, I was them. All of them."

"All of who?"

"Evan Campbell has been hunting talented like they're animals, and the pieces that survived their deaths are all screaming out for help." She ran a hand over her mouth and jaw, unsure of what to say next.

Lu watched her carefully, her eyes flicking back and forth until she decided something. She held up a finger, then produced two whiskey tumblers.

"If he's actually back on the damn board, I need a drink, and you sure as hell look like you could use one."

"You drink on the job?"

Lu shot her a deadpan glare as she poured them both a measure of alcohol. "I'm not on the clock for procedures today. I came in to show you what was going on upstairs." She topped the bottle and pushed the second glass toward Emilie.

Emilie grabbed the glass and took a small drink, the heat of alcohol racing down her throat. She held the glass close to her chest. "Why did security go up, Lu?"

Lu drained a third of her drink in a single swallow. "We treat hunters and the people who work with them. That includes talented, and even a few casters. Some folks don't like that very much." She took another swallow. "They'll have to get the fuck over it."

"There were so many of them," Emilie said. "How could there have been *so many of them*?" She put the glass down on the desk, watching the amber liquid slosh.

The droning was growing louder, and her shields were already as tight as she could wrap them. She could hear the slight pause between words, the longer pause before they repeated each time, but Emilie still couldn't make out what the words were.

"How do you know it was Evan Campbell, of all people?"

"Not everyone got to die fast." Emilie's words were clipped, barbed at the edges. "He likes to hear himself talk."

Lu's lips drew into a flat white line, and she finished her drink before staring at the empty glass as though it had something to tell her. She put the it down, rubbing at her forehead, eyes far away and moving back and forth. But Emilie couldn't focus on her because the droning was getting louder. *Closer.*

"Do you hear that?"

Lu didn't answer, caught up in her own head. Emilie turned toward the hallway, but there wasn't a window. In the corner of the room, the shade was unmoving, but she could tell it was the final remains of a spirit. One that had probably been here for a very long time now.

"*—sw—h—all—sw—he—all.*"

The droning continued growing louder and closer, and now she could hear some of the letters, the shape of sounds. It still wasn't clear enough to make out the exact words, though. Behind her, the door opened, and Dani marched inside, eyes blazing. Emilie caught the telltale twitch of her lover's right hand.

"We have a problem."

Lu turned and raised an eyebrow. "Another one?"

Dani spotted Emilie's glass of whiskey and snagged it off the table, finishing most of it in a single swallow before answering. "The Scions are on the hunt, and for whatever fucking reason, the old man let Jackal off his fucking leash."

7

DANI

The whiskey glass hit the desk with a thud as Dani stared at Lu. They hadn't known each other back then, but the doctor had her own tangled history with Evan and the Scions. She didn't want him running around without someone to mind him anymore than Dani did.

The silence grew around them, air growing thick with Lu's silence, Dani's anger simmering just under the surface.

"Do either of you hear that?" Emilie's voice broke the silence.

Lu looked toward the hallway. "Hear what?"

"Someone. Maybe several someones all saying something." Emilie scowled. "But I can't make it out, and I was really hoping it wasn't just me for once."

"No dice, killer." Dani shook her head. "Is spirit radio acting weird?"

Emilie shot Lu a guarded glance before answering. "Maybe." She rolled her eyes. "Okay, probably."

Dani gave her a long, assessing stare, and Emilie returned it in kind, her icy blue eyes flinty. As they had their staring contest, she picked out the little things about Emilie. The curve of her jaw, the slight tremble of her fingertips, and the way her eyes were shifting to a darker blue.

"You wanna explain that a bit more?" Dani asked, waving her hand at the room around them. "Go ahead, share with the rest of the class."

Emilie groaned, and her hands caught her head, slender fingers running through her curls. "Lu had a spirit...problem. When I went to deal with it, I got more than I'd intended."

"More than you intended," Dani repeated, deadpan.

Emilie rubbed at her temple for a moment. "They're...victims of the Scions. Of Evan Campbell. And they were reaching out for help." She threw up her hands helplessly. "It's not like there are mediums of my *caliber* all over the place." Emilie shook her head. "And now, I can hear them saying something. I just can't understand what it is."

Dani collapsed into an empty chair in the office, hunching over so her elbows were braced on her thighs. Emilie had seen Evan Campbell. Had seen him killing talented. Who were now calling out to her, of all people, for help. For years, there had been a wall between the way Dani'd become a hunter and the choices she made each time she took a job, each time she decided to hunt the monsters that were so fond of eating people.

She had walked away from the Scions when she'd realized the kinds of monsters they were without any help from magic. Had run until she'd found Joe and Graham and the rest of the hunting world. One where they weren't stalking people who were just trying to live their lives.

Dani had thought—hoped, prayed—that she'd managed to leave her mistakes with the Scions behind her. Now, in a matter of twenty-four hours, she'd stumbled face-first back into them, and this time, it wasn't just her. The words kept repeating over and over in her mind. *Not just me, not just me, not just me.* When she'd run from the Scions, the compound half on fire behind her, she'd done it with no one to worry about but herself. Graham's own history with the militia meant that he'd had the same fears and avoidance that she did.

Emilie was a new element, and one that sent Dani's heart leaping to her throat. She'd seen Emilie handle herself plenty, but the Scions weren't a job. They weren't a one-off. They were a threat to anyone who used magic. Whether it was by choice or because talents bloomed in their blood, it didn't matter much to them. Anyone who embraced magic, embraced their talents, embraced anything past their narrow viewpoint of what made a person *human* was tagged for extermination.

Dani let out a slow, ragged breath, calming her mind from the bleating fear that was trying to consume it.

"Mateo and Nova found me down in the parking lot," Dani said. "They were looking for me because Mateo knows that Jackal—that *Evan* has had a hard-on to take me out since before shit went sideways." She paused to collect her thoughts for a moment before continuing. "There have been more attacks."

"Attacks?" Emilie asked.

"Scions," Dani answered wearily. "They've run into two hunting parties. They know of at least nine others in the last month. And that was before I told them about us nearly running face-first into the welcoming committee in Illinois yesterday."

Lu paled but didn't say anything. Emilie's head cocked to one side, her eyes growing brighter and more luminous in her face.

"Do you hear something?" Dani asked.

"Same thing, but I can almost make out what they're saying." Emilie frowned. "But that's not important. Why would they come to talk to you about Scion attacks?"

Dani rubbed a hand across her forehead, trying to find the right words. She didn't talk about how she got started as a hunter. She and Joe had whitewashed the truth of it years ago, as much to protect her as to ensure they didn't get the wrong kind of attention. She'd kept her nickname but not much else, and over the years, her past had faded out of being something she was always distracted by.

"Everybody becomes a hunter somehow, right?" She quirked an eyebrow and looked down at her hands. "When I was fifteen, I managed to slip the lead at a facility for *troubled young women*. A group home run by the state for problematic foster children. I got away, and I ran as far and as fast as I could and wound up falling into a nest of umbra."

Dani sighed, stood up, and began pacing, unable to keep the nervous energy raging inside of her under control. Fighting monsters was easy. Trying to find a way to explain to Emilie that she'd been one once was much more difficult.

Emilie opened her mouth, but Lu waved a hand at her. She'd heard all of this before, years ago, when it was still fresher than it was now.

"They tried to take a few bites out of me, but I wasn't going down without a fight. They took me down, and a group of hunters appeared." A bitter smile crossed her face, there and gone again. "They fought off the umbra, kept me from bleeding out. If they hadn't been there, I'd have been dead before I was old enough to buy my own smokes. They wound up taking me back to their safehouse, patching me back up, and making sure I didn't die. I was mostly on the mend after a day or two. And that's when they sent in Julia."

She stilled her movement and looked over to Lu, who gave her a barely perceptible nod. Dani started pacing again, but slower this time. A measured pace instead of the frantic energy that had infected her after talking to Mateo.

"Julia explained what had happened. What had *really* happened. Told me about hunters." She paused and bit her lip. "She offered me a choice. I could go back to the shitshow of the normal world, or I could leave with them, go to Kansas. They'd train me to fight monsters like they did. It would give me a roof over my head, food in my belly, and for the first time in a long time, I wouldn't be alone. So, I went with them."

Emilie's eyes were so large in her face, but Dani didn't want to meet her gaze. Didn't want to see the questions swimming there or to try and figure out what her girlfriend thought of all of this. This conversation had been on a timer from the moment they'd left Dawson last year. If anything, Dani was lucky it had taken so long for things to come to a head.

"I didn't know that what they were telling me was horseshit.

Okay? I need you to know that. I was a kid, and I was scared, and they offered me an out that didn't have any bars on the windows. But it was *Julia Campbell* and her old man Isaac who took me in. The Scions were how I became a hunter, where I learned to shoot and use a blade when I wasn't in a street fight." Dani ran a hand through her wavy hair, wishing she had a drink. Wishing for a smoke, even though she hadn't had one in years and years now.

"Isaac Campbell had a flair for the dramatic. He ran the Scions like something between a church and...something more. He liked getting hunters young because they were easier to mold that way." She paused, choosing her words carefully. "He taught us that magic was an affliction. Talented and casters alike. A precursor to the corruption that consumes some talented. And we believed him." She let out a broken laugh and flopped back into the chair, every nerve in her body on fire, waiting for Emilie to start yelling.

She deserved it, truth be told. The things she'd done when she'd been under the Scions' thumb had been horrific, and she'd done the job happily. Thinking she was making a difference, saving people, doing what needed to be done. It couldn't have been further from the truth.

Emilie had gone stock-still in her seat. If Dani concentrated, she could have homed in on what was happening beneath Emilie's skin. Sense how fast her heart was beating or the precise rhythm of her breath. Instead, she waited for a blow that did not come.

"I thought you said that Graham trained you to be a hunter?"

"I did." Dani nodded, face drawn. "Isaac didn't train hunters. He trained killers." She wiped at her mouth with one hand, trying to pare down everything that happened into something palatable. Understandable.

"Wait." Emilie frowned like she was recalling something. "There was a riot or a fire or something."

"There was. Isaac's son, Evan...We were on a job that went bad. Evan nearly got a bunch of us killed, but rather than dealing with it, Isaac just wanted to muzzle him and keep him on a tighter leash." Dani frowned, flashes of old memories cascading across the front of her mind. "There were some of us who had realized something wasn't right, and when we expressed that opinion, shit got violent. We all used the opportunity to get the hell out of dodge."

"What happened next?" Lu asked, her voice carrying in the small room.

"A few weeks after the riot, people came after those of us who got out. To them, we're no better than traitors to the cause. It got bloody. After two years, Isaac cut a deal. We stayed out of their territory, and they stopped working outside those borders. Period."

Dani looked down at her hands, old shame washing back over her. She hadn't wanted the deal. Not at twenty, working with Graham and willing to do whatever it took. But it hadn't just been about her. It had been a deal to spare all of the survivors of the riot who'd run for the hills. Some of them had siblings to take care of, or children of their own. A small slice of territory for peace that would let them sleep in their beds without fear, that would ensure the Scion massacres stopped outside that territory? She hadn't been able to argue that it was a bad idea, much as she hated it.

"It was a good deal." The words still tasted like ash on her tongue. "Not perfect, but...better than the alternative." Better than running and hiding, attacks in the dead of night, back and forth until they were all bloodied and bruised and so angry, it seemed it wouldn't ever end.

"Do you believe that?" Emilie raised an eyebrow, but the look in her eyes was gentle. "Or is that just what you told yourself because you had to?"

Dani licked her lips, trying to find the words. Except, words had never been her strong suit, and this was no exception.

Emilie got up and moved across the room, settling in to kneel at Dani's feet. Her smaller hands took Dani's in her own, looking up at her until Dani caved and met her gaze. The anger and malice she'd expected to find there was absent, and it took her breath away.

"I think you were a kid when Isaac found you, and he offered you something you didn't have." Her thumbs rubbed tiny circles across the calluses in Dani's palms. "But—he used you as a literal child soldier."

Emilie bit her lip and met Dani's eyes. Dani wanted to be angry at the tenderness she saw in them, because it hurt. It sliced at her like pity, and if it hadn't been Emilie, she never would have let it happen. As it was, it was uncomfortable, and she didn't like it. Least, that's what she'd tell anyone who tried to ask.

"When you found out who Isaac Campbell was…that what he was doing was wrong…did you stay?"

"No." Dani heard the quiet desperation in her voice.

"Then you did the best you could in an impossible situation." Emilie shook her head, and a small, gentle smile curved her lips. "Did you help who you could on your way out?"

"Yeah, I…did what I could." She frowned at the memories of fires and explosions and screams as the compound burned. It had been impossible to save everyone, but she had opened the locks, made sure the gate couldn't close behind her. "But there were so many people left behind."

"You're not blameless, but you're not the culprit of all of this either." She stood back up and took her seat. "Trust me, I get it."

"It was a devil's bargain, and I took it."

"You weren't the only one, though, right?"

"Right, right." She sighed. Last night had thrown her off more than she thought if she'd gone off on a tangent like this so easily. Usually, she was better than this. "Isaac was a piece of work, but his children are—worse, in ways." She breathed out through her nose, unsure of how to explain the codependent dynamic that was Evan and Julia Campbell.

"I don't know *what* happened, but something has gone sideways," Dani said, reaching out for Emilie's hand again. "I don't know if Isaac has lost his mind or just decided he doesn't care anymore."

"Do you think they're coming for you?"

"I don't know," Dani said. "I don't know how bad it is, because when I left the compound, I left behind everyone I knew. When I showed up to the grill the first time, I was a stray. I had no one, and Joe took me in."

Thinking about this had been bad enough, but now that she was talking about it, she couldn't stop. It was all rushing out in a torrent, giving her no choice but to try and channel which direction it went. Dani got back to her feet, frenetic energy zapping her from the inside and making it impossible to sit still.

"Evan Campbell is probably going to come for me sooner or later, and when he does, he can't find you." Dani stopped and met Emilie's eyes. "The things they do, that he did? If I don't already have a target on my back, I will soon, and he'll use you just to hurt me. He'd do that even if you weren't talented."

She could hear the ragged edge of panic in her own voice, and Dani didn't really know where it had come from. She had worked with Graham for years, and it had never felt like this. Never this yawning abyss of loss that threatened to overtake her at the idea of losing Emilie.

"Fuck Evan Campbell." Frost spattered around Emilie in a protective circle that glistened under the fluorescent lights before wisping away to nothing.

"You don't know what you're saying."

"I know exactly what I'm saying, Dani." When Emilie looked up, her jaw was set and her eyes were shining otherworldly bright. "Mama's family ran and hid from Spectre for generations. For *centuries*." She hissed the word like it was a curse. "And it got them nothing but dead. I am not gonna hide from some Humans First fanatics, and I'm definitely not gonna stand to the side and let them hunt you down like an animal." Her eyes were half-wild in her face.

"Oh, I like it when Emilie gets riled up," Lu drawled from across the room.

She hadn't moved from her position in the chair, but she was clearly taking in the situation at hand and everything that came with it.

"I'm not saying I'm gonna go like some sacrificial lamb," Dani scoffed. "But it does mean operating with you as a talented, and with me period, just got a helluva lot more dangerous." Her mouth drew into a white line. "I mean it, Emilie, I'm not gonna hold it against you if you draw the line here." She opened her hands, palms up, aware of the old scars that ran across her knuckles and palm. "This isn't what you signed up for—"

"I signed up for you." Emilie closed the distance between them and grabbed Dani by the hips. "But I couldn't bail now even if I wanted to." She leaned up and kissed Dani with a pressure that left no room for argument. "And I don't want to," she added, leaning back just far enough that they were watching each other intently.

"If you say so."

"I do," Emilie answered, almost cutting Dani off.

"So, what's the play, *Reaper*?" Lu asked.

Dani tucked one of Emilie's curls behind her ear. "I'm going to have to do things I don't like." She turned her head so she was looking at Lu, still holding onto Emilie like a lifeline. "I reached out to our favorite fence."

A complicated wave of emotions filtered across Lu's face before she nodded. "Sawyer is tricksy, but he won't screw you over."

"He owes me."

Lu smiled, and it was nothing but teeth. "And I'm his doctor."

Dani turned her attention back to Emilie. "This means I have to go somewhere, and you can't come with me. I'd bring you if I could, but it's too dangerous. The place I'm meeting Sawyer is…"

"I get it," Emilie said, pressing one hand against Dani's sternum. "I don't like it. At all. But I get it. Just stay safe. I'll stay at Crossings."

"Okay." She nodded, more to herself than to anyone else. "Okay."

8

EMILIE

Crossings was quiet this late at night. Emilie had promised Dani she'd stay put, so that's what she was doing, but there was nothing comfortable about what was happening right now. No matter how hard she concentrated, no matter how tightly she shut herself off from spirit radio, the droning buzz of the voices speaking to her kept growing louder.

Answer the call. Answer the call. Answer the call. Masculine and feminine voices, the tones of young children, teenagers, adults, and the elderly all layered over each other in three words that kept repeating. She'd tried going upstairs, going outside, even going down into the sub-basement, as though the thick cement walls could block out the voices of spirits reaching through the veil for her. For Emilie specifically.

She rubbed at her temple again, eyes shifting across the office, carefully sliding past the shades in the corner. Plural. When she'd entered the first time, there had only been one, but at some point in the last few hours, they'd begun to multiply. There were three in one corner, and two in the corner behind her. If she turned, she was fairly sure there was at least one more in the other corner, but the last thing she wanted to do was investigate.

Shades weren't usually violent. They were the *remains* of spirits, what happened when one slowly began to fade away from the real as they slipped farther into the veil. They were a smear of grey against the faded blue of the walls, no form or shape to tell her who they had been or why they were here. Except they didn't really move much. And right now, she had a pack of them following her.

There was no movement from them to tell her they were interested, but she didn't need movement. Something deep in her chest told her they weren't just interested in her; they didn't belong here. These shades were only here *because* of her. The door opened, distracting her from the shades and whatever was happening with spirit radio as Lu swooshed through the room and flopped back into her chair.

"Long term ward is quiet, and Dani just left the lot. She should be back in a few hours."

Emilie nodded, but her attention was split between the shades, trying to keep her shields clamped shut as tightly as possible, and talking to Lu.

"Good. That's good..." Emilie trailed off, eyes flickering between Lu and another shade that had just stepped through the wall behind her.

"Something up?"

"Can we take a walk? Maybe up to the roof?" Emilie licked her lips, trying not to let the underlying unease crawling through her system translate to Lu. Not yet, anyway.

Lu narrowed her eyes but nodded. Emilie turned, spotting not two but four more shades in the corner that had been out of her eyeline. She shot out the door, making a beeline for the stairs. The echo she'd seen earlier was still there, but there were shades flooding the hallway. None of them moved, there was no malice, but Emilie could see them. And they knew she could see them.

Up on the roof, the air was sharp and clear, and there were no shades lurking in the darkness. Lu followed her out and directed her over to where a small sitting section was set up with camp chairs and a little folding table. The doctor took a seat before waving Emilie into one of the others, leveling her with a penetrating look as she got settled.

"Wanna tell me why we're up on the roof? It's not warm," Lu said, rolling down the sleeves of her jacket.

"You know that I can see spirits, see the veil and hear it."

"Yes, I'm aware."

"Usually, my shields keep blinders on what I see. Except that right now, they're as tight as I can make them, but there are shades filling the clinic."

Concern flared in Lu's eyes. "Should I be worried?"

"No?" *Answer the call. Answer the call. Answer the call.* Emilie flinched at the voices floating up and around her, coiling like a snake. She sighed. "But I'm also hearing more than usual. Just three words, but they aren't stopping."

"What words? Do you know who's talking to you?"

"*Answer the call,*" Emilie said, voice syncing up with the spirits for a moment and sending goosebumps prickling along her arms. "It's not...It's dozens of voices. I can't isolate any of them, but they're all speaking together. Saying the same thing."

Lu stared at her for a long minute before turning her gaze out toward the mountains in the distance. She didn't say anything for a few minutes, but it was a comfortable quiet. Both of them mulled over what was happening, even if neither of them had a real grasp on why. Finally, she turned in her chair so she was fully facing Emilie.

"Are the shades violent? Pushy?"

"No." Emilie shook her head. "But shades aren't usually so mobile. I've never seen so many in a single place before."

"What does 'answer the call' even mean? What call?"

"I don't know." Emilie threw her hands up in the air. "It's been the same problem for the last year. Mediums were never a common talent, and Spectre did his best to wipe out any new ones that popped up. It makes trying to figure everything out way more difficult than for some talents."

"Your Dad isn't helping?"

"My father would prefer I come back and help him run the

auction house instead of *'gallivanting across the continent with that hunter'.*" Emilie mimicked her father's pitch perfectly.

Lu only raised an eyebrow in response.

Emilie groaned and ran her hands through her hair, feeling a telltale tremor starting in her left leg. In the distance, two sets of headlights came racing out of the darkness as a walkie-talkie on Lu's hip barked to life.

"Charon, we've got a full chariot incoming. I need you down in receiving to make sure nobody tries skipping the ferry."

"Duty calls." Lu gave her a quick two-finger salute and headed for the stairs.

Instead of staying up there alone, Emilie followed on her heels, nearly skidding to a halt when she got into the stairwell. It was packed with shades, more people than could have ever fit otherwise. She could feel the echoes of personalities as she moved through the stairwell. Glimpses of memories, the voice of someone they'd loved, and under all of it, those same three words still repeating over and over again.

It was getting louder, and panic was starting to eat away at her carefully constructed composure. Lu was just a few stairs ahead of Emilie, talking on the walkie again, but she couldn't focus on it. Everything was spinning in and out of focus. When they hit the ground floor, she nearly lost her footing but caught herself on a wall.

With each step, each heartbeat, spirit radio was getting louder and louder. She could see medics running back and forth and a hunter standing out near reception with blood on his hands, but Emilie couldn't seem to make her eyes focus past trying to count the dozens of shades.

The voices grew louder until they were all she could hear, the echo of their words bouncing off the walls around her. It was too much. This was why she'd learned to shield so young: it was easy to get overwhelmed by the cadence of people who had been stripped of their lives. But right now, there was no escaping it. Emilie tripped over something and hit the ground hard, barely managing to slap her hands down under her in time.

She rolled, pressing herself against the wall, and a medic appeared in front of her. A young man she didn't know. He was trying to talk to her, tracking the movement of her eyes. She shook her head no and tried to tell him she couldn't hear him. Couldn't hear anything but the voices of the dead as they thundered around her, as more shades filled the space until Emilie was trapped.

Ice bloomed in her throat, and panic made her swallow it down. Pressing it back into the core of herself where it wasn't going to get her called a witch in a clinic for hunters. Lu didn't like the Humans First fringe, but they got an occasional Firster in the clinic.

The medic disappeared, and Emilie pressed herself harder against the door. Each reverberation of the words flayed her skin, laying her bare, until even muscle and bone, sinew and vein, were taken and destroyed, leaving her with nothing but a spirit attached to an empty husk.

Someone else appeared in front of her, and she managed to clock Lu's eyes, gone bright green with worry. She gestured to another person, and suddenly, there were gentle hands helping her into a wheelchair before moving her seamlessly through the clinic hallways. Everything around her was painted grey, and each time she was pushed through a shade, it stole her breath for a second.

They broke out into the cold air, and then she was being moved through the lot until they stopped outside an RV. Once again, gentle hands helped her to her feet, helped her move up and into the vehicle, laying her down on a bed in the back. It was quieter in here, the absence of shades making the intensity slightly less. But only slightly.

"*Answer the call. Lighthouse, lodestone, conduit. Answer the call. Lighthouse, lodestone, conduit.*"

She whimpered, and Lu appeared next to her, a cool compress in her hand, which she laid across Emilie's forehead.

"It should be better out here. Bertha is charmed six ways to Sunday and warded twice as well."

Emilie nodded weakly in answer, but her throat was raw. Had she been screaming?

"Something about you lit up, and I think that's why the shades are here. It's *possible* they're exacerbating whatever happened when you got zapped earlier. I sent out some feelers to a few people in the network. If anyone knows anything, we'll know in a few hours. I think you need to rest, without feeling them watching you. Do you trust me?"

Lu's voice was low, even for her, the words tumbling over each other as they came out of her mouth. Something was happening, and Emilie didn't have the tools to deal with it. Her brain was sloshing around inside of her skull, and her muscles ached as though she'd just run a marathon.

The doctor held up a dose of something in a needle. "I'm gonna give you something to knock you out and have someone keep an eye on you and Bertha for the night. Okay?"

Emilie gave her a weak thumbs-up from where she was lying in the bed. She winced at a small pinch in the crook of her arm, then was distracted by the flood of cold in her veins before the darkness swallowed her. Those same words chased her down into oblivion.

9

DANI

What Dani needed was time. Space. From under her breastbone, the urge to fight, find a hunt, and rip its perpetrators to pieces echoed, sentiments from the veil-blade etched onto her bones like graffiti.

It had been a long time since she'd called herself a Scion, but not forever.

Hunting, in her experience, was as much about sacrifice as it was about anything else. Hunters would say it was about retribution, revenge, maybe protection if they were wearing a white hat. They put their lives on the line, and when that was no longer possible, they hung up their hunting boots and found a different kind of life.

For her, it was about how much you were willing to give up in order to get the hunt handled. She had her own list of failed jobs, but she knew of just as many where the sacrifice required had ended with good hunters dead—or as good as.

When she'd run away from the Scions, she'd also left so much of the life she'd started building for herself behind. Some of it had been cut-and-dry; places like the pool hall had been harder to leave behind.

The American supernatural community had shattered long

enough ago that nobody really had the details on what had gone wrong, or where, or with who. Not that it mattered now. The divide between hunter and talented was so wide in some places that she and Graham had avoided them whenever they could. But hubs were the best way to get information she could trust, and Sawyer still had a life at The Double Shot Den.

Dani cracked her neck and settled inside of her skin. Tonight, she needed to pretend to be someone else, someone like the girl she had been and not the woman she'd chosen to become. So she'd dressed like she was going to war: black boots, black jeans, black shirt, black and grey flannel, black leather jacket. Looking in the rearview mirror, her eyes were dark caverns in her face, hair wild under the fold of her knitted cap. She looked like someone going a punk show, and not like the thought of walking back into this hub was shredding her into pieces.

She spoke to her reflection. "You've got this. Survive, right? We can deal with whatever later."

The past year had been one of the best of Dani's life. Lazy mornings curled up in bed, prepping for jobs side-by-side with Emilie, learning how to fit together in a way that was new and comfortable and right, as so few things in her life were. If Graham had had his way, she'd have retired entirely after a job like Dawson. Being initiated as a bladesinger made that difficult, but even with the jobs, it had been different. Better in a way she hadn't realized ever actually existed.

And it terrified her. Emilie wasn't a born-and-bred hunter. Not really a talented like she'd been used to, either. But the thought of losing her on a hunt? Having her torn apart because Dani was too slow, or because she hadn't had eyes on their six, were what her nightmares were made of. Thanks to Spectre, she had memories of her lover cool and lifeless to supply them with too.

That was why she was here. She needed information, needed to know whether there was already a target on her back or if she could go deep undercover and wait out this newest chaos. She opened the door of the truck, and each step away from it let her fall back into the person she had been. Dani wasn't sure anymore that she'd ever really been this person, but her own memories called her a liar as she slipped back into the skin of a weapon made of flesh and bone with a pretty smile.

Dani could look back along the hunts that made up her life, the ones she had chosen and the ones she had stumbled into. Instinct or not, fancy pedigree or not, most people came into the life bloody, and she wasn't any exception. She liked to talk a good game, and she was good—hell, she might have been second only to Valkyrie, because while she'd been there and done that and gotten the scars to learn her lesson, she wasn't working solo these days.

After a year of Emilie in her truck and her bed and thoroughly entwined with her life, she couldn't imagine working without her. Except she'd never had to build up the scar tissue that would keep her alive.

Thing was, Dani knew about scars. The ones you carried and the ones you hid and the ones that you never, ever, *ever* showed anyone. Once, she'd thought she was made of scars. Nothing but ribbons of stretched pale flesh connecting her to the person she'd been, the things she had done. Some were easy to identify: A caster who'd shifted into a big cat. A wraith raking claws along her back. Fingers broken one too many times. Those were easy to explain away, gloss over. They were the life she'd chosen, and they fit the narrative, paid for in blood, sweat, and tears.

It was the invisible scars that ruined you. Graham lying broken and surrounded by fire. Emilie dead-eyed in her lap. Julia standing over a corpse as she continued to fire into its mass.

Double Tap Den was a pool hall that looked like it had been transplanted out of the '80s. How it had managed to avoid the bullshit that put the other halls out of business one at a time she'd never know, but Dani was pretty sure it was because nobody had the balls to try and tell Miller that he needed to close up shop.

Honest to god, she didn't judge them for the sentiment.

Her eyes roamed over the parking lot, checking out tonight's clientèle. It'd been years since she'd set foot in this part of town, and she didn't want to run into any old faces unexpectedly. The Double Tap didn't dick around with questions either.

Next to the front door was a Humans Only sign carved in wood that was impossible to ignore. In any hub Dani frequented, there were wards to keep track of who came and went. Here, there was only the understanding that magic was unwelcome, and in most cases, as good as a death sentence. She'd spent more hours here than she could count, burning time between jobs while working hunts or looking for intel in the early days.

Now or never. You're running out of time. She blew out another long breath before entering the hall, eyes adjusting to low light as she scanned the crowd.

She crossed the threshold, holding her breath, but there was no outcry from the patrons. Nothing to indicate that she was on their DOA list. There was a bar on one side of the room, and a dozen pool tables set up on the other. Some of them were empty, others surrounded by hunters bantering back and forth.

She paid for an hour of play at the bar and claimed one of the empty tables, racking the balls. Dani played against herself, but soon enough, a brunette with dead eyes sauntered over, watching as she lined up her shots.

To anyone who didn't know what was going on, it wasn't much. A few pocket shots, no pattern between stripes and solids, numbers, or where the balls went. For those that frequented Double Tap, it was as good as ordering what she was here for. Recent news, gossip, maybe a peek at their bounty board. Making sure they weren't following in the militia's footsteps.

"These are private tables." The woman caught Dani's eyes, smiling with too many teeth.

She cocked her head and gave the girl an appraising gaze. She was somewhere between nineteen and twenty-five, skinnier than was strictly healthy, eyes sunken into fair skin with bruises smudged underneath.

"And I've met the owner, same as anyone."

With a practiced gesture, she plucked a silver coin out of a zippered pocket and placed it between them. A raven skull looked up at them, and the woman's eyes narrowed before she nodded.

"Been a while between visits, mm?" Her eyes flicked to Dani's from the coin.

"You know how it goes." The coin was tucked back into a pocket and out of sight. "Life on the road."

She aimed and cracked the eight ball into the corner pocket, grinning as she stood back up. The woman made a disgusted face and disappeared back behind the bar.

A few minutes later, a handsome man with dark wavy hair, dimples, and a smile made to make women swoon appeared where she had been standing.

"It's not nice to terrorize the help."

She raised an eyebrow but continued to rack her balls without further comment.

"Eight years is a long time to stay away, Dani."

She played with the chain of a necklace hidden under her shirt and leaned back against the wall, measuring him up. Sawyer wasn't a card-carrying member of HF last time she'd checked, but he spent enough time in their hangouts that he was guilty by association. Shame, too, because the man was cute for a guy.

"It was easier for me to move on. You know I had my reasons."

Her voice was brusque, but Sawyer took it as an invitation to join her.

"I know you've always had a soft spot for people, and it's gotten you into trouble more than once. Stripes are mine."

She watched as he dropped two balls before scratching and resetting the ball for her. Tall and slim, she could see the ripple of muscle under his shirt, the half-smirk that never seemed to disappear. Dani circled the table, looking for the right shot but never letting Sawyer out of her sight.

Hubs were supposed to be neutral territory for hunters. Places to trade information, pick up jobs, track down safe places to hunker down if a job went bad. Each one had their own rules of operation, and Double Shot was more hazardous than most.

"I heard some of the old pack was moving again. First time in years." Dani sank a pocket, circling the table to find her next shot.

"I don't tussle with fanatics," he said carefully while lining up another shot. "But I heard something about crews farther west saying there were people on the move again."

Dani's breath stopped short in her chest, and she forced herself to breathe through the gasp. She couldn't let anyone who was watching know that a comment like that would matter to her.

They kept playing, trading barbs back and forth as though she had all the time in the world. Her attention was split between Sawyer and the woman behind the bar who'd first approached her, now speaking with the bartender.

"Heard *Jackal* got off his leash and is seeing red."

Sawyer twitched, sending a ball bouncing off one of the side walls. He shot Dani a warning look that she easily translated, but she knew nobody was close enough to overhear her. She wasn't the first to refer to Evan Campbell as a wild dog, and she wouldn't be the last one, either.

"I can't confirm or deny," Sawyer finally answered, carefully navigating with his words. "But I will say, I've seen his other half recently. And let's just say, with things that have been happening, I wouldn't be remotely surprised."

He sank the last ball left on the table before putting his stick back up against the wall where he'd found it. Dani watched him disappear into the dim lighting, heading for the other side of the room. A moment later, the door opened, admitting none other than Julia Campbell.

Every muscle in Dani's body tightened. She hadn't set eyes on Julia since before the riot at the compound. They'd been teenagers back then, wild and crazy and obsessively in love with each other. When Dani left, it hadn't just been the Scions and Isaac she'd turned her back on. It had also been Julia. Julia, who knew the kind of monster her brother was and did nothing. Julia, who had pulled her out of an umbra nest, made sure that she didn't bleed out in some seedy back alley. Even now, she took Dani's breath away.

Long deep-chestnut hair tightly braided down her back. Black pea coat over a black shirt and slacks. She moved like liquid. Dani wasn't sure she'd ever seen someone who exuded violence in quite the same way. Then again, Emilie said the same thing about Dani when they were on a hunt. She spotted Dani, tossed her a look, and knocked her head to the side in the universal gesture for "let's have a chat." Dani followed Julia outside, willing to sacrifice the last of her allotted time at the table.

Blood rushed in her ears, and it sounded like the ocean crashing against her eardrums. The veilblade whispered to her from where she'd stowed it in her jacket, and when Dani threw open the door, the cold wind didn't cut through her the way it should have. Right now, she wasn't sure if that was a good thing or a bad thing.

Julia was on the far side of the lot, standing next to a shiny black SUV. On her own for once. That was new. To Dani's credit, she didn't gasp, didn't take the half step forward that her body tried to demand from her. Instead, she watched carefully, tried to guard her heart against the woman she'd been in love with ten years ago, before everything had gone so wrong. Before she'd realized exactly who the Campbells were and what they were trying to turn her into.

"Dani. I wasn't sure if you'd be willing to talk to me." Julia's full lips curled into a dark smile, and the girl that had loved her clenched in Dani's stomach, begging her to reach out.

"Why are you here? This isn't Scion turf."

She kept her eyes on Julia, looking for any trace of the small tells she'd known so well once. Julia's soft curves had sharpened over the years, every detail chosen for the reaction it would evoke. Seemed like they'd all three grown into the tools they'd been intended for, one way or another.

Julia leaned back, her smile fading but not disappearing. "Some things change with time. Other things do not."

She cocked her head as she looked at Dani. Dani felt remarkably similar to a mouse that had been spotted by an owl. Except that she was not prey and had not been for a very long time now.

"Seems that way."

"My brother is...erratic, and according to my father, he's acting outside the will of the community."

"Erratic? You call hunting people down *erratic*?"

A snarl flitted across Julia's features for a heartbeat, and Dani was reminded that she was just as dangerous as her brother. In her own fashion.

"This is beyond the pale. *Even for him.*" Julia swore under her breath. "Is there *any* other reason I'd come talk to you?"

"What does that even mean?" Dani shook her head, trying to get Julia to talk sense. Evan had always been the most brutal of the three of them, willing to do what other people weren't. Always crossing the line. "Why the hell isn't the old man handling him?"

"I don't know!" Julia threw her hands up in the air wildly before her lips thinned to a white line. "Dad has been getting more unstable too. Something is going on. Maybe it *has* been going on? I don't know, but it's bad, Dani. It's bad enough that I'm here talking to you of all people."

"Why? What set him off? Why the fuck do I suddenly have a target on my back after all these years? Didn't I stay the hell away, stick to Daddy's deal?"

Julia's nostrils flared, and she looked at Dani with eyes that were dead and cold in her face. "He wanted you dead before"—she waved a hand—"everything. You're only lucky it took him so long to find a way to do it."

Fury rolled through Dani, and she felt the telltale pulse of the veilblade from inside her jacket. "*Lucky?*" Her voice was a malevolent whisper, and her vision washed red before clearing again. Her phone vibrated in her pocket, and Dani took a step back from Julia before opening the message.

Lu: Something's wrong with Emilie. Get back here. Get back right the fuck now.

Fear crystallized inside of her, the fight that had been brewing between her and Julia still thick in the air. She bit back a snarl and shoved her phone back into its pocket.

"I don't have time for this bullshit right now." Dani shook her head. "If your brother has put me in his crosshairs, just you remember, that puts him in mine too."

Julia snarled this time, rage transforming her features. "You hurt my brother, and I'll hunt you to the ends of the earth."

"Your *brother* is murdering people in their beds, hunting down people who haven't done anyone wrong. He should have been put down years ago like the rabid animal that he is. But so long as he was under your daddy's thumb, he was manageable. The body count is rising, Julia. I'm not the only one who's noticed, and you know if my people have put it together, the Sentinels almost definitely have their eyes on this. On him."

Fear flared in Julia's eyes, and her shoulder slumped ever so slightly.

"Get your house in order before the council decides to descend on us, or I will."

Dani pivoted and sprinted for her truck. Something was wrong with Emilie. She needed to get back before anything else decided to go wrong.

10

EMILIE

The cold woke her up, the sharp *tat-tat-tat* of ice as it spattered against the wall chasing away oblivion. Sleep left Emilie slow and languid, until she drifted back into consciousness from wherever she had escaped the thunderous sound of voices she'd been unable to ignore or drown out.

She blinked at the unfamiliar surroundings, the dim faerie lights draped through the RV. Emilie sat up, flinching when she felt the telltale *slip* as her spirit separated from her body. She could still see herself lying there like she was asleep. The raucous voices that had been screaming for her were gone now, but the silence was heavy.

The calm before the storm.

She made her way to her feet, moving through the wall of the RV until she was standing on asphalt. A weak moon looked down from a sky dotted with poisonous green clouds and stars that were brighter in the veil than the physical world. And around her, around the RV, were dozens of mangled spirits. Their eyes stayed on her as she moved, but they didn't open their mouths. The ones that still had mouths, anyway.

Most of them were little more than the shades she'd seen on the alive side of things. Their forms were faded, blurred away at faces and arms. Not one stood without visible blood and wounds; not one had died easy or when they were ready to go.

Emilie narrowed her eyes and turned to look behind her. Even more were gathered around the back of the trailer where her body still rested. *What the hell is going on?* Not everyone who died left behind an imprint. It usually took an extremely strong force of will or a particularly violent death for a spirit to form. There were outliers, like certain entities that lived in the veil and fed on spirits as they crossed over, but she'd never seen anything like this.

"We were asking for help."

The spirit that emerged from the crowd was wrong. Emilie could see pieces of her stitched together with the fading remnants of another spirit. One of her arms didn't match, and the upper left quarter of her face was someone else. She was shards pushing together, mangled and still fading. All of the color had faded from her countenance. Her cardigan and matching dress were liberally splattered with gore, turning her into a sepia-stained video.

"Ever tried, I dunno, not screaming so loud you drive me insane?" Emilie was surprised she had the wherewithal to be quippy.

"You don't like picking up calls unless you know who's calling." The woman shrugged. *"We tried it the polite way, but we are out of options and running low on time."*

Emilie rubbed at the place between her eyebrows in frustration. "What is it that you want?" She waved a hand at the shades surrounding her. "Because you all want something from me."

"They told you before. When they were calling your name."

Emilie narrowed her eyes. "Earlier tonight. When the spirits hijacked those hunters?"

"Yes." The woman's image jittered, shards dislodging before they slotted back into place, anguish rolling off her in waves. *"They addressed you as what you are. The lighthouse and the lodestone. Our light when the radiance of life has been taken from us. The one we gravitate toward."*

"I'm not just a for-hire ghost problem solver, you know." Emilie paused for a moment. "At least, not always. Why...why me? There are other mediums, other hunters."

"No there aren't. Your kind were never common, and a conduit of your power hasn't been available for a long time. They have been calling out for years. You're just the first one who could hear them. We cannot scream; we can barely whisper."

Emilie shook her head, confusion robbing her of precious equilibrium.

"You know who killed us, but he's not the only problem."

"Murderous lunatic on a killing spree not the priority? Great," Emilie muttered under her breath, then blew out an exasperated sigh.

Panic was bleating at the edge of her consciousness the longer this conversation went on. She'd known it was more than that meeting with the spirits, aware that the shape of this was larger than Dani wanted to admit, because it had to be. There were dozens of spirits here, all of them shredded so badly, they were fading into oblivion by simply speaking to her.

"Don't you see the storm?" The spirit turned, facing the poisonous clouds Emilie had spotted earlier. *"Storms in the veil don't mirror the living. I think you know that."*

A cold shiver crawled down the length of her spine. It gave her strength, the ice curling through bone and muscle alike, armoring her.

"That's where the problem is?" Emilie asked.

"Where it started." The spirit pointed.

The throngs of spirits moved for the first time, their bodies moving around each other in a seamless dance that ended in a path between Emilie and the place she was going. The place they wanted her to see. She moved faster than on foot, scenery flying by, always bracketed by that same divider of spirits.

Until they were gone, and Emilie was standing in the middle of an isolated town somewhere in the mountains. It was overgrown and clearly abandoned. A broken sign for Tenacity Mill told her the name of the town but not why she was here.

Above her, the sky was green, and thunder rolled ominously. Emilie could feel the wrongness of this place, the ground shifting under her foot like it didn't know where it belonged. With each step, the town rushed past her. Homes, broken storefronts, empty streets, an old church butting up against the edge of town.

Lightning flashed, turning everything red for a heartbeat. The wrongness of that church soaked into the air and the ground, and even without physically being here, it was an assault that she didn't know how to fight against. Emilie took another step forward and saw a hole in the back of the church that defied explanation.

It was a hole to nowhere.

A hole in the world that was black and purple, sharp, infected edges slowly crumbling away. A wound in the fabric of the veil that punctured the world as it should have been. Thunder rolled in the distance, and Emilie backed away from the church, back down the main thoroughfare of town. The first chance she had, she ducked around the corner of a building so she couldn't see the church anymore. *And it can't see me.*

The panic that had been braying at the edges of her perception tried to claw control from Emilie, and she white-knuckled her way through it, breath coming in short, aborted gasps.

A hole in the world. There was a hole in the veil, and a hole in the world, and somehow, it was connected to Evan Campbell and the people he'd killed. Emilie didn't know what she was seeing, how it was even *possible*, and there was no one she trusted to ask. If what she kept hearing was true, there was no one alive who had firsthand information.

Lightning shook the ground, and Emilie scrambled away, willing herself back to her body. One moment, she was in Tenacity Mill; the next, she was back in the lot outside the RV. Most of the shades that had been there were absent now, leaving the parking lot feeling eerily underpopulated.

The same spirit who had spoken up before was still standing there, barely a wisp of anything now. She smiled a sad, wan smile.

"*Now you see. We need you. And we need your bladesinger. Help us. Before it gets worse.*"

Before Emilie could answer, she faded away into nothing, leaving Emilie standing alone in the parking lot wondering what could possibly come next.

11

DANI

Dani's truck slammed to a stop at the edge of Crossings, and she jumped out in a ground-eating stride, breaking for the front doors. During the drive back to the clinic, her mind hadn't been any more calm than when she'd received Lu's message. She should have been here, shouldn't have left Emilie here when things were so unsettled.

"Dani! Over here!" Lu's voice broke across the asphalt.

Dani skidded to a halt and looked across the parking lot to where her friend was standing outside of her RV and waving. She pivoted and sprinted over, heart clenching in her chest.

"She's okay. *Emilie is stable.*" Lu's words spilled out of her mouth, hands held up in front of her.

Dani's eyes popped from Lu to the trailer behind her and back again.

"She's okay?"

"She is *now*." Lu ran a hand through her hair.

"What the hell happened?" A shudder raced through Dani, and she swallowed a hysterical laugh.

Lu bit her bottom lip and blew out a long breath. "I don't have details. But something overwhelmed her, she couldn't talk, she was almost seizing. Her breath was starting to frost, so I brought her out here."

"Did anyone notice?" Dani resisted the urge to throw a look over her shoulder at the clinic.

"Hopefully not." Lu pursed her lips. "But I can't control their politics, and I don't turn away people who need the help." A shadow crossed her eyes. "The Scions would rather be caught dead than show up on my doorstep, though. You know that."

"It's not the actual Scions I'm worried about." Dani scuffed a boot against the pavement. "Hunters love to gossip, and Emilie is a new player on the board. The less people know, the less they can talk about, around someone who's extra interested in listening in."

Fear constricted her heart, a deep tumorous pain that seemed to weigh her down more than she'd ever anticipated. The past year with Emilie had been like stepping out from shadows into the light of the sun, except she'd never realized she was in the shade to begin with. It wasn't even that she didn't trust Emilie—while her medium wasn't quite at her level of prowess, she'd put her nose to the grindstone. Made sure that she wasn't a detriment, not dead weight for Dani to cling to.

"She's not an unknown," Lu pointed out.

"She's not," Dani agreed, two fingers rubbing at her forehead. "Is she awake? Inside?"

"I am," Emilie's hoarse voice spoke as she stepped out of the RV.

She looked haunted, her eyes dark and a fine tremor running down both arms. She took one shuddering breath, followed by another, as Lu hustled over and started to take her vitals. Emilie swallowed and closed her eyes before reopening them and pinning Dani in place. Something stretched between the two of them, instincts from the veilblade surging inside of her, speaking to her in a language she did not know.

"The spirits that Lu called us about were like the tip of the spear." Her eyes went far away for a moment, and she swayed. "When I tapped in earlier, the...others started to reach out. They were *drawn* to me." A tiny furrow appeared between Emilie's eyebrows as she began to pick at her hands. "There were too many of them." A tiny, bitter laugh broke loose from her lips. "They need help, and there isn't anyone else they can ask. They're weak. But there are so *many* of them."

Dani rushed over as Lu propped up several folding chairs. Dani eased Emilie into one of them and gave her friend a nod of thanks. All of her attention was on Emilie. On making sure she was actually okay and wasn't just pretending.

"Who?"

"Victims." Emilie blinked, eyes glassy with unshed tears. "They were all victims of Evan. Of the Scions." She shook her head, and her eyes cleared up a bit, going steely with determination. "That's not the whole problem, though. They showed me something."

"What kind of something?"

Dani dropped into a crouch, her hands on Emilie's knees in front of her. Their fingers tangled together as she rubbed her thumb along the edge of Emilie's smaller hands. Emilie frowned down at her, the furrow between her brows deepening as she bit her lip, eyes bouncing back and forth.

"The veil is almost a reflection of the world we live in. There are echoes of old events, and things other than spirits that exist there. Locations tend to make a mark, but weather doesn't usually exist there. Not like it does here." She looked at Dani again, and her features smoothed out. "But there was a storm in the distance. Green sky and lightning, the kind of storm that doesn't—that *shouldn't* exist there. So, I took a look. A closer look."

Horror filled Emilie's pale blue eyes like water filling a glass. A slow and steady increase as she tried to explain what she'd seen.

"You don't have to tell me right now."

"I do." Emilie grabbed Dani's hands tighter. "I do, because when I got to the storm, I was standing in a town. *Tenacity Mill*. There was a church, and the closer I got, the bigger the storm got, until I came around a bend and I saw what was causing it. There was a hole. A rip, a tear, in the fabric of the veil." Emilie swallowed. "So I ran. I came back and slipped back into my skin."

Dani loosened her hands, surging closer to Emilie, ensnaring her in a tight embrace. Emilie grasped onto Dani, fingers clutching her like she'd forgotten what physical touch felt like. The veilblade came to life at those words, instincts that were still foreign to Dani coming alive inside of her. She understood, viscerally, that a tear in the veil of that kind, that magnitude, was more than a threat.

"A tear."

Emilie nodded.

"In the veil."

Emilie nodded again.

Lu got up from her seat and ran a hand through her hair, fidgeting where she stood.

Dani swallowed against the lump in her throat.

"We can't ignore it." Emilie pulled back from Dani. "They came to me for help because there wasn't anyone else. *Isn't* anyone else. If you could have seen what I did?" She shuddered and shook her head.

"No." Dani breathed out. "No, we can't ignore it. Why there, though?" She turned to Lu. "Have you ever heard of Tenacity Mill?"

Lu shook her head, and Dani stood back up. Emilie let go of her hands as she did.

"The spirits said that was where 'it started.'" Emilie shook her head again. "But I'm not sure what they meant. Not sure of a lot they said before that, either."

"I can see if it rings any bells for Joe. If something is wrong on the veil side, we don't wanna walk in blind."

"You can crash in Bertha." Lu's voice was quiet. "You need sleep. Both of you." Her eyes drifted toward the mountains, where the sky was no longer pitch dark. "It'll be dawn soon enough, and if you're not asleep by the time the birds start, you'll be awake for hours."

Dani opened her mouth to argue, but Lu held up a hand, a cold mask slipping over her face that clearly communicated she was not to be argued with right now.

"You've been in the middle of shit since last night and on edge since you hit that burnt-out collective. If Emilie is right—and she is—then you're gonna need to drive tomorrow to figure out what the hell is causing a rift like that. Whether it's showing up on our side or if the tear goes, I don't know, somewhere else."

She pointed at the RV.

"Go climb in bed. I'll text Joe and tell him to send Emilie everything he has. It'll be waiting for you in the morning."

"Is it safe?"

Lu jerked her chin at the clinic. "I keep guys on lookout up on the roof. If they suspect anything, someone'll be out here before shit gets twisty."

Emilie stood up and took Dani's hand, tugging her quietly toward the RV. Dani nodded at Lu and let herself be led to the RV. There was more room inside than she'd expected, but Dani's attention wasn't on the decor. Instead, she spotted small charms and lines of wards that probably did any number of things. She would have asked Emilie if things were different.

Right now, she didn't care. Now that she was inside, the exhaustion bore down on her like a weight, curling over her shoulders. Emilie crawled onto the bed, tucking herself against the wall while she waited for Dani to follow. She shucked her boots, jeans, and jacket before crawling in too.

Emilie tucked herself against Dani, snuggling into her under the thick duvet. Dani breathed in the sharp smell of her—snow and cinnamon—and took in the soft curves of her lover's body as she stroked a hand up and down the length of Emilie's thigh.

"I love you," Emilie murmured against her skin.

"I love you too," Dani answered, moving her hand to play in Emilie's curls.

Emilie swallowed but didn't say anything else. A few minutes later, her breath evened out as she drifted off to sleep. Dani didn't follow right away, content to lay there and stroke her hair. She had learned over the years how to listen to her instincts. Sometimes, they noticed things far before she would have otherwise, and it'd saved her bacon more than once.

Right now, it was dread pooling deep in her belly, a sure knowledge that something bad was on the horizon. The moment Emilie had mentioned the tear, it had felt like a sharp laceration, and now everything that made her a hunter was screaming that she needed to get there. Needed to see it. Because this wasn't just bad. It was catastrophic.

Outside, the sky was turning grey and silver. Dani closed her eyes and drifted off just as the birds began to chatter.

12

EMILIE

Fifty-two years ago, Tenacity Mill had been a mill town white-knuckling it through each fiscal year while the world continued to turn around it. It had been helped, in no small part, by its supernatural residents, which included two talented families, a small pack of werewolves who used the nearby wilderness as cover, and a small community of casters who still practiced the herb witchery they'd been taught in childhood.

Until a hunter wielding a veilblade had turned the town into a bloodbath. Cooper Campbell had been a bladesinger, and he'd made his veilblade sing a sanguine song as he carved his way through the town with no mind to the innocence of his victims. Sixteen people died before Sentinels converged, bringing with them hunters, talented, and casters.

When the dust cleared, the Campbell bladesinger was dead, the Campbell veilblade was AWOL, and Tenacity Mill was devastated. The town limped on for a few more months until the mill closed and the remaining denizens fled for greener pastures with things like jobs and hope.

In the years since, a number of jobs had cropped up in or near the town. Emilie wasn't surprised as she swiped through the history and documents that Joe had sent over this morning at Lu's request. Physical locations were as good as spiritual sponges, soaking up all the events and emotions that occurred somewhere. They seeped into brick and drywall equally, leaving a mark on the place that most people would never see with their eyes.

Those events and memories manifested in other ways, like bad vibes or places that seemed cursed by the things that happened there again and again. If Tenacity Mill hadn't been attracting spirits, she'd have been more concerned.

Outside, a thin strip of asphalt wound tightly through green fields overgrown with thick branches that drooped from the trees above. Emilie wasn't sure if it was just the storms that had pushed them this way or whether the trees always looked as though a strong breeze might knock them over.

Around them, the wind shook the cab of the truck, but Dani barely even blinked. With nothing but this road and field for miles, it was easy to see they were by themselves out here. It should have made her feel better, the idea that there wasn't anyone out here to cause trouble. But the closer they got to the coordinates Joe had sent over, the tighter the tension inside her chest ratcheted up.

The whisper of spirits somewhere nearby was growing larger, if not exactly louder. It was almost like they were all whispering to each other instead of reaching out to her. She wasn't sure what to make of it, but the rising suspicion that this may not have been the best idea surged through her.

"We're close now." Dani looked over, one hand reaching for Emilie's while she kept her eyes on the road.

She happily tangled their fingers together, thumb rubbing idly over the webbing between thumb and index finger. This morning, for a few minutes, things had seemed almost normal. Bodies tangled together under the sheets, Dani's heart beating under Emilie's ear pressed to warm flesh.

It hadn't lasted. It couldn't last, that perfect shining moment as they just lay there. Got to exist instead of running from one job to the next. Not with what was waiting for them in Tenacity Mill.

If anyone asked—and they didn't—she was already exhausted. She'd been tired before things had gone to hell at the library. A year on the road, no roots, the constant shift of faces as she introduced herself to the hunters and integrated herself into a new community. The fact that Dani had been doing this for a decade was almost impossible to wrap her head around.

She wasn't made for the road like Dani was; it wasn't home for her. But Dani had stolen her heart one cocky smile at a time. It made the long stretches in the truck easier to acclimate to, and she wouldn't trade her wild, dark-haired hunter for a quiet life. It was a choice she made, and kept making, even when it felt like she was moving against the grain.

Today was different.

She'd never been more sure that they needed to go to Tenacity Mill and see what had happened. If the echo from beyond the grave had ruptured through to the physical world. It was possible but beyond rare. And more dangerous than even she had words for.

Dani pulled the truck off to the side of the road, out of the way, where nobody would notice for the few hours it'd be parked nearby. Ahead, Emilie could see the stark ROAD CLOSED sign that kept anyone from driving down the road that had once led to Tenacity Mill.

Emilie checked her tablet one last time before stowing it and strapping her bag across her chest so the weight was on her hip and out of the way. There was no telling what they might find in town, and she wasn't about to take any chances. At Dani's behest, she'd started carrying in case things got dicey, and she checked the blessed iron knife on her hip to make sure it was secure.

When her feet hit the ground, voices crackled to life. A swirling singing mass of lives that had lived out their purposes and passed without dilemma. Dozens of them noticed her, whispering about their lives before their voices faded again.

"You with me, killer?"

Emilie gave Dani a nod and met her on the side of the truck. "I'm with you. This area is chatty."

"Chatty?" Dani raised an eyebrow, lips turning in a feline smirk.

"Nothing bad—not yet, anyway. But this place used to be full of life and people who loved it. This silence?" She gestured around them at the abandoned roadway. "It's not natural." Her eyes shifted toward a small path that led deeper into the woods, swathed in thick shadows. "What happened in town rippled out, and it was bad enough that even this far out, people felt it and decided not to stay." She shook her head.

Dani watched her, eyes going dark as the voices flowed over Emilie and through her like a current. Emilie's eyes slipped closed, hands drifting to her sides as she took a half-step forward. When she reopened her eyes, the blinders that let her navigate the world without seeing magic or what existed past here and now were gone.

The air around her chilled, but she barely noticed it. Instead, her eyes clipped across the road and trees. There were memories of a few houses that had been across the street once, an echo of children playing in the woods. It felt golden and bright and alive, and once she saw them, they faded away again, as though the spirits who had lived and died here wanted her to know it wasn't all darkness and blood and madness. This place had been more than that once.

Not anymore, though. Without her blinders, Emilie could see the faint taint that had spread—was still spreading. Grey tendrils of power reached out from a place beyond the woods that faced them right now. Emilie nodded, more to herself than anyone else, and headed for a small worn path into the woods, Dani hot on her heels.

The path wound through the undergrowth in a twisting labyrinth, but the closer they got to town, the more prominent the grey tendrils became. They coiled around trees, draining the vibrance from their leaves so even Dani noticed it. No animals in the trees, not a bird to be seen or heard in the sky around them.

Emilie knew she hadn't slipped her skin, but the world was losing its color, as though all the life had been drained from it. Neither of them spoke as they slipped past branches and thick vines, as if speaking about it would confirm that what they were seeing was real, and it was worse than Emilie could have imagined.

When they emerged from the undergrowth into Tenacity Mill, the pressure from the veil drove Emilie to her knees with a wheeze.

A boom of voices cried out their pain, the tragedy of their lives having ended so quickly. There were those who had been killed here originally and mill workers who had died under unfair conditions, but there were others too. A least a dozen, maybe more. They were angry and grieving, and they slammed into her like a freight train.

"Hey, no falling out before we even see what's going on," Dani teased, concern lighting up her eyes as she knelt next to Emilie.

"I'm good. I'm—" Emilie wheezed out a breath and nodded. "This place is..."

"I know," Dani murmured.

Firm hands helped Emilie get back to her feet, and she took another look at the town. Dark tendrils wrapped through and around the buildings, digging into the ground and driving all life from the place. Nature had overtaken the edges, encroaching unchecked year by year, with thick branches and dark, poisonous looking leaves.

Emilie swallowed, pointing down to the path ahead of them. "This is where I came in the other night. We follow that path, and it leads us right to the back of town."

"Well, I hate that." Dani shook her head. "That is a murder tunnel." She squatted down and traced out how the town was put together with a twig. "That wide street was the main thoroughfare, but we're already at the edge of town. If we just keep to the wood line, we should be able to skip around to the side."

"That should work." Emilie bit her lip. "You feel it, though, right? The wrongness of this place."

"Yeah. I feel it." Dani stood back up and turned toward the town. "This is recon today, deal? We see what the hell is going on, get photos or whatever, and get out of dodge."

"Deal."

"Good."

Dani tugged Emilie closer and kissed her, and Emilie melted into the contact. For a brief moment, everything else fell away, and it wasn't life or death. It was just her and Dani, and the world held its breath. They parted, and she looked up at Dani, smirking like the cat that caught the canary.

"You know that's a rude way to calm me down, right?"

"Works, though." She pecked another small kiss on Emilie's nose.

Emilie sputtered, heat crawling up her spine and warming her cheeks as Dani danced backward out of their embrace—and Emilie's reach. She tried to frown at her girlfriend, but then Emilie just shook her head, suppressing the small smile trying to emerge.

Something terrible was happening here, and they had to go find out what. Part of her was screaming that she should run, hide, and never ever, *ever* stop. Emilie smothered it ruthlessly. That instinct to hide instead of fight was what had cost her years of her life, what had cost so many women in her family their lives. She owed it to the spirits calling out for help to find out what was happening here.

Somehow, it was connected to the Scions and their reign of terror. She'd seen it, experienced it, and if she didn't at least try, the shards of spirits would drive her mad. There was no way but forward.

"I don't like that you're right, but I'm not going to argue." Emilie held out a hand.

Dani moved back into range, dropping her hand into Emilie's. "You ready to do this?"

"To go see if there's a *hole in the world*?" Emilie slowly blinked at her girlfriend. "Absolutely not. But I'm doing it anyway because we have to."

"We don't *have* to. There are other hunters, locals who would check it out."

"They don't know what I know." Emilie shrugged. "They can't see what I see. I have to help. I have to."

Dani huffed out a tiny laugh. "And you say you're not a hunter. I think that's the most hunter thing I've heard you say."

"Time to go be heroes?"

"Not heroes." Dani turned to the town ahead of them. "Time to be sneaks. In and out. We just gotta get in and back out without making a ruckus."

13

DANI

Dani knew that this wasn't going to be easy. She could smell it in the air, see it in the tension of Emilie's body, and hear it in the lack of any kind of wildlife. Winter hadn't fully arrived yet; there should have been squirrels running amok, looking to fatten up before the long freeze; there should have been birds somewhere.

Instead, a strange silence seemed to muffle the ruins of this town. It sent every instinct inside of her screaming. Ahead of them, a building stood, rotting into the ground, overtaken by vines and effectively ending their strategy of keeping to the wood line as they crept along the boundary of town.

A step ahead of her, Emilie paused and cocked her head to the side. If she turned and looked, would those pale blue eyes be shining like aquamarines in her face? Or would she look like something from a doctored photo, eyes milky white and translucent as she looked at what the veil separated them from?

Dani tried not to think about it.

Graham's talents had been a source of shame for him. A double-edged knife where he had to harm himself to even access it. When he'd started over as a hunter, he left his old life behind, the supernatural equivalent of witness protection allowing who he had been to fade away.

"I hate that half of our life is climbing into buildings that definitely have tetanus." Emilie's voice held no shadow of the beyond hiding within it.

"You get tetanus from an infection, not from a carrier." Dani grinned and sauntered past her along the edge of the building.

"It is deeply troubling that you know that."

"You know you like it." She winked and sauntered forward with a little sway in her hips.

"Do you hear that?" Emilie's voice had gone far away.

"Hear what?" Dani turned, watching Emilie like she was wild animal liable to bolt if it got spooked.

"There's a..." Emilie frowned, a furrowed V appearing between her eyebrows. "Tug. Someone...something that wasn't here the other night." She cocked her head, eyes focused as she tried to listen for a signal Dani would never hear.

Dani pressed her lips together and turned in a circle. Over the years, she'd learned how to sniff out a job when she walked on location. It wasn't a perfect science by a long shot, but she'd learned to trust her gut when it told her something was waiting for her behind a locked door.

Wherever people existed, there was a breath, a feeling that you weren't alone. Even with monsters, she could always tell that places were occupied. Sussing out the sense of residency had kept her alive more than once. A way to feel out what might be waiting inside to pounce on her. Pounce on *them*.

Even now, after a year with Emilie tangling deeper into her life every day, it was easier to think in the singular. It'd been habit. Old hat, even when it was her and Graham on the road for weeks at a time. Things were different now. Emilie was different.

With Graham, there had always been a tension filling the air. Not a bad thing, but it was there, and pretending it wasn't had done nobody any good at all. The weight of things unsaid, opportunities never seized. Two ships passing in the night, both choosing over and over to pull back instead of moving forward. The understanding that eventually, life as a hunter would only leave one of them with two feet on the ground and air in their lungs.

She'd just never figured that she would be the one who came out the other side.

Killing Spectre was supposed to make Graham's loss easier to carry. The loss of his presence, of all the things he was supposed to do, the person he was supposed to be. Somehow, she'd swallowed all of them and never noticed so long as she was running or hunting or looking for a way to make the bogeyman pay for what he'd done.

Instead, it felt as though she was floundering—and bringing Emilie down with her. Surviving was more than just her now. She'd found Em against all odds and brought her into the carnage that a life of hunting entailed. Maybe, if she was very good at her job and very lucky along the way, she would never have to watch the light drain from those pale blue eyes.

It was doubtful, though.

She knew it, and she hated it, and she hated herself for thinking it even for a moment. That was how things ended for hunters who lived on the road the way she'd chosen to. Hunting didn't have to be a career or a lifestyle choice. Plenty of folks handled their shit and returned to their lives a little more bruised, a little faster to move when something in the shadows made an unfamiliar noise. Problem being, she wasn't most people. Never had been.

This life came with a body count and losses that only mounted year after year. But it wasn't just about killing things in the dark. It was about helping people, the idea that you could protect someone from all the things a person could survive. Survival broke a person, and she'd been broken long before Graham or Joe ever laid eyes on her.

She looked back to Emilie again, fully lost in whatever she was hearing. To look at her was to underestimate her. With her soft curves, she was the kind of girl hunters saved. Kind and so smart, it took her breath away sometimes. Emilie blinked and met her eyes, and for a brief moment, Dani was caught in her orbit. Her brilliant girl, who had stood up to the bogeyman and come out the other side swinging, who had decided to become a hunter because she could do the kind of good some hunters begged for.

There was no meeting that gaze and not seeing the armor Emilie wore like a shroud around herself. She had her own demons, her own losses, but seeing all of her meant Dani couldn't underestimate her. There was power behind those eyes waiting to be acknowledged.

"Whatever it was, I'm not close enough or it's not loud enough." Emilie pursed her lips. "But there are lures on a few of the buildings." She gestured with her chin across the road. "There could be more of them, and if they're capturing spirits, the spirits don't like it much. They might get..." She waved her hand in an erratic motion. "Swarm-y."

"Noted."

Emilie moved ahead of Dani, staying close to the building as they crept through Tenacity Mill. Nobody would look at the two of them and peg Emilie as the dangerous one. She was capable and talented, but nobody ever read her as a threat. There was a simple reason for that, one Dani didn't bring up.

Only one of them was a weapon, and it wasn't Emilie.

Dani pressed past her girlfriend and peeked around the front. They were still a few blocks over from the main road Emilie had walked, but she wasn't about to take any chances. Slender fingers wrapped around her shoulders, and Emilie was peering over her shoulder.

"Anything?"

"Nothing blatant?" Emilie stepped back. "The same...infection? In the land and the buildings, but nothing like what I was seeing the other night."

Dani nodded and moved them around the corner of the building, angling for the back of town, where the buildings were pressed up against the woods. They moved cautiously but swiftly, passing broken homes and empty lots where other buildings must have existed once.

The deeper into town they moved, the more the air seemed to thin. There was no vibrancy or color to anything here either. Something old and predatory came to life inside of her, the magic of the veilblade reacting to a threat even when she couldn't clock what it was yet.

When they got to the corner and peered around it, a broken church of rotting wood was all that still stood on that side of the street. There were spaces where buildings had existed, but directly in front of the church was an old scar. Blasted earth and signs of damage to nearby buildings told the story of where Cooper Campbell had been put down when he'd lost his damned mind.

"Do you feel that?" Emilie murmured next to her.

"The unending spookiness of that church standing by itself, or the fact that this whole town feels like a graveyard?"

"The second one, I think." Emilie rocked back on her heels for a moment. "There's this"—she mimed scratching with one of her hands—"scraping on the inside of my head, like something trying to get my attention, but when I check, there's nothing there."

Dani's focus narrowed on Emilie, but there wasn't anything telling her to cut and run. She checked around the corner again before turning back to her girlfriend.

"We're almost there. You ready to see what we find?"

"Ready as I'll ever be."

They broke out in a run, and Dani had rarely felt so exposed as she did crossing that faded broken street. As they crossed the empty lots, all the hair at the back of her neck stood on end, skin crawling as though they were being watched from behind clouded windows.

With each step, dread pooled in her footsteps, climbing up the length of her legs until it nested in her belly like a malignant growth. Dani started moving faster, twining her left hand through Emilie's long fingers, tying them together with skin and bone, as if something might try to whisk her away.

The edge of the church's property line had a rusting iron fence that only had a few small sections remaining. Once they crossed it, Emilie gasped, and from the far side of town, there was a sound like a building collapsing. At the back of the church, a light lit up, glowing pale, pale blue.

"Around the back, in the cellar." Emilie's voice was a choked whisper, and horror filled her eyes as they began to glow, the temperature around them dropping by several degrees in response.

Dani moved in front of Emilie and found a door into the church but nothing that would let them access the basement from outside.

"We have to go inside."

Emilie choked on a whimper but nodded, and they moved toward the back door. It opened on oiled hinges, making not a sound as they entered the broken building. The floorboards were warped and rotting in places, but none of the windows or doors were broken. The alarm bells that had started moments ago began screaming, and she tasted metal in her mouth as adrenaline flooded her system.

Outside, there was another loud boom, and in the distance, Dani heard motors. *Someone was coming.* Emilie swallowed whatever had terrified her and hauled Dani down a hallway until she found a door and flung it open.

The basement was darker than it should have been, shadows thick like a living thing, and every instinct in Dani's body told her not to descend. The smell of rot and old death wafted up out of it, trying to choke her. Emilie gasped next to her, eyes flaring bright white as she slammed door shut again with a gasp.

"Em, baby, are you okay?"

Sweat had broken out on her forehead, face robbed of all color, as her eyes faded from white back to their pale blue.

"It's a tear from there to here, and it's getting worse." A broken sob slipped through Emilie's lips before she clamped her jaw shut, cutting off the sound.

Outside, the engines were getting louder, and Dani rushed to the front of the building to see what the hell was going on. A thick cloud of dust rose near the entrance to town, and at least one building had collapsed. As she watched, two SUVs swerved to a stop and spit out bodies clad in black and grey fatigues.

No, no, no, no, Dani's mind screamed, knowing exactly who it was but not why they were here. Not how they knew she and Emilie were here. Not any of the details she wanted. The panic ran rampant for a few long moments before Dani shut it down.

We fall apart later, we survive now. Graham's voice ran through her head as she took a long breath, grabbed Emilie by the hand, and ran toward the back of the building. Before they got to the door, she heard voices from outside. A handful of men, including a voice she remembered far better than she wanted to admit. Her vision washed in crimson as she turned to Emilie.

"Hide."

Emilie's eyes went too big in her face, and she scrambled through a door behind the altar, carefully hiding herself from sight. Dani let the predator locked under her ribs out of the cage she kept it in, letting those instincts that told her when to fight and when to run, when to duck and when to shoot, become everything she was. She sank into that quiet hunter place in her mind and leaned back against one of the pews near the middle of the room.

By the time the men broke through the front door of the church, she had a blessed iron blade in her hands as she picked dirt out from under her fingernails. From the outside, she would look relaxed, almost lazy. Most people didn't know how wrong that image was until she launched into action.

Three figures in black and grey fatigues threw open the doors and took long steps inside. Their eyes went wide for a moment, and they broke formation as a fourth figure came striding into the church.

She could feel the wicked smile as it graced her lips, noticed the feral thing that lived inside of her shift as it sized up the competition.

"*Reaper.* In-ter-esting."

Evan fucking Campbell. Her lip twitched, curling into a snarl as she took him in, trying to smother the urge to surge across the room and end him here and now.

"In the flesh. You know how I *hate* to disappoint," she replied in a vicious croon.

"Oh, I do." He stepped farther into the building, until his men were a few steps behind.

Evan looked like he belonged on a soap opera, with a trim frame that topped out at six foot two, sparkling blue eyes, a boyish smile, and golden-blond hair that fell exactly where he wanted it to. At seventeen, he'd been cute, but the years had cut away his baby fat, leaving him devastatingly handsome. So long as you didn't pay too much attention to how cold his eyes stayed, to the way his smile never reached them.

"To what do I owe this little reunion?" she asked, voice saccharine as she raised an eyebrow and stared down the Scion goons like they were gutter trash.

In all fairness, she had been here first.

Evan's eyes danced past Dani, across the rest of the room, looking for something. *Someone.* She didn't so much as twitch. They didn't know Emilie worked jobs in the field, didn't know why she was here, and she could work that in her favor.

The fact that Evan hadn't launched himself at her was proof that something was up. Hatred bled off every pore in his body, eyes dark with the emotion as he refocused on her.

"We got a tip from some locals that a trap had been set off."

Dani narrowed her eyes and wagged her finger at Evan like an errant schoolboy. "Aren't we a bit far from your old man's territory? Tsk-tsk, what will the sentinels think?"

Evan's face exploded in anger for a heartbeat, and he surged forward before restraining himself. The pretty mask peeled away, leaving a man consumed by rage and hatred standing in its place.

"Ahh, see, there we go." Dani stood up and tucked the blade back into its sheath. "That's the monster I knew was waiting under all that pretty skin."

"Takes one to know one."

"Monsters?" Dani barked out a laugh. "I'm a different breed than you altogether, sugar."

Evan's eyes narrowed on her again. "I doubt you're here by yourself. You always seem to have one afflicted or another hanging off your arm."

Behind him, his men were still standing, not reacting to anything happening in front of them. *Was I one of them? A lapdog for Isaac instead of Evan?* She banished the thought, more concerned with the developing situation snapping than whatever questions her mind had for her in this moment.

Evan made a gesture with his hand, and two of the men moved outside before advancing along opposite sides of the building. *Sorry, boys, no prizes for you here.*

"Mmmm. Are they going to find someone back there all filled up on delusion?" His eyes narrowed, watching her, and Dani could see the place where humanity was supposed to exist and where, in him, it was empty of anything at all. He paused, standing just to her right, where he could watch his man toss a room with nothing in it. "One of the afflicted?" His voice tangled on the word like it was a curse. "You know how we have to handle those." She remembered the way his lips would curl when he managed to make a comment he intended as a barb.

Joke was on him. She wasn't a teenage runaway with a body count this time. Technically, she was probably a felon in like twelve states, but if they couldn't find a body, did a crime really count? Probably not. The Campbells would know better than her, though. She'd seen their blacked-out vans go out full and come back empty more than once. That compound was closer to a meat grinder than anyone but Isaac and his generals ever realized.

"Are you threatening me, Evan?" She turned and knew there was something dangerous about her voice. It was too soft. Too careful.

Her right palm itched, the veilblade reaching for her from where she'd stashed it. It wanted to taste the air. It was built for protecting what was hers, and nothing was worth protecting if not Emilie. Hunting was a calling, blood called to blood, and in this moment, her blood was singing, demanding that she strike first and make it fast.

The woman and the legend wrestled for control of the hunter, knowing both that Evan was a bigger problem and that trying to end him here and now wouldn't end things. It'd just mean more blood, and she was swerving hard to try and avoid that. Probably wouldn't matter in the end, but she had to try.

"Course not, Black." He pulled back, a particular gleam in his eyes. "We're on neutral territory, after all."

She watched him with hooded eyes until he moved past her, pausing at the altar at the back of the church. Having him behind her made Dani's skin crawl, and she moved quietly and confidently toward the front door. She got halfway there before stopping and turning back to Evan.

He'd been like her brother once. In another world, he would have been her brother-in-law if she and Julia made it, the matching weapon to her own skillset. Joe and Graham had taught her to be a hunter, how to clear houses and find the monsters that hunted people. Isaac had taught her to be a killer, had trained her to be an extension of his own trigger finger.

"Neutral territory." Dani's lips curled back into that wicked smile. "Is that so?"

When he didn't answer, she sauntered for the front door again, heart beating too fast inside her chest. He was too close to Emilie, and all she could do was try to draw him to herself. Poke at him until he didn't care about anything else.

"You are lucky I don't ruin you where you stand." He shook his head and looked at Dani, eyes wild with a fire of equal parts grief and rage. "You destroyed *everything*, and you stand there like you're innocent. Of the blood on your hands, of good men and women who died because of *your actions*." He spat out the words with a grimace, like they tasted of rotten meat.

Dani stopped at the doorway. It didn't matter what he was saying. It didn't, and she knew that. She'd spent years going between guilt for walking away when she did and not walking a long time before then. She had her own sins to pay for, and more than a few had been committed shoulder to shoulder with the man standing in front of her when they were both still barely out of childhood.

Except. Except, Joe and Graham had shown her a better way. Except, Emilie was hiding, trying desperately to keep from being noticed. Except, none of the victims of the Scions that had been reaching out had deserved what they'd gotten. None of this, not today, not the deals after the riot, or the riot itself, or the job that had been fucked…none of it was her fault.

"You're *lucky* that I decided not to take your head when I cut the Scions off at the knees," Dani declared, voice carrying through the high-chambered church. "You're lucky I didn't come back and wipe all of you from the earth. You're lucky that I loved Julia enough not to leave your body for her to find."

Evan snarled and surged toward her again, and all hell broke loose.

14

DANI

Dani's body moved before she asked it to, instincts surging past her thinking mind, calibrating for Evan. Outside, someone was yelling, the sound punctuated by the sharp crack of gunfire. There was no time to say or do anything other than respond to Evan in kind.

She danced past his fist, staying just outside his range while she got a feel for the way he moved again. The way he fought. There was no gleam of a blade in his hand—no, this was a fistfight, pure and simple.

Evan was fast and accurate. At sixteen, he'd been capable of thoroughly thrashing her. But they weren't sixteen anymore.

He jabbed a fist at her face and tried to push in, but Dani blocked it and sent her own fist crashing into the side of his face. Evan snarled with a guttural, animalistic sound, and something *other* flashed in his eyes before rage filled them. They circled each other, and as much as Dani knew how he'd operated when they were teenagers, there was an edge to him now she hadn't anticipated.

She didn't need to kill him, but she couldn't leave him here either. Not when Emilie was stuck back in that room. He scored a punch while her mind was being pulled in two directions, hard enough that it knocked the wind out of her for a moment.

Evan let her back up again, and Dani realized that the altar—and Emilie—were now behind her. He sneered, lip curling back and eyes lit up with a wild light.

"The same broken little girl you were when we were teenagers, I see." He laughed, a cruel bark of a noise.

Dani breathed in through her nose, frantically trying to come up with a plan. She didn't know if the room Emilie was in had a window. If her girl was watching what was happening. And there were still the rest of the Scions outside and whatever was happening out there. She had little time and needed to make a choice.

Evan grinned and pressed forward, and Dani acted like it was difficult to put her arms up. When he threw a punch; she defended and backed up. A few steps, a few weak jabs. The point wasn't to hit him, it was to let him push her into the room where Emilie had fled. After a few shots, she threw a jab toward Evan's shoulder, and she didn't pull the punch.

The impact threw him back a few paces, and Dani fled into the room. The door slammed behind her, and with a cold rush of air, Emilie glazed ice over the doorway. She stood there, chest heaving, eyes blazing like pale blue fire as she stared from where she'd been standing behind the door. Her skin was ashen as Dani grabbed her by the hand, pulling her toward the back of the room where there was a small window.

Outside, Evan was yelling and pounding on the door. The ice held for now, but a massive crack was forming through it.

"Out the window, we have to *go*, Emilie."

The side of the building shuddered, and Dani lost her footing, heard the crack as the ice split from the door and fell to the ground before wisping away. The door opened, and smoke poured in, obscuring everything as she scrambled to her feet. She heard Emilie do the same thing behind her. A shadowy figure surged in, and Dani went to throw a punch—until she saw the gas mask being shoved into her hands and Mateo's face on the other side of one, looking absolutely frantic.

She grabbed Emilie by the hand and let Mateo grab her and propel them through the smoke, past Evan hacking in between the pews as he crawled to the front door. They slipped out the back. Mateo didn't slow down once they were outside, breaking for the trees as fast as their legs would take them.

Next to her, Emilie was coughing, but Dani looped an arm around her middle and kept her moving until the church and whatever was wrong under it were hidden by the green of the trees. She ripped off the gas mask, taking in deep breaths as they slowed down, but there wasn't time to stop.

"Nova and I got a tip there was a Scion convoy going *fast*," Mateo said, throwing the words over his shoulder as he led them on a winding path that cut back and forth through the thick woods. "We weren't expecting them to wind up here, but we parked down the way and passed your truck."

Nova materialized from the trees ahead of them, a gas mask on top of her head. "You got lucky today, Black. What happened?"

Dani's eyes darted to Emilie, who paused before answering. "I got a tip from beyond the grave last night that something really wrong was here. We came out to see if it was only on one side of the veil. Spoiler: it is not."

"We were about to beat feet when Evan and a trio of goons showed up," Dani said.

"Two of the goons are down, but there are more coming," Nova added, leading them up a side path. There was a streak of blood along the side of her neck, and her eyes were glowing.

The four of them moved through the woods as fast as they could, listening for any indication that the Scions knew they were here. They'd gotten out too easily, and neither Dani nor Mateo was buying it. By the time they got to the vehicles, everyone was throwing paranoid looks over their shoulders.

"Follow us. I have a place nearby that's safe." Mateo said quietly.

15

DANI

Nearby was relative, it turned out. But Mateo led them from one back road to another, winding east for almost an hour before they pulled onto a small property with an extended garage and no other cars. Dani eased her truck in next to the SUV, but it wasn't until the garage door went down that the tightness in her chest eased just a little bit.

Next to her, Emilie was quiet. She was still too pale, but she'd stopped looking like a ghost in her own skin. She hadn't spoken since they'd gotten into the truck, and the silence was deafening. Now that the truck was cooling, a fine tremor worked down her arms, making her fingers twitch uncontrollably. Dani took those hands in her own, rubbing some heat into them.

"Are you okay?"

Emilie blinked and shook her head like she'd had to tune into Dani. "I'll be good. It's just the adrenaline dump now that we're safe." She paused. "Safer than we were."

Dani raised an eyebrow.

"You didn't feel it when we crossed the property line? This place is warded six ways to Sunday." She gazed out of the windshield, pointing with her chin. "You can probably see some of the smaller ones there on the inside of the door. But I felt the zap when we crossed over." She gave Dani a weak smile. "I'm not falling apart on you now. This is just. A *lot*."

"Agreed."

Dani let her hands go but leaned across the seats and gave her a long, slow kiss. Emilie melted under her, hands grasping her shirt like she thought Dani would disappear from in front of her. When she pulled back, a flush had colored Emilie from her throat up through her cheeks.

"I like you looking like this much better." Dani said with a wink. "With some color in your cheeks."

Emilie swatted her as she ducked out of the truck and found Mateo and Nova waiting for them.

"'Nearby' was a bit of a stretch, wasn't it?" Dani asked.

"Closest safe house we had. This one's new," Mateo said.

"One from Joe's network?"

"Yeah."

He didn't explain further, just turned around and began walking inside. The house didn't look much different from any cottage out in the middle of nowhere. A country kitchen connected to the garage, living room, and dining room. Upstairs, Mateo explained, there were three bedrooms and the bathroom.

It wasn't the first time Dani had been in one of the homes that the network used as safehouses, spots where hunters could rest up between jobs or keep their head down if shit hit the fan. The four of them meandered through the main floor, and Dani twitched the curtains aside to look back out front, to check yet again that nobody was out there watching, that they hadn't been followed.

"How did we get out that easy?" Dani turned and looked at Mateo. "If Evan wanted me dead as much as it seems he does, why didn't he try to actually kill me?"

"Because you baited him, babe," Emilie said from where she'd curled her legs up under her on the couch. "And before that, he was scared."

All three of the hunters turned to look at Emilie like she'd just grown a second head. Her eyes grew wide, but she held her ground.

"Okay, maybe scared is a strong word. *Nervous* works too?"

Dani threw Mateo a look before she sat down next to Emilie. "Why do you say he was nervous? Scared?"

Emilie let out a shuddering breath and flicked her gaze between Dani, Mateo, and Nova, then back again. *Is it safe to tell them?* Her eyes asked the question she hadn't voiced out loud. Dani gave back a tiny affirmation, just a squeeze of her hand and a wink to the woman sitting next to her.

The tension that had been pooling inside of Emilie drained out, leaving her eyes looking ancient.

"Last night, before I got tagged into whatever is happening at Tenacity Mill, I went to Crossings because Lu asked me for help with some spirits." She frowned for a second before continuing. "While I was helping them, I saw enough of Evan killing people to last me a lifetime. Several lifetimes." Her lip curled into a tiny snarl, but she smoothed it out again. "He was always in *absolute control* when he was killing those people. Today was different."

Dani opened her mouth to reply, closed it, and thought about it. Why had the Scions shown up? She'd assumed it was a bad draw of luck, but Evan being that close was fishy. Having that tear in the basement, in that town of all places, wasn't an accident, and the Scions were involved. They'd shown up in a panic because something had happened, but she didn't know what.

"The two buildings that collapsed today weren't us," Nova said. "And it wasn't them either. It was like there wasn't enough building to hold it together anymore. Just grey and rotten, through and through."

Emilie shot Dani a cautious look. "Whatever tore the veil open and came crawling out, it's having an effect on everything in the area. I've never seen anything like it."

"Excuse me. *Tore the veil open?*" Mateo asked, panic creeping into the edges of his voice.

"There is a hole. In the world," Emilie said, exhaustion weighing her words down.

"We didn't know what we were walking into," Dani said. "Was that an ambush, or did we set them off?"

"Six of one, half a dozen of another," Nova answered. "It doesn't really matter why you were there, just that you two got out alive. We've got more attacks on the map, and it's reaching way farther than it should, unless they've been recruiting every hunter with a grudge they can get their hands on."

"What?" Dani said, leaning her arms on her knees.

"We took off to check on some more leads, and they panned out, which led us to a few more. That's why we got the tip when that Scion cell came hurtling at you."

"And we do mean hurtling," Mateo added, flopping himself lengthwise into a loveseat with a dramatic sigh. "We lost them toward the end. We'd just figured out where they were going."

One of Emilie's fingers twitched, and Dani caught the motion out of the corner of her eye, but she didn't move a muscle. A moment later, Emilie shook her head and stood up.

"I'm going upstairs to lay down, but Dani knows what I know." She frowned. "You know what I mean. Somebody wake me up when we know what's next." She wandered out of the room and up the stairs, her steps echoing quietly through the house.

Dani charted the progress until the steps stopped, then turned her attention back to Mateo and Nova.

"We don't know what caused the tear. Which side ripped it open. Whether something is holding it open..." She ran a hand through her long hair, trying to distract herself from what needed to be said. "We were hoping it was only a veil-side problem. But there is...something in the basement of that church, and that's where the tear exists."

"You didn't get close to it?" Mateo asked.

"No," Dani said. "We opened the door, confirmed it existed, and were about to beat feet until our very unwelcome guests arrived."

Nova stood up, pacing across the small room in slow, measured steps. "How are they involved?"

Mateo scoffed from his place on the couch. "How are they *not* involved? That's the town where the council took Cooper Campbell down, and the church is where he was keeping the people he'd 'cleansed.'" He bit the last word off as if its existence offended him.

Dani shuddered, suddenly very glad that Emilie had been upstairs for that little piece of lore. She might know already, but if not? She shook her head, erasing the image her mind had supplied her with, and narrowed her eyes at Mateo.

"Do you think that somehow he ripped a hole in the world there?" Dani asked.

"No. The veilblade can't tear through the fabric of the universe," Mateo answered.

"Did the Campbells get weird before the murders?" Nova asked, her voice distant as she worked through the thought. "The big Humans First stuff, the fundamentalist ideology. Was that before Cooper died?"

Dani held up her hands. "If Mateo doesn't know, I have no clue."

He shot her a dirty look but didn't answer his partner.

"What if Campbell showed up to town because there was a job and it went wrong, and that's why he went apeshit?" Nova asked, head cocking to the side like she was onto something.

"What, like he was possessed or something?" Mateo asked.

"Maybe?" She frowned. "I just can't imagine the Scions doing something that would rip the fabric between places like that. I mean, a talented on the warpath or a circle of casters? It's possible, I guess, but these guys?" She made a sarcastic noise. "They couldn't summon water from a faucet."

"They wouldn't even consider it," Dani said quietly. "Magic, even charms and wards? They don't touch any of it. It's all 'afflicted' to them."

"Wards? But they aren't even—" Nova stopped moving and clamped her mouth shut, staring at the ceiling for a long moment before she calmed back down.

"We know," Mateo said.

"It doesn't make any damn sense," Dani agreed, flopping against the back of the couch. "But it's true anyway. They don't touch magic. Just good ole human brutality."

Nova joined her on the couch with a sigh. "So, what next? I mean. The Scions are ramping up for something, and they're not gonna be happy after whatever today was."

"Emilie and I are due back at the grill. You're free to join us, but we need to regroup and see if there's a pattern." Her eyes traced up to the ceiling again. "And I want her closer to Dawson. If shit really hits the fan, she's safe there."

Mateo's eyes lit on Dani. "You're sure?"

"About Dawson? Yeah." She made a noise. "That's where we took Spectre down last year. Two Sentinels live in town. If she'd be safe anywhere, it's there."

Nova shot Mateo a penetrating look, but instead of answering, he just closed his eyes. She glared at him for a short moment before shaking her head.

"We have some other stops we have to make, but we'll be in touch," Nova finally said. "I think whatever they're doing, these are just the opening salvos."

"What's the endgame, though?" Dani asked. "They're killing people, but it's not even like clearing a town. These are...Wait." She smacked the couch next to her. "Do you have the map? Open it up, I wanna see something."

Mateo sat up as Nova pulled the folded map out from an interior pocket in her jacket, then moved to the dining room to unfold it. Dani's eyes roved over the patchwork of attacks they'd managed to confirm were Scion related.

"When I was in, every target was a target for a reason, yeah?" Dani looked up and met Mateo's eyes over the table, and he nodded in agreement. "So why these targets? These aren't coming from the old man; he never liked working east of the Mississippi." She traced the area around the old compound. "Out here is where we'd be seeing shit."

Mateo frowned and narrowed his eyes at the paper in front of him.

"So why these targets?" Dani asked again.

"A few of these"—Nova indicated them on the map—"were opportunistic. They literally ran into the Scions, and it went bad."

"But not all of them. They hit the spot Emilie and I were casing a *second time* because they were looking for something. So, what is so important that they're tagging people all over the country?"

"That's what we need to figure out," Mateo said.

He stood up from the table and meandered back into the living room. Nova folded up the map and followed after another long moment, leaving Dani standing there, wondering exactly what was in that journal that Emilie had found in Illinois. They'd had to run for the clinic right after they got back from that job, and since then, it'd been one thing after another.

She wasn't sure Emilie had even cracked it open to look at it yet, but she had a feeling whatever was inside might give them a clue about what Evan was looking for.

***

"Emilie asleep?" Nova asked.

Dani had been lost in her own head, with a beer she'd found in the fridge after they'd scraped together something that resembled dinner. "Resembled" being the keyword. She'd thought everyone else had already crashed out, but she didn't have Nova's habits memorized.

"I think so." Dani took a long sip from her drink, watching as Nova leaned against the doorjamb.

Dinner had been mostly uneventful, none of them talking much. She knew *someone* was talking to Emilie from the way her head kept cocking to the side, but her little medium hadn't been interested in sharing. All of them were thinking about something they didn't want to voice out loud.

"She's surprising. For you, I mean." Nova ambled into the dim living room and sat down on the armchair, watching her carefully. Her tone was light, playful even. Dani didn't buy it for a second, and she pinned her with an intense gaze.

"I'm gonna need you to explain what that comment means, Nova."

She watched Dani calmly, shaking her head before answering. "Graham was surprising at first too, if I'm being fair. After J, I thought you liked people as dangerous as you."

Dani's lips twitched, and she took another drink. "You think my girl doesn't have teeth?"

She met Dani's stare and leaned forward, steepling her fingers over her knees. "Of course she has teeth. She wouldn't have lasted ten minutes with you if she didn't. But..."

"But the Scions aren't a normal threat?"

"But she's not a hunter."

Dani shook her head in a sharp, violent motion. "Emilie gets to make her own choices, Nova. That's the deal with me and her; that's been the deal since day one. She cut her teeth, she works the job, and she knows more about the things we deal with than most hunters."

"She's soft." Nova leaned back, looking furtively toward the stairs before turning back to her. "She's soft, and the Scions will eat her alive if they have half a chance."

Dani's lip curled up into a snarl as she surveyed the woman in front of her. Nova hadn't been with them when she and Mateo spent their time with the Scions. She was smart, capable, talented beyond just her magic...but Nova was sharp as a knife. And she'd been known to cut more than just monsters if push came to shove.

"She's not as soft as you think," Dani answered.

"I don't wanna see what the Scions would do to her any more than you do. But you can't think she's cut out for what's coming."

"She's the only reason we know how bad it actually is." Dani finished her beer and set it down. "Emilie isn't a fighter like we're fighters, maybe. But underestimating her is a bad call."

"We're leaving first thing in the morning. You're sure about this?"

"I know what I'm doing, Nova. Trust me, don't trust me, that's your call. But don't think I put in anything less than one hundred percent, and don't ever think that Emilie is some kind of dead weight I'm just hauling around as a bed warmer."

Her voice was deadly soft and even, but Nova paled, her eyes going wide for a moment before she recovered herself. Dani swiped her bottle and deposited it in the bin in the kitchen before she went up to bed.

In the moonlight, Emilie's hair was a glowing halo peeking out over the covers. Dani stood there for a long minute, watching her lover. Then she stripped off her clothes and climbed into bed. She was suddenly far more exhausted than she'd realized.

16

EMILIE

Useful. Until this morning, sitting on the back porch with a hot cup of coffee clutched between her hands, she'd never found the word to be hateful. She'd trained and fought and clawed to get to a place where she wasn't just Dani's plus-one. Someone picked up in a sleepy mountain town who didn't belong in this life. She wasn't an A-list hunter by any stretch of the imagination, but she wasn't a bystander either.

Dani hadn't said it, hadn't even insinuated that Emilie wasn't part of the team. Sitting out here alone as dawn slowly crept across the world, all she could think of was the way she'd fled behind the door inside that building yesterday. The panic in Dani's eyes when she'd escaped into the room with her, in those moments before Mateo and Nova had blown the doors off.

There had to be something she could do. A way to contribute instead of hiding and wishing things were different than they actually were.

Was this what Grandpa wanted for me? The thought caught her by surprise, robbing her of composure in one fell swoop. Falling apart would have been easier, but she couldn't right now. She didn't have that kind of luxury, even as her hands trembled, sending hot coffee sloshing over the edges of the mug. With a sigh, she set it to the side as a familiar pressure pressed in against her mind, followed by a warm tenor voice.

"Are you going to listen to me today? Or are you still ignoring me?"

Emilie raised an eyebrow but inclined her head toward the voice.

"I know you can hear me, Emilie. Ignoring me isn't going to help when you're lit up like a beacon in the darkness."

She sighed and threw a look back inside the house—still quiet, no sign that anyone else was awake yet—before answering.

"Yes. I hear you."

Emilie bit her lip and gently lowered her shields until she could see the man leaning against the railing at the edge of the porch. She'd recognized his presence following her for the last two days, trying to get her attention. *Graham.*

Face in profile as he looked out toward the woods, he was handsome. Bronze skinned, with locs pulled away from his face and gold rimmed glasses perched on his nose. Emilie's heart skipped a beat, seeing him here in front of her. She'd met him before she ever knew him, before the binding was shredded to pieces in Dawson, when he'd slipped into her skin to warn Dani about Spectre.

"Took you long enough." He turned his attention away from the scenery and to Emilie. *"I've been trying to get your attention since you decided to sprint at Tenacity Mill."*

"Not sure if you noticed, but I was kind of preoccupied." Emilie took a sip of coffee. "You know. With the dozens of victims who nearly drove me mad before I agreed to help them."

"You were walking into a trap. Both of you were walking into a trap!" He shot her a furious glance and took a bracing breath he no longer needed.

"Why are you here?" Emilie shook her head. "You've been dead for years, Graham, why haven't you moved on?"

He shot her a look, like she was being intentionally obtuse.

"We thought that after Spectre was handled, you'd be able to move on too."

"Hard enough to let go before you lit up the veil like a damned lighthouse. Anyone with a scrap of anything left is being drawn to you."

Emilie sighed and rifled a hand through her hair, cursing the lack of other mediums she could talk to. Someone who understood what she was and what she could do. It was true that spirits faded the longer they were connected to the physical world, degrading over time until they became things that hunters were called to handle. It was also true that Emilie had been able to see spirits older than Mama long before she hit puberty. Spirits that should have been at rest—or monsters causing havoc.

"There's not much I can do about that. I'm locked down as tight as I can be without cutting off all my talents and pretending I'm just a person. And that is never going to happen."

"I'm not blaming you, little lodestone. I'm just telling you what's what. You asked, remember?"

"Lodestone?"

"Lodestones are naturally occurring magnets. Physical ones attract iron. You attract spirits."

A small smile played over Emilie's lips, and she took another long drink of her coffee. "Okay, it's not the worst nickname I've ever had. But I asked why you hadn't crossed the Styx yet, Graham."

He leveled her with an intense stare, and Emilie watched him assess her in that moment, finishing the last of her coffee as she tried not to fidget. Inside the house, she heard people moving, and Graham disappeared in the blink of an eye. She waited until she heard Mateo praising the existence of coffee before standing up and moving back inside.

***

The parking lot at the grill was mostly empty, and after twelve hours on the road, Emilie was ready to stretch her legs and bang her head against a table. They'd sat in traffic for two hours in Kentucky, and Emilie couldn't seem to get her mind off of the conversation with Graham this morning. One she hadn't immediately told Dani about because she wasn't sure what to say.

What exactly was the best way to tell her hunter girlfriend that her former hunting partner wasn't at rest on the far side of the Styx but was instead waving to get her attention about something? She wasn't sure what yet, and that made her hesitate too.

Dani had seen enough, had watched Graham die and then made sure that Spectre paid for it. She didn't deserve a new wound to torture herself with where he was involved. If Emilie caught shit for it later, she'd deal.

It wasn't really the priority right now, anyway.

No, tonight was for strategy. Making a plan to get people out of harm's way and try to figure out what the Scions wanted. Emilie let herself out of the truck, following Dani across the asphalt, stuck in her own thoughts.

She'd paged through the notes they'd recovered from the library in Illinois, but they hadn't been illuminating. Light research on the veil, some potion for minor wounds and cuts, but nothing that should have put them on the radar of the Scions. Nothing big or flashy.

Inside the grill, it was quieter than usual. There were a few familiar faces at one of the tables on the far side of the room, but nobody was paying much attention as Dani and Emilie entered. Joe was sitting at one of the larger round tables, three beers and an awe-inspiring quantity of bacon cheese fries in front of him.

"Oh, you *do* love me." Dani grinned, making grabby hands for the fries as she snagged a seat.

Joe just rolled his eyes and gestured for both of them to get comfortable.

"So, I hear y'all had an eventful visit to Tenacity Mill." He tossed a fry into his mouth and pinned Emilie with his attention.

"Why am I getting the third degree? Dani's the one who's supposed to be a professional."

Emilie looked at Dani, who was currently shoveling fries into her mouth like they were about to be made illegal. She paused when Emilie and Joe looked at her, then shrugged, continuing as if they should expect this sort of behavior from her.

"Okay, I see your point." Emilie took a swig of her beer and collected her thoughts. "What did Dani tell you?"

"You got nabbed by some spooks who roped you into a job at Tenacity Mill," Joe said.

"Not exactly right, but not wrong either."

Dani shrugged and continued eating.

"So, what happened?"

"I was…made aware of a problem in the veil. At Tenacity Mill. We went to see if it stretched into the physical or not."

Joe sat forward in his seat, eyes intense, but let Emilie keep talking.

"When we got there, it was like something was draining the land of its life. I could see growths I'd expect in the veil, but they were on our side. We got to where the rift was on the veil side and…confirmed it's stretched through to the real."

"Fuck." Joe sat back before snatching his beer and draining a third of it in a long swallow.

"That's not all," Dani said, punctuating her sentence with a swallow from her drink. "My least favorite asshole showed up, and shit got dicey."

"Jackal?" Joe asked, eyebrow raised.

"The one and fucking only."

"And he was spooked by something. The guy was not on his usual murdering A-game," Emilie added tartly.

"This is very bad," Joe said.

"Yeah. That's why we bailed back here soon as we knew they weren't tailing us," Dani said. "He's been targeting talented all over the country. Mateo and Nova have been tracking him. They showed up at Crossings to ask me if I'd seen anything, right before spirit radio grabbed Emilie by the ears."

Joe finished his beer and stood up, slapping his hand on the scarred wooden table. "Closing early, folks. Unless you got one of my rooms out back, you need to beat feet. Finish your drink, I've got boxes for your food."

His booming voice filled the space of the grill, and the hunters that had been on the far side of the room cleared out in a few minutes with minor muttering. He turned back to Dani and Emilie, face more serious than she'd ever seen it before. Usually, Joe was a giant teddy bear of a man, big smiles and warm eyes. Right now, he looked more like the hunter he must have been in his heyday, eyes gone dark and his jaw tight.

"Call the Sentinels. If Tenacity has been breached, I'll bet the bar it has something to do with what happened there with the Campbells."

Emilie felt the telltale tremors in her hands as her bones froze inside of her body, frost flickering at her fingertips unbidden and fear fissioning up her spine like a livewire.

"It's that bad?" she asked in a frozen whisper.

"It is," Joe answered. "Firecracker, you need to get in touch with the fence and see if he knows what the hell is going on. If the Scions are on the hunt like they were in the old days, we need to get word out to the talented and anyone else we can get ahold of. They need to get to cover or keep their heads down."

"Joe, what do you think is happening?"

He glanced at the ceiling for a moment. "I was on the ground at Tenacity Mill when everything went to hell in a hand basket. The Sentinels from the council made the call about what happened, but they didn't go into Cooper's murder hole under the church." His eyes flickered from Emilie to Dani and back again. "The things he did live with me, and with everyone else who went down there. If there is a tear or a rupture from the veil to here, there is no way that it was accidental. We need to find out if anyone knows what the hell Jackal is up to and how long he's been at it."

Dani finished her beer and stood from the table. Emilie followed suit.

"Leave the plates on the table, and I'll deal with it tonight. I need to make some calls. Y'all do too." He pinned them with another intense gaze, before disappearing down the back hallway to his office.

Dani twined her fingers through Emilie's, then led her down the same hallway and out the back door. A small paved path led them back to where Joe's house and a small block of apartments sat. Much as the cold bit at them during that slow walk, all she could think of was the warmth of their hands clasped together.

17

DANI

Dani sat on the tailgate, knife scraping against the edge of a whetstone as she waited for Sawyer to show up. She was parked on a two-lane dirt road, not much to see where it ran next to a river. She wasn't sure which one; right now, it didn't matter all that much.

She moved the blade against the stone again in long, steady strokes as she made sure her hip-knife was sharp enough to slice through bone and muscle like warm butter. The cold air bit into her, but she'd gotten used to it. It was only in the '40s, so she wasn't a shivering mess quite yet, and she wanted eyes on Sawyer as soon as he turned down the road.

From where she'd parked, the main road was visible, but she wasn't as easy to spot. She wanted to make sure the fence wasn't about to try something stupid and bring a Scion squad rolling up when she'd called him for a chat. A chat that Joe had insisted she have again this morning when they'd dragged themselves out of bed for breakfast.

The too-loud exhaust of a mustang caught her attention, and she watched as Sawyer took the turn and started the mile-long drive to get to her. She tracked its movement by sound when it turned back out of sight, rolling down the rutted road toward her.

Dani didn't stop what she was doing. Just kept running that long, sharp knife along the whetstone, muscle memory taking over as she locked eyes with Sawyer through the windshield. His eyes widened at the sight of her, and Dani grinned a smile that was a predatory show of teeth. Her "threat display" as Emilie liked to tease.

As Sawyer put the car into park and slowly stepped out, she stopped the rhythmic motion of sharpening the blade. She didn't need to be looking at Sawyer as she held the blade up to the light, moving it back and forth to inspect it before returning it to the sheath on her hip. She could feel the tension in the air, the weight of his eyes on every move she made. *Good.*

Her eyes flicked up, bouncing over Sawyer before resting on his face. He looked wan, and there were bags under his eyes. Maybe he'd been running into his own trouble while she and Emilie had spent the last few days running back and forth.

"You rang, *Reaper*?" He raised an eyebrow and pulled a pack of cigarettes from inside his jacket.

She scowled at the old nickname and shook her head. "I think we both know why I decided to ring up you of all people."

"Trouble in white-hat paradise?" He mimed gasping, rolling his eyes before lighting a cigarette. "I'm shocked. Absolutely *floored*, I am."

"If you're just going to be a brat, then you can leave," Dani said.

He glared at her, smoke curling from his nostrils in two thin tendrils. "Coming from you, that's real rich." He put the cigarette in his mouth again and threw his arms out wide. "Here I am. You rang?" Sawyer plucked the cigarette back from between his lips and watched Dani carefully.

She narrowed her eyes, making him wait a beat before answering. "I need to know how much work you've been doing for the Scions and their cronies lately."

"Oh, come on, you know me better than that, don't you?" He

scoffed. "A lady never kisses and tells. That's what lets me do what I do."

"What you do?"

"Don't get nasty now, Black. I work with whoever can pay my rates or has work worth doing. You *used* to understand that, if I recall. Before you picked up your newest sidearm in Dawson."

"Careful how you speak about Emilie, Sawyer." Red washed over her vision in a fine haze as the veilblade woke up at a perceived threat.

He blanched again and swallowed before answering. "I can't tell you if I've been working with them or in what capacity. I do that, and I'm as good as signing my own death warrant, because the other side will want the same damn thing."

"The other side?" Dani jumped down from the tailgate, pinning Sawyer with a murderous gaze. "The other side is monsters, Sawyer. It's rogue talented and casters summoning demons to eat their exes and things that kill people for no good reason."

"Don't be naive." Sawyer snapped, embers glowing bright at the end of his smoke. "There has been a war inside the big war for as long as we both have had feet on the earth." He held up a hand, stopping her rebuttal. "The Scions are the latest generals in the war, and you and Joe stand on the other side, and we both know it. We've both known it for a long, long time. Ever since you did what you did and everything exploded."

Dani's lip curled up in a snarl, and she suppressed the urge to snap her teeth at him. Wondered if he'd flinch if she did. He held up his hands, the way she might if an animal was poised to attack her.

"There are the Humans First hunters, and then there are those of you who haven't gone completely off your rocker. It might not be pretty, but it is what it is. I'm a mystical fence Dani, the only thing that keeps me alive is the fact that my clients know I don't talk about anything. *Anything.*"

Dani nodded, and some of the red haze drifted away, leaving her calmer but still simmering with a rage that sharpened everything.

She swallowed against the hot coal of her anger so she could speak, and it burned all the way down.

"Emilie and I were working a job farther north. A rift in the veil up in *Tenacity Mill*." She paused and watched the fear slowly fill Sawyer's eyes. "When we got on site, we realized it reached through to the real and nearly got gutted by Jackal. I don't know how he knew we were there, but he was not on his A-game. If he's been doing something up there, if you know anything about it, I need to know."

Sawyer's nostrils flared, but he'd stubbed his cigarette out and stuffed the butt into a pocket. Now he flicked his lighter open and closed against the leg of his pants, eyes distant as he seemed to work something out.

"I don't work directly with the family," Sawyer said finally. "But some of my other contacts have...heard things."

"What *kind* of things, Sawyer? I'm not asking for my health, here. Joe told me to come talk to you real specific-like. Does he think you know something?"

"The Scions haven't been working outside the region, but their friends have. They've been expanding, pulling more people into the militia. Telling them that the reason things have gotten so fractured is that the affliction from talented and magic users has made it too dangerous to exist."

"People are listening to that drivel?"

"Not a lot of them, but enough. And the ones that do are living up on the compound. But it's something else too."

"What do you mean?"

"The casting community down south, they're convinced something has gotten its hooks into a lot of hunters."

"Something like what?"

"I don't know. Really." Sawyer shook his head. "It's a lot of back and forth. A few of the collectives that got raided, they shouldn't have hit anyone's radar. They were doing research into some shit in the veil, but it was all theory, Dani. Nothing practical, nothing that should have put them on *anyone's* radar, much less the Scions."

She frowned at what he was saying, tapping one foot in agitation.

There was too much energy thrumming in her chest, and she didn't have a good way to get rid of any of it right now.

"There's no way it was a coincidence that he was there. No way it's a coincidence that there have been targeted attacks all over the country or that they're accelerating. I can't just sit down and watch this happen again, Sawyer. You *remember* what happened last time." She spit the words out like acid and couldn't stop the poison that spewed out of her next. "You remember that last midnight raid when Jackal dragged us out and murdered a family while they slept and wept and cried." Her lip curled up into a vicious snarl. "You have as much blood on your hands as I do, so fucking *help me, Sawyer.*"

He tipped his head to the sky, hands clenched into trembling fists. Dani watched him until he finally looked at her again.

"I remember that raid, and too many others to count, Black. Don't ever think that I don't. We both work the job in our own ways. Don't mean either of them is better than the other. You walked out and didn't look back at the people who got stuck in the middle. Least with me, they know they're not gonna get sold out."

"And with me they are?"

"There is no you out there!" Sawyer yelled. "There's the HF hunters and not much of anyone else because of the fucking deal that Isaac set down. That didn't mean there weren't talented or casters or the packs that live out there!" He fumed, watching her and shaking his head. "I get why you had to walk away, and I'm not blaming you, but I didn't have a good option. I did what I had to do."

"So do better now. *Help me do better this time.*" Dani could hear the desperation in her voice, and she hated it. "Whatever they have done, whatever they *are doing*, it has torn a hole in the fucking world, Sawyer. One that is draining the life from everything it touches. And it's only going to get worse. *They* are only going to get worse."

Sawyer closed his eyes, and his shoulders slumped. When he opened them, he looked more tired than she'd ever seen him. "I'll see what I can find. No promises, but I'll look. There was a collective up in Illinois. Johnstown, maybe? Last I heard, the woman who gathered them all up was collecting dirt on the whole family, the entire operation. Maybe Emilie knows them. Maybe they knew something." He turned back to his car and opened the driver's door. "I don't know anything concrete yet, but I'll be in touch. We're not gonna let it get that bad again, Dani." He ducked into the car and pulled out a folded piece of paper with her name on it. "But it's good you called. Someone wanted to talk to you."

He held it out, and she waited a beat before walking over and grabbing it. As he drove away, she slammed the tailgate up and stalked back to the cab of the truck.

It was too late to keep it from getting bad. It was already just as bad as it had ever been, they just hadn't noticed. She slammed the door and threw the truck out of park before continuing down the road. It all felt like too little, too late, but she knew that was just her anger talking.

They might not have made the first move on the board, but they could still stop Evan and his cronies before things got worse. They had to.

18

EMILIE

Joe's house was a colonial, and he'd taken what had probably been a sitting room in another life and turned it into his personal library. It was filled with occult texts, research, and titles that Emilie had reverently ran her finger along, the age of them visible from the wear on the leather covers.

Today, while Dani got in touch with Sawyer, she was staying away from the grill. She needed to see if she could find what might have caused the rift in the veil, and if she could narrow down what was pouring out of it. There was something about it that kept scratching at the back of her brain. Something her mind had clocked but that she couldn't quite remember. Every time she grabbed at it, it slipped through her fingers, elusive and shadowy.

So she'd set up camp in Joe's house, where she had room to spread out without any nosy hunters poking in or anyone trying to distract her from what needed to be done. Here, it was quiet. Just her and the books, and maybe the answers would reach out and bite her. That had been the idea when she'd crawled out of bed that morning and given Dani a kiss on her way out the door.

It was now well after noon, the pile of books she'd gone through was only growing, and she still wasn't any closer to figuring out what could have caused the kind of damage it would take to tear through from the veil into the real. Generally, there were few people who could cross the veil or magical means of reaching through it to touch the other side.

While certain creatures could cross over, it was usually under very specific circumstances. Spirits who still had a tie to the living world or rituals that opened a door within a small space. But this was different. It was a breach, a tear, a wound in the fabric of the world that separated the living and the dead. If Emilie hadn't seen it herself, she wouldn't have believed it *could* have happened. Yet, here she was. She tapped her fingers on the table and looked at the front door. The very closed and quiet front door.

She did have access to options that no hunter she'd met had access to. If the Scions kept raiding locations, it was only a matter of time until they found out she existed and tried to use her against Dani. They weren't counting on a medium who wasn't so much bound to her body and where that body was located as she was...tethered to it.

Slipping her skin—or astral projection, spirit walking—there were plenty of words for it depending on who was talking, but they all amounted to the same thing: leaving her body unoccupied and defenseless while she took a better look at what was happening in the spirit world and peeking through to watch people in the real.

Stepping outside her body was dangerous for any number of reasons, and doubly dangerous when she didn't have anyone to keep an eye on her body. But if she wasn't safe in Joe's house, Emilie wasn't sure she'd be safe anywhere. The veil was dangerous enough all on its own, so her choices were danger, or a different danger. At least if she got a better look, she might find a lead, and if she stumbled on the Scions, she might be able to see something. Hear something. Revulsion crawled over her skin at the idea of running into Evan Campbell again, but at least in the veil, she was more capable.

Emilie ran a hand over her face and realized she'd made up her mind. Evan Campbell was hunting them, and somehow, he was damaging the balance of the world. But he'd never dealt with anyone like her before. She quickly re-shelved the books she'd paged through earlier and settled herself on the couch in the living room. She willed her body to relax, even as her mind revved up, possibilities flickering through her mind in rapid-fire.

What if something terrible is waiting in the veil? Her throat seized at the thought, but Emilie pushed past it even as fear roared in her ears, rushing around her like the ocean.

She didn't have to do this. Nobody would know until after she was back, and there was every chance that nothing would come of it. Emilie bit her lip and let her eyes slip shut as she controlled her breathing. Inhale and exhale, each breath held longer than the one before it, until her ribs stretched, lungs filled to their capacity before billowing out again.

As she breathed out, she stepped outside her body, slipping into the periphery of herself. It left her weightless, only vaguely connected to the body she called her own. She held up her arms, turning them back and forth as she got a peek at herself. Behind her, her body looked as if she'd fallen asleep on the couch, but exhaustion was easy to see on her face. Not knowing what was coming next was beginning to take a toll, even if she didn't want to admit it in the moment.

Instead of dwelling, she moved, bypassing the doors and finding herself outside. Joe's wards glowed here and there, but there weren't any spirits here. From far away, she could hear hushed voices speaking to themselves, shards of spirits lost in their own loops as they lived out the ruins of what had been their lives.

She concentrated, and in the distance, there was a tug. The rift. She could feel it, as if a cord connected her to that place. She moved through the veil quickly, landscape and spirits alike moving past as she followed that tether. *There's something else I need to see.* Emilie frowned at the thought, unsure of exactly where it had come from, but she didn't slow herself.

She reached the edge of Tenacity Mill and paused to look around. The same wicked green storm was billowing over the church, and a strange vertigo made her feel as though everything was upside down.

Instead of running straight at the storm, Emilie took the time to look at everything. No detail too small.

The wild growths she'd seen in the physical world were everywhere. Here, they undulated, black and purple streaked with poisonous swirls of green. She could feel the wrongness of it pulsing through the world and realized they were reaching out from the town itself. Today, there were no other spirits, and the tunnel vision that had made her disregard the town was shocking. Grandpa would have given her a look and made that face that said he'd taught her better than that.

The thick growths stretched toward the world at large, and if she traced them back, they led to the church. Several of the buildings had lures around the edges, drawing in spirits and trapping them within. Emilie gave them a wide berth as she navigated through the narrow streets, taking her time and looking for any signs of something malevolent. As she moved deeper, she found pools of oily darkness. A light sheen on some of the porch railings and doorways, puddles of it along the streets and alleys.

Emilie looked at it from a distance but avoided them as best she could, moving slowly and carefully. When she turned the corner and found the church, the world tilted on its axis again, and if she'd had a physical form, she'd have stumbled. The ground outside of the church had a thick miasma of darkness, roiling and writhing.

It stayed within the confines of a charred spell circle, but Emilie wasn't sure if that was by choice or design. The dark storm clouds still hovered over the church, painting the sky black and green, but the lightning only flashed ominously within them instead of spearing up toward the ground.

This time, she could see fissures splitting the ground, spiking out toward the west side of town, where she hadn't looked yet. More of that oily darkness lingered there, pulsing as if it was alive, squatting there and making itself at home. The ground groaned as the mass of darkness within the circle surged again, and the fissures grew as thunder rolled overhead.

From the way she'd come in, a pack of black SUVs rolled into town in formation. Emilie ducked behind the side of a building but tracked them until they pulled up in front of the church in a line. A dozen Scions poured out of the vehicles, all in matching dark fatigues. She stayed in the shadows, acutely aware of how vulnerable she was like this, looking for any sign of protection on the Scions. They were hunters, after all; they had to have something they were using to protect themselves, right?

The longer she watched them from a distance, the clearer it became that not only were none of them wearing even simple protective charms like most lifers, but the same oily darkness saturated them like they were showering in it. It shone in their hair, tucked into the shadows of clothing, or coiled along their collars. Insidious little fingers of infection reaching across them.

Until Evan hopped out of the SUV at the front with a cold look written across his face. The darkness curled around him, tendrils reaching across his skin in sinuous loops that hugged skin and shadow alike. It was hard to tell where actual shadows stopped and the darkness began. It undulated, twining tighter around Evan with every moment.

Emilie moved, getting a better angle, but still kept her distance. There was a cruel whisper, and she'd bet it was whatever was wrapped around Evan. Every instinct inside of her was screaming that she needed to get back to her body and make sure she stayed as far away from Evan as it was physically possible to be. Run and run and keep running so that *it* never knew she'd seen it. Seen the way it was nesting inside of Evan, glutted and pleased.

Instead, she dug her heels in. Emilie hadn't survived Spectre and reclaimed everything he'd stolen from her to run away from whatever this was.

"Clear the building. Drop the bodies into the basement." Evan gestured with two fingers, and the assembled commandos surged into action.

Half of them moved into the church, and she heard them shouting back and forth as they cleared it room by room. They finished as the rest of them pulled two bodies out of one of the trucks.

They were limp, no shard or sign of their spirits, as the bodies were moved into the building. Emilie wanted to know what they were doing, but she wasn't going to push her luck while they were still here. There were bad moves, and there were stupid ones, and she was only willing to push it so far.

"*Well, aren't you a curious little morsel.*" The thing clinging to Evan like a vine stretched out, reshaping itself into a bad reflection of a person. All bad angles and contorted limbs, moving in the space behind Evan toward Emilie.

She froze for a long second, like a deer caught in headlights, before she steeled herself and looked at where this thing's eyes ought to have existed. Instead, there were dark holes, the shape of a person drawn from memory and distorted in glass. She'd never seen anything quite like it, and the shape sent dread galloping into her belly.

"Is that so?" Her voice was a murmur, drawing it farther away from Evan and toward herself, even though that was definitely not her best idea ever.

"What are you?" it asked.

Its voice oscillated between different tones, never settling on a single voice. It reminded her of nails on chalkboard as the sound scraped along her spine. Emilie took a step backward as it curled toward her, not allowing it to fully close the distance, careful not to step into one of the pools of ichor that lingered through the town.

"I could ask you the same thing," Emilie said, cocking her head as she tried to memorize everything she was seeing.

It reached toward her but could only stretch so far from Evan, and it seemed to have found its limit. This thing—because it wasn't a person, had never *been* a person, much as it wanted her to believe otherwise—was dangerous and old. It was also familiar, somehow. The way it moved, or spoke or…

"Maybe I chose wrong with my current pet." Its mouth curled into a smile that made Emilie step back, ice freezing inside of her even though her body was nowhere close.

It reminded her of Spectre. A cold fury washed through her, and she reared back and away from it, curiosity evaporating as her face turned into a cold mask. The smoke-thing recoiled and sneered back at her.

"Medium," its voice hissed, more sibilant than it had been before. It pulled back, retreating in something between fear and hatred. "You're not in charge here, *lodestone*. I'm not to be trifled with. Not here, and not out there." It whipped itself back and forth, scenting the air. "Where are you hiding? Why keep to the darkness and not come find me yourself, little sweet?" Its voice turned saccharine sweet as it returned its attention to Emilie.

Fear and anger warred for dominance in her chest, and she wasn't sure which would win. Emilie wasn't sure what she'd expected to find, but it wasn't this.

She wanted to flee back to her body, but she wasn't willing to let this thing make her run. She might have been terrified, but she was also furious. Instead, she stayed where she was, watching it slowly return to Evan as the Scions filed out of the church and began to load back up into the vehicles.

"I'm not sure what you mean."

"I wouldn't abandon that sweet body for long." It cackled. "We know you're out there, and we're coming for you."

Before Emilie could respond, she felt a hand on her shoulder back in the physical. Her spirit shot through the veil, and she slammed back into her body with a gasp that turned into a coughing fit. Standing next to the couch was Joe, and someone was yelling outside.

"Welcome back," he said. "Time to tell the Sentinels what's happening. Merc is here."

19

DANI

Dani pulled her truck into the nearly empty parking lot. Rather than going back to the grill, she'd made a detour for another conversation. She backed into a space a few down from the only other vehicle, eyes slotting to the person waiting for her.

Julia Campbell leaned against the quarter panel, arms crossed against her chest as she watched the truck park. Dani adjusted her sunglasses, then made sure the veilblade was hidden in a pocket and that her newly sharpened iron knife was snug against her thigh.

Why am I here? It would have been easier to go back to Joe's and see if Emilie had found anything. Instead, she was still two hours from the grill, meeting up with a woman she thought she'd firmly left in the past. Eventually, she hopped out of the truck and leaned against it. Looking at Julia, Dani noticed all the little things she'd missed the other night at the bar.

The pin her father had given her when she was sixteen was still attached at the shoulder, but the silver was tarnishing. Black jeans, boots, shirt, but they were ruffled. Yesterday's clothes doing double duty? Or a rough morning? Hard to tell with the gulf of years between them, but she still cut a figure. Dani drank it all in, but Julia didn't have the hold over her she'd once had.

Julia settled herself, her eyes dark pools of curiosity, but didn't say anything for a long minute.

"It's rude to stare," Dani said.

"I used to dream about what it would be like if we got the chance to talk again." Julia's eyes were far away, searching for something she couldn't see. "When you...decided to leave us, I didn't understand." Her arms tightened across her chest. "Why you'd run off like you did after we took you in, what you and I had..." She trailed off.

"You know why I left. After the accords, I stayed away. That was part of the deal we all cut with your pops."

Julia was talking around what had happened when they were still kids, barely out of school. Dani had no such issue with calling a spade a spade, and it needed to be done here and now.

"The Accords." Julia repeated the word like it was in a foreign tongue.

"C'mon, he let you in on everything." Dani shook her head. "Wasn't a damn thing that happened in this place"—she gestured vaguely—"that you didn't end up finding out about."

"Well, that's not really true, now is it?" Julia asked in a venomous, saccharine voice. "Or I would have known what was coming. The kind of danger that we were in."

Dani narrowed her eyes. "I'll tell you what I told your old man all those years ago. One of these days, Evan is gonna cross someone who isn't gonna be backed into a corner. And when he does, there won't be much of him left to find." She shook her head again. "Why are we even talking about this, Julia? You don't care what he's doing. You never have. Not really. Nothing he does ever sinks in."

"He's my brother," Julia said. "I don't know what else I can say. Of course you wouldn't understand. You're not just an only child, you're an orphan. Obviously, the idea of loving somebody else more than you love yourself is anathema to you. You're selfish."

"I survive." She spat the words out before she could stop herself and watched Julia's eyes go wide at her tone. "You're right, though. I don't have siblings or parents. Not really." If Joe could have heard her, he'd wring her neck right now. "I have morals, though. Standards. Rules."

"Do you, now?" Julia pursed her lips. "You weren't so picky when we pulled you out of that nest and taught you how to fight back."

"I was a kid. Same as you and your brother."

"We picked you up off the street."

"And then Daddy turned me into a good little child soldier." Dani didn't blink, didn't budge. "He taught us all to be killers, you just got to go a different route than the rest of us."

"We all have jobs."

"Isn't that always how it goes." Her voice went quiet. "Why are you here, Julia? Is it to argue about what happened, because we can do it blow by blow. I'm down." She crossed her arms over her chest. "But I don't think that's quite it, is it?"

She waited for an answer, but Julia just stared at her.

"Why come talk to me now? Why do it at all if you think your brother isn't in the wrong?"

Julia opened her mouth, snapped it shut, and looked away.

"You think something's wrong." Dani cocked her head. "Very wrong, if you decided I was the person to talk to about it."

"You have to understand—When our father—After the riot—" Julia kept starting and stopping sentences, eyes darting back and forth as she tried to find the right words.

"What is going on, Julia? What the fuck happened?"

Julia let out a breath that rocked her slim frame, hand clenching over the pin on her chest. "My father died ten days ago. Before that, his health had been...deteriorating rapidly." Her eyes bounced all around, never settling in one place for more than a few seconds.

Dani watched Julia try to string together the chain of events in the most sanitized way possible, picking each word and syllable to say what she wanted to say and *only* what she wanted to say. Julia had always been strung tight, but this was more than that. It was like watching someone on a tightrope and realizing once they were halfway across that they had no backup.

"He'd been saying the compound was haunted. That there was something influencing us all." Julia's head shook in small tremors, eyes too wide in her face. "I mean, can you imagine?" She met Dani's eyes. "Can you?"

"Isaac was a believer in his cause," she answered carefully, unwilling to send Julia careening off balance.

"Dad went from teaching us to—" She clamped her mouth shut so tightly, it was a white line, nostrils flaring as she fought for composure. "Something wasn't right. I knew it, and Evan knew it, but Dad was locking himself in his office.

"And then he died." Julia bit off the words. "There wasn't blood. The coroner determined he had a massive stroke and died in his sleep." Her forehead crinkled, and she looked skyward, trying to compose herself again. "Evan took off on a tear and..."

"And you were left holding the bag. The way your pops always planned," Dani said quietly.

Isaac Campbell had been in the second generation of Campbells to live on what had started as a farm but now housed the Scions of Seraph and oversaw their operation. He had been groomed to take over the business as a boy and chose his daughter to do the same. He'd always known he was mortal, that in this life, so few things were promised to anyone, much less the people who faced what lay in the darkness.

Julia hesitated and looked around, as though someone was watching them. Even odds they had at least one pair of eyes on her if she'd actually taken over for her father.

"Evan said Dad had gone soft. After the riots. He hated being told where he could work and when. I haven't seen him since the night we found Dad."

"Oh, don't worry, plenty of other folks have. He's been murdering his way across the east coast, and it looks like he's got some friends doing the same over in the southwest. People who did *nothing*, Julia. They're dead, and there are a lot of them."

"My brother's methods aren't pretty, but they get the work done."

"I can't believe you right now." Dani snapped, tongue running over her canines. "I always thought you had a good head on your shoulders. But not when it comes to your brother. You have a blind streak fifty miles wide and twice as deep."

A shadow slid behind Julia's eyes, and if Dani hadn't been paying attention, she'd have missed it. It looked identical to what she'd seen in Evan's eyes. The creeping suspicion that they hadn't believed their father because they were already under the influence of something else dawned on Dani.

"People just living their lives, Julia. I did the background myself to check. He's attacked *children*."

"Sometimes sacrifices have to be made for the greater good."

"The greater good? *What* greater good? This isn't greater anything. This is a psychopath murdering his way through his daddy issues."

"I didn't want it to come to this." Julia's voice had gone cold. "He is my brother, Dani. My right hand now that Dad is gone, and I'm alone."

"You don't have to be alone. Help me stop him, stop whatever he has gotten himself into. It doesn't have to be us on different sides."

"Yes, it does." Julia shook her head. "I didn't *want* it to come to this. But if you hurt my brother, I'll end you."

"You can sure as hell try." Dani said with a sharp smirk as she felt the veilblade react to the threat.

She took a deep breath, but violence was screaming for blood, riding the edges of her bones. *How dare she.* The veilblade whispered to her from the pocket of her jacket where it lived. Come for her people, and she'd destroy them, she'd pull them apart piece by screaming piece until they were nothing but red and wet and a warning.

Julia gritted her teeth. She'd never looked more like her father than she did at that moment. Dani almost wished she had been the one to hose Isaac Campbell. The man would have been a war criminal if the council had done their damn job, and he'd done a lot of people dirty over his years running the family business from his farm. There was not an endless list of people who'd wanted him dead, but there were plenty of folks who'd celebrate and cheer his passing without shedding a tear.

"I'm not seventeen, and I'm not playing about your brother. He's a psycho." She smiled and knew it was all teeth.

Any good humor left in Julia's face drained away, leaving her wan and looking far more exhausted than when Dani had parked.

"Hold onto that spark, Dani. With what's coming, you'll need it."

20

EMILIE

The tremor in her hands was worse than usual and adrenaline dumped into her system as she processed what she'd just seen in the veil. She'd asked Joe to give her five minutes, but the longer she sat in the living room, the more the encounter batted at her. She knew what she'd seen, but she didn't know what it was. That thing made of oil and shadows.

Emilie looked up as Merc swept into the room. As one of the closest sentinels to the grill, it was natural. Sentinels helped to keep the balance between the magical and non-magical world, drawing on the power of the earth itself through their affinities. He was tall, Black, and absolutely radiated power. His locs had gotten longer since the last time she'd seen him, and he'd pulled them back and away from his face. He was dressed to the nines in a plum dress shirt with the sleeves rolled up the elbow, charcoal slacks, and a bracelet with silver charms on his wrist.

"Welcome to the shitshow," she said.

"Joe calling me personally is the only reason I'm this far from home." He twitched. "It's itchy."

"Itchy?"

"Sentinels who watch over a town. Over time, we become tied to the land. Some of us, anyway. Being this far away is uncomfortable." He shrugged. "It'll pass. So, why am I here, Emilie?"

Emilie sighed and waved him over to sit down in the armchair across from her. "Well, that's more complicated as of five minutes ago."

"Oh?"

She paused and rubbed a weary hand over her face. "The other night on a job in Illinois, Dani and I almost got jumped by a pack of Scions. Then I got tag-teamed by a host of his victims begging me for help, who proceeded to show me a—" She waved her hand idly. "Tear in the veil."

Merc opened his mouth, but Emilie kept talking.

"It breached the physical. We went to check, and ran into the Scions *again*."

"Where?" Merc had gone still as the stone that was his element.

"Tenacity Mill. There's more."

"More?"

"I took a look at it again with fresh eyes on the veil side. I saw Scions dropping a body inside the church, and I saw...something attached to the Scions there."

Merc leaned forward, face in his hands, for a long moment before he sat back up. "There is bad, and there is worse. This is worse."

"I noticed," Emilie said, wringing her hands together. "The Scions have picked up their activity where they left off all those years ago. We know of a dozen attacks in the last week or two, and they're getting worse."

Merc's eyes flicked back and forth, and Emilie recognized it as him rolling through the facts in his head. "You know what happened at Tenacity Mill."

"I know what happened to Cooper Campbell, if that's what you're asking."

"The council stripped the Campbell veilblade from the family after what he did. They viewed him as a grave threat to the balance. To everything that we exist to do, including protecting the people who don't know what's out there."

Emilie felt the tremor in her hands finally calm. "They had a veilblade?"

"*Had* being the operative word. It was passed on to the hunters." He raised an eyebrow. "Valkyrie holds it now."

"What?"

"Oh, you heard me." Merc shook his head and looked down at the floor for a moment. "It was before my time, and not our territory, but that veilblade wound up going to Valkyrie before she was...well. Valkyrie." He shrugged. "I'm not sure why it went to her or how any of it happened. It's the only reason there was still a veilblade in Dawson for Dani to find. The blade she carries, it's been in the Black family for a very long time now."

Emilie rubbed at the space between her eyebrows and added one more complication in what they were dealing with.

"Do you think he's targeting Dani because he thinks she has his family heirloom?"

"Evan? Maybe, but he's had a grudge since Dani left. This might have been what set him over the edge, but he's been a rabid dog for years."

"Why didn't anyone do anything about it?"

"You mean the council?" Merc sighed. "I wish I knew. Truly. There are less of us out west, and I know there was some kind of deal." He shook his head. "Things have been deteriorating for a very long time. Since the last Watchtowers fell in the '80s. The American community has been fractured for decades, hunters and talented at each other's throats, and everyone else trapped in between them."

"They've been killing people for a long time, Merc. A lot of people. And something happened when they died. These spirits were in bad shape. Some of them had...stitched themselves together to try and combine themselves, others were missing pieces of themselves, like their souls had been fractured by whatever happened. I saw their deaths as they experienced them."

Merc's eyes went wide, and an unreadable expression passed over his face before he answered. "What the Campbells did in Tenacity Mill, it was bad, Emilie. So bad, nobody will even really talk about it.

It left a mark on that place, even after the town was abandoned. You know that bad shit can seep into a place. If anywhere in the world was soaking up something terrible, it was that town."

"It's like something is connected from the veil side and trying to crawl out. It's squatting under it, I'd almost swear." Emilie frowned. "But I've never seen anything like that. Never even read about something like that."

"I can take a look and see what I find. If there is a breach in the veil, I have to let the council know. I don't deal with the spirit side often enough to know how to patch it, how go about fixing something like that."

"Fixing the patch doesn't deal with the Scions. If they started something there, what's to say that Evan hasn't taken up his uncle's mantle?"

Merc stood up, pulling at his collar. He looked deeply unwell, and she wondered if that's how she'd started to look too. Everything was piling up, and Emilie felt the odds shifting out of their favor with every new piece of information. Right now, she didn't know anything helpful, anything that could stem the tide of all this bad, and it was flowing over her and through her whether she liked it or not.

"It's possible. I just don't know. I'm out of my depth here."

"We can at least put out the call to the talented, the casters in the area. Warn them."

"That I can handle." He nodded. "I have to get back to Dawson. Clue Andry in and start making calls. If I find anything, I'll be in touch. Try to stay on this side of the veil, yeah?"

"Yeah."

Emilie watched Merc stride back out of the house at a ground-eating pace before looking around the living room, unsure of what to do with herself. She was built for research, she knew how to do this, but what she didn't have were the vast reserves of knowledge she'd grown up with. Worse, since she was dealing with hunters, it was entirely possible they were playing by rules she'd never learned in the first place. The temptation to wallow or let the creeping despair infect her with its inaction was almost strong enough to bring her to her knees.

Instead, she took a deep breath and then blew it out, digging her fingernails into her palms until the pain cleared her mind. Before she realized it, she'd plucked a notebook out of her bag and started writing everything down, starting with what she'd seen in Tenacity Mill today.

She filled a page, and another, pen sliding across the paper as she poured every detail down onto the page. Emilie tried to remember everything she'd seen and heard over the last few days so that she had the salient details laid out in front of her, where she could try to put them together.

Too much had been happening all at once, and she'd been overwhelmed by the magnitude of it occurring so quickly. Now that she was writing it down, piece by piece, she could see it hadn't started recently. There was so much fallout from decisions that had been made years ago, and now she and Dani were both caught in the middle for different reasons.

By the time she'd written everything down, Emilie's mind was looking at it from different angles. Moving the information this way and that, trying to find how it all fit together. The spirits that had come to her hadn't all been recent. Some of them were decades old, if not older.

How much older? Emilie cocked her head, and her eyes slid to the floor where her bag was lying. From inside, she snagged the journal that they'd found in Illinois. She'd flipped through it on the drive out to Tenacity Mill but hadn't been able to focus.

She skimmed the pages, looking for anything that might help, unsure of what exactly she was even looking for. There had to be a reason they'd been looking for this. Something incriminating, something that told her what the Scions didn't want anyone to know. What they were killing to protect.

Emilie slowed down, stopped skimming the pages and started reading them. Mostly journal entries from a talented who had been researching the veil. Along with spirits, there were any number of other entities that existed in the veil, but not beyond the cold reach of the Styx.

No, they had found a home in the shadowed darkness of the veil and adapted to it. Devoid of a material form, they wanted the heat and the life of the world without being able to access it. At least, unless they found a host. Some of them were symbiotic, and there were stories of smaller beings who hitched a ride during summonings and the like. Most of the time, they were trapped within the summoning circle that had opened a door through the veil.

But not all the time.

Outside the house, the Scions were still on the hunt, attacking talented and looking for something. But inside its walls, everything but the information in front of Emilie fell away. There was nothing but Miriam's research.

The hours passed quickly, and she had to turn on the lights to see as the sun went down. As night swept over the building, the shadows curled heavier in the corners of the room. Emilie didn't pay them any mind. As she read, she took her own notes, getting words down on paper as fast as she could.

There was a pressure in the air that hadn't been there earlier today, and much like yesterday at the safehouse, she could feel Graham's presence pushing at the edges of her perception. Technically speaking, it shouldn't have been possible. Joe had warded his home thoroughly. It was probably almost as well-warded as her childhood home, from intruders, spirits, and anything else that might try to poke around on the property without invitation.

"I needed some time to think, and you were busy."

Emilie regarded him carefully, shutting Miriam's journal but leaving the other notebook open in front of her. "Seems like I'm always busy these days. How are you even here, Graham? This place shouldn't let any spirits through."

"I helped Joe ward this place more than once. I know where the gaps are." He looked around the study idly. *"I spent years of my life in this place. The wards are meant for spirits who are uninvited. This was my*

home too." He ran spectral fingers along the spines of books, a sad expression in his eyes as they sank through the physical.

"Why are you back?"

"I know what you're looking for. I don't know the answers, but Joe might. He was there when the Campbell bladesinger was put down."

"I'm listening."

"He doesn't like talking about most of his hunting days. It's a bloody business, and he's been doing it for a very long time."

"Was he in the basement? Was he the hunter they gave the veil-blade to?"

Graham side-eyed Emilie before turning back to her and leaning against one of the walls, legs disappearing into an armchair in the corner. *"I don't know. I know your grandfather was involved. He was the representative of the northeast talented collectives."*

"That sounds like him." A faint ghost of a smile drifted over Emilie's lips as she replied. "He was always doing too much. 'Til the very end."

"Sounds about right. You remind me of him." Graham tilted his head, a canny intelligence filling his golden-brown eyes.

Emilie watched him, but she didn't know what to say. Grandpa had been her favorite person, more of a parent to her than Dad in the years when the binding had held her tight. There were far worse comparisons that he could have made in that moment.

"Because I'm doing this?"

"Because once you get your teeth in something, you can't let it go." A gentle smile graced Graham's lips.

"I couldn't if I tried. The spirits who want vengeance have no one else to turn to."

"Would it make a difference if they did?" He cocked an eyebrow.

"I don't know," Emilie said, raw honesty flavoring her words. "I want to run, but my family ran from Spectre, and they still died for it in the end. Hiding doesn't do any good if there is something hunting you."

"The Scions weren't hunting you."

"Because they didn't know I existed. Mediums were never

common like some talents. Spectre took a whole lot of them out of commission, and it seems like the Scions are keeping up that work."

Graham sighed and watched Emilie for a long moment. *"I don't know what the thing is that has latched itself onto the Campbell family, but I'd bet it's some kind of parasite. What you need is to figure out which one."*

"You're sure?"

"No. But it makes the most sense. They're not usually this much of a problem, but the Scions don't protect themselves the way anyone with a brain does." He raised a hand, showing off the spellwork tattooed onto his wrist. *"Shields, charms, or wards. Hunters pick their protections, but the Scions don't truck with any of it, and it's biting them in the ass now."*

"That gives me more than I had before." She paused. "What I said the other day still stands, though. Why are you hanging on? Why haven't you crossed over, Graham?"

"Dani has a target on her back. She was never the bright and shiny one, Emilie. Why do you think?"

"You're keeping an eye on Dani?"

"She was the most important person in my life." He smiled briefly. *"The Scions nearly destroyed her. I couldn't stand by knowing that Evan was out there. It was only ever a matter of time until he slipped his leash and came after her."*

Emilie breathed out, a shudder rocking through her chest. "Okay. Then we make a deal. Dani and I are going to deal with this, and when it's done, you find peace. You finish crossing."

"What kind of deal is that?" he asked, his form becoming more solid for a flash as his eyes lit up.

"The kind where you never become something holding onto the world and losing themselves in the process," Emilie said. "We both know what happens to spirits who aren't meant to stay. You can feel the degradation already. I know you can, and you know it too."

"It's not as bad when I'm near you," Graham admitted. *"You're a bolstering influence. I'm sure you've noticed it before. Why do you think those shards of spirits reached out to you?"*

Emilie's eyes narrowed. "Lighthouse and lodestone, right?"

"*Right. Spirits are drawn to you, but you're a reactor. A power source, in a manner of speaking.*"

"Stay close, then," Emilie said, the words popping out of her mouth before she had time to stop them. "Stay close, and you can help me do this. Help Dani survive what's happening."

"*I'll try,*" Graham said, voice fading as he flickered back out of sight, leaving Emilie alone with her notes.

She picked up the pen and started writing again. Dani would be back soon, and they'd need to talk about everything Emilie had learned. She didn't want to miss anything, and there was too much flying through the ether for her to keep it all locked up inside of her head. Graham further complicated things, but she'd have to tell Dani that he wasn't gone. That he wasn't crossing over because he wanted to make sure she was safe first.

21

DANI

Dani wasn't sure where she'd been expecting to find Emilie when she got back to the house. Curled up in bed with a stack of books piled around, a notebook in hand, and a plate of snacks definitely wasn't it though. She leaned against the door frame and shot Emilie a wolfish smile. After a long day on the road, this was exactly what she'd been looking forward to.

"You're back!" Emilie grinned, and excavated herself from her research, clambering out of the bed and nearly tripping herself in the process.

Dani choked back a snicker, and let Emilie launch herself into her arms. Her hands found their way to Emilie's hips as her little medium smiled up at her. She could still see the edges of exhaustion at the corner of her eyes, the slump of her shoulders.

"I'm back," Dani said, dipping down for a soft kiss.

After a year, Emilie still melted into her, eyes slipping closed. When they reopened, the exhaustion had faded, replaced inside by a quiet warmth.

"I have things to tell you," Emilie said. "I got some intel while you were out of the house."

Dani cocked her head. "Research?"

"I mean, *partially*—" she said evasively. "The thing is, going through the library wasn't exactly helpful when I didn't know what I was looking for." She pulled out of Dani's grasp, and scooped a notebook off of the bed.

"Mmhmm." Dani made a noncommittal noise, watching Emilie as she squirmed where she stood.

"I know we generally don't like me going out of body without someone to keep an eye on me—"

"Emilie!"

"Look! If I'm not able to slip my skin here of all places, then where would I be safe? I made a calculated risk."

"Calculated." Dani repeated the word, scowling at Emilie.

"And it paid dividends."

Dani sighed, and suppressed the urge to run her palm over her face. Instead she waved her hand and let Emilie continue.

She hemmed and hawed for a minute before finally sitting down on the edge of the bed. "I went back to Tenacity Mill on the veil side, to try and get a better look. While I was there, Evan and a pack of Scions showed up." Emilie winced at the dark look Dani threw her, and continued. "There is something that has...attached itself to Evan. To a bunch of them, but to Evan in particular. There are also traces of it all over the town."

Dani rubbed at her temples, and tried to smother the groan that wanted to escape her. "So you decided to go veil walking without anyone to keep an eye on you, watched the Scions...and found something attached to them?"

Emilie nodded in a tiny motion. "It...saw me. Didn't recognize me as anything at first, but then it seemed to realize I was a medium. And it was...big mad about that." She licked her lips. "Threatened me but it didn't try to attack."

"Why not?"

"I don't know." Emilie admitted. "Surprise maybe? The Scions were up to something while they were there, but I couldn't keep an eye on them once the...thing...noticed me."

"Okay. So you think the rift might be tied to whatever has attached itself to the Scions?"

"Maybe. It was all over that place babe. I mean, pools of oily darkness. The ground is splitting on the veil side, like it's squatting under everything in that town. I need more information, that's why I moved in here."

Dani sighed and moved to sit next to her on the bed. "I see we both had eventful days then." She ran a hand through her dark hair. "Sawyer had rumors from the community down south that something had its hooks in them, so now we know what." She frowned. "Kind of anyway. He's checking on some information for me." She paused. "I also...you should know that I talked to Julia Campbell today. The other night too actually."

"What?"

Dani paused and lifted her eyes to the ceiling for a moment before the words began to pour out of her. "When the Scions took me in...I was close. With Isaac, and his daughter, Julia. Evan's sister." A broken laugh burst out of Dani. "She was my first love, and when shit hit the fan over Evan she wasn't there. The other night when I went to that hub? I ran into her in the parking lot. Today I got a message that she wanted to speak."

"And you went?"

"I had to try? Try to convince her to help us, that Evan couldn't be helped. That he was out of control?" Dani looked over to Emilie, tangling their hands together. "Isaac Campbell is dead, that's what probably set Evan off but Julia doesn't know what he's up to. She isn't that good at hiding her tells."

"Does she know he's coming after you?"

"Yes, but she didn't seem to care all that much." Dani shook her head and gave Emilie a bitter rueful smile. "Julia is more loyal to her family than anything. *Anything.*" She snorted. "I did however tell her it was only a matter of time until someone was capable of fighting back. And if he comes for me, I'll leave him behind on the floor."

"Good." Emilie's voice was cold, and there was frost ghosting the tips of her fingers before it smoked away into nothingness.

"Cold as ice, killer. I approve."

Emilie looked down to where their hands were still wrapped around one another. "It feels like everything is going so fast, all piling up in front of us. Like we're waiting at the gallows for our names to be called."

"It does that sometimes." Dani nodded, and raised Emilie's knuckles to her mouth.

"There's more." Emilie whispered, quietly. "Graham hasn't passed over."

The words hit her like a freight train, and vertigo washed over Dani, confusing which way was up for a long moment. Time stretched out like taffy, and she gripped at Emilie's hand like it was a lifeline. Maybe in that moment it was.

"What?"

"He...came to me today. He's trying to help."

"Is he...I mean what's..." Dani was at a loss for words, trying to wrap her mind around what Emilie was saying.

"He's not...degrading. Not yet anyway. But he told me that the veilblade that was stripped from the Campbell family in Tenacity Mill? It's the one Valkyrie has."

"Oh." Dani said, the words not entirely sinking in.

"I wasn't sure if I should tell you, but I don't—" Emilie breathed out. "I didn't want to hold out. Not when it comes to this." She waved a hand around them. "You deserved to know."

Information swirled around Dani, all of it locking her in place. She wanted a drink. She wanted a simple, no frills monster job where she could fulfill the bloodlust that had been singing through her veins all afternoon. She wanted to forget, even if just for a little bit.

She turned, and Emilie mirrored her, questions swirling in her pale blue eyes.

"I'm glad you told me," Dani said. "But I don't want to talk about this anymore."

She curled a lock of hair around her finger, gently tracing the shell of Emilie's ear as she fixed it. Emilie's eyes unfocused for a moment, blush draping across her cheeks and down the line of her neck.

"I don't really wanna talk about much of anything." Dani continued, voice gone low and husky.

She moved her hand down, ghosting above Emilie's skin, watching the bob of her throat as she swallowed.

"Then let's not talk anymore."

Emilie surged in the space between them, freeing her hand as their lips crashed together. Dani surrendered to the heat rising between them and rolled so Emilie was beneath her. She gave her a wolfish smile before nibbling her way down the column of that pale neck, hands roaming under her shirt. Emilie gasped, a low moan breaking from her lips.

Dani couldn't stop everything outside their room, but for the next few hours, nothing else mattered but their bodies twining around each other.

22

EMILIE

Emilie groaned and dropped her head onto the table in front of her. She had plenty of notes on what was happening and where it was happening, but she could feel the shape of the information she didn't have. Something had attached itself to the Scions, she'd seen it for herself, but Dani had told her there were rumors about it farther south too. Something was going on in Tenacity Mill, and it linked back to both the Scions and their bloody history with the town.

But that didn't explain everything. Not the souls that were in pieces and trapped in the veil, unable to fully cross over, screaming and begging for help. Dani's own history with the militia might have explained if they'd been hunted, but so far, that wasn't it either.

The Scions had been looking for someone. *Or something.*

Emilie picked her head back up and scrambled to the far side of the table where she'd put a fresh map with the Scion attacks from the last few weeks. The hunters hadn't seen a discernible pattern, but she knew the militia was targeting talented. It made sense that they didn't know what they were looking at.

Talented had spent centuries running and hiding and fighting for their lives. It seemed as though every generation had their own spin on how to eliminate the people different from them, and it was no different in the magic community. Whether it was the church, witch hunters, or people hissing *"afflicted"* at them at the slightest indication of ability, her people had learned how to hide in plain sight. Talented and casters alike had learned how to integrate with the world in different ways, but both kept their heads down and avoided hunters unless they knew them personally. It was just safer that way.

Her finger trailed across the paper of the map, and she frowned. She didn't have every location that had been targeted, only the ones Dani could remember. Seven in total, and she recognized half of them. The library collective in Illinois, an archive in Texas, and two smaller collectives that had worked with Lockgrove Antiquities when she was younger. There were larger, flashier operations between them, but every spot that she recognized had been an archive.

What are they looking for? She wracked her brain, trying to remember what each of them had specialized in, but things changed month to month and year to year. She'd been out of the loop for too long, and too many things had changed while she was away. The attacks had been scattered, but the more she looked at them, the more the pattern etched itself indelibly into her mind.

"What am I not seeing?"

"Depends on what you think you're supposed to be seeing," Graham's voice piped up from behind her in a bored drawl.

She glanced over to see him peering down over her shoulder, his eyes narrowed at the map as well. "There's a pattern here." She waved a hand over the map. "But not the one the hunters think they're going to find."

"What do you mean?" He moved along the edge of the table until he stood across from her.

"You know the same as I do that these collectives were small. *Quiet.*" Emilie tapped on the map. "What would have drawn the Scions all the way out to Georgia? I mean, Louisiana, Illinois, and Texas, sure. But Georgia? Maine?" She shook her head. "Nah, that's not random. There's something here, I can *feel it.*"

Graham watched her carefully, and she got the feeling that he had come to some kind of conclusion about her. She wasn't sure what it was, but the fact that he kept showing up had to count for something. Right now, she needed all the help she could get.

This morning, she'd watched Dani pace back and forth across the room like a caged predator. They were running in circles, and she hated it. Hated the way it made her feel cornered, like she was nothing more than a scared prey animal. She'd been taught how to hide, to keep from being noticed, even while spirits whispered their secrets and regrets to her. Emilie was over it. She was done running. But if they were going to fight back, they needed to know how.

"You're not wrong," Graham said, frowning at the map. "*I didn't even know about most of these.*" His eyes flicked from the map to Emilie. "*I know of larger populations with a flashier reputation. Do you know what they were doing?*"

Emilie shrugged and snatched her notebook before turning back to Graham again. "A few were archives or rare book dealers. The collective in Illinois had research on the veil and some of its nastier citizens." Emilie shook her head. "I don't know what they were looking at, but I do know *Jackal* was the one searching. He tore that library apart, but they'd hidden the notes well enough that I found them first."

"*You said you'd seen the thing that has the Scions...wrapped up?*"

"In the veil," Emilie answered, watching his face for a reaction as she talked. "It's sentient, and it was...not pleased about noticing a medium."

"*It sounds like a parasite. You know there are varieties that have been known to hitch rides from the veil into the physical.*"

"Knowing it could be a parasite isn't specific enough. I need to know what *kind* for it to be of any help." Emilie huffed in frustration. "Nothing I have on me covers them, and this is niche enough that Joe's collection doesn't touch it either. I know the book I need, but it's not here."

"*You can't get it nearby?*"

"At the auction house, maybe. But *Carroll's Compendium of Parasitic*

Fiends is only worth anything before the seventh edition. There aren't many floating around anymore."

Emilie's finger traced idle patterns on the table. *Carroll's Compendium* was the most informative text on the subject, but the seventh edition was the only one that'd have what she needed. It was rare enough that even Merc wouldn't have a copy just lying around.

Graham blinked at her, opened his mouth, then closed it again. "*You think you need a copy of Carroll's?*"

"It's got everything, including the additional appendixes from the last edition without the weird witch hunting nonsense that replaced the rest of it." Emilie drummed her fingers on the tabletop and bit her lip. "The only wrinkle is that I'd need to go to Lockgrove Antiquities to find a copy."

She'd avoided going to the auction house for a laundry list of reasons, but she'd been aware that it was only a matter of time until she'd need to return. Were there other places she might be able to hunt down the book? Yes, but there was no telling how long it would take. She knew for a fact that the archive at the auction house had several copies.

"*You think that's a good idea right now?*"

Emilie watched him for a long moment before answering. "It's my only idea." She shook her head and started to stack her notebooks and reference materials. "We can't do anything until we know *what* we're dealing with."

"*You could eliminate the Scions.*"

Emilie stopped moving, watching Graham carefully. She licked her lips, then answered him quietly. "Eliminating the Scions only deals with one problem. Once we know what's coiled itself around them, we'll know what we're dealing with and we can make a plan to destroy both of them."

This time, Graham paused, and Emilie continued to clean up her research, acutely aware of his eyes on her. "*Ice cold. I see why Dani calls you killer.*"

She looked up, a protest forming, only to find that Graham had left her alone. A moment later, the front door opened, and Dani appeared.

"You're done hitting the books?" She leaned against the doorframe, crossing her arms under her breasts as she smirked at Emilie. "I came to strongarm you into breaking for lunch, but you're all packed up. I thought I'd never see the day."

Emilie scowled at Dani for a moment, but her lip twitched and gave her away. She sighed, and it turned into a light chuckle as she eyed her lover watching her expectantly.

"I break for food and caffeine," she finally said with a sniff. "But I realized we don't have what we need."

"Yeah?"

"Yeah," Emilie said. "I know the book I need, but it's rare, and I need the right edition."

"Why do I not love the way this is headed?" Dani shook her head, stubbornness settling over her features.

"Because I need to go to the auction house."

"Lockgrove Antiquities? Why?"

"Because they keep a massive archive, and I know they have the book. Maybe a few others too. Trying to source it down here would take time we don't have."

"So we go to Maryland."

Emilie winced. "...*I* go to Maryland. Alone."

Dani's eyes flashed, and a muscle in her jaw twitched. "In what world is it a good idea for you to travel alone right now?"

Emilie leaned back against the table, taking a moment to collect her thoughts before responding. "The Scions won't notice me. I'm still under their radar, and the auction house doesn't have what they're looking for. At least, they don't *know* it has what they're looking for."

"What do you mean?"

Emilie pointed her left thumb over her shoulder where the map was laid out. "Their targets have been smaller specialized archives and research cells who did work on the veil and the things that live there. We don't advertise everything we do at the auction house, and it's old enough to have serious protections. If the Scions target it, they'll be on the radar properly, and I don't think they want that right now."

Dani circled the table to look at the map, settling into the same space Graham had occupied just a few minutes ago. Emilie pointed out the locations she was talking about and watched Dani as the gears in her head started to turn. After a long minute, she rubbed her hand across her jaw, watching Emilie with a distinctly displeased expression painted across her features.

"And why should I stay here while you make this run alone?"

"Because if they *are* somewhere in the area, they'll notice you." Emilie could feel the telltale tremble at the tips of her fingers as adrenaline surged through her system, but she stood her ground.

Was this the best idea she'd ever had? Probably not. Would she be safer if Dani came with? Probably. But Emilie knew the auction inside and out. If she did this right, she could slip in, get what she needed, and slip back out without anyone being the wiser. With her girlfriend in tow, things got more difficult, and right now, they didn't need difficult.

Dani let out a slow exhale, and her eyes slipped closed for a long moment. When they reopened, her shoulders slumped. Before she ever opened her mouth, Emilie knew she'd won her over.

"Fine. But we're negotiating, and I want to know exactly what you're doing." She narrowed her eyes. "And lunch. You need calories."

Dani headed for the door, turning to look at Emilie. "C'mon, let's go get some bacon fries so you can finish convincing me that this is a good idea and not an absolutely terrible one."

Emilie scuttled over to join her, tangling their hands together as they moved from the house over to the grill. They snagged a booth in the corner, and Dani disappeared for a few minutes before returning with two plates of bacon cheese fries and a drink for each of them.

"You're too good to me," Emilie said with a smile, reaching for her root beer.

"Oh, *now* you wanna butter me up," Dani said with a dramatic flourish. "You're just trying to get on my sweet side so that I agree to this plan of yours."

"It's not a *bad* plan," Emilie said. "There's a degree of danger thanks to the Scions, but not as much as driving around in your truck." She traced idle patterns on the scarred tabletop.

"And you don't think they have Dawson or Lockgrove in their crosshairs?"

"I don't," Emilie said, the levity draining out of her voice in an instant. "This is a calculated call, babe. It's not me going off half-cocked or something."

"It's not your style anyway," Dani muttered. "I'm the impulsive one."

"Exactly. Most people don't know about everything inside of the auction house, but I do. Mostly."

"Mostly?"

"There have been new acquisitions, but nobody goes to Lockgrove Antiquities for books." Emilie raised an eyebrow and popped another chunk of cheesy potato product into her mouth.

"You're sure what you need is there? You're positive?"

"I'm sure enough that we're having this conversation at all. Do you think I'd bring it up if it was just a fleeting chance? The fleeting chance is hoping there's a bookstore down here that we can trust with what we need." She licked her lips. "Sawyer's source, or whatever, down south...the one that said that something had its hooks in the Scions? They're right, and I saw it with my own eyes. What I don't know is exactly what it *is*, and this book can solve that little problem."

Dani leaned back in her seat and took a long drink from her beer before idly picking at the label. "Fine. *Fine*. I hate it, but you're probably right." She threw her head back and groaned. "Keep your phone on you. Text me, call me, if shit goes sideways. And if you're not back by sunrise, I'm coming after you."

Emilie swallowed and reached a hand across the table. "Deal."

23

EMILIE

Emilie stared up at the narrow brick building that held Lockgrove Antiquities. From inside the car, she could see the telltale shine of the wards that layered every inch of the exterior. She knew them all by heart, but sitting here, she could see where a few were starting to weather and fade. Dad had never been a clever hand with wards, so Grandpa had handled it, even after retiring.

The auction house wasn't just a building, at least not to the family. It was a seat of power, independent from talented society and their sneering backbiting. It was also one of the single largest accumulations of relics, artefacts, and knowledge in North America. When her family had fled Europe due to rising violence from witch hunters, they'd eventually settled in Frederick and opened shop.

The oldest wards were archaic enough that Emilie wasn't entirely sure what they did, and Grandpa hadn't known either. They'd originally been copied from the old seat of power in Europe, and there were no precise records of exactly what they did, only that they would protect the building and everything contained within it from threats. It was rumored that they had come from the first Watchtower, but nobody had ever been able to confirm or deny it.

While none of them had ever worked out the precise purpose of the wards, their maintenance had always been important. Lockgrove Antiquities was hidden from non-magical eyes with security that protected it from any number of issues ranging from thieves and malcontents to fire, storms, and mold.

The building itself was quiet now, the windows on the main floor reflecting the brilliant orange light of the sunset. A few people were on the street, but none of them acknowledged the red brick building that stood alone, the river behind it.

Coming to the auction house had been the right call. Emilie could feel it in her bones. But that didn't make it any stranger. It was less the nostalgia of returning to a place that had mattered so much to her, and more the sensation of an old friend reaching out. As if the very brick and mortar of the building itself was happy to see her.

"It's now or never, Lockgrove," Emilie muttered to herself and shook her head.

Grabbing her bag, she steeled her spine and headed for the building. At the top of the small staircase, her fingers lingered on the brass plate next to the door. Lockgrove Antiquities Est. 1762. This time, it wasn't in her head. The building sighed, and then the front door popped open.

Maybe it had missed her as much as she had missed it.

Inside, she crossed the reception area and found another door. As she reached for it, she heard the lock click, and it popped open as well. A tiny smile curled the side of her mouth, and Emilie entered the arterial system of the building. A wide room with a dozen tables and corridors branched off to the left and right. Above her on the ceiling was an intricately painted mural with a broken watch tower in the center. Talented, casters, and hunters fighting back against the darkness with magic and weapons alike.

Her heart stuttered in her chest, and a fond smile curled her lips. Home. The smell of ink and parchment, burnt herbs, and fragrant smoke permeated the space, and the sensory memory it inspired made her stop moving.

Staying away had been a calculated decision for a number of

reasons, but right now, she couldn't seem to recall any of them. As she breathed in, she lowered the strongest of her shields and cocked her head as spirit radio crackled to life. Gentle murmurs of scholars long dead echoed down the hallways, and somewhere upstairs, a woman was singing. None of them were reaching out for her; they were simply existing in this place in their own ways.

Emilie shook her head and took one more lingering glance at the mural above her before scurrying across the room and taking one of the corridors on the left. She bypassed a staircase that led to the lower floors and found a pair of tall oak doors. They were engraved with a rounded art deco depiction of a library, beams exploding out from the arc at the top.

She pressed three fingers against the wood and pushed gently as her eyes slipped closed. Some parts of the building had stayed open, and the main library with texts that were for sale was on the opposite side. She'd gone for the archives that weren't open to the public. This library was one Emilie understood better than most.

The doors popped open at the contact, and a warm tendril of magic slipped over her shoulders. Shelves in neat rows dominated the space, with a handful of research desks against the walls to her left and right. Along the right side of the room, tall windows let in the dying light, narrow slats of orange that splashed along the floor.

She let the atmosphere wash over her as she wandered down the aisles, fingertips dancing across leatherbound titles. Emilie made it almost halfway through the room before a rush of cold air raised all the hair on the back of her neck.

"The library is not open to the public. Infiltrators will be removed. Are you an infiltrator?"

One of Emilie's fingers twitched, and she turned very, very slowly. Standing in front of her was a wisp of a spirit. Her countenance was faded, so translucent that the shelves behind her were fully visible. A young woman in a knee-length black and white polka dot swing dress and a black cardigan with a pin of an open book over her heart. Her red hair was pinned back from her face. Gore matted the bottom of her dress, splattered halfway up her torso, and speckled her cheeks, painting them red and black.

"Aggie?" Emilie asked. "Do you remember me?"

Agnes Crawford had been a librarian here in the forties. A summoning in the basement had gone wrong and released a demon that killed more than a dozen people. She'd held it off at the doorway, protecting her books and binding the demon back to its dimension. Emilie had known her since she was a child.

The woman's eyes widened, and she surged forward until she was a few scant inches from Emilie. She cocked her head, eyes wide as she peered at Emilie's eyes and hair. She zoomed around Emilie, investigating her from every angle, and with each movement, she became more solid. After a few long seconds, she stood back and smiled at Emilie, no longer translucent but still bleached of color.

"*Emilie Lockgrove. The prodigal daughter returns.*" A smile twitched at the corner of her mouth now that she looked like a person again. "*It's been so long since I've seen you, my girl.*"

"Yes, yes it has," Emilie agreed quietly. "Aggie, I need your help."

The woman cocked her head again, eyes suddenly gleaming bright blue in her face as color started to fill back in. "*My help? Dear girl, you know I don't leave my library untended.*" She clucked her tongue. "*You wouldn't believe the mess some people try to leave in here.*" She sniffed.

Emilie bit her lip. "I need to check out some books, and I can't be sure I'll be able to return them."

She braced, waiting for the spirit to snap. Instead, Agnes regarded her carefully.

"*Which books?*"

"*Carroll's Compendium of Parasitic Fiends.* The seventh edition." Emilie swallowed. "There are a few others I'd like...but I *need* the compendium."

"*Need?*" Agnes raised an eyebrow and twitched her lips. "*You were always a good girl and a quick study.*" She began to move down one of the rows as she talked, and Emilie trailed after her, listening. "*Such a bright girl, and such a bright talent.*" As she spoke, the color painted back onto her until she seemed nearly as alive as Emilie. *"Did you know I don't allow most children in my library? Sticky fingers and no regard for the books. But not you..."* Agnes trailed off, turning to face Emilie.

She plucked a book off the shelf behind her without looking and held it carefully in her hands. Reverent fingers ran over the embossed cover before she pinned Emilie with a shrewd look. *"I know you wouldn't come at this hour unless you were desperate."* She pursed her lips and handed Emilie the book. *"Treat her kindly. If you don't, I'll know."* Agnes paused. *"But there are a few other texts you'll need."*

"Oh?"

"Mmm." Agnes clucked her tongue again, then zipped into a side room and back in the blink of an eye, now holding three more books. "Protective Spellcraft: A History of Sigils and Wards, Conduits and Clairvoyants, *and* A History of Watchtowers." She handed the books over to Emilie with a nod. *"I've had these held for you for a number of years, but I knew you'd be back for them eventually."*

Emilie took the books, confusion written all over her face. "Did I...request these? I didn't think I had any holds here."

"You didn't." Agnes smoothed her skirts, twitching them so they laid properly. *"After your mother passed, she lingered at first."* Agnes clucked her tongue, watching Emilie. *"She was worried you wouldn't have anyone to teach you. About who you are and what you are."*

"You spoke to Mama?" The words fell out of her in a broken whisper.

"Not me. Marie, your grandmother. She passed the fear along, so I pulled a few titles that would help. I never anticipated it would be so long, but as I said, you've always been a quick study."

Emilie tucked the four books into her bag and was thankful yet again that she'd upgraded to something big enough over the summer. Her old bag could never.

"Thank you, Aggie...I don't know what to say."

"Say you'll come back before it's been another ten years." Agnes winked. *"You help me to stay rooted, dear girl. I'd hate to leave this place*

unprotected. Spark only knows what those unruly scholars would do to the place without someone keeping an eye on things."

"I think that can be arranged." Emilie nodded. "You look more... yourself than you did when I got here."

Agnes smoothed her skirt again and nodded. *"You're a beacon in the darkness, Emilie. It's why you can hear the scarcest of voices, and you've always had a good ear. Your presence...grounds those of us who aren't ready to let go of the physical."* Agnes smiled, but it was a sad, wistful expression shining from her eyes.

"As long as I'm breathing, I'll make sure you don't fade. Not unless you're ready."

Before Agnes could respond, a long shadow appeared at the window to their right. A young man stood outside, peering in with a frown. He wore the same pin she'd seen with her earlier run-ins with the Scions; she recognized it immediately. Ice ran through Emilie's veins, and she retreated away from the window.

From outside, they were nothing but brick, but the fact that there were Scions outside at all was bad. Very, *very* bad. Next to her, Agnes snarled, and her face began to warp in proportion and form: wide eyes and a slavering jaw, her limbs growing and distorting.

"Time for you to go, dear. There are infiltrators peeking through my windows."

Agnes' voice hadn't changed, a sweet voice coming from this terrifying apparition. The building around her shuddered, and the quiet murmurs of spirits went silent. Emilie took one step back toward the entrance, then another, not turning her back to Agnes along the way.

She had never been predatory toward Emilie, but that didn't mean she wasn't capable of it. Better to be safe than sorry. Emilie made it halfway across the room before spirit radio crackled back to life. This time, it was a voice she'd never heard before, one that rumbled through her bones in a register so low, it was a drone.

"Protect them. Protect us. Wake up, dear friends, your assistance is required by bond and blood."

Around her, scarlet wards winked into sight, dozens, then hundreds. The blood wards were all archaic, but listening to the droning voice as they appeared, Emilie had an idea of what she was looking at. A dangerous idea, and one she'd be keeping in her pocket for the moment. Wards that could call on the spirits still tethered to this place, protections old enough that no one had known what they were for because they were a "smash in case of an emergency" plan.

"*Down the stairs and out the door at the end of the hallway, dear,*" Agnes called across the room, nodding. "*You won't be able to get out the front. Lockgrove is sealed to the physical.*"

Emilie nodded and stumbled out into the hallway. Around her, spirits were peeling themselves from the walls, more wards lighting, sigils stamped into the bricks flaring to life in a vicious array.

Emilie navigated on memory, senses overwhelmed by the auction house coming to life around her. Spirits echoed the call for aid on spirit radio, and she could see them as they emerged, rising from the walls and the floors as if they'd been here the entire time. As she moved through the hallways, she could see the spirits shifting from thin, translucent apparitions into people she almost recognized.

She nearly tumbled down the stairs but clutched at the railing as she begged her legs to do their damned job. Two floors down, the stairs terminated in a long hallway lined with doors. Down here, the floor and walls were almost vibrating, and the same sense of someone there that she'd gotten when she first arrived surrounded her.

Emilie ran as fast as her legs could carry her and nearly tripped twice, but she felt someone, something push her forward toward the door. She slammed into it, both hands slapping against the faded wood, and the door popped open with a sigh. A phantom hand pushed her again as something spectral began screaming, and Emilie tumbled outside as the door clicked shut behind her.

24

DANI

The beat-up wooden floor was smooth under Dani's boots as she paced a circle into its surface. Three hours since Emilie had hit the road, and the hunter was slowly starting to crawl out of her skin. The urge to take her truck and follow had been nearly overwhelming, but Dani trusted Emilie, and she was right. Her little medium knew how to take care of herself, and Dani was a walking target.

That didn't really make any of this any easier. She couldn't seem to sit still as she tried to distract herself from the fact that if something went wrong, she was over an hour away.

"You have to realize pacing like that isn't gonna help anything." Joe raised an eyebrow at her from behind the bar.

"You've been polishing the same glass for the last ten minutes, not sure you have room to talk," Dani said.

Joe scowled at her, put the glass in his hand to the side, and picked up a fresh one to start all over again. "Emilie knows how to spot danger, and she's been riding with you for a year. It's going to be fine."

"It better be." Dani took a seat at the bar. She plopped her elbows down and raked both hands through her unruly dark hair. "I hate that I'm not there with her right now, Joe. What if they spot her? What if they're casing the auction house?"

Joe snorted. "If they try to raid Lockgrove Antiquities, the Scions have another thing coming. That place has its own security systems." He put the glass to the side. "If we're lucky, they haven't clocked Emilie yet. You might be a good smokescreen when it comes to this. They're so focused on you, they're not asking questions."

Dani freed her hands and rubbed her fingers across her forehead, suppressing a groan. "Just tell me it's gonna work out and I don't need to panic."

"Panic is overrated," Joe said as the front door to the grill slammed open behind them.

Dani turned in a flash and spotted Mateo and Nova, with another figure supported between the two of them as they stumbled inside.

They fell into the first table, depositing a long, lanky figure into an empty chair before straightening up. Dani checked the lot outside to see if anyone was following them, but it was empty. When she closed the door, she threw the lock and turned the sign.

She leaned back against the locked door and raised an eyebrow at Mateo and Nova. "What's goin' on, guys? You seem a little stressed."

Nova narrowed her eyes, and Mateo tipped his head toward the ceiling, pinching his nose. After a long moment, he recovered from his agitation and let out a long-suffering sigh.

"If you'd been dodging Scion raids for the last three days, you'd be a little stressed too."

"Where?" Dani asked.

"Where not?" Beside Mateo, Nova let out a bitter laugh and left the table, aiming for the bar. He watched her for a long moment before turning back to Dani. "We started farther south, looking for leads again after you told us about the rumors down there." His eyes slid to the prone form at the table.

"You found them down south?"

"No," a feminine voice piped up groggily, still facedown at the table. "I found the hunters first."

A woman with deep auburn hair and green eyes looked up from

the table with a shrewd expression. With a small button nose and a smattering of freckles across her nose and cheeks, she looked sweet, but there was something sharp watching from behind her eyes. A lot of people would have clocked her as a victim without ever thinking about it. At that moment, Dani knew that was a very bad call.

"And you are?" Dani took a seat across from her at the table.

"Maggie Caspar." She brushed hair out of her face and cracked her neck. "I've been on the run from the Scions for three years. You?"

"Longer," Dani said.

Mateo slouched into one of the chairs at the table and watched the two women talk, but he didn't try to add to the conversation. Smart man. Maggie rolled her eyes and tapped two fingers on the table.

"I was looking for them because I needed to find you." She shrugged. "Well, you and the medium, but in the short term, you'll do."

"And why. Pray tell. Would you be looking for a medium?" Dani asked in a quiet murmur.

Mateo paled. Maggie smiled, a predatory baring of her teeth. Dani recognized it from looking in the mirror.

"Not a medium, *the* medium," she corrected carefully. "Emilie Lockgrove is the strongest medium in a hundred years." She shrugged again. "On this side of the Atlantic, anyway. I've got information that can help her handle her side of the cultist problem." Maggie raised an eyebrow and pinned Dani with an intense look.

Dani exhaled through her nose and relaxed just a little bit. "You've got information?"

"It's my favorite currency," Maggie said.

"And what do you want for your information?"

"I want the two of you to handle the cultists. It was bad enough when I had to leave the midwest, but they've burned me out of three states now, and I'm over it."

"Burned you out?"

Maggie sighed. "I was a caster. A witch. Kind of. It's complicated."

She shook her head. "I attracted their attention, they grabbed me, and I...sparked."

"Sparked?"

Maggie paused before answering. "My magic backfired, and I lit them on fire." She paused to examine her nails. "Look, who I am and how I got here isn't really the thing to chat about." She cocked her head and moved her gaze to Mateo.

Nova waltzed back over before he could answer, eyes flickering between them all. "Maggie is a conduit. A real-deal, these-don't-happen, magical conduit."

Dani frowned. "Wouldn't the talented have scooped her up?"

Maggie scoffed and knocked on the table. "Talented are a bunch of stuffy assholes who like to protect their pedigree." She started tracing an index finger across the scarred wood. "Not all of them, but the ones who bring new people in, for sure. The line between caster and talented is a whole lot thinner than most people think."

"So you have intel for us, and all you want us to do in return is handle the problem," Dani said after a long pause.

"In a word? Yes. I have a vested interest in surviving. I like my skin, and my soul, firmly attached to my body, m'kay?"

Dani blinked. Twice. She flicked her gaze up and found Joe watching her as he returned to cleaning the bar. When he caught her eye, he nodded slowly. She exhaled, feeling the tension under her skin ratchet up again. This was the worst possible time for this woman to show up, but if she knew something, they needed to know what it was.

"In that case, I'm all ears." Dani flipped her chair so she was leaning against its back while facing Maggie. "What'cha got?"

"The Scions are trying to help an evanescent parasite transubstantiate into a physical form because they think it's an angel," Maggie said simply. "Also, it's got its hooks in dozens of them at this point. I couldn't tell you for sure who is doing it because they like it and who is being magically manipulated."

Dani paused, unsure of what to say, just before the sound of glass breaking behind her caught her attention. Joe was staring across the empty space, worry etched over his face.

"I can tell the parasites infecting hunters thing is bad," Dani said slowly. "But I'm getting the feeling I don't actually know how bad."

"Evanescent parasites are usually bottom-feeders," Joe said, abandoning the bar to join them at the table. "They exist in the veil, but occasionally, a few small ones get out by riding the coattails on a summon." He shook his head. "They're nasty little buggers, but there's an easy charm to get rid of them in the early stages."

"This isn't the early stages," Maggie piped back up. "It's been squatting for decades."

"Decades?" Joe repeated, eyes bugging in his face.

"The coven who trained me knew about it." She pursed her lips. "They'd seen it, or felt it, I don't know the details." Maggie bit at the nail of her thumb idly. "Best they could tell, it caught a ride on a demon summoning that went wrong somewhere in the '70s. They figured it got its talons into a hunter who didn't notice and started to feed."

"It feeds on magic," Mateo said, choosing his words carefully. "But it doesn't use its sources for food. It manipulates them into creating discord and strife…flushing magic folk out and getting them killed. Since it doesn't have a physical body, it's not the kind of threat we usually see."

"It's why we hand out those charms to the new bloods," Joe added. "I've seen these little bastards before. The easy way to keep 'em outta you is just by wearing a ward. Once they've gotten a chunk, it gets harder the longer they've been embedded."

"Wait, wait, wait. Go back." Dani shook her head. "It doesn't have a physical body? And why would the Scions feed it?"

"Get this." Maggie leaned over the table conspiratorially. "It latched onto Grandaddy Campbell first, way back in the '70s, right? Convinced him it was an angel and he was doing god's work. Once it had him convinced, anytime it wanted a new host, they already believed it was an angel. Latching onto that family was like a cash cow for this thing. It calls itself Seraph." She leaned back in her chair, watching everyone else at the table gleefully.

Dani could feel the new information sinking into her brain, but right now, she wished Emilie was here. Her girlfriend would know the right questions to ask to get everything they needed out of this woman.

"Don't look so giddy about dropping that bomb," Joe rumbled, eyes flashing. "You just told us that the militia that has been hunting people for fifty years has been doing so because of a parasite infestation." He shook his head. "I knew these people. I saw them change." He got up and made himself busy behind the bar again.

The mood in the room sobered immediately, and Dani's mind started to come up with questions nobody here could answer. Was Julia infected? Evan? Had they already been doomed when she'd met them, or had there been time? Had the Campbell family started by hunting talented, or did they become the preferred target because of the parasite's feeding preferences?

"Look, I'm not trying to be an asshole here," Maggie finally said. "It's a lot, okay? I know it's a lot, and now, so do you. But I've had to have this conversation a dozen times now. I've watched them ruin people's lives and kill them because of charms in the window and magic in their blood. I'm sorry that y'all know some of the hunters who got infected, but as far as I know, there isn't a safe way to deworm them. When we sever the connection between the parasite and the host, it's a toss-up on if any of them survive it at all."

Joe reappeared with a bottle of whiskey and a few glasses. He poured everyone a finger, then slugged his back all at once before refilling it. Dani sipped at the alcohol, letting it smooth her frazzled edges.

"It's almost better, though," Nova ventured after taking a sip of her drink. "That it isn't just hunters being stupid and cruel and terrible."

Dani's phone chose that moment to ping from her pocket, and she pulled it out, still paying attention to the conversation in front of her. Then dread crashed down over her as she saw the notification that Emilie's phone signal was no longer available.

Panic clawed at her throat as she scrambled through the menus in the find-a-friend app she and Emilie used to keep tabs on each other. She'd watched her travel up to Lockgrove Antiquities, but the last time she'd checked, before everyone got here, Emilie's little ghost icon had been firmly on top of the building.

Now it showed a greyed-out icon, indicating that her phone had gone offline. Tension radiated from her, and the urge to scream or flip the table or do anything was choking her. Emilie had been in trouble, and she'd been sitting here instead of being up in Maryland with her. She'd known better. She'd known.

"Emilie's phone is offline." The words were deadpan, but the burble of conversation around her died. "I don't think it went fine at all."

Joe nodded. "Rescue run?"

"I can't just sit here with my thumb up my ass."

"If her phone is offline, and it was them, she's already gone." Mateo stood from the table, holding his hands up to Dani, palms out, like she was a predator. Maybe she was. "You know I'm right."

"Are you sure?" Dani pressed him. "Can you be absolutely sure?"

"You know he's right," Nova said, still nursing her drink.

Maggie held up a finger and concentrated, eyes slipping shut for a moment. Her eyelids fluttered, and she gasped in pain before they reopened. "Something happened at Lockgrove Antiquities. Might still be happening. But that's not a small-time collective." She shrugged. "They poked a bear when its cub was there. Bad call."

Adrenaline flooded Dani's system as she watched Maggie. She recognized the mannerism. It was the same thing Emilie did when she was tuning into spirit radio. Except for her, it always seemed like second nature, something intuitive and ingrained. The strain on Maggie's face had shown her concentration, and that gasp of pain meant something too. Right now, Dani didn't really care.

"Bad call how?" Dani pressed.

"That place doesn't just have protections, it has security measures."

With teeth." Maggie shook her head. "Nobody is getting in or out of that building before dawn."

Dani started to pace back and forth again, the excess energy pouring out of her. She felt like a big cat stuck in a small cage. Right now, she was practically gnawing at the bars of her enclosure.

Maggie watched her carefully, then leaned over to Nova and asked a quiet question. Dani didn't pay attention to what was said, but the witch's entire demeanor changed. Instead of simply passing on information for Emilie, there was a new degree of...respect? Understanding? It was hard to place, but the change was undeniable.

"You didn't tell me you were bringing me to Reaper." Maggie shook her head. "When I said 'all the salient details,' I really did mean it." She sighed at Mateo and Nova, who rolled their eyes in unison. "I've been trying to get Valkyrie's attention about this for years. There are two good methods for dealing with an evanescent parasite: mediums and veilblades." Her lips curled into a wicked grin. "Lucky us, we have both."

Dani paused, then turned her head to regard Maggie. She clocked it when Mateo and Nova went stock-still at the look on her face. It was easy to forget the way hunters gossiped, the way a job turned into a story, turned into a legend. They were calling her Reaper, and already, the person she was behind the moniker was fading away. The people who knew, knew. It would have been easier if it hadn't been what the Scions had called her when she was a teenager.

"You said this thing lacks a physical body," Dani said.

"Yes," Maggie answered. "But it does have tethers from the node where it emerged to its hosts. The depth of the infection is hard to tell, but if you could see the tethers, the veilblade could probably sever them."

"Probably."

Maggie shot a look around the room, then pulled out a thick notebook bristling with notes and photos pinned inside. She flipped open to a specific section and read through until she found what she was looking for. "'Evanescent parasites may be excised with weapons capable of cutting past the real and into death's realm. These weapons are rare but have been witnessed alongside the legendary bladesingers when eradicating nests near the first Watchtower.'" She finished reading from the notebook before tucking it back into the bag coiled at her feet.

"The other method is a medium?" Dani asked.

"...Yes, it's what I was banking on by coming up here to talk to Emilie." Maggie shrugged, a tiny wrinkle appearing between her eyes as she frowned. "Between the two of you, this is much more doable. On her own would have been...tricky."

"Tricky how?" Dani bit out the words from between clenched teeth, her temper far too close to the surface.

"These parasites only have access to the physical because of their hosts. If you sever those connections, most of the time, the place where it ruptured the real will heal on its own, and the parasite will try to find a new way to reach through. This one is...different."

"I gotta say, I am getting really tired of you beating around the bush here, Maggie. I can tell you know what you're talking about, but I can't do anything about it unless you get to the damned point."

"Seraph is large. It's attached itself to dozens of hosts in the real and has been devouring the souls of people they kill. Trying to sever all of those connections is just the first half of the problem. The parasite needs to be cast back into the river, into the vastness of the veil, so that the spirits can reclaim what was stolen from them."

"And you want Emilie to cast it out. Why don't you just do it?"

"If I was capable of that, I wouldn't be sitting here right now." Maggie's eyes flared brightly, and then the flare died unexpectedly. "I'm a conduit, not a medium. I don't hold onto power, and this requires someone who can move between the physical and the veil without thinking about it. I don't get through the veil for a listen without some significant mojo." She flashed her hands, the fingers covered in rings of different sizes, with and without gems.

"Emilie is different," Maggie continued. "Think of it like a pyramid. A conduit is a building block of Emilie's abilities, but only one channel or avenue or whatever. That's all I have easy access to. I am the bottom of the pyramid. But your girl? She's sitting pretty up on top."

25

EMILIE

Emilie landed on the floor in a heap, not entirely sure what had just happened. Above her was a grand vaulted dome, painted to depict stars shining in a violet sky before it soared into tiered floors she could barely make out. She blinked, pulling herself back up and looking around. Behind her, the narrow wooden door she'd traveled through was gone, replaced with a wide marble archway with glass doors.

Ahead of her was a library that made Lockgrove's archives look like a personal collection. A dark wooden desk separated the room, a few small signs sitting on either end. Beyond it was a wide circular area with stacks leading off in different directions, warm light washing over the collection. Emilie gaped, unsure of what the hell she'd stumbled into this time.

She knew every inch of the auction house, and there was no way this had been hidden in the basement the whole time. This was grand and beautiful, like the dream of a library she'd never been quite able to remember upon waking. Her eyes traced the corners and spotted the tell-tale curvature of wards and sigils, but she didn't recognize them. Not any of them.

Emilie licked her lips, blinking away the shields that kept magic from blinding her, and the room flared with power. Archaic wards and sigils crawled along the walls and the titles of some of the books. They imbued this place from top to bottom. A finger on her right hand twitched as she tried to identify what she was looking at, to figure out what or where she'd been pushed into.

"Welcome to the library. Is this your first visit?"

Emilie's attention whipped to where a librarian was now standing beside the desk, watching her. The woman had a short pageboy cut of blond hair, bright blue eyes shining from behind a pair of holographic glasses perched on her nose. She was wearing slacks and a button-up with a dark blue blazer, and she would have looked comfortable in any occult library Emilie had ever visited. But something about her felt different in a way she couldn't place.

She was out of her depth here and didn't like it.

"It is." She wandered closer to the desk, every instinct she had focused on whether she was in danger or not. "I'm not...entirely sure how I got here."

"It goes that way sometimes." The librarian moved behind the counter. "I'm Olivia, and I can get you acquainted with the place. You're Emilie...Lockgrove, yes?"

Alarm shot through Emilie as the woman reached for something behind the desk. She'd never been here before, but they knew who she was, and that was rarely a good sign. Ice flooded into her fingers, her innate magic responding to a perceived threat. The front door was still behind her, and if she was fast, Emilie might be able to make it out. Who knew where it would toss her later, but that was future Emilie's problem.

Olivia looked up with a half-smile and produced a small, laminated library card with Emilie's name on it. "Here we are. If you're a patron, you'll need a library card." She slid the card across the desk.

Adrenaline drained from her system, magic curling back up inside her as the panic receded like the tide going out. It was a small generic card that had "Library Card" written across the top, her name printed on it, and a small number in the lower right corner. Tentatively, she swiped it from the counter, turning it back and forth.

"How did you know who I was?" Emilie finally said, curiosity burning through her.

"Perks of being the librarian," Olivia said with a small smile. "We aren't your usual establishment, and we have a select clientele. Everyone who will come here already has a card waiting for them."

"What?" She'd heard the words just fine, but it was like they weren't entirely computing at the moment. "What do you mean? Not your usual establishment..." She shut her mouth and narrowed her eyes. "Where am I?"

The woman gestured around her with a wave. "Welcome to the library. A few of the stuffier patrons call us Library Prime." Olivia wrinkled her nose. "But it's an easier explanation for you to say we were the Library of Vesper, from before it fell."

Emilie blinked. Vesper was the name of the town that had grown around the first Watchtower, until it fell during the schism and the early wars. It had held a legendary library filled with old magic, and during the siege, it disappeared. The raiders found a hole where it had existed, but the building and everyone inside was simply gone.

"Vesper is a story," Emilie said, shaking her head. "A way for the families to try and rationalize losing what they lost during the schism wars. For talented and hunters to deal with that kind of loss and how it catapulted us into the dark years."

Emilie had always believed it was just a story. There were rumors of people stumbling into it before it disappeared again, but they'd been like fairytales. A mystical library that showed up exactly when it was needed seemed a little too on the nose, but here she was. She definitely wasn't in the auction house anymore.

"The best stories start with a nugget of truth, don't they?" Olivia raised an eyebrow, lips tipping into a wry smile. "Vesper was a prayer against the darkness, and for those still seeking to light up the world, it can be found."

Emilie took a deep breath and let the new information sink into her brain. "So, then. Where are we? I was...somewhere else, and I went through a door...and now I'm here."

"The first time is always interesting," Olivia agreed. "Sometimes, it's people entering a library. Sometimes, you get pushed through if you're looking for something." A small smile graced her lips. "I'm betting it's the second one with you."

"Yeah, I came through a door, but not that...door," Emilie said, glancing back over her shoulder.

"Well of course not. Those are the library doors. They only exist here. In Vesper. We exist in a sort of...extra space. Tucked between here and there." Olivia picked a bit of non-existent lint from her blazer. "When you're here, you're only here. But you won't ever be able to find us on a map. The library is everywhere and nowhere. Open the right door if you have a library card, and Vesper might be on the other side."

Emilie nodded absently. "And I already had a card waiting for me?"

"Everyone who shows up does." Olivia shrugged. "Not my department. I'm here to help the people who do arrive. So they can find what they're looking for."

"What I'm looking for," Emilie repeated.

Olivia nodded. "Mmm. We're an archive and a library. We have all the books." She frowned. "Most of them. It's hard to keep up some years. New releases can be a bitch to get ahold of." She shook her head. "But most people are here for older texts, unabridged, before the church got their firebug fingers on them."

Emilie's eyes lit up. "Wait. How—" She shook her head. "Nevermind. It doesn't matter. What if I only know what I'm looking for information about?"

"Finding the references you need isn't hard. The card catalog is inside to the left. Think about your subject when you grab onto it, and anything relevant will be inside when you open the drawer."

"How does checking a book out work?"

"Books on the main floor can be checked out by new patrons. Additional floors require a longer membership period, but there are research desks in each section that can be used during your stay."

Emilie nodded absently, already considering the things she needed to look at. The books she'd acquired from Agatha would cover some of it, but not everything. They were a start, not a full reference run, and she knew there was more information here.

"Thank you."

"Of course. Just pop back over here if you need anything." Olivia put a small silver service bell on the counter. She gave Emilie a polite nod, then left the counter, pushing a cart of books that needed to be reshelved.

Emilie made a beeline for the card catalog. Ahead of her was a giant bank of small cubbies made from a gleaming dark wood with shiny silver inlay. As she walked closer, the cubby in front of her shimmered before her name appeared on the front in a flowing script.

"Just concentrate on what I need to find and open the cubby," she murmured to herself as her fingers alighted on the drawer.

She needed more information on all of it. The parasite, the Scions, and the veilblade. The thoughts tumbled one over the next as she tried to concentrate without much success. After a moment, there was a small spark of magic, and the drawer popped open. Inside, Emilie found three cards, all for books on the ground floor.

It didn't take long to find the books that had been recommended and make her way back to the reception counter. Olivia reappeared as Emilie approached and nodded approvingly at the books in her hands.

"Found what you were looking for I hope?"

"I think so." Emilie swallowed, putting the books on the counter. "I'd like to check all three out. How long can I have them?"

"Until you return to us," Olivia said simply, waving a hand over the books. A small wave of magic washed over them, and then she pushed them toward Emilie again. "The books will return to the library if you no longer require their information or with your physical return."

"Okay." Emilie nodded. "How do I return?"

"Intention and a door usually does the trick," Olivia said. "It works best with a library or an archive. But if you need it badly enough, most doors will pay attention."

Emilie nodded "Okay, okay. Got it." She shot a look at the doors. "Will they drop me back where I came in?"

"Usually." Olivia grimaced. "Unless the physical location has been destroyed. In those cases, it will take you where you need to go."

"Once more into the breach, I guess," Emilie murmured, heading back for the doors.

She tucked the new books into her bag, then readjusted the weight on her shoulder before putting a hand against the tall doors. Right now, Emilie wasn't sure whether they'd drop her back into the basement at the auction house or somewhere else entirely, and dread pooled in her belly. With a long exhale, she pressed against the doors, closed her eyes, and walked through them.

Her feet hit thin carpet, and Emilie reopened her eyes to see the familiar hallway of Lockgrove Antiquities. She let out a long, shaking breath and reached for the wall, grateful beyond belief that it was still standing. The building hummed around her, pleased she had returned.

She stayed quiet as a mouse, opening her senses for any sign of what happened while she had been away. The seething chaos that had chased her to Vesper was gone. No more bass voice speaking through the veil, no more spirits answering its call. Emilie wasn't sure whether that was a good thing or a bad thing. Her eyes tracked up the ceiling, waiting to hear any sign of intruders on the main floor above her.

A vibration in her pocket made Emilie jump, scaring her before she realized what the noise was. When she pulled it out of her pocket, a string of notifications were coming in, delayed by her jaunt to Vesper. Apparently, pocket dimensions didn't get signal. Her stomach dropped as she saw four separate messages from Dani, and just now, one from Andry up in Dawson.

> Dani: Did your phone die?

> Dani: I swear if you hit airplane mode I will strangle you. With love.

> Dani: You have 90 mins to check in or I'm
> driving up.

The last message was from less than an hour ago, but she fired off a quick reply. Dani must have been climbing the walls by now. She was lucky she hadn't come back to her hunter trying to take the place down to studs to find Emilie.

> Emilie: Alive. Unharmed. My phone lost signal
> and went offline, but there was a sighting.

She paused before hitting Send, rewriting the message twice. She needed to tell Dani she was okay, but she wasn't sure what she'd be walking into upstairs. Emilie rocked back on her heels and lowered her shields so she could hear spirit radio clearly, which also meant any nearby spirits noticed her in return.

"Is there an ambush upstairs? Do I need to be worried?" she asked out loud, hoping someone would answer.

"*No, and yes.*" Graham shimmered into sight in front of her. "*You got damned lucky tonight.*" He shook his head, giving her a stricken look.

"Yeah, I noticed," Emilie hissed back, not in the mood to be scolded by a dead man.

Before he could continue, she checked her other message.

> Andry: Scions tried to raid LA, but your
> Gramp's security measures kicked on. They
> might have their sights on you at this point.
> Keep your head on a swivel. Merc went down
> to the shop to scare the cultists back to their
> hidey hole.

"*Most of them beat feet after the blood wards on the doors went off.*" Graham made an exaggerated grimace. "*Serves them right, but they were nasty. They didn't get in the door, but they probably still have someone on the street watching the place.*"

Emilie readjusted her bag and nodded. That meant going back out the front door was a no-go. Had they been out there already when she'd gotten here? Had coming here alone been the wrong call after all? She didn't think so, even right now, but with danger lurking outside the building, she wasn't so sure.

"So I go out the side door, get to my car a few blocks over, and beat feet without them noticing."

"Noticing more, you mean," Graham said pointedly.

"Did they actually see me come in, or are you just giving me shit?" Emilie leveled a measured stare at him.

Graham held his expression for a long moment before it faded and he rolled his eyes. *"It's the principle. If you knew there was a quieter way to get inside, why did you come in the front door?"*

"The building has feelings about which doors we use for what things, and I hadn't been here in a decade." Emilie scratched at the back of her neck absently. "I wasn't sure it would recognize me, and if it didn't, then trying to go in through one of the other doors could have ended very badly for me."

Graham blinked, then shrugged. *"Well in that case, I suppose it makes sense. When you get outside, I'll make some racket near the front door. Should keep them distracted long enough that they won't notice you."*

The spirit's form suddenly blinked away, and from upstairs, Emilie heard the creak as someone moved from the reception area into the building above her. She licked her lips, moving as quietly as she could down the hallway. To get out of here, she needed to get up one floor and make it to one of the exterior walls. There were plenty of magical one-way doors keyed to her family, but they were useless unless she could get to them. Ice surged in her veins, and when she breathed out, vapor hung loosely in the air around her.

Carefully, keeping to the shadows and moving slowly, Emilie made her way up the stairs and took a right. She'd made it halfway to the mark when a man turned into the hallway ahead of her. Merc, armed with a flashlight and looking less than enthused, was sweeping the building.

"You got here fast," Emilie said.

Merc startled but recovered. "I knew there was someone with a pulse in here. The security wards went off, was that you?"

"No, that was the Scions casing the place."

Merc swore under his breath. "Did they get in?"

"Not sure. I got yeeted through a door into another archive I'd forgotten about," Emilie said, choosing her words carefully.

The librarian hadn't told her she needed to keep her access to Vesper a secret, but with those books in her bag, she had the sudden urge not to tell anyone about it. Not yet, anyhow.

Merc nodded, looking around absently. "I don't think they breached the place. It looked untouched to me." His eyes shot across the building toward the main library. "The doors to the library sealed themselves, though. Is that normal?"

"Yes," Emilie said with a smile. "The spirit that protects it has feelings about after-hours guests coming to fondle her books."

Merc stared at her and shook his head, muttering about spirits with too much time on their hands. "Emilie, why are you here? It's nearly midnight."

"Had to see a spirit about a book," Emilie answered with a shrug and a slight smile. "I didn't want to run into my dad, and coming at night when nobody was doing business seemed like the right call."

Merc watched her, and she could feel his judgement, but he didn't try to admonish her out loud for once. Emilie was glad that he'd decided to grow as a person.

"If you say so," Merc finally said. "The Scions were gone by the time I got here. I probably scared them off for now." He sighed, opened his mouth, and shut it again.

Sentinels weren't supposed to get involved in squabbles between the different parts of the magic community. Their job was to keep the balance, ensure that everyone was able to try and coexist in the world without destroying it in endless wars. That regular people could live their lives without being kidnapped for blood rituals and talented could use their magic without being hunted down like dogs.

Except. Except that right now, a whole lot of people were dying at the hands of the Scions, and so far, the Sentinels hadn't done anything.

"I need to send people to Dawson," she blurted out suddenly.

"Maybe a lot of people, and maybe some of them are hunters or talented or casters."

Merc stared at her like a deer caught in headlights. "That's not usually the way things work."

"I know," Emilie said. "But there are people at the clinic. If it gets targeted, they will need a place to go. A safe place."

"From Crossings? Andry thought this might come up. Most of them shouldn't have a problem getting into town. Some of the hunters might get turned around by the wards, but I'll keep an ear to the ground."

"Thank you." Emilie shifted from foot to foot. "Now, let's get the hell out of here. I have research to do."

26

DANI

Dani turned a small resin charm in her hands, over and over. It was simple: a locator charm that would break if the person it was tracking died. She and Emilie had made them last winter as a stopgap to panicking if they got separated. Dani usually kept it on a necklace that stayed hidden under her shirt with a few other charms, but right now, she wanted it in her hands. She needed the magical confirmation that everything was fine and Emilie would be back to the grill any minute now.

Emilie had called when she'd hit the highway, confirming that she'd made it out without any trouble. That didn't make the fear that curled around Dani's spine any easier to deal with. She'd gotten used to the fear of dying, but losing Emilie to the Scions was something new and terrible. Worse now that Maggie had finished unveiling what she knew and why it mattered.

They didn't know if all of the Scions were infected or just some of them. They had no idea how many hunters had been infected, if it was just the Scions, or whether there was anything they could do about it. She'd come outside when Emilie called, but right now, the cold night air was bracing. It reminded her that she was still alive, and as long as she was alive, she could figure this out.

Despair was an indulgence she didn't have time for, though she'd never say it out loud where someone could hear her. There was too much to do, too many people who needed help, to allow her mind to convince her that what she was doing was useless. She knew it wasn't because she had seen the other side when she'd run with the Scions during that first year. In the absence of good hunters helping people, there were bad hunters willing to kill someone over it. If that was the dynamic, then what choice did she have but to step up and do the job? To keep doing the job, no matter what it cost her.

When Joe unofficially adopted her, it had been like a mantra. If she worked hard enough and did it right, maybe she could atone for the things she'd been a part of back then. Em could tell her she'd been a kid, that she hadn't known any better, all she liked, but it didn't erase that some part of Dani had known what was happening was wrong. Maybe not all of it, but enough, and she'd waited, and people had died because of it.

A car pulled into the lot and parked, dragging Dani out of her head and back into the real world. Emilie stepped out of the car, and before she could shut her door, she was in Dani's arms. Dani hadn't meant to bum-rush her, hadn't intended it really, but during those ninety minutes when Emilie had been greyed out, the panic had been all-consuming. Even the attempts at planning had only worked so much.

Emilie clutched the back of her jacket, burying her face in Dani's chest. Tiny frissons of stress broke out of both of them as they stood there, holding onto each other like they were the entire world. This late at night, only the flickering sign of the grill watched over them.

Dani finally breathed out and leaned back enough that she could tilt Emilie's face up to her own. Fear shined brightly in those pale blue eyes, but there was something behind it that Dani recognized. Determination. The kind that showed up when you knew what you had to do, even if you didn't know how to do it yet.

"I know I agreed that this was the right call," Dani said. "But I hated every second of it."

Emilie laughed lightly, and Dani leaned in for a kiss, her hand reaching up to cup the curve of a cheek in her palm. She kissed Emilie like they'd been separated by sea and war, like her little medium was air and she'd been suffocating for too long. Dani poured the panic and the love and everything in between into it, and when they came up for air, Emilie was flushed, and the fear was gone from her face.

"I—yeah." Emilie opened her mouth, closed it again, and shook her head. "I had a response, but I think you kissed it out of me."

"Couldn't have been that important, then," Dani said, detaching to grab Emilie's bag from the car.

"It wasn't not important," Emilie protested.

"What is even in this bag? It weighs a ton." Dani shook her head and closed the door, reaching for Emilie's hand as they wandered toward the grill.

"Books." Emilie grinned. "I found exactly what I was looking for, and then some."

"We got some new information while you were out too." Dani paused outside the door. "Mateo and Nova brought in someone who escaped from them. She was looking for you."

"Me?" Emilie squeaked, then paled. "Why me? Is she a hunter?"

"Not a hunter." Dani's eyes slid to the doors. "She's a caster I think. But she knows about the thing that you saw. It's a parasite."

"I knew it!" Emilie crowed. "That's why I had to go to Lockgrove."

"Was it still worth it if she waltzed in to tell us what we're dealing with?"

"Yes." Emilie winked. "The books I got weren't just for identification. They also have information on dealing with the problem in the veil."

They pressed into the grill to find Joe behind the bar cleaning glasses again. Mateo and Nova were quietly talking to Maggie at the giant round table they'd claimed. Dani steered Emilie over to the table, and Joe appeared a moment later with drinks for the two of them.

"Find what you needed?" Joe asked.

"I found everything we should need," Emilie said, piling her stack of acquired books onto the table.

"Is that a first edition?" Mateo's eyes bugged in his face, and Emilie grinned triumphantly.

"It is." She handed the book over while looking at Dani. "The later editions were heavily redacted by the church once they figured out where they were being printed. Caused problems for a few centuries. We can technically get everything from the first edition elsewhere—"

"But it's a pain in the ass," Mateo muttered, gently paging through the book. "Four other books and none of it as well organized."

Dani raised an eyebrow and met Nova's eyes across the table. *Book people.* The other hunter gave her a small nod. They'd both managed to wrangle book nerds as their partners, and while it was handy on jobs, there were times, like right now, where it was a little weird.

"Don't get that look on your face." Emilie elbowed Dani sharply. "I can almost hear you calling me a nerd."

"I said nothing," Dani answered, holding her hands up in surrender. "Nova, you've got my back here, right?"

"Your face said it all," Emilie teased again, knocking her hip against Dani's.

Nova gestured at Dani, then leaned back in her chair, smirking from across the table.

"So, since you found what you were looking for, does that mean we know what's going on?" Dani finally asked, running a hand over the old books on the table.

"Kind of," Emilie said. She grabbed a book from the stack and started flipping through it.

"Maggie said it was an...effervescent parasite?" Dani asked.

"Evanescent parasite." Maggie and Mateo corrected her in unison.

"So do we think all the hunters are infected by this thing?" Emilie asked, paging through one of the books, looking for the right entry.

"Does it matter?" Maggie was looking at the rest of the table fiercely. "These people have been murdering talented for years."

"And apparently, they've also been under the influence of a parasite that causes strife and chaos to feed off it," Emilie shot back. "There's a recipe here for something that might be able to de-worm them." She blinked. "I mean, magically speaking, anyway."

Dani grinned as she watched Emilie spar with Maggie. She'd been ready to say some of the same things—in far less pleasant words.

"If they're still going for the throat after we try it, then we can handle it," Dani announced.

"There are few enough hunters as it is," Joe said quietly. "We're spread thin, and there are never enough hunters working to cover the bad in the world…" His voice trailed off, but Dani could hear what he wasn't saying.

If there were people who wouldn't have done this, didn't they have to try? Not everyone who ran with the Scions was infected when she was there, but there had been more of them then. Things had changed after she left. And the people who did this on purpose… What about them? She ran a hand over her jaw, listening to the burble of conversation as the table weighed the pros and cons.

They were all talking around what was coming though. Dani knew it, and everyone else at the table knew it. Maggie was just the only one who had the balls to say it with her whole chest. Whether the Scions were all fully under the control of Seraph or not, they'd still done enormous damage. To the magical community and to the veil itself. They had to go.

It suddenly felt heavier than it had a few minutes before. Dani left the table, everyone else still arguing, and made her way back out front again. It didn't take long for Joe to follow her outside. The two of them leaned against the building, and she shot him a sidelong glance.

"Do you think it's worth trying?"

"It's worth considering, at the least," Joe said after a long minute. "I want to think some of those hunters were somehow forced to do this."

"But some of them weren't. Or it matched what they wanted to do anyway." Dani scuffed her boot against the pavement. "They talked me into terrible shit because I didn't know any better." She bit her lip and sighed. "But I think the people who stayed or joined up later... they didn't have the same kind of excuse."

He watched her carefully. "You know that means people you know are gonna end up dead."

Dani nodded. "Even odds, I'll be the one to kill them." She looked over the mostly empty parking lot. "Evan Campbell has to die either way. I'm surprised he hasn't gotten the council's attention already."

"It's probably only a matter of time," Joe said. "Unless we put him down."

"We put him down, it means Julia too." Dani shook her head and looked back at Joe. "I know the kind of monster Evan is, but I don't know about her."

"Still?" he asked.

She shook her head. "You weren't there. Their pops raised them like soldiers, not kids. Julia is the only reason I'm alive. You know that."

"I do. And I know that Isaac Campbell was a good man once. But I don't know if that matters when we weigh it against what they've done."

"Yeah," Dani agreed. "I know."

Emilie pushed her way through the doors, her bag of books back over one shoulder. "It's late, and I want to sleep somewhere that isn't one of those tables."

Dani gave her a small smile and moved so Emilie could duck under one arm. She gave Joe a two-finger salute as they headed for the house to get some rest. None of this was settled, but it would still be waiting in the morning.

27

EMILIE

Emilie kept staring at the books as if they were hiding information from her. When she'd left for Maryland last night, she'd been convinced she could find what they needed to handle the rift and fix the hole in the world. The problem was that even if she stitched that rift up, so long as Seraph had a hold on the Scions, it was only a matter of time until it tore open again.

Without dispatching the parasite, anything they did was just a stopgap. It wouldn't fix the problem, and it wouldn't help the spirits who were still trailing her to find some kind of peace and cross over. And there was no dealing with the parasite so long as the Scions were still on their own personal witch hunt. Emilie could feel the pieces shifting on the board and knew that the walls were starting to close in on them.

According to Nova and Mateo, the Scions had been getting ballsier in the last day or two. They'd stopped a raid on a magic shop in Tennessee in broad daylight and had word that a collective in Kentucky had gotten out of their place only minutes before another one. People were scared, and when people got scared, they panicked. All it would take was a talented collective panicking too close to humans, and the council would be breathing down their necks.

And nobody wanted the council to cross the ocean with their judgment.

She traced the words on the page, as if by reading them again, she'd know what she was supposed to do next. Instead, there was the sharp scent of ozone, and Graham shimmered into sight leaning against the far wall. Emilie looked up and met his eyes but didn't say anything at first. At this point, she didn't know what to say.

Last night, listening to the table discuss how to deal with the Scions, she'd realized that there had to be a better way. Something more than just killing them or deworming them. Emilie didn't think about the problem in the same way as a hunter. They saw a job, a problem that needed to be dealt with so they could move onto the next one. It was hard to deal with spirits causing chaos or monsters eating people when you couldn't trust that the other hunter who showed up wasn't there for you.

But Emilie saw it more like a disease. The reason Seraph had been able to convince the first Campbell that it was an angel and that it had messages for them was because of their beliefs. Seraph was an infection, and it had been chewing its way through immunocompromised hunters for a long time now. But the infection had spread past just the Campbell family, stretching its influence toward other hunters and latching onto the ones that were weak enough to fall under its sway. Nobody had noticed it until now, and the people who had tried to speak up had been silenced. And now everyone associated with the Scions was standing under the sword of Damocles without ever looking up.

"*You're quiet today. That's not a good sign,*" Graham said.

"It's not like I never shut up," Emilie said without looking up from her passage.

"*Answers not hiding inside those books?*" He raised an eyebrow and watched her.

Emilie met his gaze, trying to find the answers to questions she hadn't asked in his eyes. Unfortunately, they weren't there yet.

"The Scions are infected by an evanescent parasite that calls itself Seraph," she said, thumping the large tome closed and pushing it away. "To close the rift, I have to detach Seraph from its hosts, but if I do it the wrong way, they all die. I have the recipe for something that could deworm the Scions, but we have no way to tell if they are in control of what they've been doing." She frowned, running a hand through her tangled curls. "I don't want to be responsible for killing all those people...but I don't think that detaching Seraph and just letting them go is the right call either. I don't know what to do."

Graham nodded and moved closer. *"Hunters tend to come at things from one direction. Most of their problems are solved by a blade or a gun. Violence is the language they're all fluent in."* He paused, watching Emilie and sighing before he continued. *"Talented and casters, they come at things sideways. Magic, charms, and enchantments. But people like you and I, we don't do either of those."*

Emilie didn't say anything but kept her eyes on Graham as he moved around the room as he spoke.

"We learn to move diagonally. A little of this and a little of that together might be able to do something that couldn't be done on its own." A small smile tugged at one side of his mouth, sad and solemn.

"Diagonally..." Emilie murmured, an idea coming to mind.

"Thatta girl," Graham said quietly.

Emilie looked up, ready to thank him and ask why he'd decided to show up today, but Graham was already gone. She frowned a little, then shook her head and started to take notes. The Evanescent parasite didn't have a physical form, so its influence in the physical world was directly limited by what its hosts had access to. That didn't mean there weren't tangible things that could weaken that influence.

Plenty of herbs were useful in clarifying spaces or weakening spirits' grasp on the real. Creatures and beings that reached from the veil had a tenuous hold on the physical world. It was why spirits tended to phase in and out, even the particularly malevolent ones. If she could just weaken Seraph's hold on a Scion, there might be a way to untangle it without overtly harming the host. If they did it in a controlled environment, there was a chance she could see what the reaction to coming back to themselves was.

Dealing with one hunter claiming to be something they weren't was a whole lot easier than dealing with a dozen or more. She needed a plan to bring to Dani and the rest of the group, but she wasn't willing to believe that her only options were to kill all of them or detach them and let them go. There had to be a third way. Some method to separate the people who had reveled in the violence and bloodshed and those who didn't. It was hiding here, if she just had time to find it.

Time wasn't on her side, but Emilie was used to having the deck stacked against her. There had to be an angle she hadn't considered. The spirits that had cried out to her deserved more than peace. They deserved justice, and they had decided that she was their arbiter.

She stacked the books on the table, then went to raid Joe's workshop and see if he had what she needed for sachets. If hunters only wanted to fight, and talented always reached for magic, how did she move between the two? How did she get justice for the spirits, stitch up the veil, and make it out the other side alive?

Right now, Emilie just wasn't sure. From the way Maggie had been talking, Seraph knew that a medium—a true medium—was capable of expelling it back into the depths of the veil. It knew she was out there, and if they did any deep digging about the auction house, the Scions would find her. Right now, it felt like the only one in more danger than her was Dani, and that was because of Evan's psychotic grudge.

"*Figure it out yet?*" Graham materialized again as she entered the workshop and started looking for rosemary and lavender.

"I have to find a way to thread between talented and hunter patterns," Emilie said carefully. "But I'm not straddling two worlds; for me, there are three. I have to account for the veil and the spirits trapped and unable to cross over because of what is happening here." As she talked, she carefully ground the herbs and began to put everything together.

"*Sounds like you're starting to figure it out.*" Graham smiled and shook his head. "*Least you aren't as dense as Dani.*" He shot a wistful glance down the hallway, then looked back to Emilie again. "*You are a lighthouse in the darkness. Means there are spirits and other things in the veil drawn to you. It also means you understand that place better than most of the living. You understand why a rift is so dangerous."*

Emilie sighed in response, pouring the ground mixture into small cloth bags before she met Graham's eyes. "I can't be the only one who understands how bad it is. We're lucky that it's only a parasite trying to crawl through right now. I still don't know how bad the damage is because Seraph is in the way."

"You'll figure it out." Graham winked. *"You're a survivor."*

He faded out of sight again as Emilie tied up the sachets and tucked them into her pockets. They might not work at all, but at least she'd try. If it didn't work, she could hold onto that. When she got downstairs, Dani was leaning against the table with her books.

"Time to shake a leg. We're heading for Lu."

"Crossings?" Emilie asked.

"Crossings," Dani agreed with a grin. "Before Lu scored that location, she ran Crossings as a mobile clinic. Some of her old crew still work as a satellite, and they've all pulled back to her place. Things are getting dicey out there."

"Dicey?' Emilie asked, fidgeting as she gathered her things.

"There was a raid nearby, so she has a bay full of patients, more than usual, and her security can't cover everyone. She's twitchy, and I don't like it when Lu gets twitchy," Dani said.

"Yeah, that's never good. Give me five minutes and I'll be ready to go. I just need my backpack from upstairs."

Dani hefted the back from where it had been hidden under the table. "Already got you covered." She winked.

Emilie leaned in and gave her a long kiss, hands tugging at Dani's hips. "I love it when you think ahead."

Dani leaned in for another kiss, and Emilie surrendered to the feel of her lips, the way Dani seemed to press in all around as if she could be consumed. When she pulled away, she had a wicked glint in her eyes. "It's hot, right?" She snickered, then pulled back, hauling Emilie's bag over her shoulder.

Emilie slipped the books from the table into her messenger bag, checked to make sure she had everything, then followed Dani out. Just before she closed the door, she thought she saw Graham watching them from the hallway. But it was a fraction of a second. Too dark and too fast to tell. Something had been different about him today. She just didn't know what.

28

DANI

Dani's boots had barely touched the dirt outside when the phone started ringing. She shot Emilie a look over her shoulder as she grabbed the phone, making sure everything was in order. When she saw Sawyer's name flash across the screen, her instincts sharpened in an instant. She picked up the call, holding up a palm telling Em to hold for a moment.

"Sawyer. This better be good. Shit has gotten worse. Fast."

"There's an incoming raid on the halfway house." Sawyer's voice was breathless on the other side of the line. "I'm on my way, but there's a full house right now, and you're closest."

"*What?*" Dani's heart stalled in her chest, and she gestured toward the truck, panic blooming inside of her.

Emilie moved at a lope, tossing her bag into the truck, Dani's panic infecting her.

"The proximity wards that Lockgrove set up for us all those years ago went off. They aren't there yet, but they're circling the area. I think they're looking for K."

K's place was a landing pad for young talented, a place they could go to catch their breath and keep their heads down. It was kids.

Nothing but kids who needed help. And it'd been there for over a decade.

"I'm on my way," Dani said, leaping into the truck. "We're not abandoning the kids. We are on the way."

She cut off the call and accelerated the truck onto the road, away from the grill, fast enough that they spit rocks under the tires. The weight of the veilblade pressed against her ribs from inside her jacket, and it pulsed in time with her own heartbeat. Dani wasn't sure if the magic was reacting to her desperation or if it was something else, but right now, it felt like someone was holding her hand.

"It's Brightfields?" Emilie's voice broke the silence as they pulled onto the highway.

"Yeah." Dani moved past the few other vehicles on the road at this hour. "Sawyer got pinged by the wards your gramps set up back in the day."

"Okay, I know those wards. Some of them are set to beguile and distract. If we're lucky, we'll get there before the Scions."

Dani shot her a quick look. "You know about the place?"

"I helped Grandpa design the wards." Emilie's hands fluttered in her lap with nowhere to go. "Kalliope is a null, did you know that?" Emilie nodded more to herself than anyone else. "If she exerts her talent, it shuts down all magic in proximity to her. That's why she opened the halfway house originally. To help talented kids whose magic was too flashy or dangerous."

"Did you spend time there?"

"Not unless I was helping with something," Emilie said. "My magic wasn't dangerous in a way that Kalliope could have helped me with. I always had a good grasp on how it worked. It was what came through the receiver that was a problem."

***

Brightfield Academy was a modest property just over the West Virginia state line. An old farmhouse shielded from the road by trees, a "No Trespassing" sign, and a dozen broken wards.

Dani rolled onto the property using the dirt road that led out the back way. There had been no more word from Sawyer, and K wasn't answering her phone. If they were driving into a firefight, she wanted the advantage of surprise.

Instead, the area was silent. Dani was out of the cab first, gun drawn as she cased the property, trying to get an idea of what had happened. The house was untouched except for the screen door hanging from only one hinge, but the front yard was a mess.

Multiple sets of deep tire tracks and a slurry of mud from too many boots. No shells, no smell of gunpowder hanging in the morning air. *We didn't get here in time.* The thought cut through her mind like a razor.

Behind her, Emilie let herself out of the truck. Dani watched as she blinked, and her pale blue eyes clouded with white as she scanned the yard. After a long moment, she shook her head, and her eyes returned to normal.

"There's nobody here." Emilie bit her lip. "No spirits floating around."

"I can't decide whether that's very good or very bad," Dani said.

She moved toward the house, putting herself between any danger and Emilie. The quiet was stressing her out. As soon as she put weight on the first step of the porch, Emilie grabbed her by the back loop of her jeans with a hiss.

"This place is crawling with wards. Wards I *didn't* help with," Emilie said.

"Do you recognize any of them?"

"*Intruders unwelcome, breach hospitality and perish, breach the perimeter and perish*, and *locked down*...I think." Emilie squinted at the house, tracing shapes idly with one finger. "But they're all overlapped, and I can see blood wards in there." She shook her head. "If we try to go in with force, we're not leaving."

"Well, that's bad." Dani stared at the house and spotted a few of the wards, but without her truth-sight charm, she had no clue what she was looking at.

Around them, the wind picked up, flowing from the other side of the house toward them. As it did, a familiar metallic tang blew into her face. Dani knew that smell, but she didn't want to admit it. Didn't want to acknowledge what it would mean.

"See if you can figure out whether there's a way to ask nicely and get through the door. I'm gonna look around the side."

Emilie nodded absently and kept tracing wards with her fingers as she talked to herself. Dani moved around to the side of the house and stopped short. Dark red letters were painted in drips. *Thou Shalt Not Suffer a Witch to Live.* Under the words was a familiar broken circle.

Blood. They had left their message in blood. Her throat worked convulsively, afraid those psychopaths had butchered one of the kids to leave a warning in their wake. Better she found them than Emilie. They still needed to get inside the house.

She went still, instinct surging through her as her right hand twitched, wishing the veilblade was in her grip. Dani's head cocked and she heard Emilie clearly at the front of the house and a low gurgle from somewhere out back. Her steps were quiet, lip curled away from her teeth as she moved silently around the corner of the house.

For a moment, she didn't understand what she was looking at.

A dark mass of flesh was pinned up against the back of the house like a macabre art installment. Wet black and red flesh, interspersed with flashes of white bone. It was a person. There was a rattle and a gurgle as their chest moved, and Dani surged into action. It was a person—a *not-yet-dead* person.

Dani sliced through the binds that held them up, leaving wet smears behind on the house. Emilie was suddenly beside her, helping to guide the body onto the patio, leaning against the house.

It was Kalliope. Those bastards had tried to take her apart piece by piece. Skin sheared away from raw flesh where they had skinned her, bruises blooming in dark swollen patches that disguised her with violence. The odor of burned meat where they had pressed a brand of a broken circle into raw flesh. The Scions had left her behind to die, ruined and broken, with that fucked up message on the house.

Kalliope let out a wheezing noise as she struggled to breathe again, eyes cloudy with pain and pinned on Dani. Her mind tried to catalog the breadth of wounds she was seeing, but there were too many, too severe. All she wanted to do was load her into the truck and race for the closest hospital, but she knew there wasn't enough time. There had never been enough time.

"Reaper...glad you could...make the trip." Her breathing was labored, each word a struggle. Her eyes skipped to Emilie for a moment. "Lockgrove? Didn't realize you'd joined the fight." Her breath rattled in her lungs, eyes far too distant for Dani's liking.

"You know I can't stay away." Dani knelt next to her, blood soaking into her jeans.

"Prox wards warned us, and the Fence was here to move a few anyway. Gave me enough time to get most of them out. Last few are... in the basement. Locked the place down...Ran out of time." She reached out and grabbed Dani by the front of her shirt. "Jackal is coming for you and Lu. He wanted you to know you're next." She began coughing and spat a thick wad of blood onto the ground next to her.

Dani reached out and took one of Kalliope's hands in her own. Next to her, Emilie was nearly vibrating, and her eyes had begun to glow as they grew cloudy and white in her face.

"Kalli..." Emilie's voice was a choked murmur.

Kalliope shook her head in a sharp motion. "Talking crazy about making the traitors pay. Wiping out the affliction until Seraph could bring revelation to the world." Her breath rattled in her chest again, and Kalliope's grip weakened in Dani's hand.

"We have to get you to a hospital." The words tumbled from Dani's mouth before she could stop them, even though she knew they had no time left.

"No," Kalliope said in a sharp exhalation. "Need you to get the last ones out...Make sure those bastards don't circle back around."

Kalliope tugged her hand from Dani's grip and snatched at Emilie's instead. She traced a figure into her palm in blood, and it glowed a deep red. "House won't bite now." Her hands collapsed at her sides, and she looked back to Dani again. "They wanted the kids, but I didn't give them up. I held the gate shut. You tell them I kept them safe." She nodded, and her eyes slipped shut for a moment.

Pain lanced through Dani's chest. The only reason Evan was still a problem was because she hadn't dealt with him herself years ago. She wasn't sure she'd ever be able to forgive herself. *Fuck that.* No, she'd never forgive Evan for turning what she had done into a personal vendetta. This wasn't on her, but she would make sure it ended with her.

Kalliope reopened her eyes. "Told me they turned some of ours. That Tucker joined up." Her voice was weak, hoarse, as she tried to speak, and Dani had to lean in to hear her properly. "No way he turned tail. Not on me. We kept his sister safe for years. Don't you let this happen."

"I won't," she promised, emotions warring inside of her.

Kalliope nodded, then her eyes slipped shut again, and she was gone.

Dani moved her hand down to the ground and stood up. The world was a blur around her, and she didn't know what to do. Did she leave Kalliope here? Did she go into the house to find the kids?

She stood and realized that she was covered in blood. In Kalliope's blood. Rage, hot and incandescent, burned through her veins. She wanted to throw back her head and howl. She wanted to tear the Scions limb from limb. Next to her, Emilie rose slowly as well, eyes faded back to their normal hue.

"I'm gonna see how many kids are downstairs," Emilie said quietly, voice warbling slightly.

"Good call. I'm gonna grab a towel from the truck and try to take care of some of the blood."

Both of them moved around to the front of the house, Emilie ducking inside while Dani grabbed a towel from the back of the truck, trying to wipe the blood from her skin. It was tacky and wet, leaving behind scarlet stains. When she had done the best she could, she followed Emilie into the house.

Kalliope had run Brightfield for over a decade, and it was a comfortable, lived-in space. Thick knitted blankets, photos of people on the walls, and bits of character peeking out from unexpected nooks and crannies. Dani moved quietly, grief crashing over her in waves. She wanted a drink. She wanted blood for the blood that had been spilled.

Emilie was sitting in the open doorway that led down to the basement. Warm yellow light shined up the stairs, and when Dani peeked down, she saw three teenagers staring up from the basement, all of them pale with wide eyes.

"We're here to help," Emilie said, trying to cajole them up and out of the safety of the basement with a soft voice. "Kalli sent us."

One of the kids took a step toward them, bronze skin, ebony hair, and golden-brown eyes peering up at her suspiciously. "Only her friends call her Kalli."

"I know," Emilie said. "She knew my Grandpa. I knew Kalli when I was younger than you are now."

The kid nodded and turned to the other two teens. The three of them huddled together, whispering as they decided whether they thought Dani and Emilie were a threat. Before they'd come to a decision, a siren began to whine from the other side of the ground floor.

Dani moved through the house in practiced motions. "Proximity alarms," she hollered to Emilie, hitting a switch outside of Kalliope's office to silence it.

The quiet rankled her, the world both too quiet and too loud all at once. She moved toward the front of the house and carefully twitched the curtains aside to see what they were dealing with. She wasn't ashamed to say that she almost wanted it to be the Scions. She wanted to eliminate their presence from the world, and if that meant leaving them a ruin of meat in the front yard, so be it.

"Is it Scions?" Emilie asked, appearing next to her.

"No," Dani said, agitation curling around her shoulders. "It's my fence." She shot Emilie a careful look. "Stay inside, keep the kids quiet. I want to know exactly how this happened."

29

DANI

Anger moved slowly under her skin, the roaring fire of magma hidden only by the crust of the earth—or in this case, the thin sheath of skin that separated it from air. She had been a hunter for a long time now, longer than a lot of other people, and she'd seen more than her fair share of death in that time. Kalliope's would crawl into the depths of her soul and torture her like a deep splinter.

What if they'd been faster? What if she'd called for more help after Sawyer reached out? How many kids had been here, and where were they now? The questions punched at her, knocking her off balance, and Dani didn't have answers for any of them. She didn't know, and Kalliope was dead behind the house.

Left to bleed out and expire as if she was nothing more than roadkill. An inconvenience turned into a message made of meat.

And now Sawyer was back, rolling in like the cavalry when the battle was over, while Emilie tried to convince those kids that they weren't the bad guys. She might have been firmly on the right side of this thing, but Sawyer's motivations were more suspect. No way was he getting in this house. She didn't care if he'd been here this morning, didn't care that he'd called her for help.

Either he could drive away, or he could die in this place. Right now, she didn't really care which option he took. Violence and grief were multiplying inside of her, and she moved on pure instinct, stalking halfway across the front yard and staring at Sawyer as he sat behind the wheel of an older black RAV4.

When he saw her, his eyes went wide, and his shoulders slumped. *Interesting.*

"What. Happened?" The words crawled with violence as they escaped her throat.

"I'm here to *help*." His voice was hoarse, and after jumping out of the car, he reached into one of his pockets and produced a cigarette and lighter. "I was due to move a few kids today, but Kalliope called me. Said the prox wards were going nuts and she had a full house." He eyed Dani wearily. "I got here *before* the Scions did. And I loaded up the truck with as many kids as we could fit into seats." He huffed a bitter laugh. "But it was a full house, and I didn't have space for everyone. No way to fit in the oldest, and Kalliope wouldn't leave anyway." He ran his tongue across his teeth, eyes blinking too fast.

"You came to help," Dani repeated his words slowly.

"I called you, didn't I?" he asked, pain painted over each syllable. "I was hoping maybe, somehow…" His voice sounded a thousand miles away. "Maybe the wards would hold out. The kids know how to work together, they can obfuscate things sometimes. But Kalliope is a null, talents don't work right around her. It's why she runs this place. She can turn off magic when she needs to."

"You swear you're here to help," Dani said again.

"Black, if I walk into that house, am I going to find a bloodbath?" Sawyer flicked his eyes from Dani to the house and back to Dani again.

She watched him for a long minute, weighing her choices and trying to ensure that she was doing the right thing. The truck would only fit one more person, maybe two. But no way could she fit all three of those kids between her and Emilie. They needed help to get them out of dodge before things got even worse.

"No," she said finally. "K held the gate closed." Her breath hitched in her chest, and her throat felt like it was full of glass as she forced the words out. "She's dead, Sawyer. Kalliope is dead." Her gaze flickered from his face to the space beyond his shoulder.

It was too hard to break the news and watch his eyes while she did it. Grief was already clinging to him, and as much as Sawyer might drive her insane, he didn't deserve the blow of this. None of them did.

"She locked the house down. Didn't let them get to the kids. The Scions turned her into a message. Tried to torture it out of her," Dani said, noting absently how her voice was devoid of any emotion. "We got here before she passed, and she unlocked the wards for Emilie. The kids are still alive in the basement, but I can't fit all of them in my truck."

"I have space," Sawyer said carefully.

"Can I trust you?" Dani's voice cut through the air like a knife. "Were you the reason this place was raided? It's off the map. It was protected. It's *kids*, Sawyer."

"*I know*, and *it wasn't me*." He stubbed out his smoke with a snarl. "I was one of Kalliope's Ferryman. I brought new kids in and helped the ones who graduated to get to their next stop. I've been doing it for years."

Dani narrowed her eyes, looking for any sign of a lie, but her gut told her that Sawyer was telling the truth.

"Does Joe know?"

"Has for a long time now, but we agreed the less folks who knew about me being involved, the better."

"Why is that?" Dani asked, toe scuffing into the dirt.

"Because some of the kids came from Scion territory," Sawyer said softly. "Not a lot of them, and not often, but a few. Mostly kids who had started to manifest magic. Not even the big leagues like your girlfriend, but any whiff of magic in that place was as good as a death sentence."

Dani ran a hand through her hair, trying to take Sawyer's measure again and realizing she'd been falling for his disguise for a very long time now.

"You could have told me. I wouldn't have tried to make you eat your teeth quite so many times."

"Nah." Sawyer cracked a weak smile. "Every time you kicked the shit out of me, the Humans First crowd took it as proof that the rumors couldn't possibly be true. After all, if I *was* helping the other side, wouldn't they have thanked me and not, oh, I don't know, broken my nose?" He shook his head. "Your animosity was a smokescreen, Reaper. Best a fence could ask for."

Dani sighed and rubbed at her forehead. She wanted to trust him. Wanted to believe what he was saying. It made sense. Hell, she even respected the hustle. But if she was wrong, it would mean more blood on her hands.

"If I find out you're lying, I'll gut you myself."

She turned back to the house and waved at Sawyer to follow her. The door remained open, but she still winced as she crossed the threshold. There was a tiny zap of power, the magic in the house recognizing the veilblade on her hip.

Before she gave Emilie the all-clear, she turned to Sawyer. "Where are the other kids?"

"I handed them off to other ferrymen."

"All of them together?"

Sawyer shot her a disgruntled look. "Do I look like this is my first rodeo? No. Seven riders, three ferrymen, and I don't know where any of them were headed." His voice softened. "That's the way it works if we have to move fast. The less I know, the less they can try to drag out of me."

"Good." Dani looked back over her shoulder and lowered her voice again. "We're taking these three to Lu at Crossings."

Sawyer frowned and made a gesture that told her to keep going.

"Kalli said the Scions are gunning for traitors. That's me, Mateo, and people on Lu's staff. The clinic was packed, but maybe there is safety in numbers."

Sawyer bit his lip, thinking about it, but didn't answer.

"We can't bring them to the Grill, someone might clock them. At least at the clinic they'll be easier to hide until Emilie and I can bring them up to Dawson," Dani said.

"Dawson?" He raised an eyebrow.

"It's got two sentinels, Phillip Lockgrove, and enough magical firepower to take on an army if someone tries to threaten it. The place has old mojo, and right now, people need all the help they can get." She gritted her teeth. "The sentinels already know, and folks in the area are being told to head there if they're afraid for their safety. Those kids need a safe place to lay low and catch their breath, and between Emilie and me, we have the space and then some."

Sawyer finally nodded. "I'll help you bring them to Crossings, but I don't know what comes after that."

"You'll *actually* come to Crossings?" Dani pushed, aware of the history lingering between him and Lu.

"Yes." He sighed and shook his head. "I might have been a fuckup, Black, but I did it because someone had to."

"And now?"

A bit of light came back into Sawyer's eyes. "They came after the kids. We all have lines. It's about time I made a decision anyway, don't you think?"

"Mmm." Dani watched him as he moved past her into the house before turning after him and trailing him to the entrance of the basement.

Emilie was sitting on the floor, the door open beside her as she murmured to the kids. She went quiet and stood up when she saw Sawyer, but Dani gave her a nod to let it go as he popped his head around the doorjamb.

"Told you I'd be back, didn't I?"

A moment later, three teens had charged up and out of the basement, crushing Sawyer into a hug that slowly moved away from the basement and into the space of the living room. Emilie met Dani where she was but didn't ask anything out loud. Questions swirled in those pale blue eyes, but she didn't voice them. Not yet, anyway.

"He's gonna help us transport them to the clinic."

Emilie nodded. "We need to convince as many people as possible to head for Dawson. It's the closest place that might be safe."

"Agreed."

A moment later, the huddle of people across the room broke up, and Dani nodded. "We need to beat feet. Is there anything we need to seal up?"

"Everything was linked to her. Her private study was down in the basement, but everything went up in flames when the Scions broke through the wards," one of the kids said.

"Security measures," Emilie murmured. "In case they got into the house. This way, she was the only one who knew."

Dani took Emilie's hand in her own and felt the crackle of ice before it wisped away into nothingness. She squeezed her girl's hand, encouraged when that squeeze was returned in kind.

30

EMILIE

Useful. Until today, standing in the parking lot of the clinic that was now almost overflowing with vehicles, Emilie had never found the word to be hateful. She'd trained and fought and clawed to get to a place where she wasn't just Dani's plus-one she found in some sleepy mountain town. She wasn't an A-list hunter by any stretch of the imagination, but over the last year, she'd learned to give as much as she got, and then some.

Even though Dani hadn't said it, hadn't even insinuated Emilie wasn't part of the team, right now, failure was cresting over her in a wave. All of the spellcraft in the world wouldn't do a damn bit of good if there were more days like today waiting in their future. The spirits of the Scion victims were counting on her, and at Brightfield's today, she hadn't even been able to coax those teenagers out of the basement. She had a specific skillset, and right now, it didn't seem that it was particularly helpful.

There had to be some way to contribute to what was happening instead of simply wishing things were different from the reality she found herself in.

Fear rode the edge of her consciousness, a yawning pit that took residence in her stomach and threatened to eat her alive if she succumbed to it. Emilie was well acquainted with fear. Fear of failure, fear of the things she didn't know, fear of people who hated her because she was different. Had *always* been different. The Scions of Seraph had been a bogeyman when she was a kid, but they weren't anything new. Instead, they were the most recent in a long line of people who saw magic as something dark or evil or unholy.

Emilie had thought—had believed to the core of herself—that the world had improved. Moved past the dark intertwined history into a new future, one where talented and hunters and everyone in between were all working together to build a better kind of world.

Before, the danger had been amorphous. Distant stories and warnings from the people who'd survived the dark times. Now, it was standing on her doorstep, yelling into her ears, and there was no way to ignore it. To pretend that the better world had already been won.

The Scions of Seraph were hunting, and anyone with even a drop of magic in their veins would find their head on the chopping block.

She didn't know what to do. The helplessness that had consumed her during the years that the binding held had been mostly absent for a year now, and she resented its reappearance. There was a part of her—and not a small part—that wanted to run back to Dawson and hide. She'd be safe behind the wards.

But none of the people she'd come to know over the last year would be. That choice was no choice at all, and Emilie smothered the urge, hoping she could extinguish the instinct to flee entirely.

Was this what Grandpa wanted for me? The thought caught her by surprise, robbing her of what little composure she'd been white knuckling in a single snatch. Falling apart would be easier than facing this, but she didn't have that kind of luxury anymore. None of them did.

"You still with me, killer?" Dani asked.

Her voice was softer than usual, as if coaxing a stray dog out from under a car. Emilie wanted to resent her for it, but it made her feel a little bit better.

"I'm here." Emilie gave her a wan smile, but her heart wasn't in it.

"Sawyer and the kids should be rolling up any second. We need to find Lu and let her know..." Dani's voice trailed off, unable or unwilling to finish her statement.

"Let's go find her." Emilie nodded and opened the door, hopping down onto the battered blacktop.

Almost as an afterthought, she grabbed her bag, glad she'd been writing everything down. She didn't want to forget any of this, terrible as it was.

She met Dani at the front of the truck and tangled her hands together. Emilie took comfort in the warm calluses on Dani's fingertips as they traced over her own knuckles. So long as they had each other, they could figure this out. They didn't even make it across the parking lot before Lu came striding out of the double doors. She gave them a two-finger salute and gestured with her chin to where her RV was parked.

Lu didn't waste any time. "The look on your face tells me something happened."

"We got a call this morning," Dani said flatly. She squeezed Emilie's hand in her own before continuing. "Early. From Sawyer. It was an attack on Brightfield."

All the color drained out of Lu's face, and her lips thinned to a white line. Anger and grief warred for dominance in her eyes as she shook her head, as if she could stop what was being said.

"By the time we got there, Kalliope was too far gone." She huffed out a bitter laugh. "We were just in time for her to die in my arms." Dani squeezed Emilie's hand again.

"The kids?"

"Safe," Emilie said. "A ferryman grabbed them this morning, but he couldn't fit all of them. There were three holed up in the basement."

Lu frowned. "How did y'all get into the house? It was locked down like Fort Knox."

"She transferred the glyph before she passed." Through the numbness infecting her bones, Emilie heard the lack of emotion in her own voice. "My grandpa was the one who set them in the first place."

"Sawyer will be here any minute with the surviving kids," Dani said. "Lu, it was a raid. The fucking Scions raided Brightfield."

Horror washed over Lu's face all at once. "What?"

"You heard me," Dani said quietly. "They raided Brightfield on purpose. They left a message that nowhere is safe. Kalliope said they're coming for Crossings."

Lu pulled out a cigarette and lit it, pacing back and forth. "What the fuck has the world come to? Crossings isn't—We aren't—" She shook her head as she talked, words coming faster and faster. "We've been fucking packed since you left. Jobs gone bad, people jumped. Guess you could figure the first half by all of this." She gestured wildly to the parking lot. "I have patients I can't fucking move, Dani. Why the hell attack us? God damn them!" Lu shook her head again, fury pouring off her in waves.

"Because they're fucking lunatics." Dani hissed back, malice coloring every syllable. "We can't get everyone out, but it's only a matter of time before they're knocking on your door. We need a plan, or we're gonna get caught with our pants around our ankles."

"You're right. Shit. Come with me." Lu stubbed the cigarette out under her boot and made her way back toward Crossings in a ground-eating stride.

Emilie was a step behind Dani when she walked into the chaotic thunder of the clinic. People were jammed into the space shoulder to shoulder, some of them bloody or injured, and all of them wearing exhaustion on their faces like a death mask. She moved through the waiting room and down hallways where the chaos was traded for quiet determination from the doctors and nurses.

The second floor was quieter, but a frenetic energy seemed to possess everyone Emilie saw. Patients were stacked two and three to a room, some of them on cots instead of full medical beds.

Lu waved them into her office and shut the door behind her. The last time Emilie was here, the hospital had been overrun by spirits. This time, every person was very real. She didn't know which was worse. Lu fired off a quick text before collapsing into her chair, the desk separating them. Emilie took one of the chairs, while Dani paced the small space like a caged animal.

"The wave started last night. I've got a full spread of patients: talented, casters, hunters, and a few folks who fall in between too. At least four more Scion raids before you got here, and dozens injured. Some of them have been running for days." Lu flipped a map open over the desk. There were red marks through the locations that were no longer there. "Where do I send them if it isn't safe here anymore?" She gestured at the map. "The hunters have hubs at least, but my talented patients? The casters? The folks who are still getting caught up in this anyway? Where the fuck do I send them? What are my options?"

"Dawson," Emilie said quietly. "We tell the talented, the casters, anyone with magic…We tell them to go to Dawson."

Lu paused and looked at the map. "Why do I not have Dawson on my map?"

"Because it's hidden from hunters for a reason," she said. "But it's their best shot. Two sentinels, my father, and enough wards to keep almost anything from getting through."

"They're just going to let a caravan roll into town?" Lu asked.

"The sentinels are expecting it," Dani said. "Dawson is a special spot, but they can handle the influx."

Lu nodded and flopped back in her chair for a moment. Emilie sat down as well, heart thundering in her chest. *This is actually happening.*

"I don't know what happens next," Dani said. "I'm a weapon, no two ways about it. You point me in a direction, and I can take out the monster threatening to eat someone. But…"

Anger surged through Emilie like a frozen spike at Dani's words, cold and clarifying, and for the first time, she wanted to hurt them back. To make the Scions realize they couldn't just terrorize people like this and get away with it. More than that, she wanted to erase any reminder that Seraph had ever breached past the veil and orchestrated the symphony of pain and ruin that had infected the magical community.

"The Scions *are* monsters," Emilie said. "My parents used to tell us stories, my sister and me, when we were little. Of the way things used to be when they were younger. I don't know why you'd tell kids something like that unless you had to. Unless the world was so dangerous that the not-knowing was scarier than realizing what was outside. They aren't hunters. Not *real* hunters. They target magic, and they want to eradicate us because our magic is an *affliction*." She spat the last word like it was poison. There was a fine film of ice coating her hands, and she wasn't sure she cared. "If the Scions show up here and find talented or traitors, they'll kill them. They'll kill all of us for helping them."

Dani's face turned into a cold mask as she gestured at Emilie. "You know what you have to do. Charon, we are out of choices."

Lu winced at the codename but pulled an old-school walkie-talkie off her hip. "Code Black. I repeat, we have a Code Black." She set the walkie down on her desk and flicked her eyes toward Emilie. "It wasn't supposed to be like this." She bit her lip and tipped her head toward the ceiling.

A man's voice crackled to life on the desk. "Code *Black*? You're sure?"

Lu picked it up and sighed before answering. "You heard me. Code Black. Activate Charon's Last Ride protocol." She pulled out her phone and fired off a text. "I've just sent coordinates for the ferryman. The Scions are out for blood, and they want their pound of flesh. Get out or get ready for a fight. Do it fast and quiet, boys."

The walkie crackled again. "Understood."

Then the walkie began to squawk, and Lu switched it off before turning back to Dani. "You know I was a medic during the war?" She raised an eyebrow and looked around the room. "Active duty, right up until I wasn't." Silver flashed along the bottom of her leg from the prosthetic under her jeans. "I got home just in time to see my brother die from a job that went wrong. Torn up by something." She shook her head. "I needed a reason, and that's what Crossings is." She shook her head and stood. "C'mon, we need to get everyone ready."

"Ready how?" Emilie asked.

"An ounce of preparation is worth a pound of cure, yeah?" Lu pulled a handgun from inside her desk. She strapped on a shoulder holster as she talked. "First few years I was running Crossings, we didn't stay in one place long. RVs, SUVs, we were a mobile clinic operation. We've been here almost three years, but that wasn't long enough for me to get comfortable."

Lu walked past them and opened the door to organized chaos. Wheelchairs were lined up outside of rooms, staff rushing in either direction carrying supplies or helping ambulatory patients to the elevators. Everyone had something to do, and moving through them was literally like going against the current.

It didn't take long to get down to the garage layer that Emilie hadn't known was even here. A dozen vehicles waited, doors open as people swarmed around them.

"Welcome to Charon's Last Ride," Lu said. "The backup plan for my backup plan. We've got four RVs in the lot, the old mobile clinic vans around the corner, and what you see here. I'm not gonna let them knock us out of the game. Not yet."

"I hear a 'but' coming," Dani said.

"Equipment and personnel are easy enough to move. We've run drills, but not all of my patients are safe for travel. I've got one in surgery right now, two in recovery...and that's not accounting for the long-term ward upstairs." She shook her head. "Ambulatory patients are leaving now. we're trying to get word to the magic folks quietly."

"People are gonna notice what's happening upstairs," Emilie said.

"Upstairs, yes. But we're moving differently on the main floor. It's mostly emergency, so it's easier to mask." Lu turned her attention to Emilie. "Do you think you could tell if a patient was infected by Seraph?"

Emilie went still and looked at Lu for a long moment before she answered, "Probably. If it's latched onto them. It doesn't take much to see."

"Lu, why are you asking?"

Lu sighed. "Because when we go upstairs, I need to know if

anyone in the lobby is infected before I start giving those patients the evac plan."

Emilie closed her eyes and felt her stomach drop. She still didn't know how much of a link Seraph had with all of its hosts. She had more to work with than she had a few days ago, and she had the sachets she'd put together at Joe's place, but it still didn't feel like enough.

She'd wanted to be more of use. Wanted a way to contribute. And now it was staring her in the face.

"Okay." She nodded. "I mean, not alone, for obvious reasons, but I can check, and we can make a plan. We need to get everyone and everything out of here as fast as we can."

31

DANI

Crossings came alive like a well-oiled machine. Scrub-clad workers moved people down into the basement with talented patients, medical supplies and equipment were rolled out of the freight elevators so they could be loaded into the vehicles. For a few short minutes, Dani thought there was a chance they could do this before all hell broke loose.

It wasn't that easy. It was never that easy.

The plan had been simple. Go upstairs, scope out the waiting room, and make sure there weren't any Scions playing at being people who needed help. The ground floor was quiet compared to the frenetic energy consuming the rest of the building. Dani heard the timbre of their voices before their words. Angry and sharp, violence cloaked in communication.

"It's time to clean house, boys and girls," a masculine voice rang out from around the corner.

The air was thick, like a summer storm right before the skies opened up. Dani almost felt the world slow down around her, and she was glad yet again for the veilblade in her pocket and the strength the weapon lent her. Tonight, she'd need it.

She threw a hand up and heard Lu and Emilie stop short. No way was she letting Emilie anywhere near these psychopaths if she had any choice at all. Dani turned and met their eyes, the predator she kept caged inside slowly stretching under her skin. She watched as her friend and her lover saw the change as she let the darkest aspect of herself out.

A sharp patter of gunfire and glass and screaming broke the rising tension, and all three of them dropped to the ground. Ahead was the staging area for emergencies, connected to the waiting room, where hunters waited for their friends and hoped they weren't dead. There was no return fire, just the screams of people who had come to Crossings for help.

This was supposed to be neutral ground. That was the point of hubs and places like the clinic. Places people could come for help without fearing that telling the truth would get them sent to a locked ward and pumped full of drugs. Red washed over Dani's vision, and suddenly, the veilblade was in her palm, humming with power and potential.

"Get everyone out. As far away from me as possible." She winked and blew Emilie a kiss, then vaulted to her feet as she surged into the fray.

With the blade in her hand, she could feel everything happening. The kind of betrayal Evan was visiting on the community couldn't be tolerated. *Wouldn't* be tolerated. His vicious nature had caused enough pain and bloodshed to last a hundred years, and he'd never stop so long as he had breath in his lungs. The piece of self she'd sacrificed to the veilblade came alive, and the power of being a bladesinger danced through every atom of her existence until she was consumed by it.

The veilblade became an extension of Dani. She moved like something between a shadow and the wind itself. An hour ago, the waiting room had been filled with people looking for help, and now it was painted in scarlet splashes of blood. Two men in black were sweeping back and forth, convinced they had dealt with everyone.

Dani kept her eyes on them as she flanked around to the side. They never saw her coming.

Years ago, Isaac Campbell had given her a moniker: *Reaper*. In this moment, she became death, and for the first time in years, she embraced it wholeheartedly. She swept up behind the first goon, stabbing through him like he was made of fabric and straw instead of flesh and blood. Before he had time to shout, she took his gun, looked down the barrel, and shot the other Scion in the face. As bone exploded and the bodies dropped, she felt...nothing.

Once, Dani had made rules for herself. Rules about what it meant to be a hunter, what it meant to live this life and be able to sleep at night when she laid down her head. Rules like: no matter what happened, no matter how bad it got, she didn't gun down other hunters. Maim them, leave them ruined, but leave them alive. It was a line she wasn't supposed to cross, and it was gone in the flash of the muzzle. She'd held onto that belief like a lifeline for years, but it was gone now, and everything Isaac had taught her back on the compound slipped back into action, smooth as silk.

She let the Scions lie where they dropped and moved the way they'd come. Doing what she had been built for, what she had been trained for. Hunting. Distantly, Dani understood that something was off in this moment, the way the fury pounded through her blood and stripped her humanity away, the way she was moving faster and quieter than she ever had before. It would be a problem for the future, because the only thing she held onto now was her need to protect the clinic, the hunters, Lu and Sawyer, those kids, and Emilie. Her Emilie. It overrode everything as it propelled her into violence and madness.

One more Scion was waiting around the corner, and she dispatched him without a thought, snuffing out his life like blowing out a candle. She finished clearing the waiting room, and once she realized the threat was gone for the moment, the rage bled out of her quietly, leaving her standing in an abattoir. On the ground around her were the bodies of patients and staff alike, blood pooling in violent puddles that had been people just a few minutes ago. She didn't speak, even though she knew there must have been survivors.

Instead, she wiped the veilblade clean on her jeans and tucked it back into the pocket of her jacket.

Her ears were ringing, and the blood drying on her skin left it tacky. She was exposed, a raw nerve, a weapon that wore a face. Right now, exposed was the opposite of what she wanted to be. She hadn't wanted any of this. She'd left the Scions behind, spent years trying to undo the damage they had done to her and to the community, and none of it had been worth a fucking thing. They hadn't done anything to deserve this. Not the people of Crossings, and not her. And yet, she was hip-deep in all of it all over again.

It woke something dark inside of Dani that she tried to keep hidden as much as possible. Under Isaac's wing she'd trained to kill monsters, to take down talented and keep them incapacitated until they could be remanded to the custody of the other Scions.

Transported back to the compound to be locked in dark cells, poked and prodded until they gave up everyone in their life who was afflicted by the "disease" in their blood. Changed by what they allowed themselves to become. Looking back, it was easy to trace the way the Scions had manipulated her and ensured they had her loyalty. Right up until they didn't. She'd left it behind and tried to become something different, something better.

Dani didn't want their blood on her hands, but it seemed like her wants were no longer relevant. The harder she ran from her past, the more it rushed to catch up with her. And now her mistakes, her *leniency*, had led to the deaths of all these people. No more. There would be no more negotiating. No more talk. If these bastards wanted a monster, she'd give them one that they would not survive.

She moved back through the bloodshed and into the hallway where she'd left Lu and Emilie. They weren't here. There wasn't anyone remaining in this part of the clinic. Good. She didn't want them to see her like this, when she felt like a monster for the things she was best at. Dani needed time to gather up the fragile scraps of composure left to her.

The door to the stairwell cracked open, and Sawyer appeared. He paled when he saw her, which told Dani everything she needed to know about how she looked right now.

"Is it done?" Sawyer asked, stopping into the hallway ahead of her.

"For now," Dani said. "But this wasn't a full raid. This was just their opening salvo."

"They're loading everyone up in the basement. Upper floors are as empty as they're going to get." He paused, watching her with hooded eyes. "Emilie says she knows of a place where the kids will be safe."

"You can trust her. She grew up in a safe haven. She's bringing the convoy to her hometown."

"Then why do you look like you're ready to walk to the gallows?"

Dani paused, breathed out, and waved him into one of the exam rooms. It looked strange, cupboards open and empty, scraps of paper littering the floor.

"This was their opening blow, which means there are more on the way," Dani said. "And I need a favor."

"A favor," he repeated slowly.

From outside, she heard horns honking in tandem, and her blood ran cold. They were out of time. The horns cut off abruptly, and a familiar voice began to speak with a loudspeaker. Evan. She snarled but swallowed the anger. For now.

"It didn't have to be this way, you know." Evan made a sympathetic noise over the bullhorn. "Hospitals are supposed to be safe places, but you gave quarter to traitors. *To afflicted*. To those that are driving our world into darkness. And now you're paying the price." He clucked his tongue, and Dani's left eye twitched uncontrollably.

She bared her teeth, still looking at Sawyer. She was powerful and dangerous, but she was still human. *Mostly*. She couldn't protect everyone here from what was coming, and they both knew it.

"But I'm not without a heart. My people know what they've signed up for. To cleanse the world is not an easy thing, and they have been returned to oblivion knowing they were fighting the good fight."

Dani held a finger in front of her lips, still listening to Evan's words. Knowing that every second they held out, more people were being loaded into vehicles that would take them to safety. Knowing that they were outmatched and outgunned.

"Send out the afflicted, and I won't have my people take this place down to studs. Give us what we want, and we'll let you leave with your lives. You have twenty minutes to think about it. Don't make me wait too long."

The silence afterward thrummed around her, and Dani licked her lips. Evan might have been saying that he wanted the afflicted, but she understood something very clearly in that moment: He'd give all of it up if it meant that he had her.

"I need you to play your part one more time," Dani said.

Sawyer watched her, gauging her words, gaze flickering over her bloodstained form. What she was asking wasn't fair, and it wasn't right, but in the moment, she didn't see another option. To be a hunter was to put herself in front of the threats that tried to ruin the world, and right now, she was the only thing standing between the Scions and all the people who had fled to Crossings looking for safety.

"I need you to make Evan believe you're on his side. I need you to deliver me to him. And I need you to get Emilie to Dawson. Can you do that?"

Sawyer heaved out a shuddering breath. "You don't know what it is you're asking for."

"I know better than anyone what I am asking and what it means. But you know, and I know, that we don't have a choice. Even if we handed over every talented in the building, Evan isn't going to stop there. Nobody here will see the sunrise if we roll over and show him our bellies."

Sawyer swallowed. "Why? Tell me why this is the play."

Dani bit her lip and sighed. "Emilie is powerful. Powerful enough to sever Seraph from his bonds and shove him back into the veil. But if she dies here? If the Scions get their hands on her? Everything we are seeing will get so much worse. She has to get to Dawson, and she has to be the one to end this. Not me. *Her.*"

"You're sure?"

"Evan isn't going to bring me back to the compound, and he isn't going to kill me fast. It'll be slow, and it'll be bad, and he'll want me to watch what comes next. That gives you time. Gives *her* time. So I need you to do this because nobody else can."

Her mind kept going back over what she was asking, what they were facing, looking for another option. Problem was, she didn't see another way out. Not for her, and not for all those people who had come to Lu for help. Who'd still be coming in the weeks and months and years to come if she did this right. But *only* if she did this right.

Being a bladesinger was about more than being a badass with a blade, much as she hated to admit it. It was about protecting her people. And they were all in danger. The kind of danger she could shield them from if she was willing to go all the way. When hadn't she been?

"I'll do it," Sawyer said. "But only because it's you. Because you understand what it is you're asking of me."

"Better me than all of us."

She heard the steel in her own voice, wished that it didn't have to go this way. That she could tell Emilie what was coming. But her girl would never let it happen if she knew. Dani wished she could tell her it'd all be okay in the end as long as she followed through.

Out front, she could hear vehicles revving and wondered what was going through Evan's mind. Did Julia know what he was doing? Did he think they were up to something? That Dani would let him walk in here and kill these people like they were nothing?

Maybe. Knowing what he'd been like years ago, probably. He believed the worst of everyone because he was the worst all by himself. That had been her theory, anyway, on the rare occasion some of the Scion's survivors got together to drink and commiserate about what they'd escaped. To remember the people who hadn't.

Even without his voice echoing through the empty halls, she could feel the time ticking away.

"I am going to do this because it's what needs to happen," Dani said. Her eyes bored into Sawyer, needing him to understand that this was a sacrifice, but it wasn't suicide. Not for her. She needed him to understand so he could explain it to Em. If anyone could understand sacrifice, it was him.

"You think he won't be able to kill you?"

"I think he is going to try, but it won't be clean, and it won't be easy. It's not his style. You and Em are gonna bring the cavalry so he doesn't take me apart piece by piece. I am doing this for Lu and Emilie and every person whose life has been shattered by this bastard." She ran a hand through her hair. "Give me a few minutes, and then we'll do this."

Sawyer nodded, his face a grim mask.

Dani let bravado carry her back into the hall. She had to, because if she didn't, she'd break and run for Emilie, and everything would go ass-up before anyone could stop it. Being a hero was about more than doing the right thing when it was easy. It was about the hard choices. And if this is what it took, then she'd do it. Dani believed Emilie would come for her, and if she was lucky, she'd have all of her extremities intact when she did.

As she opened the door to the stairs, she could almost smell Graham's aftershave. For a moment, it seemed like he was here with her, even now.

32

EMILIE

Patients and hunters and staff alike crushed into the garage basement, some of them huddling away from the violence on the floor above, others being guided carefully into vehicles or toward the garage door that was currently closed. Emilie had taken up guard, staring at the door, waiting for Dani to come strutting through it like she always did. Like she had to do.

The vehicles idled as they filled, one by one. Every time the door opened, she hoped it was Dani coming to tell her the problem was handled. Instead, the hair at the back of her neck was standing straight up, and a susurrus of whispers surrounded her. Not loud enough for her to pick out a singular voice, but enough to tell her that she wasn't alone. A moment later, her wish was granted when Dani entered the basement, Sawyer hot on her heels.

"Oh, thank god." She threw herself at Dani, frantic hands checking her for damage and finding none. "Are you hurt?"

"Nah, killer, I'm okay." Dani's voice was low and husky, and there was something hiding in her eyes, but Emilie didn't question it, because she was alive and whole and in her arms.

"The truck is parked outside—"

"We can't go outside right now," Dani interrupted her quietly.

"What?" Emilie shook her head lightly. "No, because the truck is out there, and we need to get to it so we can lead the convoy."

Behind them, there was a horrified gasp, but Emilie didn't turn. None of her usual curiosity was in effect, not when Dani was looking at her like this.

"The Scions are outside. They want Lu to hand over all of the talented and casters that are here, and we can't do that."

"No, we got here in time. We got everyone down to the basement..." Emilie's voice trailed off as fear choked the air out of her.

It wasn't fair. It was a silly thought in the moment because when in her life had things ever been *fair*? It hadn't been fair when she'd been manipulated by Spectre, or when she'd watched Mama and Lizzie die, or when she'd had her talents bound to try and protect her. Why should that have changed now just because she wanted it to?

"We did," Dani said. "And I'm gonna deal with this. I have a plan, but you have to trust me. You have to get these people to Dawson, and you have to figure out how to deal with Seraph."

"No, *we*," Emilie said again, shaking her head.

Dani kept saying that Emilie needed to do this, as if she wouldn't be standing there the entire time. Except that was ridiculous. She was Dani Black! A bladesinger! Of course she would be standing next to Emilie, the muscle to her brains.

Dani's voice was so painfully gentle when she spoke again. "I have to keep them distracted long enough for everyone to get away, and that includes you, killer."

"No." Emilie reeled back, but Dani held onto the loops of her pants, keeping her from moving. "No, that's insane."

"Em, Babe. We either hand over the people the Scions want so they can kill them, or we make a distraction big enough they don't care that everyone got away. And we both know the first option is a no-go."

"Do not pass go, do not collect $200," Emilie murmured. "There has to be another way. There *has to*."

"Tell me the play, and I'll run it," Dani said. "But I keep running it, and this is all I've got. I need you to trust me. Can you do that?"

"Of course I trust you," Emilie hissed, anger coloring her words. "Please, please do not ask me to do this, Dani. Not this. Not us."

Dani pressed their foreheads together, and Emilie melted into the embrace. She wrapped her arms around her hunter, as if by pressure alone, she could keep her from doing this. Keep her in the basement where there were no Scions. Keep her in this moment where it was just the two of them.

Except she knew that wasn't an option. She had spent a year with Dani, had met her during some of the worst days of her life. This was what Dani did, who she was, and even though Emilie understood it to her marrow, right now, she hated it.

Before Dani could say anything, the door slammed open, and a tall Black man stood in the doorway wearing dark fatigues. Emilie clocked several things all at once: the silver pin over his heart, a deep-notched scar on his jaw, and a shadow wound tightly around his neck. Her hands grasped at Dani's shirt as Emilie made a discontent noise.

"Tucker? Why are you out of bed? We had someone coming for you," an orderly said, moving past Emilie.

Dani detached herself, but Emilie didn't let her eyes leave Tucker's form. Oh, he was infected all right, but his eyes slid right past her with no sign of recognition. The shadow was wrapped around his throat, but it wasn't the perfect gleaming darkness she'd seen at Tenacity Mill. She rocked on her heels and nudged Dani.

"He's attached to him," she murmured.

Emilie palmed the sachet in her pocket. There was no guarantee it would work, no promise that if she lit it on fire and tossed it across the floor that it would have any effect to Tucker at all. But she couldn't let him get on the bus, couldn't let him join their convoy while Seraph was wrapped around him.

Dani glided through the thinning crowd, and Emilie quietly pulled the sachet from her pocket. She pulled out a lighter she'd gotten on a snack run yesterday and quickly lit the wick. It took, fire climbing until it reached the sachet of herbs and magic. With a murmur, she pushed a spark of magic into it, then lobbed it onto the floor as it began to smoke. It rolled, leaving behind a thick stream of pale purple smoke as it went, the fragrant aroma of lavender and rosemary filling the space in moments.

Tucker began to hack and wheeze, and Emilie lost sight of Dani in the thick smoke. The susurrus of voices was louder now, and one of them was louder than the others. A woman's voice, soft and gentle.

"He never would have crossed that line. He promised me. He promised."

Her voice was like a spring breeze, and for a moment, Emilie was surrounded by roses, the scent so thick, she could almost taste it. It lasted barely a moment before it was gone, but Tucker was on the ground, coughing and trying to crawl out of the smoke.

Without even thinking about it, Emilie followed him. She forgot her shields existed, forgot that she usually kept them wreathed around her like a protective cloak. There were shades of spirits everywhere, and they were watching what happened next, keeping their distance, but circling Emilie and Tucker both. Next to her was the gleaming form of a light-skinned Black woman with braids that brushed her shoulders. She had a hand on Emilie's shoulder and her eyes on Tucker.

"He promised me. You remind him of that, and he'll come back. He can still come back." Conviction colored her words as she faded away, but Emilie continued forward until she was standing over the man.

The coil of Seraph's influence was still wrapped around the column of his throat, but it had faded from black to a pale grey thing, its grip loosening coil by coil. Cold surged through her with the fury of a winter storm, and Emilie could hear the crackle of ice as it wrapped itself around her limbs.

She reached out with a clawed hand, instinct moving her as she wrapped it around something no one else could see. How dare Seraph? *How dare it?* Bring its soldiers to a clinic meant to help, take the people who were here to render aid and use them to heal its hosts. Not if she had anything to say about it.

Emilie's temper flared. Ice glazed the floor as she wrapped her fingers around the sickly coil attached to Tucker and yanked. He screamed and began to vomit black bile onto the floor, on all fours as his body convulsed. Spirits howled around her, and Emilie saw ghostly hands wrap around her arm. She could feel the veil, the otherworldly cold of the Styx, the chill of the mist that filled that place, the sepulchral power that she'd never accessed before.

There was a wild scream from somewhere far away as Seraph felt the connection server, and Tucker hit the ground, boneless.

Emilie relaxed her hand and straightened back up. Under her, the sachet had burned out, and the smoke was wisping away around her. This was not the night Mama died or the trap Spectre had left her at Cedar Terrace, and this time, she would not be a victim. She was not who she had been, and the Scions would learn it too. She took a long breath and found Lu just a few feet away.

"You good?"

"I am now," Emilie answered, amused at the tiny puff of vapor that accompanied her words.

"Infected?" Lu cocked her head at Tucker on the ground.

"Not anymore." Emilie cracked her neck. "I had a Hail Mary."

"One hell of a Hail Mary," Lu agreed.

The doctor gestured, and several people surged forward to check Tucker and move him to one of the vehicles. Lu moved closer, concern written all over her face, and Emilie realized she was holding something in her hands. A beaten leather jacket.

"No," Emilie said, and a peculiar numbness overtook her.

Lu had a leather jacket in her arms, and Emilie's mind didn't want to tell her what that meant. She didn't have to ask to know it belonged to Dani, who wore it even in the middle of winter when a parka was a better idea. No way would she have taken it off. It was a second skin, armor of a modern variety.

Her legs nearly gave out under her, and Lu caught her by the elbow, walked her to a curb, and helped her to the ground. Emilie's thoughts spiraled wildly and she wrapped her arms around her middle to try and ground herself before she snapped into a thousand little Emilie-shaped pieces. Been there, done that.

"Lu, why..." Her voice was hoarse, like asking the question out loud would bring the worst circumstances to life in front of her.

"Dani said you'd know why I had this. What she had to do," Lu said quietly, eyes red rimmed.

Shock washed over her in a cold wave, and pale shards of ice crackled along her spine, spattering onto the ground at her feet.

"No. No, because Dani wouldn't just leave, she wouldn't—"

Lu put the jacket in Emilie's lap, and it was too heavy. Emilie buried her hands in the soft leather, running her thumbs across the worn material before she slipped it on. It didn't fit quite right, fitted to Dani's frame, and hung heavy on one side. She put a hand into one of the pockets and felt the shape of the veilblade there, waiting.

"God damnit, I'm gonna kill her." Emilie jumped to her feet.

"She said you might feel that way," Lu agreed.

Around them, the vehicles were starting to queue up in front of the garage door, and Sawyer reappeared from wherever he had disappeared to.

"We have a window, but it isn't long. We need to go *now*," he said, out of breath, eyes wild.

Lu gestured to the convoy and grabbed Emilie's hand. They ran for the garage door and ducked under it as it cranked open. The parking lot was empty. There were no Scions, no threat, no Dani. Just the truck and Lu's RV, parked and waiting for them. Something in Emilie's chest cracked open, and she realized what her lover had done.

Lu took off for the RV. Emilie turned to Sawyer.

"What did you do?" Desperation made Emilie's voice raw.

"What she asked me to do," he said, shaking his head as if he couldn't believe it either. "I did what she asked me to do. Now, we need to get to the truck. Once that thing realizes you can remove it, they'll be back, and this time, the target is going to be on your back."

Emilie sputtered, and pain flared sharp and bright inside of her. Dani had given herself up like a sacrificial lamb, and Sawyer had helped her do it. With a snarl, she slugged him in the jaw and then swore, shaking her fist. That was gonna leave a bruise.

"I deserved that, but we didn't have a choice. Once we get to

Dawson? We have choices. But not until then. Do you understand?" Sawyer asked, rubbing his jaw.

"I understand," Emilie said, then made a break for the truck.

Sawyer hopped in on the passenger side, as she got behind the wheel. Dani's keys were still in the breast pocket where she kept them, and Jezebel turned over without complaining for once. Emilie pulled to the edge of the lot, and when Lu joined behind her, she took off, heading for her hometown. In the rearview mirror, she watched the swarm of vehicles as they rolled away from Crossings in clusters, none of them going the same way, even if they were going to the same place.

They had gotten out, but all her mind kept asking was: *What was the price? What was the price? What was the price?*

33

DANI

The light above her didn't change. She slept, and it was morning. She stayed up, and it was morning. A black bag was thrown over her head, and she was dragged from one stone-walled room to another with a recessed drain in the floor and back. Sometimes Evan threatened her, and sometimes Julia asked why she insisted on such stubbornness.

Being asleep and being awake weren't easy to pull apart from one another. Her head was swimming, and she didn't know which way was up. She had no concept of how much time had passed, or was passing, or could yet pass. All she had were the things she had sacrificed. All she could hold onto was the fact that Emilie knew she was out here, Emilie had the veilblade, and her people would come for her. She had to believe they would come for her.

Over the last year, Dani had listened to Emilie as she talked about the veilblades. It used to be that they were family heirlooms of a kind. Handed down, one generation to the next, sacred artefacts built to fight the malevolence hidden in the night. They had been created to give those able and willing to fight a weapon capable of pushing back the darkness.

The problem came when a generation was born with no one

willing to take the mantle of responsibility. Or worse, no one capable of doing it. The veilblades were fearsome weapons imbued with power, but in the end, they were extensions of the bladesinger. Of a person capable of knowing when something was right or wrong, able to untangle those threads and find the truth of the matter.

Dani's path back and forth, in and out of the supernatural world was always leading her back toward the blades. Inert creations that they were, they craved the hand of a hunter filled with the understanding of *why*. They were the last defense, or the first offense, or both, or neither. The hand that held the blade was nothing without the people they stood for.

"It doesn't have to be this way, you know." Julia was looking down at Dani again. She didn't know how long she'd been on the ground. She opened her eyes at the voice, and the light was dimmer than it had been. Time finally catching up to her presence, perhaps. "We aren't evil, Dani. Perhaps our methods are *unorthodox*, but we get the job done."

"It has to be like this," Dani said, scowling up at the other woman. "Evan has been hunting people who never did anything wrong."

"You've been cavorting with afflicted for years." She shook her head. "You're lucky you even got to that clinic at all. And look, it still stands, even if the roaches scattered after my brother collected you." She paused, regarding Dani for a long moment. "Willing to flee and let us take you without a second thought."

"Injured people. People who needed safety," Dani said, head swimming as she remembered those last moments with Emilie. Reminding herself why she had done this. Why she was alone now. "Evan threatened to kill them. Sawyer saw an out and took it. But even now, even after what he's done, you don't blame him, do you?"

"He's my brother. Not that I expect you to understand. You never ever did," Julia said.

Dani's head was heavy and fuzzy, but she dragged herself to the wall, leaning against it as Julia's eyes captured hers, nailing her in place.

"You can come back, you know. Back home, with me," Julia

continued in a murmur that threatened to swallow her whole. "Hunters are supposed to help people, aren't we? Don't we help people?"

Dani licked her lips and tasted blood at the edge of them. She was getting lost in her own mind, in Julia's duplicity, but she couldn't seem to stop the slow, maddening descent as her mind desperately tried to keep its balance. The darkness below wanted to swallow her, but she fought it every step.

"You're not hunters," Dani said, blinking as some of the fog that had been blanketing her mind rolled away at the edges. "We killed people in their beds. Innocent people murdered on your brother's word, and nobody ever did anything about it, did they?"

Julia's face twisted into something ugly, and the illusion faded further. It was like trying to dig herself out of sand at the beach, her mind obscured by something she didn't know how to fight.

"We've done what we thought was right, no matter the cost. That's a bitter pill to swallow for some people."

"Unless the cost was holding your brother accountable for his crimes," Dani said, fury swelling inside of her throat. It cleared her head a little of the cobwebs, brought her back to the here and now, even if she had no idea where she was or how long she'd been here.

"There's no talking to you anymore," Julia said, darkness sliding behind her eyes. "You spent too long letting the afflicted sully you." She made a disgusted noise low in her throat, then clapped twice.

The door of the cell opened, and a trio of goons in fatigues with masks over their faces swarmed her. Dani fought to get to her feet, feeling the crunch of bone under her fists as she tried to keep them from dragging her away again. The spirit was willing, but somehow, the flesh was weak, and before she knew it, she was being hauled down a stone hallway.

She didn't fight like her life depended on it. Not yet. Sometimes survival didn't require fighting. It required enduring. If she could outwait them, survive when they expected her to collapse, then she could win.

In the back of her mind, there was a screaming chasm that

wanted her attention. It wanted her panic and her rage and all of the darkest aspects of herself. She couldn't fight it, so she ignored it. Instead, Dani wrapped herself around the space that Emilie had carved out in her heart. The hopes of a future with a comfortable house and a warm bed. Of a world that wasn't always coated in blood. It smelled like grave dirt and petrichor, and she would not surrender it. Not for Evan, not for anyone.

Somewhere outside of this place, she could still sense her connection to the veilblade. It was a tether, and it was out there. Far away, but not as far as it had been, not destroyed, not sullied, not broken.

The men threw her into a chair, and she took in another room with a rust-colored floor and a recessed drain in the ground. Torture session, apparently. *Classy.*

"I see we're going back to torture vibes," Dani said, grasping for her wit, using sarcasm like a shield.

"That's cute, Black. Make jokes. I like jokes," Evan said with a smile.

Even now, with a stained leather apron on, he looked so pleasant. The kind of man someone might ask for directions or expect to see in ads for some new small town. He looked like an advertisement, like what a commercial thought a person ought to look and sound like.

"You know, we have to stop meeting like this," Dani whispered. "People are going to talk."

"Enough of your bullshit, Black. I know your secret."

"That I'm gay?" She feigned shock. "Dude ,I came out *before* boning your sister. And that was a decade ago, at least." She winced. "I might be getting old. I don't wanna think about it too hard, you know?"

Evan looked at her, confused for a minute, before shaking his head. "No, I don't care that you're—" He breathed out slowly through his nostrils. "I know you're a bladesinger. I know the blade you hold. And I want it back."

When she was a kid, she'd been in a decent foster home for a few months. With a backyard that held a giant oak tree with a tire swing. It was the kind held up on all sides by rope, so she'd sit inside and spin and spin and spin until the world turned into blurs of color and she stumbled back to the ground only to collapse and stare at the sky as it churned above her.

Seemed like that dizziness had followed her ever since. Through a string of foster homes, the group homes, a few dances in juvie, and the months she spent on the street. As if she had always been standing still while the world whizzed past her. And now it was here too.

Dani's palm itched for the familiar heft of the veilblade, and there was a hollow ache in her chest that whispered east. Not here, and not specific. If she was lucky, it was hidden behind wards in Dawson, where the Scions couldn't reach Emilie, couldn't turn her into bones and blood and dust and meat.

It's not yours. The thought was a stone dropped into a quiet pond, and it sent a shockwave rippling through her. The veilblade didn't belong to anyone, and it chose its wielder. If Evan had never gotten his mitts on one, there was a reason, and she knew it in the same way she knew the sky was blue.

"The blade doesn't want you," Dani said finally, meeting Evan's eyes and letting him see the hate in them. "If it did, it would have found you. But it didn't, because your family is broken, and the magic knows it."

A mocking smile twisted his lips but didn't manage to make it to his eyes. "I'm tired of playing these games. Why don't we talk. As equals."

"Equals?" In his dreams, maybe. "Sugar, we're not equals. We will never *be* equals. You're a murdering psychopath playing second fiddle to a monster, and I'm a tried-and-true hunter."

"You know, it's funny." He raised an eyebrow. "People look at us like we're monsters. Just because we care more about normal, everyday people than the afflicted that have infected our world." His lip curled up. "Talented, casters, the subhuman species…sentinels." His voice ended in a half-hidden snarl.

"They're people. Just…people. Living their lives until they end up in your crosshairs. We are not judge, jury, and executioner."

"Why not?" A dark light lit up his eyes. "The afflicted kill people. Treat everyday folks like chattel. So we fight fire with fire."

"They were sleeping in their beds!" The words exploded out of her and left Dani heaving, head swimming wildly. Were there fumes down here? She'd never felt so off, as though her perception was warping with each beat of her heart.

Evan narrowed his eyes, nostrils flaring as he looked down at her. "They were afflicted and deserved to be dispatched. None of them would have had anything worth knowing." He shrugged like he had all those years ago when he'd forged a job for the three of them.

It'd been a few short weeks before initiation, when they would become full members of the Scions. Ready to become boots on the ground in the war for survival against the darkness. Evan always got them the juiciest gigs, and with Julia shadowing Isaac more and more, jobs like that had been few and far between. Except.

Except he'd tacked it onto intel they'd already gathered. Except Julia looked nervous when he announced it, stayed back when she was usually the tip of the spear. Evan was up the stairs before Dani got through the door, and by the time she hit the stairs, he was already firing. She found a few people around her age huddled together inside of a warded circle and curled into a puppy pile for warmth against the chill. Dead before she made it into the room. Dead before she could ask why they were there or what they'd done.

Julia didn't say anything. She never did, not when it came to Evan. He was her blind spot, and Dani wanted to understand, even if she couldn't. Loving Julia meant Evan had to be her brother too, and she knew it. So Dani buried it for weeks.

Until she realized they were innocent. The wards had been to warn them of danger as they tried to flee east. Except that Evan found them first. He murdered them and made her party to it, and he never once understood what that meant.

Dani thought the horror of that night had been left behind with the kid she'd been, but apparently not. Some wounds festered deeper than others.

"Don't pretend you're so high and mighty, Dani. I know your sins."

He smiled, and this time, it was almost charming. It was so easy to see why so many people believed him when he talked. Bad people weren't supposed to look like Evan Campbell. Didn't seem to matter much to him.

"I'm not perfect, but I'm not you." Her lips twisted at the words.

"I'll tell you what. You tell me where you stashed the veilblade, and I'll let you walk away. Alive." The cadence of his voice slowed, a mesmerizing tone that tried to captivate her and failed.

Laughter burbled out of her in a hysterical bark as she doubled over. "It's gone and hidden." She snickered. "Handed it off before I walked out the door, and now it's behind wards even you can't break." She fell into a fit of giggles as Evan started to pace around her menacingly.

"What am I supposed to do, then?" he asked. "Valkyrie isn't an option." He paused, as if listening to someone respond. "There are no other options." Another brief pause. "No, I didn't do this for nothing. There has to be a way." Another pause, punctuated by the sound of metal clanging against the ground as he flipped a platter of tools to the ground. "It's time to be done. If she isn't going to be useful, there's no reason to play nice."

He was talking to Seraph, Dani realized. The fuzziness that had hounded her since waking intensified, and she closed her eyes. A vain attempt to regain composure.

Instead, Evan snatched the chair from under her and slammed a steel-toed boot into her ribs. Worn and reeling, the pain exploded through her in an aura of agony. She gasped, curling protectively around herself as her body tried to knit itself back together, but each breath felt like breathing glass.

Bones broke and blood flowed, and her body healed, but not fast enough. It left her hovering in a grey place as Evan continued to slam his boot into her, rage bubbling through her as blood frothed on her lips. Finally, he knelt down and grabbed her chin in his hand, fingers like a vice.

"Reach out to the veilblade and live, or come to the church tomorrow and die," he said pleasantly. As if this was another

Tuesday to him. Maybe it was. "Those are your choices. Your only choices."

She managed to spit a bloody wad at him, and it landed on his cheek. With a vicious snarl, he stood back up and snapped a foot into her chest. Something cracked, and pain ricocheted through her for a bright, sparking moment before the dark swallowed her completely.

34

EMILIE

Surrounded by people, and Emilie had rarely felt so alone. The drive to Dawson had been thankfully quiet, and the town was waiting. Merc was as good as his word, and there was room for everyone between the motel, a new bed & breakfast that had opened on the outskirts, and folks in town who opened their homes.

Dad was AWOL yet again, and at this point, Emilie wasn't even surprised by his absence. She'd brought Lu, Sawyer, and the kids to Lockgrove House, wanting the extra protection of wards. The kids needed somewhere quiet to decompress, and Emilie found herself wandering from room to room wearing Dani's leather jacket.

She'd stayed up until nearly dawn, making sure everyone who had joined the convoy found the town before she collapsed into bed, too tired to dream. Today, she felt like a puppet with its strings cut. Lu was checking on her patients, and Sawyer had taken the kids to wander Main Street. All Emilie could think of was the fact that the Scions had Dani, and she had no clue where they were, and Sawyer had helped her.

"What am I supposed to do next?" she asked out loud, more to herself than anyone else.

Graham flashed into existence next to her in the hallway. *"You do what only you can do. But I think you know that already."*

Emilie ran a hand through her messy curls and bit her lip. "Andry might be able to help with more sachets, including some options that pack a bigger punch, but I don't know how to do this alone."

"So don't." Graham raised an eyebrow with a cheeky smirk. *"You're not cut off from people, you're surrounded by them. You've been meeting and helping hunters on the road for a year. People remember things, little lodestone. Don't think it's gone unnoticed."*

Emilie stopped short and looked at him carefully. "I was just trying to help."

The truth was, when she'd started working jobs with Dani, she'd been desperate to be useful. She hadn't been great at combat or marksmanship, but from day one, there had been information she just knew. Access to the kinds of texts that kept hunters alive. Why hadn't she considered any of that?

"And you did. You brought these people to Dawson, and I know for a fact it wasn't just talented and casters. Each of those hunters has their own patterns, their own networks. Maybe it's time to put out the call that it's time to come together before the Scions tear down the world."

"Do you think they'll listen to me?"

"It can't hurt to try. I wouldn't be surprised if there were a few spirits sticking close to make sure their people finish this. Let your shields down, and there's a host of folks willing to help."

Graham disappeared, leaving Emilie alone in the living room.

Shielding lessons were some of her earliest memories. Mama and Dad both teaching her how to protect herself from the spiritual world, to block out the things she saw and heard, that most people would never perceive. It'd come back naturally in the weeks after killing Spectre, an understanding of how to keep those shields up so that she could ignore the things she didn't want to see.

Now, she needed to see all of it.

The walls that protected her from the wider world of magic eased away until they were gone. Static wards carved into the walls and floor now danced in a riot of color, and the murmur of spirits on spirit radio were a quietly burbling river. For a moment, it was overwhelming. Then her system adjusted, and they became part of the world instead of separate from it.

She had spent so much of her life with blinders on at the behest of her parents. Blocking her own abilities under her parents' belief that it would protect her. But it hadn't. Instead, it had stripped her of recognition of the breadth of her talents. Another way her parents had held her back instead of teaching her to embrace who she was and what she could do.

Emilie nodded to herself, then opened the front door to find Lu walking up the driveway with a stormy expression painted across her face.

"What happened now?" Emilie asked, shutting the door behind her.

"Tucker's awake and wants to talk to you. Sawyer is already getting on my last nerve. Joe wants to know the plan, and I need you to take point."

Emilie tried not to squeak.

She was used to being the sort of person who faded into the background. It was a superpower in a lot of way, knowing that, more often than not, she could walk into a room and no one would be distracted by her presence. This about-face had thrown her.

"Okay, okay, okay." She paused. "Tucker first, then I'll talk to Joe. Can you do me a favor while I talk to Tucker?"

"What kind of favor?"

"There's an apothecary in town, right across from the coffee shop. I need you to tell Andromeda that I need as many spirit smoke bombs as she can whip up." Emilie blew out a breath before adding, "She'll know what I'm talking about. I got the recipe from her. It's time to get to work."

***

Emilie found Lionel Tucker sitting outside in an Adirondack chair. He looked wan and still a little green around the gills, but the cold presence that had coiled around him at Crossings was entirely absent.

There was an empty chair next to him, so she curled up there, glad that it was a rare warm day before winter gave up its grasp entirely.

"Emilie Lockgrove," he said in a gentle baritone, stating her name instead of asking it. "You're Dani's girl." He nodded his head. "When you touched me, I heard my sister."

She watched him for a long moment before answering. "I am, indeed, Emilie. Lu told me you wanted to talk."

He nodded again and looked down at his hands before he began speaking. "You're the one who…detached Seraph. I owe you everything."

"You didn't want it?"

"No." He shook his head. "A few months ago, I was on a job and ran into some Scions. It broke bad, and I woke up in a stone cell." His eyes went faraway, and Emilie recognized the look. "I could feel Seraph…worming its way into my head, but I couldn't stop it. That place…it put me off balance. I couldn't seem to collect my thoughts. One day, I woke up, and it was just…easier. I lost my baby sister last year, and it almost broke me."

"I'm sorry for your loss," Emilie said, the pang of grief driving into her heart. "Losing people is never easy."

"It's not." He turned and watched her, his eyes searching hers looking for something. "But when I lost Myra, I…lost myself too. I was so angry, and I think Seraph fed on that. Once it had its hooks in me, the anger was still there but it…changed. I changed?" He shook his head. "I'm sorry, I know this probably doesn't make much sense."

"Why did you want to talk to me? What was it you wanted to tell me?"

"They were keeping me in Tenacity Mill," Tucker said. "Not in the church but in one of the buildings across the street. Evan's been there almost constantly the last few months. If he's the one who has Dani, that's where he'll take her."

"Why?" Emilie frowned, mind poring back over the data points she'd collected. "Why bring her there if that's where Seraph came through? It'd be like inviting your archnemesis into your lair."

"I don't know exactly," Tucker admitted. "But I know there was more than me locked up in those stone cells. And I know that Evan wanted something from Dani. I never spoke to him much."

Emilie nodded. "And the attack on Brightfield? Was that you?"

"No. They picked up a talented who'd been there as a kid, and Evan broke them. That's where they got the intel. Even with Seraph wrapped around my throat, I wouldn't give up the halfway house. Myra would have reached past the veil and smacked the shit out of me." He chuckled.

"Damn straight I would have," a woman's voice said quietly. *"Tell him that we need his help. Tell him I said he owes me. Tell him I love him and that I'm at peace."*

Emilie gave him a small smile. "She loves you to death. Myra says…she would have, and that we need your help. To get Dani back. To end this." Emilie paused for a moment. "Kalliope is dead, and Brightfield is shuttered. Crossings is gone now too. If we don't fight back and end this once and for all, then I don't know what comes next. But it's about more than talented or hunters or casters or any of it. It's about what comes next, and I think we're gonna need hunters like you, Tucker."

He smiled, and for the first time, it was genuine. "Well, can't argue with Baby Sis. She sure as hell knows how to send a message." He pulled a necklace out from under his shirt, rubbing a medallion between two fingers. "Yeah, I'll help how I can. I don't know how many people here will trust me after what I almost did, though. What I was party to."

"You weren't, though," Emilie said gently and felt her words ring true. "You were tortured, and they tried to break you. Even under Seraph's influence, you didn't give up the halfway house, and you've seen how they operate in Tenacity Mill. I need your help to rally the hunters before it's too late."

***

Joe was waiting for her on the front porch of the house. He tracked her as she walked up in Dani's jacket, but he didn't say anything. Each step weighed heavier than the last, but in no time at all, Emilie found herself on the porch, standing in front of him.

"Lu said you wanted to talk to me."

A slight smirk tugged at the corner of his mouth. "I did. We need a plan, and I think you're the woman in charge at this point."

"In charge?" Emilie swallowed a whimper.

"You're the one who got everyone back here, aren't you?" He raised an eyebrow and watched her carefully.

"I couldn't just stay quiet. They would have massacred everyone."

"I know," Joe said. "You rallied the troops, even after Dani turned herself over like a sacrificial lamb."

"So you know what she did?"

Joe sighed. "Yes, I know what my firecracker did. Girl made the sacrifice play, all right." He cocked his head at Emilie. "But I think I know what she was doing."

"What do you mean by that?" Emilie took a seat on one of the chairs next to Joe, curling her legs up on it until the leather jacket draped over her knees.

"Dani doesn't do anything by halves." Joe shook his head. "Evan wanted her worse than he wanted anyone else in that building. You and Lu included. But she handed over her jacket and the veilblade both. She didn't tell you ahead of time, either. Does that seem like something off the cuff to you?"

Emilie sighed and rubbed at the space between her eyebrows. "No. No, it doesn't."

"You know more about Seraph than anyone else. You're the one who understands what we're actually dealing with. Dani was buying time. Ensuring that you'd be able to figure this out. That you'd come for her."

Emilie looked down at her hands for a long moment, unsure of what to say. It was one thing to know what Seraph really was and how it had gotten its claws into so many hunters. It was another entirely to realize that the duty to destroy Seraph was a weight she needed to carry.

"I can't do it alone, but I have an idea," she hedged carefully. "It will take more than just hunters to do it, which means working *together*."

"I'm listening."

"Seraph breached the physical in Tenacity Mills." Emilie frowned, thinking of the basement in that church. "It's where it is strongest, but it's also where it is destabilizing the area. Creatures that are born in the veil aren't meant to stay here, and the longer they do, the more damage they're capable of. We have to eradicate it at the source to ensure that all of its hosts are removed from its influence."

"So you want to raid the spot where Seraph has been squatting all these years?"

"Decades," Emilie said. "It's slowly corrupting everything it touches, manipulating the hunters it finds weakness in, and Evan has been feeding it."

"The Campbell kid hasn't been around all that long."

"Yeah, but he's always been unhinged, right?" Emilie pressed. "Isn't that how Dani found out what the Scions really were?"

Joe watched her with dark eyes for a long moment before nodding. "It is."

"Seraph, all evanescent parasites, they feed off of negative emotions and amplify them. If Evan was already consumed by it, then it's not a stretch to think that Seraph saw a host that was more than meat."

"You think Evan is working with it willingly?"

"I don't think any of the Scions who know about Seraph realize what it really is." Emilie looked down the driveway, frowning, her mind going a million miles a minute as she tried to make sense of everything. "They think it's some kind of avenging angel, and it plays right into all of the oldest hunter and talented problems. The Scions aren't a new phenomenon. People have hunted talented and casters and witches...by whatever name...people with magic have always been hunted by people without it. Something as old as Seraph knew that. Knew exactly what buttons to push in order to get what it wanted."

Joe was quiet next to her, but Emilie could feel the weight of his gaze. She let him watch, let him see the anger and fear battling for supremacy within her. She kept her eyes on the road, thumb rubbing at the leather jacket as if it were a worry stone.

"You know there are going to be hunters there waiting for us."

"I'm betting on it," Emilie said. "Some of them didn't buy all the way in, but now they're stuck all the same."

"There is no way to separate them, though. If they fire on us, we're going to fire back, and people are going to die. Ours and theirs."

She nodded quietly and looked back at Joe. "People are going to die, but you're wrong. There *is* a way to separate them, and I proved it last night."

"Keep talking."

"Seraph is essentially a spiritual infection. So, we hit it with the same stuff that gets spirits to stop clinging to a place, person, or object. If they don't actually believe in what they were doing, they won't get back up."

"And the rest of them?" Joe asked.

"They'll get what's coming to them one way or another," she said, a glaze of ice skittering over the chair.

Joe nodded. "Good."

His eyes were harder than she'd ever seen them, and Emilie was reminded that long before he'd handed out jobs from behind a bar, he'd been a deadly hunter in his own right.

"Lu is getting more sachets from Andry, and Tucker is talking to the hunters he knows. I can ask Lu to see which talented or casters from the clinic want to come as well. This is an all-hands-on-deck situation. We need all the firepower we can get."

"Heard. I'll put the call out to my people as well. Call in some favors. Want to go over the finer details?"

Emilie stood up and raked a hand through her hair again. "Yeah. We need to pin down what we're doing and how, but we can't take long, Joe. If we drag our feet, I'm afraid we won't get there in time."

35

DANI

The itching woke her, a stinging burn that crawled under her skin and made it impossible to focus, impossible to rest. It also reminded her that she was alive and that Evan didn't care about taking her apart if he got what he wanted out of it. Her heart stuttered inside her chest, the bruises and aches from her last face-to-face making it clear that even her enhanced abilities were working double time to keep her breathing.

"You're awake," Julia said quietly, watching her from a chair on the other side of the room, looking more wrung out than ever.

Her perfectly combed hair wasn't quite perfect today, and there were dark circles under her eyes. Wrinkles in her shirt, as if she'd slept in it. Maybe she had. Each time she reappeared in Dani's life, she seemed to fade further away. They were too young for this shit, and weariness rolled over her in a wave that made her want to lie down and sleep for a thousand years.

"It would seem that way," Dani said roughly.

Dani forced herself to sit up and take in the small room she found herself in. A battered couch, windows hidden from the outside world with weak sunlight breaking through the curtains. Not the cell where she couldn't think straight, and not the cell that Evan's people had dragged her off to.

"Why were you in Evan's cells, Dani?"

She raised an eyebrow at Julia. "You were there when they dragged me off, Julia. You know exactly why I was down there."

"You were supposed to be taken to an isolation cell. Not into my brother's custody."

"Well, that's not the way it went down." Dani buffed her nails against her bloodied shirt. "The better question is, why am I still here?"

She watched Julia as they talked, picking up on every tiny movement. The way her nail beds were red and bloody, the exhaustion writ large across her face, and the fact that she wasn't on a concrete floor somewhere.

"See, I don't think you want to answer that question. You're willing to believe his lies—that he's here for revenge or that I was somehow responsible for your Pops's death." Dani leveled Julia with a disgusted look. "You know that he's gone off the deep end, that I shouldn't be here, but you just can't admit it, can you?"

Julia's nostrils flared, retorts flickering through her eyes before she answered. "My brother has always been brutal." Her gaze danced back and forth. "Our calling requires brutality and a steady hand."

"It requires you to bury your humanity. Your morals." Dani shook her head and coughed wetly.

"What do you want me to do? It was all so *easy* for you. Walked away and left me behind like I was nothing."

Dani's lip curled up as she snarled, unwilling to play any more games. Much as she'd wanted to save Julia, the petty cruelties were all she had in this moment.

"I left because your brother is a psychopath who was murdering people and calling it hunting, and neither you nor your father were ever willing to deal with him." She sneered. "You're lucky I didn't set fire to the place while everyone was asleep in their beds."

No shock on Julia's face, no horror. Only a deep resignation that sank over her in a dark shroud, making her shrink further.

"He is my brother. My only living family." Julia's voice wavered. "You never understood what family meant."

"*We* were supposed to be family!" Dani swore under her breath, and a thick silence filled the space between them. "We were in love. You were my fucking future, and then your brother did what he did, and instead of backing me up? You defended him."

"We could have found a way through. *Together*," Julia hissed. Her voice was barbed when she spoke up again. "You ran away and let everything burn behind you like we were nothing. Like I was nothing."

"You weren't there, and it was my best chance to get those people out. I wasn't going to become part of the legion. Wasn't interested in gunning down people in their beds. Being a murderer whenever someone higher up didn't wanna get their hands dirty."

Julia nodded grimly, mouth pressed into a white line. "So instead, you took up with the east coast riffraff. Joe and his little networks, his pet talented willing to do his bidding."

"Keep his name out of your fucking mouth," Dani spat. "Joe is better than all of you combined."

"I guess we'll see. When the sun goes down, someone will come for you. You can do what Evan asked of you, or you can be marched out to the square to die like an animal. It's your call, Dani. You get to make the choice."

Julia stood in a single fluid motion and all but fled, the door locking behind her as she left Dani alone with her thoughts. Her mind was topsy-turvy, and even away from the oily presence that had pressed in around her in that last room, she wasn't even keeled. She didn't know if her people would get to her in time, if Emilie had a plan to ensure that Seraph's influence was cut out of the world at the root.

Emilie would fight for her, Dani understood that to the marrow of her bones. But if she didn't get here in time, it wouldn't matter. There was a wet darkness growing inside of her, whispering that she could trade all that fear and anguish for power if she simply allowed it to swallow her. Was this what it had been for Valkyrie—her mother—after fighting Spectre when he'd come for her?

She didn't like to think about it. What it must have been like after the attack, thinking the people she loved most were gone. The magic that lingered inside her from the veilblade numbed her to the fear and left something else to fill its place.

She knew who had caused this chain reaction of damage and pain and bloodshed, and they would pay for it. Evan Campbell had been trying to destroy her for more than a decade. His actions had led to the riot, the attack at the hospital, and dozens of people were dead by his hand. She'd known him before Seraph had him in its coils of power, and even then, he'd been wrong.

No more. There was no more pretending this could end without blood. His blood. And anyone else who'd aided him was nothing anymore. Distantly, Dani was aware that she was slipping away, but she had no interest in stopping the free fall anymore. Instead, she steered her way into it, trying to keep ahold of herself as something so vast that it went on forever attempted to inhale her like she'd never existed outside of it.

Julia could try to stand against her, or she could fall to the wayside, but the bladesinger inside of her was no longer interested in allowing her human side to control their actions. Evan needed to die for what he'd done. To her, to the people she called family, and to all the people and hunters killed or maimed or injured along the way. Without him, how many people would still be alive today?

It was a question without an answer. Not here, and not now. Dani blinked, and the darkness receded, but not enough. She was still unwell. After this, Dani thought she might always be unwell. Once, she had thought Julia was her future. Instead, she had been prey pretending to be a predator.

In the hallways, she could hear people moving and talking. The last time she'd been this close to so many Scions had been at the compound. Some trying to get in and others fighting to get out, chaos breaking through the compound like a fever running its course. She hadn't meant to start everything, but her presence had become a catalyst, as if she was just the match that started a pyre waiting to be burnt. Violence built as those who didn't believe talented were afflicted with evil or darkness and people who were there because it allowed them to carry out the dark desires in their hearts clashed.

There was a quiet chant running through her head. *Kill Evan, kill Evan, kill Evan.* A loop she had no interest in stopping. As if she was being called to service. It felt right and necessary, and there was no part of her that pulled back from that inherent knowledge. Not anymore.

Outside, the light from the sun was fading, but Dani refused to do what Evan was asking of her. If they thought she'd go as quietly as she had at the clinic, these people had another thing coming. This time, when the darkness beckoned for Dani, she let it swallow her willingly. Survival required sacrifice sometimes, and she understood that better than most.

All she had to do now was wait.

36

DANI

It was dark when they came for Dani. She'd been sitting there for hours, waiting for what came next. Their boots cracking against the floor warned her of their approach before they ever opened the door, thunder crashing somewhere in the distance.

The door crashed open, nearly embedding itself into the wall. Lightning flashed nearby, echoed by a crash of thunder loud enough to shake the walls. Six men glowered at her from the hallway, red flashlights in their hands to illuminate the room and where Dani was sitting on the couch, elbows on her knees as she watched them.

"I was wondering how long it would take you to come for me," she quipped.

"Be silent," one of them snapped.

"Oh sugar, silent isn't how I operate." Dani unfurled herself from the couch and cracked her neck as a feral smile stretched across her lips.

"Be silent and submit yourself to judgement."

Two of them moved into the room in lockstep, shadows hanging heavy over their faces. Violence clung to them like a mantle, and the taste of ozone lingered in the air. Dani didn't have Emilie's ability to see past the real, but in this moment, she could feel Seraph's influence. Its malignancy coiled tight around each of these men. Lightning flashed again, and she could see their eyes were perfect black pools as they stared at Dani, unblinking.

"I don't submit. Not to the Scions, and not to Seraph." She ran her tongue over her canines, shook her shoulders, and let her body drop down into a fighting stance.

Her people would get here in time or they wouldn't. She would die on those stones in front of the church or she wouldn't. The possibilities loomed each way that tonight could go, but right now, she couldn't think about any of them. She surrendered herself to the power lingering in a deeper place inside her than she'd ever been aware of. Dani was no longer a hunter, no longer even really a person. She was a weapon, and this is what she had been forged for.

She exploded into action, lip curling into a snarl as she snapped her fist into the face of the first goon. Under her fist, his nose burst, and he ricocheted back into his friends with a gurgle. Dani's grin stretched across her face as lightning flashed again and the rest of them flooded into the room.

There wasn't much space, and they were bunched up trying to get to her without being pummeled in the process. It was a target-rich environment, and Dani let her body move where it needed to go without thinking. She had no weapons, even though her palm itched for the familiar heft of the veilblade. She was a whirlwind, a dervish, nothing but violence encased in flesh and muscle.

She was the dancer, and the music was the wet impact of flesh on flesh, the gurgling moans of the men as they dropped to the floor one after the other, the crunch of broken bone as it shattered under the onslaught of an unstoppable force.

Then she stood there for a long moment, chest heaving, raw wounds on her knuckles dripping quietly onto the bodies that now littered the floor.

The building around her was devoid of people. No idle chatter, no running feet, just the moaning of the men she'd put on the ground, and the storm raging outside. Dani wiped the blood from her hands onto her dark jeans and marched out into the hallway. The storm shrouded her, muffling any other sounds as she moved like the predator she was.

The walls of the building were leached of color, crumbling under the weight of their own existence. Dani moved out into the street and stopped short. The sky was burning a sickly green, and there were wide cracks in the ground that undulated with an oily sheen. To her left, the church stood against a cloudy sky and nearly glowed in the darkness.

Her eyes skipped across the landscape, mind focused on one thing and one thing alone: *Evan*. It would have been smarter to pull back. Find a way to contact her people and come in with a plan. But they were out of time. The sky was glowing, the ground was undulating, and Evan was the one who had brought all of this to pass. It would end tonight, or she would.

Dark clouds raced across the sky, and there was another crash as lightning hit something at the far side of town. It lit everything for a split second. Not long, but long enough for her to spot Evan standing on the front steps of the church, a huddled mass of bodies between the two of them.

If she had been a different person, if she hadn't surrendered to everything the mantle of the bladesinger demanded of her, Dani would have gone in quietly. But she was a weapon. She was retribution and vengeance, and now she could taste blood in the water. She moved to the middle of the street and began walking toward the church.

They would see her, and she was planning on it. If it killed her, she'd make sure every last one of Seraph's hosts bled out in this place and added their bodies to the ledger. They were anathema to everything that being a hunter was, and now they were going to pay for it. Something rolled over and through her like a wave, and in the not-so-far distance, she heard the throaty rumble of engines.

A *lot* of engines.

She walked slowly, clapping her hands as she did. Evan turned, then moved through the mass of people, who fanned out into the street and began to yell. More bodies poured out of the church and some of the buildings across the street.

"Good show, Evan, but the game is over now." Lightning struck again, and this time, one of the buildings caught fire, dark smoke billowing into the sky. "Today, Jackal meets its end."

"And what? You're going to kill me?" Evan asked, moving until only a few bodies separated them. "You're good, Dani, but even you won't kill all these people."

She clucked her tongue at him. "Don't forget that your daddy named me too." Her lips curled into a cruel smile. "Reaper."

Evan stood there watching her, and Dani wasn't sure why she hadn't dealt with him years ago. He'd tried to ruin her and destroyed the lives of so many people in the process. She had almost loved him like a brother once. She had believed in second chances. Hell, she'd needed one of her own, hadn't she? Dani had given him chance after chance after chance. Some misguided hope that he'd turn it around, that he wasn't really the monster she saw watching her from those cold baby blues.

That was over now. Evan would be given no more chances, no redemption arc. It was time for him to pay for his crimes in blood, and she had nominated herself as judge, jury, and executioner.

Evan went stock-still, as if he'd seen it in her face. Seen the cold determination written into every molecule of her being. Bladesingers were not immortal. They were not immune to injury. But they were stronger, faster, and more capable than a human hunter could ever be. And he knew that better than most. In moments where there didn't seem to be hope, having a bladesinger on your side could turn the tide.

Behind her, vehicles skidded to a stop, hunters pouring out of them and backing her play. She didn't have to look; she could feel it. Feel *them*, as if each one was an energy signature telling her she wasn't alone. She didn't have to do this alone. She had all of them.

"Kill them! KILL THEM ALL!" Evan's eyes bugged out of his face.

As the Scions burst into action, packets trailing smoke thudded to the ground around her in a grey and lavender haze. Evan was turning when Dani took off toward him. The shock and fear in his eyes were ambrosia. He was nothing but a rabbit running from a fox, and she was no longer willing to hide in the tall grass.

Evan sprinted for the entrance of the church, ducking around the side of the fence toward the back of the building. Thunder rolled again, and rain fell as the sky opened up above them. He was fast.

Dani was faster.

37

EMILIE

Emilie saw Dani in the moment before the sachets hit the ground, burning and filling the street with fragrant smoke. The air tasted like lavender and petrichor as all hell broke loose. The Scions charged into the haze, and a third of them dropped to their knees as they choked.

Dani was gone in the blink of an eye, racing into the smoke. Hunters fired their guns, muzzle flashes sparking in the obscured street. Someone screamed, but the spirits that were crowded onto every rooftop kept their silent vigil.

The sky, painted green, opened up, rain torrenting down over all of them. The ground crawled with an oily darkness that seethed from the cracks in the world, supernatural magma trying to force its way into the real. The thick fog lingered only a few feet off the ground, and the Scions scattered like roaches under a kitchen light. Wind whipped through the street, eddying the smoke into tiny cyclones, leaving the people who had succumbed to the sachets puking black ichor onto the ground.

Emilie took off after Dani, her body moving low and fast. She didn't know what she looked like in the moment, but she could feel it as the legion of spirits moved with her, granting her what little strength they had left.

All she wanted to do was find Dani before it was too late.

The demand for justice pulsed inside her, reminding Emilie that there was a timeline here. It was possible to run out of time, and she was down to the wire. The town was full of nooks and crannies, layers of stories that had sunk into the bricks, asking her to pay attention, to remember they'd existed once. Shots ricocheted past her head, and she ducked into a building, trying to find a way around the chaos to where Dani had disappeared.

Something cold and sharp churned in her stomach, crawling up her throat as frost coated her shoulders and knuckles. There were doors on either side of the hallway, metal doors with a viewing window at the top, and she didn't need to look inside to know what she had found.

"We were as good as animals to them," a man's voice spoke into her ear before he shimmered into sight in front of her. His dark eyes were luminous, but his spirit was nearly translucent, even for her. *"The Scions took us from our homes and brought us here to finish their work."*

The doors hung ajar, empty of victims, but the memories of this place threatened to overwhelm her. She wanted to scream and cry. She also wanted to take this place down to studs, as if the darkness of this world had touched only the building and not the very land that it stood on. She fled through the building and found a door that led out into a narrow alley running between the streets.

A roar of violence met her as she broke back into the damp air. Ozone was heavy around her, and it was thicker than it should have been. Something was about to happen—unless she stopped it. Above her, lightning crashed and thunder boomed, resonating through her bones. The rain was still coming down so hard that her visibility was shot, wind whipped her wet curls around her face wildly.

In front of her, several figures in dark clothing moved to block the alley. Emilie skidded to a stop, the water pooling around her boots, painting her clothing to her body.

"No place to hide now, witch."

Emilie narrowed her eyes. "Who said I was hiding?"

Two of them raised rifles, and a third stepped in front of them. "Turn yourself over for cleansing, and you don't have to die." He cocked his head to the side. "At least you won't die bleeding in a forgotten alley."

No more of this. Emilie's lip curled back from her teeth, hands clenching into fists as her nails bit into her palms. No more talented taken from their beds for the prejudices of these psychopaths. No more bloody cells where they beat the names of friends and family from people who had done nothing more audacious than living with magic running through their veins.

"Your choice, girlie. Maybe we'll pull you out in front of the other afflicted. As a warning of what people like you get."

"People like me?" Emilie asked, voice hoarse. Ice coated her arms, wrapped around her thighs, climbing the inside of her throat like some kind of poisonous vine. "There are no people like me."

The air around her went cold, each drop of rain turning to ice as it got close and becoming armor that coated her limbs. Emilie blinked and dropped her shields. The power from the spirits rolled over and through her as the Scions fired blindly. A round glanced off her shoulder, taking out a chunk of ice before a new layer was formed in its place by the rain.

Emilie took a step forward.

"You have been judged by the dead and by the living. And you have been found wanting." Emilie continued to move, step by step, and extended a finger toward the Scions.

Spirits burst through her and rushed the soldiers in a wave.

They screamed at the sight, shooting and swinging, but it didn't last long. Their cries snapped whatever tension had filled the air, and violence flooded Emilie in a racuous torrent.

Emilie surged behind them, past the wreckage that had been the Scions. Another block over, she could see the church. It pulsed like a beacon, white wood wrapped in dark tendrils that undulated with the same green light peeking through the dark clouds in the sky.

She paused at the corner of the alley, taking in the chaos that had erupted behind her. People were screaming somewhere on the far side of the church, and something had exploded on the other side of town, fire fighting valiantly against the rain.

Emilie didn't run. She walked between bodies, spirits circling her like a pack of dogs. Ice glazed the ground where she stepped, leaving a slippery trail in her wake. She was still wearing Dani's jacket, unwilling to take it off or move the veilblade from where it was hidden. It'd seemed safer that way. Now, it was dragging her toward the church like a magnet, as if it knew where she needed to go.

Around her, spirits split off as she moved through the carnage. Some of them burned out; others found their unfinished business in the Scions still fighting in the streets. A few followed in her wake: Tucker's sister, Miriam, who had reached out to start this, and a handful of others Emilie didn't recognize. As she drew closer, Graham shimmered into place next to her, walking in lockstep.

The closer she got, the more the illusion of the church melted away in front of her eyes. The doors out front were wide open, and it made the building look less like a place of worship and more like a yawning mouth waiting to swallow her and anyone else foolish enough to enter.

From inside, there was a soft glow telling her to come inside. Everything was fine here. It would continue to be fine here. So long as she did what she was told and didn't try to fight back. It was a calming, muffling sensation that blurred all the hard edges of the world.

If she had been a different person…if there had been no Spectre or fire or death, maybe she would have been content to believe the lie emanating from the church. But there had been. She had seen bitter fruits wrapped in sweet lies one too many times to believe this. She concentrated, and it shattered and fell away. There was a dark throb to the land, and to the world, and it frightened Emilie more than she could say.

Whatever this place was, it wasn't a church. Not really, not anymore. No, it was something darker and hungrier than that. It was also exactly where she needed to go. Needed to walk inside knowing what lingered in the basement, that it would steal something from her if she let it.

But *only* if she let it.

She held out her right hand and shot Graham a look out of her peripheral. "Stay with me? I don't want to do this alone."

He grabbed her hand, and she felt the cool rush of energy as he touched her. Emilie nodded and took a deep breath before ascending the stairs. She paused at the threshold and tugged the jacket closer before crossing it and hoping she wasn't making a terrible mistake.

38

DANI

In the instant between Evan taking off through the tombstones of the cemetery and Dani bolting after him, lightning struck somewhere nearby. Déjà vu glimmered at the edges of her mind not fully consumed by the predator instincts that propelled her forward, connecting this night to the night everything had gone wrong at the Campbell compound.

She'd learned her lesson the first time around. Evan would be dead before the concept of a third round could take root in anyone's mind.

The cemetery was larger than she'd realized, and the air was thick in her lungs. She pushed through it, gaining on him with every step. The wounds he'd left from their one-on-one in his murder basement weren't fully healed yet, but rage sustained her, magic soothing her aches to get what it wanted. Vengeance, bright and vibrant, in her veins.

She zigzagged between headstones and guardian angels and a single broken obelisk cracked down the middle. She'd halved the distance between them, and Evan realized as he looked back over his shoulder, eyes wide in fear or panic. Dani wasn't sure what she looked like right now. Not that it mattered. His fear fueled her, drove her forward faster, ready to tear into him and feel everything he had taken from the world. Every life stolen before its time. Everything had a price, and for him, the bill had finally come due.

Evan tumbled past the short fence that separated the graveyard from the church proper, slapping against a side door in panic. His hands flapped for the handle as he looked to see how far away Dani was. She closed the last hundred feet between them, vaulting the fence like she'd been made for it. The wild instinct to hunt, to tear flesh from bone and make him understand what he had done, rolled through her, becoming a living thing trapped in a cage of muscle and sinew. One she didn't know how to control.

One she didn't want to control.

She slowed until he was almost within arm's reach. Evan glanced back again with wide eyes, as if she was a monster, and it stirred... nothing. Distantly, she was aware that whatever was happening was very bad and that she was no longer entirely in control of herself or her actions. The absence of empathy, the utter disregard for a human life, should have concerned her. But he deserved what he was going to get, and she wasn't sorry about it.

"Anything to say for yourself, Evan?" She stalked forward and cocked her head to one side. "I'm guessing you didn't think it would go this way." She grinned, lips curling into a predatory smile. "You thought wrong."

Instead of answering, he let out a cry of relief as the church door finally gave and he tumbled into the waiting candlelight. Her hunter's smile morphed into a snarl at the idea that he might escape because she'd been stupid enough to slow down instead of killing him fast and clean. It was more than he deserved.

Before she could pursue him into the church, a familiar dark-haired figure stepped out, closing the door behind her. Every time she'd seen Julia since leaving the clinic, she'd been in what the Scions considered civvies. Now, she was kitted up for a fight. Every inch below her chin was covered in layers of dark clothing with Kevlar weave, the shape of steel plates showing through the fabric.

Dani recognized the design. She'd helped sketch out the first version of it on coffee napkins during long hours of stakeouts. Lightning flashed again, followed by an explosion across town, the thunder so close, it rattled her bones, nailing her in place as the girl she once loved stared at her with flinty eyes.

"Don't make me do this, Julia." Dani shook her head, droplets of water spraying away from her. "You're not the one I want."

"You know I can't let you do this. You know!" The wind whipped between them as the rain continued to pummel the ground wildly.

"He has to pay for what he's done." Dani didn't yell, didn't raise her voice. She didn't have to.

"Not this!" Julia paced back and forth. Her hair was pulled back in a severe ponytail. It had always been so wispy, and prone to falling out if it wasn't secured properly.

"You can get out of my way under your own power, or I can do it for you." Dani stalked forward.

Julia mirrored her movements, keeping the door behind her. "He is my brother!"

There was barely any space between the two of them. Julia was pleading with her eyes, body language begging Dani to listen to her.

"I don't care." Dani's voice dropped to a guttural snarl, and she threw a knee up into Julia's abdomen.

Julia blocked the blow, shoving Dani backward. Rain had pounded the ground into mud, and she skidded back before her boots dug into the soil. Years ago, they'd been almost evenly matched; Julia had always been a half second faster. But after a decade plus on the road, with the magic from the veilblade pulsing through her, Julia couldn't stop the flurry of attacks coming her way.

Dani knew what she was, what she had been trained for and built into by life and by blood and by everything that mattered. She was a weapon, built to strike out and as likely to cut the hand that wielded her as she was to shear away anything in her path. Once, she had hated it, what she was, how life had shaped her. Tonight, she embraced it.

They traded blows, a dance they both knew, and she remembered what it was to fight someone on her level. Even with the preternatural reflexes granted from becoming a bladesinger, Dani had to be careful, or Julia would sneak inside her guard with sharp jabs that stole her breath and pushed her back and away from the door.

A sharp kick knocked the wind out of Dani and pushed her to her knees. It shredded the last of her self-control. Whatever she had been holding back burned into nothing in an instant.

"I'm sorry!" Julia said, yelling over the ferocity of the storm.

As if she could take Dani down. As if she'd ever won in their sparring days. Julia might have forgotten, but Dani had not.

"Good," Dani growled back.

She should have been sorry for all the bullshit she'd dealt with because Julia was too scared to confront her brother. Should have been sorry or dealt with it years ago. Now, it was all too little too late.

Dani snarled as she surged to her feet and threw a nasty punch that caught Julia on the edge of her jaw. It snapped her head up and back with an audible click. Before the other woman could retaliate, Dani followed it up with a pair of jabs to her solar plexus, then swept her feet out from under her.

Julia heaved for breath, in the mud. Black eye, blood at her jaw, one arm hanging wrong, and she still fought to get back on her feet, panic shining from her eyes.

"I don't want to kill you," Dani said, surprised at how calm she sounded. Maybe it was the rain. Maybe it was the way Julia had always fought like a feral animal where her brother was concerned. "You can't fight anymore." Dani shook her head. "Stay down."

"Not just gonna lay here..." Julia struggled to sit up and kicked against the mud until she hit the side of the church. She hacked up blood and spat it at Dani's feet. "...and let you kill my brother. Not now, not ever."

Dani stared down at her, rage and history fighting each other for dominance. Julia couldn't fight, and there were no pools of darkness hiding in her eyes. Dani didn't *want* to kill her, but that didn't mean she wouldn't.

"Your brother is a fucking psychopath who tortured me, killed dozens of people, and caused this." Dani grabbed her by the back of the collar and dragged her around to the front of the church.

The cracks in the ground had grown during the battle, darkness beginning to seep out from the ruptures. The sky was a poisonous green, but the rain was starting to let up, showing off the carnage of what had been a town once. Blood and bodies littered the ground, and multiple buildings were on fire now, dark smoke billowing up into the sky.

"I ought to leave you here to die, but out of all of us, I'm not the monster."

"You are," Julia insisted, spitting more blood at Dani's feet. "You just don't look like one."

Dani squatted down until they were eye to eye. "Takes one to know one, now, doesn't it?"

Dani unfurled back to her full height, looking at where Julia was slumped on the front stairs with disgust. Once, she had loved Julia. Wanted to spend her life with her, hunting monsters and protecting the people who didn't know what went bump in the night. Now, the same woman stared up at her as if she was nothing more than trash. Maybe that was the way it had always been, and Dani had been too lovesick to notice it.

"He killed so many people, Julia. Families. *Children*. Why doesn't that register with you?"

"Afflicted," Julia said. "If the veilblade hadn't cleansed you of their taint, you'd be just as bad."

"Ah." Dani nodded and began walking up the stairs. "Good ole prejudice. You know, not gonna lie, I never figured you for one of the true zealots. I mean, you did your job, you toed the party line, but you weren't Evan. Hell, I always figured that's why Isaac wanted to hand everything over to you." She shook her head, wishing suddenly that she'd left Julia in the rain. "How the fuck did I miss that?"

Before Julia could spit more of her rancid opinions, Dani left Julia behind—where she belonged—and headed for the open maw of the church. If the hunters were here, that meant Emilie was too. If she knew her girl at all, she'd have gunned it for the place where Seraph had crossed over to end this. Which meant she was alone in this place with Evan and Seraph both.

She moved into the relative quiet of the church. The rain still pounded against the roof in a staccato beat that echoed through the room, not quite drowning out the pop and crackle of the dozens of candles scattered throughout.

Dani didn't know what she'd been expecting, but it wasn't this. Skulls and bones were clustered around the candles, some of them coated in thick wax, and around her, there was no one. A raw wound in the church where the wall had been demolished still let in a breeze from the back room, but now she could feel the darkness seeping up and into this place. It felt alive in a way it hadn't just a week ago.

She moved through the pews softly and silently, ears perked for any sign of Emilie or Evan. From below her, there was a scuffle, and she heard a man's voice murmuring. *You're going to be too late.* Dani burst into motion, skidding across the worn wooden floorboards and tripping down the stairs into hell. Evan had tried to take everything from her, but he wouldn't take Emilie.

Dani wouldn't let him.

39

EMILIE

Outside, the storm hit in earnest, chasing Emilie into the depths of whatever the church really was. An open mouth waiting to swallow her whole. The floor pulsed underfoot, alive with power in a way she'd only experienced at the auction house.

Candles lit up the interior, and there had been new additions since the day she'd scoped this place out with Dani. Skulls and bones, macabre artwork leaning where the windows had been, and underfoot, the floor flickered between stones and wood as if even it didn't know what it was supposed to be. Water washed in through the open door behind her as the storm raged on, but it suddenly felt so very far away.

The pull of the grave called out to Emilie, and though she stood alone in the real, the presence of the spirits who moved with her bolstered her. The hair at the back of her neck stood up as she moved farther into the building, bypassing the altar and the office behind it and winding down the hallway, where the basement entrance called out to her.

She'd never spent much time in churches, but Christianity was so ingrained in American culture that she could pick out the problems.

No sign of Jesus or a cross to be found inside the building, but there were hallowed figures with too many limbs and shadows that poured from behind haloed saints looking into the distance. The corners of the room were thick with a roiling darkness, veins of poisonous green leaching out across the floor.

She was uniquely aware that she was alone here, with no physical weapon to speak of, and walking into the kind of terror she was unprepared for. Except, there was no one else here who could do what she could. Emilie shook off the dread that tried to drape itself over her shoulders. Seraph wanted her afraid, wanted her hesitant, and she wouldn't give it the satisfaction. She might not have been a bladesinger, but she was more than capable of putting up a fight. Of ending this.

Emilie moved through the flickering light down the hallway and let the shadows shield her from prying eyes. Deeper in the building, someone moved, and she heard a door open and then close. She tugged the leather jacket tighter, relishing the bite of the metal zipper in her palms, grounding her. Not the same as Dani's hand in her own, dark eyes watching over one shoulder until it was time to go. The jacket was ingrained with the smell of leather and oil and gunpowder, and it almost made it feel like Dani was here with her. Ready to take on the whole world if Emilie was.

Was Dani in the building? Had she chased Evan into its depths? Emilie's heart beat a staccato rhythm in the hollow of her chest, but she refused to allow the panic to take over. She couldn't, because if she did, then there wasn't anyone coming for Dani. If she did, Seraph would get what it wanted, and none of the victims that had reached past the veil for help would ever be able to truly cross over. And that? That was unacceptable in every possible way.

"That bitch!" a man's voice yelled from around the corner, followed by a fleshy slap as hands impacted rotting wood. "Julia will handle *her*, but we can't wait any longer. It has to be tonight. It has to be *now*."

Emilie pressed herself into the darkest shadows, skin crawling.

"I should have killed the bitch when I had the chance." His voice paused. "I know what she is, and that blade belongs to me. My family. My legacy."

"*Evan fucking Campbell.*" Graham's form slipped into sight next to her, hate threaded through every syllable of his words.

She turned to look at him, staying silent in the shadows. Evan might not be able to hear the spirits, but she could. Emilie just couldn't respond without being overheard. Learning ASL moved drastically up her to-do list for once this chaos was over. If it would ever really be over. Less, maybe? She could work with less.

"*You asked for help. You said you didn't want to do this alone. This is it.*" Graham turned to her. "*Dani won't be safe, no one will be safe, not so long as he's still breathing.*"

Emilie licked her lips and nodded in agreement.

"*It's not what you think. Not like I stuck it out to chase after the girl I never said anything to. I haven't been grinding my axe against some white boy with a god complex. But this close, I can feel it, and I think you can too. Let me help you end this. End him.*" Graham's eyes glowed amber, motes of scarlet dancing in them.

Power throbbed through the building again, and the floor roiled underfoot. Wood cracked, and the wind howled, beating against the walls. Emilie could feel Seraph trying to drag itself out into the real, to become something that existed here instead of a parasitic leech drawing power from its hosts.

"We're not alone," Evan said, and his gaze turned toward Emilie, trying to see her through the shadows.

"Let me in," Graham said, panic pinching his face. "Let me in, and we can put Evan down. So long as he's here, Seraph will never be gone. Never."

Fear washed over her in a paralyzing wave, goosebumps breaking out on her arms, chased by the crackle of ice as it settled over her skin anew. Memories of a spirit trying to crawl inside her sent revulsion rushing down her spine. But this was Graham.

She licked her lips, then pushed down the fear until it was an echo and nodded. Just once. It was an invitation for him to come ride shotgun. One last job, one last monster that needed to be handled by the people who could do what no one else could. He flashed past her in a cold breeze that ruffled her hair, and she scrunched her eyes shut, instinct telling her something terrible was waiting in the bowels of the church.

In front of her, Evan was speaking again, but she was too preoccupied trying to let her body adjust to the second soul slammed inside of her to pay attention. Graham tried to be unobtrusive, but there was no way for him to fit comfortably. She felt like a very large fishbowl that had been overfilled and now balanced precariously, trying not to spill everywhere.

I won't overstay my welcome," Graham's voice echoed inside of her mind.

If Emilie thought about what was happening, a headache would begin to bloom, vicious and painful. So instead, she did her best to ignore it and pretend as if all of this was normal. She stretched in place and felt Graham's spirit fit itself as best it could to her limbs. An echo that tracked each tiny movement she made.

"I know you're out there somewhere." Evan looked right into the shadows with a cruel smile dancing over his lips. "My friend says you're right there, trying to hide from me, is that right? Too scared to come out and fight me yourself?" He cocked his head, standing in the flickering yellow light as fissures appeared in the walls around them.

Emilie stepped forward out of the shadows, Graham helping to puppet her limbs, her muscles tensing in unfamiliar ways.

"You let me take the lead, and I promise we can do this."

Emilie nodded just a little and let her gaze pierce Evan as cold power flooded her limbs. "I wasn't waiting for you. Honestly, I figured you were already toast. Dani *really* wants your head on a stick."

"Of the two of us, I'm the one who belongs here." He raised his arms, eyes bouncing along the ceiling. "You don't even know where you are."

"It's a church, in a dead town." Emilie rolled her eyes and planted her feet.

"A church, in a dead town," he mimicked her words. "I suppose I should expect as much from your kind."

"My kind." She cocked her head, eyes flickering along the hallway behind him. "You mean, like, *lesbians*?" She stage-whispered the word with an innocent look.

"No, I don't mean—I should have expected this. Afflicted lack the capacity to understand this place. To understand the future Seraph has shown me."

She recoiled as if he'd slapped her, and Emilie's lip curled up of its own accord. "Afflicted." She nodded her head and pursed her lips as power pooled in her belly, ice flooding through her system. "You use that word so flippantly."

Her voice was quiet, but power continued to fill her like a vessel. Magic drawn up from inside of her, pushing Graham to the edges of herself.

She had been nine the first time she'd seen Humans First nutjobs. People who condemned her as poisoned by the world or the sin of magic, depending on which one was talking. One had told her that if she'd been Emilie's mother, she would have strangled her in the cradle. Pruned that branch from the family tree to ensure the affliction could not spread.

Afflicted. Emilie hated that word, and the hate spread through her veins, slow and cold and unstoppable. Ice in her blood, ice in her eyes, and something older than all of it waiting for her to but ask. Her eyes slid shut, and when she breathed in, the scent of loam and rot and old flowers surrounded her. Emilie exhaled, her breath sliding from her in a cold vapor that drifted in the space between them.

"You." Evan's eyes bulged in his head, red around the iris. "I should have taken her and killed you where you stood like the vermin you are." His voice stayed conversational, even as he spewed his warped ideology into the air. "Afflicted and spreading your poison and chaos through anyone you can find. No more." He shook his head, and his body snapped toward her.

Emilie had spent the last year working with Dani and the hunters she'd met along the way until she was passable in hand-to-hand. But Evan was a better fighter than her in every way. He moved like a dark blur, fast enough that she couldn't track where he was moving or what he was doing. Even with Graham riding shotgun in her mind, she wasn't sure she'd be able to take him.

Her body dodged a blow she'd barely seen coming, his fist grazing past her cheekbone. She danced in a circle away from him, never close enough to actually throw a punch of her own. Graham marionetted her, and she could feel it, embraced it even, as her mind kept spinning. Emilie's anger at the situation billowed up inside her, a ferocious creature unleashed for the first time.

When things had started to get bad as a teenager, she hadn't really been able to get angry. Anger was reserved for Lizzie, reserved for Mama when she fought with Dad in those low, terse tones about inpatient stays and what they were supposed to do.

Anger had been foreign to her, and so Emilie had spent years pushing it down and trying to smother it. If she was careful, if she kept ahold of herself and colored inside the lines, doing as she was told even when it went against her instincts, then it'd be okay. Except, it had never been okay, no matter how many times she swallowed her rage and spit out blood from the wounds she caused herself.

Years lost due to the binding made her angry. Dani sacrificing herself made her angry. Talented collectives hoarding their knowledge, casters who would sell each other out for a new spell, the werewolves running scared, and the Humans First hunters deciding who should live and who should die made her angry. And all of it, *all of it*, paled in comparison to the fury that lit her up at Evan's words.

It wasn't hot anger, made to flash bright and burn itself out. No, this was different. It was cold and old, and it had been building inside of her for years. Years of shoving down the things she'd endured, of never being able to fully be herself, of the world that led her to a place where she couldn't even defend herself without the help of a dead man settled inside her skin.

"No cheating now," Evan said as he feinted, and his open palm slammed into her chest.

She crashed against a door that broke under her and sent her tumbling down a decrepit flight of stairs. Emilie landed in a heap at the bottom, then scrabbled to get her feet under her, coughing as she tried to catch her breath, until she was pressed against a wall. Ice crackled over her joints, vapor streaming off her.

Evan chased her down the stairs, a cold smile stretching across his lips as he got closer, brutally kicked her in the stomach, and flipped her onto her side. She coughed and spat blood, but the pain woke up something wild and feral inside of her.

She crawled to her knees, Evan looming over her, a wind that smelled like death whipping around them.

"Please." Her voice was hoarse, pain stealing her breath and making it difficult to expand her lungs.

"Please what?" He cocked his head and looked down at her, close enough that she could almost reach out for him. Her breathing began to even out. "Beg me for mercy, and maybe, if you do a good enough job, I'll kill you fast instead of slow." His face lit up in a beatific, unhinged smile.

"P-please..." she whispered, watching him from under her eyelashes, looking as vulnerable as she was able.

"That's right."

He leaned down over her, and Emilie snapped into motion. She jabbed one hand sharply into his throat, then surged to her feet, throwing a knee into his groin as he doubled over. Graham was pushed out of her, and only Emilie was left as she snapped a vicious kick into Evan, ice curling around her boots and crawling across the ground. Everywhere she touched, she left smears of frozen skin and ice crystals that clung to fabric and flesh alike.

He tried to scuttle away, but Emilie grasped him by the front of his shirt. Emilie breathed in a full breath, tasting it as it turned so cold, it burned inside her throat, and then breathed out in a curse gifted to her by the people Seraph had killed.

"Breathe deep. I hope you freeze."

It was a spell made of nothing but the malevolent anger brewing inside her. That cold magic that connected her to the dead and those who lingered in the veil between life and death. Evan's eyes rolled up in his head, and she threw him against the stairs. Anger so frozen, it felt like embracing the cold of the river and death filled her, and around her, dark tendrils that belonged to Seraph froze and began to crackle away. Emilie stalked forward, ready to finish Evan so that this could end.

Except that standing on the stairs was Dani, watching her with eyes darker than she'd ever seen them.

"Dani?"

Her heart thumped like it was going to leap out of her chest as Dani galloped down the stairs, kicking Evan in the back of the head. Hands grabbed at her as if she was a mirage. Emilie wanted to revel in it, but it wasn't over. Not yet.

40

DANI

She rushed down the stairs, afraid she'd find Emilie glassy eyed, nothing more than a broken doll in the darkness. Instead, she found Evan as a sack of flesh brushed with frost, and her girl stood there like an avenging angel.

Emilie was a sight. Curves clad in icy armor with a halo of pale curls and ice-blue eyes that burned like fire against pale skin.

"Dani!"

She rushed past Evan and crushed their bodies together, mouths colliding desperately. *Alive! Alive! Alive!* The words settled into her core, and a fear she hadn't let fully take root was erased. But the disquiet and need for blood still pounded through her, the mantle flooded with angry magic demanding its pound of flesh.

"I figured you'd want this." Emilie tugged at the side of the leather jacket. "Haven't really taken it off."

"You know that's hot, right?" Dani smiled as a ghostly wind whipped around the two of them, standing in the eye of the storm.

She didn't want to pry herself away from Emilie. She wanted to keep her safe and trapped within her arms where the world couldn't take a swing at her. Evan was still on the stairs, groaning. And at the far side of the basement was a wound in the world, slowly opening.

Dani didn't want to look at it. Her heart was beating a thunderous rhythm in her chest as she locked eyes with Emilie. Her head was swimming, and the pull from the veilblade made the world twist around her in a smear of color. She could hear each rattling breath in Evan's lungs, feel the chill of Emilie's skin under her fingers.

A twisting spark of anger and darkness continued to fire along her synapses, and she finally pulled back just enough. "I thought he'd killed you." Her voice was hoarse and hard to hear over the spectral wind around them.

Days like this were always going to come. As a hunter, as a person who fought against the darkness and the things that dwelled inside of it, she had to know how to weather them. Storms that could derail her entire life or wash away some of the blood, if she let them. This one was the former, and she knew it without having to be told. She knew as soon as they'd dragged her down into those cells that hell would come raining down on her.

"I'm tougher than you think," Emilie said softly. "And I had a badass teacher, you know?" She winked but grabbed one of Dani's hands and clutched it tight.

"Something happened once they had me." Dani frowned, trying to find the words for what it had felt like in that damnable room. "It was like I couldn't remember which way was up. I don't know how long it's been, or what happened but...the bladesinger bond... changed." She smiled wanly, all of her attention on Emilie, the only thing that felt real and right in the moment.

If Evan moved, it would be easy enough to kill him. The thought was bold, as if he wouldn't fight back. If he ran, it would be nothing to kill them and ensure this merry little chase was over. A week ago, she'd have considered not killing Evan. Of turning him over to the council to deal with. Using that thin mortal line as a way to judge herself as separate from the people who'd trained her, allowed her to become the hunter she was meant to be.

It wasn't that it was gone. She hadn't killed Julia outside when she had the chance, hadn't even done permanent damage—provided she got medical care before the bones started to mend. It would be the smallest thing to place her boot on the side of Evan Campbell's neck and snap it. Clean and virtually painless. No different than putting down an animal. She wouldn't take joy in it, but denying that the thought stirred a quiet satisfaction was impossible.

"Dani. Come back to me." Emilie's voice drew her out of her thoughts, allowed her to focus on the gentle hands at her elbows.

There was blood splashed across her front and a bruise blooming at the side of her jaw. A low grumble roiled out of her throat. The feral thing inside of her clawed to get out, to destroy anyone who had put hands on her girl.

"No," Emilie said softly. "I'm fine, but this is not over. Not yet. I am here. I am not gone, and neither is the fight."

The hair on the back of her neck stood at attention as Emilie's eyes dilated, glowing brighter until they were shining gems in her face. Power resonated off her like Dani had never experienced as she pulled off the jacket and settled it over Dani's shoulders.

Her jacket was the first thing she'd bought for herself after she left the Scions behind, figuring out who she was away from the people who'd trained her, away from the girl who'd changed her life and then refused to fight for her. She'd hand sewn the interior pockets herself, and after so many years, the leather was worn to the shape of her body. Putting it on was like coming home.

Dani breathed in, one hand reaching for the familiar weight of the veilblade in its pocket, and a jagged piece of herself smoothed itself out and settled properly into place. One finger rubbed the pommel of the blade, but she kept it hidden away, aware of how quickly she could pull it.

"Do not walk toward the darkness, my love. I do not yet wait for you beyond the broken shores." Emilie's words were a burble of language that slid over her in a tone that spoke of midnight and the darkness of being alone in a world that did not understand her.

Something about it quieted the disarray building inside Dani. It didn't suffocate it entirely, but it was no longer snarling at the back of her throat. It wouldn't last, of course. It couldn't. Dani knew the next time it reared its head, there would be hell to pay. But for a few minutes at least, the world did not feel like a whirlpool trying to suck her down and into the darkness.

"I am the shield of the people, and their pyres lit the night." The words were unfamiliar on her tongue, but she recognized the callback. She just didn't know from where.

Outside, thunder rolled, and around her, a chorus of voices answered, all chiming through Emilie. *"May your aim be true, Keeper of the Blade. Lady Justice sends her scales. It is time for judgment to be rendered."*

Around them, a chime of bells shook the walls, and something roared on the far side of the chasm that had opened up in the wall. Now that her mind was her own, Dani didn't know how she'd ignored its presence. It was a poisonous thing, a swirling miasma of black and green that reached out to infect the world. Thick, oily tendrils reached out from the other side of this tear in the world.

The wind picked up, as if Seraph was suddenly aware that they were coming for it. Evan still lay unmoving, breath rattling in his lungs.

"Seraph is waiting for us past that thing, isn't it?"

"Not us," Emilie said quietly. "*Me.*"

Emilie took a hesitant step away from Dani and toward the rip. Ice sparkled at her feet, moving with her. Dani wanted to reach out for her, wanted to stop her. Stop all of this. Wrap her girl up in her arms as if she could protect her from everything out there. But she couldn't. She understood, maybe better than most, what it was to know something in her bones. To see a threat and understand that she was the one thing standing between the world and the monster.

Except this time, she wasn't the one standing there. Emilie was. Her girl turned back to her, power still haloing around her head in an aura. She could almost see it, could feel the way death and ice rippled around Emilie like a shroud. One that had not been there a few short days ago. Her fear had been burned away, and something else took in its place. Something powerful and old and deadly.

"I can't come with you, can I?" Dani asked quietly.

"No," Emilie said in a voice that sounded like echoes. She bit her lip before turning away from the hole and back to Dani. "Seraph is a creature of the veil." She gestured with an elegant hand. "We've weakened it, stolen most of its hosts, but it's still trying to drag itself out into the real."

"You aren't sure you can end it?"

"We need a backup plan in case shit goes south," Emilie said, moving closer to Dani again. "A weapon that can destroy anything." She smiled weakly. "Sound like anyone you know?"

"For the record, I hate this," Dani said. "We should be together. We're stronger together."

"We are, but I need you for something I wouldn't trust anyone else with. I need you to protect me while my spirit is…elsewhere."

Dani heaved out a breath, grabbed Emilie by the front of her shirt, and kissed her ferociously. She poured all of her love, fear, anger and passion into that kiss. If it was the last time she had Emilie in her arms, she didn't want to spend a lifetime thinking of what she should have done. Emilie melted into the kiss, eventually pulling back, her eyes glazed.

"No distractions now. We have a world to save."

"I'll watch over you," Dani murmured.

"I never doubted it," Emilie answered, voice husky. "Not for a single second."

Emilie moved closer to the chasm and reached out to touch it. The entire world shuddered, a wall of ice glazing over the tear in the world. It curled over the edges of the wall, and the strange growths that had been reaching past it withered and fell to the floor. There was a shockwave of energy, and Emilie fell to the ground like a puppet with its strings cut.

Behind her, Evan screamed and writhed, dark foam bubbling at the corner of his mouth as his body jerked in spasms. Dani ignored him.

She scooped Emilie up into her arms, moved her carefully to a corner, and pressed a kiss to her forehead. She'd protect her girl, whatever came for them. Alive or dead. Physical or spectral. She'd watch over her until she came back if it was the last thing she ever did.

41

EMILIE

Her hand pressed to the rift, and before she ever made contact, Emilie knew what was waiting for her on the other side. Her spirit was ripped from her flesh, a thousand barbs ripping into the essence of her being and pulling. Beyond the real, beyond the veil, into something else—somewhere else.

"Your petty ice magic won't help you here," a voice hissed at her from the darkness, a chorus of voices braided together, all of them in pain.

Around her was a blasted landscape leeched of color and life. No trees, no grass, no animals. It looked like a bomb had gone off, leaving nothing behind save the dark form flitting back and forth. In this place, the illusion of humanity was washed away. It had too many limbs, thin spindly appendages that tapered to vicious points.

"It doesn't need to," Emilie said, taking a quiet step forward.

A chill wind stirred around her feet, and it smelled like loam and rotting flowers, decaying wood and old books. It was the smell of death, and for the first time in her life, it did not incite fear to bloom in her chest like a dark flower. She closed her eyes as it ruffled her hair and called out into the darkness.

There were no words, only instinct. Above her, the sky flashed green and purple, poisonous dark clouds roiling wildly. Emilie called out for everyone whose lives had been cut short by Seraph. Not just the talented and hunters gunned down but the peripheral people too. The people who had died because there were no longer hunters to take on the beasts in the darkness, the towns robbed of protection when their wards broke and there was no one to reinforce or replace them.

All her life, she had been told to bury who and what she was. To hide her talents, fold her hands in her lap, and pretend she was someone other than herself. Emilie had learned to work under the radar, but she was over it.

"I am not the one that kills you, Seraph," Emilie said, the words simple. "That's not my job or my place." She cocked her head and felt the power inside of her ripple out as the spirits appeared around her. "You attacked them when they were weak and alone and scared. When they were half-mad from torture or dragged to you dying from what your creatures did to them."

Around her, spirits appeared, one after another. Some of them were fully fleshed out; others were shreds of the people they had been. Seraph flickered in and out of sight, a dark mist that coalesced and faded.

"*You think these...pieces are enough to destroy me? ME?*" Seraph roared, and the ground trembled with its rage.

It appeared ahead of her, staring with three yellow, slitted eyes. As Emilie watched, it became less of a shimmering mirage and more of a creature. Nearly nine feet tall with thin, barbed limbs protruding from angles that made no sense. It was black, covered in an oily sheen, even in this place.

"Alone?" Emilie looked to her right, where Graham had appeared with a grim countenance. "No, they weren't. Even if they had all come for you, it wouldn't have been enough." Emilie cocked her head and looked back at Seraph. "But that was before they got ahold of me."

Seraph skittered forward, but a few of the spirits rushed it, and Seraph thought better. It prowled around the edges of the crowd but didn't push forward.

The wind picked back up, and several spirits gasped as it blew through them. They gleamed brighter as they recovered pieces of themselves, the side effect of being in proximity to her. Emilie smiled as Seraph hissed, clocking what was happening in real time.

"*I will rend your spirit to shreds so small, it will never reach the misty shores!*" Seraph crowed, then it bowled into the mass of spirits.

They descended on it like mad dogs, spirits burning themselves out in brilliant sparks of silver, gold, and green as they ripped at Seraph's limbs and tried to tear the creature piece from piece. Emilie's eyes were pinned on it, legs trembling where she stood. Evanescent parasites weren't physical creatures, and destroying them required a careful hand. The older they were, the more careful they were about hiding the core of themselves.

Emilie couldn't bring Dani with her, and Seraph was too smart to be pulled fully out into the physical where there was danger. It hadn't left her many choices, but she had one. Seraph wanted her dead and Dani out of the way. It might not have fully clocked what she was when she walked in the door, but it knew now, and it would let itself be torn to shreds rather than let Emilie power up all these spirits. It just didn't realize that Graham was standing next to her, or that she had a long shard of icy magic clutched against her thigh.

She'd been pouring magic into it since the moment she touched the rift, a slow but steady pulse so that it didn't wisp away. It wasn't entirely ice anymore exactly, but it was close enough to do what she needed.

"Are you ready for this?" Emilie asked above the roar of Seraph fighting through dozens of spirits as they threw themselves at it with abandon.

"Yeah." Graham nodded with a grim smile.

"Don't be a hero, just open it up, and I can end this."

"*You know that's not how this is going to go, little lodestone.*" He shot her a sidelong glance. "*We have to destroy it here and now, while it's disconnected from its hosts, or it'll just regroup. It's not just gonna open up like a birthday present.*"

"I'm not asking you to sacrifice yourself," Emilie hissed. "We don't know if the spirits who burn out here can even reach the river."

"We both know that's not true." Graham tapped one ear. "You don't hear it? You are a true conduit to the grave, not just the dead. The river recognizes you. Just remember that."

"I'm serious."

"So am I." Graham sighed. "When a woman with one foot in the real and one in the grave asks for help, the spirits will always answer."

Ahead of them, the mass of spirits had thinned, and Seraph was growing closer. The darkness that once coated it had been ripped away. Green, poisonous wounds bled where its limbs had been torn asunder. Graham launched into motion at the same time two other spirits did the same. Her very own dead honor guard. All three of them hunters, all trained in how to take advantage.

They circled and attacked, throwing vicious punches in a cyclone of pain. Seraph couldn't keep its eyes on all three of them at the same time. It pivoted to focus on one, and the other two attacked. They ripped and tore at its back until a massive wound revealed a glowing violet light deep in its body. One of the remaining limbs speared a spirit, and it burst in a gold rush of energy. Graham pinned its arms, and Emilie darted forward.

Seraph stabbed through Graham's chest, and he laughed maniacally as Emilie plunged a weapon made of ice and magic deep into its back. She funneled all of that cold, icy rage that roiled under the surface into it. This was for Dani, who thought it was all her fault; for Kalliope, who had simply tried to protect children; for every person who had run in fear because this thing had found them a delicious target.

Seraph screamed, talon cutting Graham to ribbons until he simply disappeared. It scrabbled at its back, the ground underfoot shaking wildly. Ice climbed from the middle of its torso out to its limbs, a white infection that brushed it with frost as it screamed.

Evanescent parasites were creatures that dwelled in the veil and hated it. They craved the warmth and heat of a world they could never have, but it was the cold of death that put them back in their place. Only if one could strike the core, they could be frozen from the deepest recesses of themselves.

She backed up, watching as the ice broke off one limb and then another as Seraph screamed. It was a world-ending shriek, and the universe shook in kind. But under the death throes, she could hear something else. She could hear fighting and the sound of a river rushing like rapids somewhere nearby.

When its torso was fully encased in ice, it cracked away to nothing. In that roiling green mass of energy at the core of what Seraph had been, her icicle still was suspended, strobing between black and ice-blue, before the entire thing exploded outward in shards of color. The shockwave knocked Emilie back a good fifteen feet, the world undulating around her.

It was followed by sharp fireworks of color as the shards of spirit that Seraph had eaten over the years were freed. The blasted landscape around them slowly faded away until she was surrounded by the town of Tenacity Mill. She should have gone back to her body, where Dani was waiting. Instead, Emilie just stood there, watching as the sky faded and the veil returned to its natural state.

It had been so easy. With numb movements, she pointed herself toward the sounds of the river. The fireworks of released spirits continued to go off around her, and she could feel it as the spirits reconstituted and disappeared into the darkness. Some of them crossed over, some of them went elsewhere, but all of them were whole in this place for the first time.

Behind her, she heard a roar as the land itself seemed to scream, but Emilie moved to the edge of the river. Mist eddied around her calves, feet dipped in the perfect cold. It felt like coming home, and she had missed it in a way she couldn't explain. For a brief moment, the far side of the river was visible, and she saw a few of the spirits who had now passed on to whatever came next. There was no sign of Graham, and her heart clenched in her chest.

From far away, she heard Dani's voice yelling for her, and Emilie looked back over her shoulder toward the place she knew her body was lying. The river was calling, asking her to wade deeper and spend her time here, but the real was waiting for her. *Dani* was waiting for her.

She took a step back, and then another. Slowly, she backpedaled away from the river, and that siren song begged her to dive into those depths, to surrender herself to the grave and what it could offer her. She moved faster and faster, rushing back to herself, back to Dani, back to the life they were building together, and as she did, the world shuddered wildly.

Emilie stumbled even without a physical body as a scream built in the air around her. The ground roiled, and Emilie turned for the church. Seraph had spent decades squatting in this place, changing it from what it was into its own personal playground. That much anger and hate and darkness had sunk into the land even on this side of the veil. Now that the thing holding everything together was gone, the world was cracking at the seams.

She rushed, moving faster than she ever could have in the physical. The world moved past in a blur, buildings turning into a grey smear as she ricocheted through the church and back into the basement. The rift was still a wound in the fabric of the veil, but it was no longer a tear that broke between the world of the dead and the world of the living.

Emilie slammed back into her body with a wild gasp and saw Dani crouched in front of her. Her back was to Emilie, veilblade shining in her hand like a captured star. There was blood splattered across the floor in a wide arc, and Emilie gasped as the floor rolled and bucked underfoot.

She was back, but it still wasn't over.

42

DANI

Evan screamed and seized for several long moments before his body stopped moving. Dani watched, predatory instincts rising to the fore. Emilie was still on the ground behind her, and the cold from the sheet of ice glazing the wall pressed at her. But Dani wasn't about to move. Not until Emilie was back, not until Seraph was left to the darkness and no longer able to reach past the veil.

From upstairs, there was a sharp patter of gunfire, and her eyes rose to the ceiling, waiting for the stomp of boots overhead. There were still Scions outside, still boots on the ground of this war that Seraph had started with its machinations and manipulations, and she wasn't stupid enough to think it was over just because they'd gotten this far. No, there was still blood to be spilled, and if Seraph was capable of reaching out to whoever was still wrapped up in its influence, it would.

There was a gurgle, she turned just in time to see Evan rush at her. His eyes were bloodshot, dark lines of ichor trailing from his mouth, and he'd never looked less like a person. He didn't move like one, either. He was faster than he should have been, motion almost a blur. Dani snarled, and the veilblade was in her hand in the blink of an eye.

Evan careened at her, no weapon in his hand as he threw a sharp jab at Dani, but his eyes moved past her to where Emilie was slumped on the ground. She snarled, and his attention snapped back to her as she ducked past a vicious blow, dancing back until her girl was protected behind her. They both had jobs to do, and in this moment, this was hers.

Her body moved on autopilot, baiting him into paying attention to her. She could see the madness shining out of Evan's eyes; there was nothing human in them. Nothing of the boy she had known as a teenager, and nothing of the cruel hunter he had been shaped into. Instead of those blue eyes, they had turned black as night, as if Seraph itself was staring out of them. Maybe it was.

Dani didn't care.

She surged forward, throwing a punch with her off hand as she swiped across his body with the veilblade. He screamed in frustration, backing toward the other side of the basement as Dani continued to press in on him. They clashed and backed away, bloodied knuckles and bruises blossoming across their skin like dark flowers. Dani didn't give an inch. Not when he slammed his fist into the side of her jaw and snapped her face to the side, not when he tried to swipe her feet out from under her.

She knew what she was. A weapon. The Reaper. And in this moment, she stood alone. The walls around them shook, and in the distance, there was an explosion. Evan screamed again, and Dani took the chance. She pummeled into him, tossing her blade from one hand to the other. Evan threw up an arm to block where the blade should have been, and it sank through skin and muscle and sinew like it was nothing. The blade sizzled as it bit into bone, and she rode him to the ground, stabbing until the remaining light went out of Evan's eyes.

The silence was deafening for a long moment. Then the world around her shook and screamed.

Dani snatched the veilblade and retreated toward Emilie's body. The ground roiled underfoot, and she settled into a crouch waiting.

"Emilie, baby, I need you to come back to me," she said, voice calm despite the chaos that seemed to rain down upon them.

Dirt and detritus fell like leaves in the fall, and Dani didn't move. She sat, still as a statue, her eyes on Evan's prone form cooling on the far side of the basement.

"I promised I would watch over you, come what may, and we're getting real close to what may out here, babe. Sounds like the world is ending out there, but I'm not moving. Not without you here with me. You hear me! I said I'M NOT LEAVING WITHOUT YOU, SO GET YOUR ASS HOME!"

The world shook again, nearly knocking her off her feet, and then there were arms wrapped around her torso. Dani gasped and spun, and there was Emilie, standing there, her eyes dark with the shadows of what she'd seen. But she was alive, and she was here, and it was time to go.

"I knew you'd kick its ass," Dani said with a wicked grin and a smile that lit her up from the inside. "But now? Now it's time to get the fuck out of dodge."

She grabbed Emilie's hand as a mighty crack thundered through the world, and the ground split. Cement crumbled away into nothing and dirt crawled through the rupture, as if the land itself was reclaiming this place and erasing any reminder of what had happened here.

Without another word, she took off, tugging Emilie along with her as they sprinted up and out of the basement. In the moment before they ran up the stairs, the world swallowed Evan's body, tugging broken limbs into the ground as if he'd never existed in the first place. Dani didn't stop to watch the way she would have a few hours ago. Seraph was gone, and Evan was gone, and Emilie was still here with her in this moment. Right now that was all that mattered.

They escaped the church as the walls crashed around them. On the front stairs, there was no Julia, just chaos. A puddle of blood sat where Dani had left her when she went inside. The ground was cracking, buildings falling into rubble, and around them, the sound of vehicles revving as the survivors fled for their lives. Dani didn't have a car. She didn't know how she would get them out before the world swallowed them the same as the fallen.

A familiar truck swerved to a stop on the street ahead, and Joe honked the horn, yelling out the window.

"Y'all waiting for a fucking engraved invitation? Get in the damn truck!"

Emilie took the lead this time, dragging Dani in her wake as they sprinted to the truck. Once, it would have been Dani pulling her along, taking the lead to get them the hell out of dodge. Not anymore. No, after a year and more hell than either of them could have predicted, Emilie'd found her sea legs. Dani kept up effortlessly, and she whooped, joy and exhilaration billowing inside her.

The two of them clambered inside the old Chevy like they were teenagers running from their parents, then slammed the door shut as Joe took off for the edge of town. Around them, fissures opened in the ground, structures collapsed, and fire ate through old buildings like they were kindling. Emilie turned to see whether the whole place was falling to pieces behind them, but Dani tugged her back into the here and now.

"No point in watching it burn, killer. Trust me." She bumped her shoulder against Emilie's and pulled her into an embrace, her arms over Emilie's chest.

Emilie sighed and clutched Dani's arms like she was a lifeline. Maybe in this moment, she was.

"Where are we headed?" Dani asked as they skidded out onto the main road.

There was a line of vehicles ahead of them, hunters packed into their rides before they peeled away. All of them dispersed as quickly as they'd come together.

"Home." Joe shot her a grin. "Heading for the grill. Got plenty of people waiting for the two of you there."

"Yeah?" Dani asked, raising an eyebrow.

"Good," Emilie said.

She wiggled out of Dani's embrace, got comfortable, and shot her a grin. "I wanna use you as a pillow."

Dani chuckled but adjusted herself so Emilie could lay her head on her shoulder. Her girl was asleep in moments, hands holding onto Dani like she was the last real thing in the world. It was a frantic grip, even in sleep, almost tight enough to bruise.

The sway of the truck lulled her into a kind of peace. Joe behind the wheel, Emilie's head resting against her shoulder...For the first time in a long time, it felt like she was walking forward into the life she wanted for herself. One where she had the things she needed, where she could build a future that wasn't just running from the mistakes of her past.

Something inside of her had shifted too. She could feel the space where something had been chipped away after those hours under the Scions' tender mercies, and they'd have to talk about it. Not today, though. Maybe when they got home, maybe a few days after that.

But for now, they'd survived. For now, it had to be enough.

43

DANI

It was late when they pulled up to the grill, but light was pouring out over the parking lot, and it was overflowing with cars. Lu's RV was parked at the edge of the lot, camp chairs set out next to it. Dani had passed out for a little while, her head pillowed on top of Emilie's, and now they were home. *Home.* The word felt strange to consider because as much as she loved the grill, it was still just a place. It was the people who had come for her, the people who had come together to end this, who were home in the way a place never could be.

Dani's innards felt as if they'd been rearranged in new and interesting ways. Not just because of what they'd done or what she'd dealt with from Seraph and the weight of the magic that coursed through her veins.

She hadn't seen this many bodies at the grill in a long, long time. And never with so many smiles. She was used to war councils, talking strategy and soldiers and tactics in a war that couldn't ever be won. Her nostrils flared. The smell of old blood and gun oil lingered in the air. Probably always would for her, in this place.

She took a long drink from her beer and let the music wash over her for a few minutes. This was the time to relax, to convince herself that everything had worked out in the end.

Except, there were still loose ends that prickled at her uncomfortably. Julia was still out there, alive and dangerous, and no way was she going to take Evan's death sitting down. No, she'd come back swinging, and it was going to be dirty. Dani couldn't relax so long as she knew it was coming for her. Waiting, watching, always peering over her shoulder until it finally hit.

Even now, surrounded by friends and allies, her attention jumped from one hunter to the next, wondering if there were people celebrating today that would have worked with the Scions under different circumstances. Hunters who thought Emilie was less because of her talents, who would have happily crucified Graham if given half a chance. Lu, Mateo...even Sawyer she could trust. Nova trusted Mateo more than her own mother, Mags had proven her worth when there was nothing in it for her, and Joe was beyond reproach. But past that? There was an uneasy churning in her gut. One that told her that when things went sideways, it was going to hurt.

"Don't go borrowing trouble from tomorrow." Lu sidled up and hip bumped her with a knowing smile.

"I don't know what you're talking about," Dani said, taking a sip from her drink, still watching the crowd.

"Of course you do," Lu said, watching her for a reaction.

Dani wasn't sure she wanted to know what she was looking for. "Julia wasn't there by the time we got out of the church. Her people... the ones who weren't dead either."

"Rats on a sinking ship." Lu killed her drink and shook her head. "She won't stay hidden forever, but it does no good to go jumping at shadows."

"You're saying I shouldn't keep an eye out?"

"Hell no. A healthy bit of paranoia keeps us alive. I'm saying it'll happen when it happens, and not a minute before. She'll need to grieve and lick her wounds before she shows up all murderous and vengeful. Enjoy the time with your girl. Might not last that long." She gave Dani a knowing look before plunking her whiskey glass down on a table and sauntering away.

Smug as hell for getting the last word in for once, but Dani wasn't going to argue. Not when Lu was right, much as she didn't want to admit it.

Her eyes settled on Emilie across the room, and she smiled. Her girl was sporting a black eye and bruised knuckles, but she was taking it like a champ, even if the bruises were stark against her fair complexion. She looked like a proper hunter, surrounded by a pack of people as they laughed and talked.

As if she felt Dani's gaze, she looked up, and for the thousandth time, Dani was caught in her eyes. Pale blue with mottled flecks of grey that caught the light when she moved just so. Emilie was too far away to see them up close right now, but she had long since memorized the exact shade, even if the words to explain it right escaped her.

Emilie trotted over with a grin, and Dani watched the whole way, drinking her in. Their time together had toughened her girl up in ways Dani never could have anticipated. That neither of them ever asked for. Her curves were still there, but now she could see muscles in her thighs and arms, the self-assured way she held herself. She wasn't a hunter at her core; she was something different. Something all her own. Not a bystander, and not a deer in the headlights. Her girl was a tempest, and Dani would happily be buffeted by her for the rest of her life.

"You look deep in thought for someone who is supposed to be enjoying a win," Emilie said, grabbing at the loops on Dani's jeans.

The tongue-in-cheek comment left her speechless before a burble of laughter burst out of her like a dam breaking. Something nasty and dark in her chest crumbled, a weight she'd not known she was carrying.

"I'm not *not* enjoying it," Dani said, but it sounded weak and flimsy, even to her.

Emilie smiled softly and cocked her head. She took Dani's hand in her own and led her through the crowd. She followed Em's lead, and it erased some of the twitchiness riding the length of her spine. It wouldn't last, *couldn't* last, but she had right now, didn't she?

Something inside of her had cracked in those dank rooms. Pieces of herself she'd never had to worry about had been filed down to shards, and it was disconcerting the way they moved out of tandem with the rest of her. A shadow self with its own thoughts about the way they should be handling things.

It was the veilblade, probably, but even that was just a guess. She wanted to laugh again but held it in until they stepped outside into the cold air. It was bracing but not terrible, and she was reminded of the years huddling with friends in the wind as they shared a smoke outside one dive bar or another. She'd kicked the habit fast, smart enough to know she wouldn't be able to afford the damage to her lungs, but the cold brought the memory back every time.

"You seem lost. Are you okay?" Emilie turned, pulling Dani close.

Those hands were softer than her own, but they'd started to develop the same calluses Dani had carried for years. Her bloody knuckles made her one of them as much as anything else, even if they didn't share the same methods, the same skillset. Those were Emilie's and hers alone.

"I'm…" She paused, trying to find a way to explain. Wishing that she didn't feel as if the world was spinning around her. "It's not really over yet, is it? I can't stop thinking about it. About what comes next."

She wanted to pour out her hopes and her fears and everything that had happened during the hours or days the Scions had her—but not tonight. Tonight was for something else, because fuck Julia and her cronies and her madness. Dani was alive and with Emilie, and they had each other. Nothing—*nothing*—was going to tear them apart again

"But that's for another time. Tonight isn't about the bad." Dani smiled at herself and pulled Emilie in for a long kiss.

Heat sparked between them, Emilie's hands on her hips, Dani's hands roaming along the breadth of her collarbone. "Tonight is for what comes after," she murmured along the shell of Emilie's ear, enjoying the way a shudder rolled over her girl's skin, leaving a trail of goosebumps in its path.

"You are an emotional terrorist, you know that, right?" Emilie gasped, laughter on her lips as she clutched at Dani.

Her girl had never looked more alive than she did right now, eyes bright in a face flushed with emotion instead of bitten by cold. Her pale hair danced around in tangled curves that waved around her shoulders. She wrapped a strand around two fingers and tugged gently.

Emilie gasped and huffed out a nervous chuckle. "Tease."

"I'm a tease?" Dani tutted, tipping Emilie's face up and kissing her like they were the last people left alive in the world. "We don't have to stay, you know."

"It's a party in our honor."

"I saw, I endorsed, and now I have plans for a different kind of party. Won't be the first time I've ducked out on a shindig, won't be the last. Let me take you home and put you to bed."

"I just need you to know that my objections were purely lip service." Emilie laughed and leaned in for another desperate kiss.

"Noted." She fake-saluted and took Emilie's hand, leading her out and around the building.

Through would have been faster, but right now, less people was better. Less people meant less distractions. They snuck past the grill and down the footpath that led to Joe's place, making a beeline for the carriage house they'd claimed as their own. Along the way, they paused to kiss, hands roaming over each other like lovestruck adolescents.

This wasn't the first time they'd tumbled into the building, barely taking their hands off one another long enough to get the doors unlocked, but there was a weight to it that hadn't been there before. Before Dani had been cracked open and put back together again.

In the dark, they fumbled through the main floor, leaving a trail of jeans and socks and half a shirt, a victim of Dani trying to rip off her own shirt and tearing it to shreds when it got stuck. Sometimes, that was just the way these things went. Before she knew it, they were in bed. Her hands were on Emilie, dancing along the column of her neck, while her girl moaned and bucked underneath her.

In the predawn grey of the morning, it struck her that this was exactly what she wanted. Exactly where she was supposed to be. Whatever was going to happen would still happen. Julia and her madness, the veilblade and its magic. There was no stopping it, just learning to roll with the punch when it inevitably landed.

Right now, she could exist in this moment and hold onto it like something precious. It was. *Emilie* was, and she'd chosen Dani all on her own.

"I want you to know I chose you too," she murmured against Emilie's skin with a smile. "I choose you when you're gorgeous and moaning in my bed and when you're stealing the covers and when you wanna punch me because I interrupted your research. I pick all of the yous in all of the ways for the rest of forever. However long that is. I pick you. I choose you. *I choose us.*"

A magic she hadn't known was there stopped straining at the bonds of herself, and for the first time, something settled deep inside Dani. Heat settled over her in a shroud, and Emilie was blinking too fast, like she couldn't see, which meant magic. Lots of magic. The kind that sealed up the wounds that had been opened by a lifetime of fighting against the darkness and knowing it was at best a war of attrition.

It settled over the crevices and cracks in her soul, smoothed away the broken edges of the girl she had been, and sealed them into the person she had become. The woman she had chosen to grow into over all these years. It settled, and Emilie surged up from the bed with a ferocious kiss, wrestling Dani down under her.

"I choose you too. What comes next isn't here yet."

Emilie kissed her, and Dani surrendered to the swell of heat and pleasure that rolled through her as the sun rose outside.

Whatever would come would come, but they'd face it. Together.

COMING SOON

DANI AND EMILIE WILL RETURN IN BOOK 3 OF LEGACY OF SHADOWS.

ACKNOWLEDGMENTS

First and foremost, thank you to my partner in shenanigans, Riggs. You might be an agent of chaos, but you make every day better. I'm so glad we picked each other, always be the Gomez to my Morticia.

Next is my favorite villain T, you're my dark haired love interest and I'm so glad we found each other again. Thank you for your endless patience as I hyper fixate on writing during our brief hours together.

My friends, family, and found family, you make my life so much better. Thank you for the lunches, the adventures in the woods, the constant memes when I am banging my head against my desk, and for always *always* believing in me. I love you all to the moon and back.

To Dad who convinced me to never stop writing, & Mom who showed me there is magic in the quiet moments.

No book appears in a vacuum and I managed to finally finish this monster after years of working on it thanks in no small part to my crew of authors. Lou Wilham who convinced me it was in fact a good book, and my dearest Discordant Owls: Charissa Weaks, Kristin Jacques, SL Choi, Holly Rose, Lisa Edmonds, Lily Riley, Megan VanDyke, & SC Greyson. Ladz who has always been my cheerleader, and all the writing friends I have made over the years but who elude me as I write this in the middle of an actual blizzard.

To Meg Dailey who wrangled all of my commas, and helped fine-tune this book with the editorial eye I desperately needed.

Last but never least, thank you to you my reader. I wouldn't be here without you, and your love for my absolute disaster lesbians gets me through all the hard days. I hope that the wait was worth it, and that I'm here telling you stories for decades still to come. I cannot thank you enough.

ABOUT THE AUTHOR

Jen Karner might just be a crow cleverly disguised as a human author. She never attended college, but she did the required reading anyway. A horror nerd, she loves TTRPGS, and talking about her fandoms.

Jen was raised in the Baltimore suburbs, where she devoured as many books as possible, and spent her afternoons running amok in the woods. She lives in Maryland with her partner, their dog, and a very large orange cat.

FIND ME ONLINE

Website: www.JenKarner.com

Instagram: www.instagram.com/articulatedream

Threads: www.threads.com/@articulatedream

Everything else: www.JenKarner.carrd.co

CHIPPED CUP COLLECTIVE

Robot Dinosaur Press
robotdinosaurpress.com

Sins of Survival was made possible with the support of the Chipped Cup Collective. A gathering of queer creators making a home for micro press and self-published speculative works.

The collective spirit of Robot Dinosaur Press reaches beyond its list, with members found throughout the creative world. Look for this stamp on projects by members of the collective who want to acknowledge that spirit.

For an introduction to our work, sign up to our newsletter at robotdinosaurpress.com/newsletter and receive a free anthology of short stories by RDP authors.

www.ingramcontent.com/pod-product-compliance
Lightning Source LLC
LaVergne TN
LVHW012033070526
838202LV00056B/5481